*"Who am I to pass up the chance of a lifetime?"*

They stood still, facing each other in front of her door. His eyes traveled from her eyes to her hair, to the features of her face, taking it all in, slowly, pleasurably, in a way that made her feel suddenly very beautiful.

Gently, he ran his fingers through her hair, and around to her neck. He lifted her chin and bent down and kissed her lips for a long time. When he backed away, he looked down at her longingly, as though he had not really wanted to stop. He stroked her cheek and smiled. "I'll call you."

Cynthia walked into her apartment still feeling the touch of his hands, the taste of his lips caressing hers.

*My God, a kiss.* A real kiss, not a hurried one, nor a self-conscious one. A truly romantic kiss. A sign of affection. When was the last time she had had such a kiss? Back in her teens? She couldn't remember. But she felt just as giddy and excited as she imagined she had felt back then…

"Linda Cashdan captures the wheeling and dealing of the official Washington, but it is her account of a very contemporary love affair that makes this book so real and compelling."
— Barbara Cohen, Washington Bureau Chief, CBS News

"Thoroughly engrossing!" —*Booklist*

# S·P·E·C·I·A·L
# INTERESTS

## LINDA
## CASHDAN

ST. MARTIN'S PAPERBACKS

"Whatever Happened to Old-Fashioned Love," by Lewis Anderson, copyright © Old Friends Music & Greenever Music. Reprinted by permission of Evergreen Entertainment Group, Inc.

SPECIAL INTERESTS

Copyright © 1990 by Linda Cashdan.

Library of Congress Catalog Card Number: 89-77950

ISBN: 0-312-92512-3

Printed in the United States of America

St. Martin's Press hardcover edition published 1990
St. Martin's Paperbacks edition/May 1991

10 9 8 7 6 5 4 3 2 1

To Edward Wollner and (in memory)
Harriet Wollner, parents who loved and inspired

Special thanks to Molly McKitterick, my candid critic and constant supporter, and to Brooks Jackson, Dr. Sandra Goldstein, Dr. Kenneth Miller, and Sheldon Samuels, who shared their time and expertise.

# SPECIAL INTERESTS

## · 1 ·

1986 IS NOT AS BAD AS IT SEEMS . . .

Cynthia Matthews scanned the invitation trying to decide which she found more distasteful, the little-girl curlicues of the penmanship, or the upbeat chirpiness of the message. Whatever. The overall effect was cloying—especially at five A.M.

She poured her third cup of morning coffee and began pacing in circles in the kitchen, the card in one hand, the coffee mug in the other. Her body was pulsating from an overdose of caffeine, and at the same time exhausted from a sleepless night.

And what had set the insomnia in motion? Cynthia opened the invitation once again—for what had to be the fiftieth time—and gazed at the message:

AN END-OF-JANUARY-DOLDRUMS PARTY!
AT: LILAH BALLUSTRUM'S
ON: JANUARY 24TH, 1986
(AFTER 8 . . .)
337–7405 (REGRETS ONLY)

Cynthia Matthews "regretted" with her thumbnail, running it back and forth across the writing, mangling the message with indented scratches.

Who sent out invitations to hundreds of people without needing to include a specific address?

1

Who, indeed? Only Lilah Ballustrom, purveyor of parties. "Verrry Washington parties," as Lilah delighted in billing them.

Cynthia walked out of the kitchen and sat down on her living-room sofa, taking care to smooth the skirt of her maroon suit under her so it would not crease. She played with a lock of blond hair as she scowled at her coffee mug. Just what she needed: another of Lilah's "verrry Washington" parties, another glorious reunion of the cream-of-the-crop, Power City's up-and-comers.

The talk would center on politics, and ironically, there would not be one native-born Washingtonian in attendance. Washington's fast track consisted of sons and daughters from the hinterlands whose aptitudes and ambition had drawn them to the nation's capital, and whose stellar achievements—or undaunted hopes—had kept them there year after year after year.

Though it was the last thing she needed, Cynthia took another sip of coffee anyway.

The guests would be a warmed-over "cream-of-the-crop," to be sure. Lilah's swinging singles tended to be a bit above the median national age for that category, but, then, in Washington you could qualify as a swinging single up to the age of fifty—if you had the right job.

Freeze-dried adolescents sprouting age lines, Cynthia thought, picturing the assembled group of divorcees, career women, and bachelors, all impassioned workaholics who divided their time between offices and gymnasiums, pushing their careers and encouraging their muscle tone at the expense of any real emotional development.

And why would they all be trekking to Lilah Ballustrom's Friday night?

In hope of mating, no doubt, but knowing, from years of experience on the Washington social scene, that that hope would probably prove elusive. "Swinging single" was, after all, just a euphemism for "walking wounded."

These were people with thick layers of scar tissue around their hearts, still smouldering from past rejections, hungry but suspicious, looking for Ms. or Mr. Perfect, but pragmatic enough to know that the best they could probably hope for was a recycling of someone they had already discovered was less than perfect.

There would be few new faces.

Cynthia smiled a little, enjoying an imagined scene in which Lilah Ballustrom stood up on a chair and asked in her famed hostess singsong: "Is there anyone here who has not *already* slept with someone else here tonight?"

Cynthia's smile faded as she faced the truth. It was a test she could not pass.

She swallowed hard and entertained another reality: Her glib mental diatribe bore a striking ressemblance to the long-distance rantings of her older sister, Georgine—rantings Cynthia vehemently denied and that usually culminated in Georgine's pleading "Why don't you move back to Indiana?" and Cynthia's screaming "Because Washington is my home!"

Her eyes wandered to the magazine on the coffee table in front of her, to the headline in the lower right-hand corner of its cover:

**SHADY DEALS AMONG WASHINGTON'S LEGAL ELITE . . .**
**page 32.**

On page thirty-two, it said in large bold lettering: "By Cynthia Matthews." Her best-looking byline yet.

Appropriate, she told herself haughtily, given the importance of the story.

Without opening the magazine, she could picture among the head shots of the culprits on page thirty-six—the blond man in the second row.

She bit her lower lip. In truth, nothing she had thought about the party had anything to do with her *real* reason for not wanting to go.

And what about Lilah's reason for inviting her? Was she to be the object of another of Lilah Ballustrom's favorite Washington party games? Was that the purpose? Was she to appear as one half of a former couple, now separated into a "him" and a "her" in separate corners of the room, each pretending to be having a wonderful time as the eyes of the crowd darted back and forth, from his corner to her corner, whispering about the scandalous way Cynthia Matthews's thirst for a major byline had precipitated the separation?

A headliner and a byliner in one room. What a coup for Lilah! What perrrfect entertainment for a verrry Washington party!

Cynthia's large blue eyes misted slightly as she pictured Rob Diamond over there in the "him" corner, long and lean and golden-haired . . . perfect. Oh, riddled with abominable moral imperfections, to be sure, but none that showed, none that kept her from irrationally yearning to have Rob move across that room from the "him" corner to the "her" corner.

She sat very still for a moment, fantasizing, imagining his agile body cutting a path toward her, deliberately, dramatically.

But the fantasy ended abruptly when Rob Diamond arrived at her side, ended because the script ended. Hard as she tried, she could come up with nothing—no excuse, no promise, no clever one-liner—*nothing* he could possibly say to make everything all right.

She played with the invitation. Lilah Ballustrom was wrong: 1986 was *every bit* as bad as it seemed.

By six A.M. Cynthia was beginning to feel the walls of her apartment closing in on her. Surely, she rationalized, she would be able to find more useful outlets for her energy at the office.

Out on the empty streets, she felt the icy January wind focusing on her, its first human victim. She pulled her hat down and her coat collar up, pushing forward, fighting it off, while casting a wary eye over her shoulder at the ominous shadows she sensed lurking in alleys and doorways.

Who would get her first? Mother nature or her fellow man?

The Adams-Morgan neighborhood in which Cynthia lived was Washington's version of the national trend of inner-city rejuvenation—another once-good area going through a rebirth after years of decay.

What made Adams-Morgan different was that the transformation had been as political as it was economic, and appropriately so, perhaps, for a region located in the heart of America's most political city.

The early "settlers" in Adams-Morgan's rebirth had come in the early 1960s—a wave of Cuban immigrants, and, simultaneously, a wave of American radicals.

The two had little in common, to put it mildly. The two groups were, in fact, diametrically opposed—Cuban right wingers plotting to overthrow Castro's revolution, and American socialists dreaming of mobilizing the masses to foment a domestic revolution.

However, they were united in their ineffectiveness and their passion, and saved from out-and-out discord by the fact that they did not speak the same language.

Each group begat other groups. The presence of the Cubans stimulated the influx of the next wave of Spanish-speaking immigrants—refugees from El Salvador, Honduras, and Nicaragua. The presence of the American radicals brought in others from the more central left. Middle-class liberals, artists, hippies, peaceniks, all delighted in living in the architectural vestiges of the past and found the Latin-Americans a delightfully colorful backdrop.

The result was American leftists (ardent supporters of the Sandanistas in Nicaragua, for example) living side by side with those who had fled the Sandanista government.

But, again, fortunately, few spoke the same language.

And there was passion. Everywhere, there was passion. Adams-Morgan quickly became a neighborhood of festivals, impromptu music concerts, demonstrations, and food stores catering to the gastronomic preferences of the new settlers: tacos and tortillas on the one hand, granola and bean sprouts on the other. If ever there was a place where people busied themselves "making love—not war!" it was Adams-Morgan.

That was the area's status in the late 1970s, when Cynthia Matthews had moved in. A former farm girl who had chosen to pursue a career in journalism in the nation's capital right after graduating from college, she had fallen in love with Adams-Morgan's urban vibrance, antiquated architecture, and scrupulous informality. Where else in Washington could she wander around in tattered jeans on a Sunday and feel, if anything, overdressed?

Not only had the neighborhood provided an escape from her fast-track professional and social life; it had also afforded her several free-lance story ideas over the years.

Thus, it was as a "veteran" resident that Cynthia Matthews had watched the latest wave of change unfold: The Latin-Americans had been followed by immigrants from other Third World trouble spots, most of whom, it seemed, had arrived with recipes. In a short time, Adams-Morgan had turned into Washington's very own culinary melting pot, with block after block of restaurants offering an eclectic mix of Latin-American, Ethiopian, Afghan, Middle Eastern, Thai, Caribbean, and Nepalese cuisine. The "laid-back" neighborhood suddenly became a very trendy night spot. People were starving in Ethiopia, but in Washington, attorneys and government officials were flocking to Adams-Morgan for "authentic" Ethiopian food.

And then, the final irony: Now-trendy Adams-Morgan had become a neighborhood of skyrocketing real-estate values where condo-seeking Yuppies were fighting each other for living space beside immigrants from the developing world.

The streets of Adams-Morgan pulsated with activity during the day and late into the night. However, between midnight and daylight, they had a dormant, seedy, inner-city ambience.

Cynthia turned to the right and took in an immobile body sleeping in the doorway of a clothing store, its gloved hand clutching a bottle wrapped in a brown paper bag.

She picked up her pace.

At the bus stop, finally, she stopped, out of breath, and shivered a little as she looked up the street.

No bus in sight. Nothing, at all, in sight.

She heard a strange semicombustible putt-putt sound in the distance, getting louder, closer. Not a bus, but an engine. Some kind of car engine.

A large vehicle with only one functioning headlight came into view. It was rumbling down the street in her direction. She raced back from the bus stop, into the shadows of an empty store doorway, admonishing herself for being so frightened. Why did she feel only unsavory people would be up and around at this hour?

The vehicle got closer. It was a large, dilapidated green van, and it sputtered across the intersection in Cynthia's direction and then heightened her anxiety by screeching to an abrupt stop right in front of where she was standing.

Maryland license plates.

The front door burst open, and a tall, skinny, sandy-haired

man hopped out and ran around to the back. He opened the rear doors and began yelling into the van's interior. *"Vamos! Vamos!"* he exhorted. As he moved into a street light, she could see he was missing a front tooth.

Nothing happened.

*"Vamos!"* the man shouted again in irritation. This time he reached in and pulled on something. It was an arm, and gradually it was followed by the rest of the small, wiry-looking man, staring into space and moving very slowly.

*"Vamos! Vamos!"*

The man did not seem to be resisting the driver. Rather he seemed incapable of moving out of the van as quickly as the driver wanted. When he finally made it out, he swayed on his feet a little, lingering under the spotlight of the street light. He seemed unsure of where he was.

Cynthia watched.

Slowly, other men began climbing out of the van—short, squat, dark-haired, dark-skinned men, in crumpled, torn clothes. Some seemed as out of it as the first man, others ran off energetically into the darkness. The fact that they were oblivious to Cynthia's presence made her less frightened and more curious. Well, this was one weird car pool, that was for sure! The passengers all looked as though they had O.D.'d on Dramamine!

What was going on here? A new shipment of illegal immigrants delivered to Adams-Morgan in the darkness of the night by an American "coyote"?

The riders certainly seemed exhausted enough to have traveled for days and nights, cramped together in the back of that van. But they were carrying lunch boxes, not sacks of belongings.

Cynthia snickered at her own high-blown sense of melodrama. Since when did illegal aliens come with lunch?

The riders' lack of energy was countered by the driver's gusto. *"Hasta luego!"* he shouted at the backs of those emerging from the vehicle and heading off in different directions. *"Hasta luego!"*

The Spanish phrase was delivered with a rural Maryland lilt. "See you tomorrow," Cynthia translated silently to herself. The drop-off must be a daily occurrence. Perhaps it *was* a car pool of sorts—Latin-Americans coming into Adams-Morgan from Maryland each day for work.

But why would they arrive before daylight when most of the area's restaurants did not begin business until noon? And why would the driver tell them he would see them again "tomorrow"?

Well, why not ask? Her fears had long since dissipated. It was certainly a harmless-looking group. She stepped forward, out of the shadows, in the direction of the van. When the driver spied her, his face froze, and he shot her a look of discomfort mixed with hostility that further fueled her interest.

Up to no good.

The driver was forcefully pulling the men out of the van now, anxious to speed up the process.

Eight, nine, ten. Cynthia counted the bodies crawling out. She noted an especially glassy-eyed man who was led away in a stupor by a cohort. Twelve, thirteen . . . They each emerged from the van in the circular spotlight of the street lamp, and then headed off into the darkness.

She moved closer.

A tall, thin man who seemed more alert than the others looked over at Cynthia as he emerged from the van. "Preeety lady!" he screeched. The shrill sound made her jump, and take a step back in the direction of the store entry.

"Me Pablo!" the man yelled to Cynthia. "Ahhee speeek Eeeenglitch wery well!"

Cynthia relaxed a little. Pablo seemed more comical than dangerous. The driver nudged Pablo irritably, and a short, cherubic-looking teenager who had gotten out of the vehicle behind Pablo began remonstrating with him in Spanish and pulling him off in a different direction.

Pablo threw his head back in laughter and then kept repeating the phrase. "Ahhee speeek Eeeenglitch wery well!" The words faded out as the boy led him away. "Ahhee speeek Eeeenglitch wery well . . ."

The driver slammed the back door shut, ran to the front, hopped in, and slammed the door behind him.

Cynthia Matthews frowned as the van hurried off down the street. She turned around, looking for a passenger. No one was left. The street was once again silent and empty—as though nothing had happened.

*    *    *

"Come in!"

The door opened and a stocky man in his late twenties with a closely cropped light brown beard burst into Senator Frederick Barker's office. Attired in a heavy overcoat and muffler, he seemed to bring a gust of wintry air in with him.

"Thad Rankerman," Senator Barker shouted, putting down the stack of papers he had been perusing. "My, you must've caught a very early flight!"

"I wanted to catch you," Rankerman said breathlessly. "Miranda said you had a long day of hearings." He shifted uncomfortably from foot to foot in front of Barker's desk, his eyes darting around the room. "I'm . . . uh . . . concerned, Senator. Very, very concerned."

Senator Barker nodded slowly and waited for more. Rankerman kept shifting. Gradually, Barker's bushy brown eyebrows worked themselves into a frown as he gazed at Rankerman over the tops of his bifocals. "Body language," the Senator muttered grimly.

"Huh?"

"Body language!" the Senator boomed. "Isn't that what my young, hip campaign staff is always instructing me in?"

"What does that have to do with—"

"I'm telling you I can tell by your goddamn *body* language that you are concerned!"

Rankerman jumped.

"It would help a whole lot, Thad," the Senator said softly, "if you stopped pantomiming and resorted to mere words." He gestured to the chair on the other side of his desk. "What's happening in the home state that's made you so . . . concerned?"

Rankerman sat down and leaned forward, thumping his fingers on Barker's desktop. "It's bad. Really bad. The guy's running the slickest ads I've ever seen—on television, cable, radio, the works. 'A new idea,' that's his theme. All over the place, 'a new idea.'"

"Appropriate for a man who's never won elective office," Barker chortled. "But hardly a new theme. Nor news to me. I've seen those ads."

"It's the *reaction* to them I'm talking about. They're catching on. For two weeks I've been moving around the state, scouting, and I'm telling you, they're all lapping it up! The farmers, the factory workers—all your big buddies, your former backers! Iowa's economy's so bad, they're desperate for help. They're willing to try anything. 'Maybe we need some new blood.' That's what they're mumbling."

"Thad, Thad, Thad," Senator Barker sighed as he stretched lazily in his high-backed swivel chair. "Relax a little, my boy. I may not be schooled in this pollster, ad-biz stuff you all love, but I've been through a lot more campaigns than you. They always start like this."

Rankerman raised his chin. "No. Not like this."

"Hell, it hasn't even started yet! The election is nine months away! Why, the man hasn't even won his party's nomination yet. What's more, he's a Republican." Barker beamed. "Just like the administration that created all of Iowa's economic problems in the first place."

"He's not a Republican." Rankerman's gray eyes snapped to attention. "He's a man with a religion—right-wing conservativism—and he's a man with an enemy—you!"

"Can't say as I blame him," Barker drawled. "I've fought him and his cult every step of the way for a decade now, and, believe me, there have been many steps." His eyes twinkled. "I've always won hands down."

"This time it's different! This is the brave new world of political campaigning! He's waging psychological warfare, with the slickest assemblage of pollsters, pulse-takers, ad men, video producers I've ever seen." Rankerman eyed the Senator significantly. "Dirty tricks too, from what I've heard."

"Oh, hell, Thad, dirty tricks are nothing new," Senator Barker laughed. "Richard Nixon popularized the concept more than a decade ago, and believe me, it was nothing new then either!"

Rankerman leaned across Barker's desk. "The man has a network of tentacles that stretches beyond the state—to right here in Washington. They're watching everything you do."

Barker broke out laughing. "Tentacles that see, huh? Now, that must be a *very* modern set, indeed!"

Thad Rankerman sat up stiffly in his chair, his jaw clenched.

"Hey, I'm sorry," Barker said softly. "I don't mean to minimize what you're saying. It's important. I know it is. I just want you to put it into perspective, is all. You're the expert on new-wave politics, but you have to remember I've been doing this a long time." Barker tried to thaw the stern visage before him with an ingratiating smile. "I'll trust my fate to the Iowa voters. They're good people who've never let me down yet. They'll see."

Rankerman thrust himself forward, reentering the fray. "They see slick ads, all the time they see slick ads, the best that money can buy from a man so filthy rich that he can keep buying and buying and buying . . ."

"So? We'll buy some too."

"With what?" Thad Rankerman threw up his hands. "With *what*! With campaign coffers that are empty by comparison?"

Slowly, Barker picked up a pencil and rolled it back and forth between his index finger and his thumb. "Now, Thad, we have plenty of time to raise money."

"From whom? From the bankrupt Iowa farmers? The laid-off factory workers? Senator, you've got—"

"Who's your contact?"

Rankerman blinked. "Contact?"

"Come on," Barker cajoled. "The one that's been telling you about dirty tricks and far-reaching tentacles."

Rankerman smiled smugly. "One of their staff workers . . . a *disgruntled* staff worker."

"Stay close to him." Barker winked and then stood up. Heeding the message, Rankerman rose from his chair abruptly and headed for the door.

"Thad . . ."

He turned around.

"I appreciate what you're doing." Barker's tone was warm and sincere. "Just relax a little, son. I've been doing this for a long, long time. Take my word for it—it's gonna be fine." He shot Rankerman a convincing grin.

The grin vanished as soon as Thad Rankerman walked out and closed the door. Barker's face suddenly froze, and his fist clenched so tightly, the pencil in his hand broke in half. The Senator stared at the broken pencil for a moment, and then hurled it into the wastepaper basket.

Cynthia Matthews opened the door that read SUITE 503, CAPITOL RADIO and was greeted by the smell of freshly brewed coffee and Sylvia Berg on the telephone at the front desk.

"Hi, honey." Sylvia smiled maternally at Cynthia over the tops of her bifocals, and then snarled at the telephone receiver. "Des Moines always put me on hold."

Sylvia's eyes traveled from Cynthia's face down her body, clouding suddenly when they got to the bottom of Cynthia's coat. "What? You think this is Miami or something? How can you go out without pants on such a cold day?"

As Cynthia put her coat in the closet, Des Moines took Sylvia off hold, thereby letting Cynthia off the hook.

Capitol Radio was a Washington, D.C., news service in the business of feeding audio programs to local stations around the country (and in Canada) that were too small or too poor to have correspondents of their own in the nation's capital.

Officially, Sylvia Berg was Capitol Radio's receptionist, and administrative assistant to Capitol Radio's owner, founder, and director, Gardiner Weldy. Unofficially, Sylvia was the office mother, a human geiger counter capable of sniffing out who needed a pat on the head, who deserved a harsh reprimand, and who was having trouble with his wife.

Privacy was a concept unknown to Sylvia, who probed and poked until she found the cause of the gleam in a coworker's eyes, or the teardrops on his copy.

A short, plump, dark-haired woman in her late fifties, Sylvia Berg had reentered the workforce after sending the last of her three sons off to college. The managerial skills developed during more than twenty years as a housewife had translated well into an office setting, especially Capitol Radio's office setting.

Sylvia's personality provided a welcome balance to the boss's. Cynthia considered Sylvia meat and potatoes to Gardiner Weldy's quiche. While Gardiner pontificated on his "concept of the role we have to play," it was Sylvia who understood the needs and interests of the customers and which reporters were best at fulfilling which assignments. Accustomed to being the real power behind the throne as a housewife, Sylvia was comfortable fulfilling that role in an office setting.

Gardiner Weldy made the assignments at the morning meeting, but all Capitol Radio employees were well aware that the assignments were placed before him on a piece of paper in Sylvia's handwriting.

"You don't have to tell me," Sylvia groaned into the telephone. "I agree one hundred percent. It's not me. It's . . ." Sylvia shot an angry glance at Gardiner Weldy's closed door. "It's not *me* who's balking, believe me." She leaned back, listening. "Marie," she sighed after a while. "I'll let you know. That's all I can tell you."

Cynthia watched as Sylvia hung up the telephone and tapped her pencil tip on the top of the clipboard on her desk. Her full, painted lips were drawn into a troubled pout, causing the loose flesh on either side of her face to droop into the ruffled collar of her white satin blouse. The combination of her jowly grimace and the shiny white ruffle on her short neck made Sylvia look like a bulldog dressed to show.

"Sylvia, what's the matter?"

"Nothing." Sylvia stood up, plucked a piece of lint from her "slimming" black slacks, and then pulled her billowy white blouse down over her generous hips, hoping to camouflage the fact that she was not thin.

She looked down at her clipboard for a while, and then abruptly turned to Cynthia. Some sort of decision had been made. "Two Iowa stations—one in Des Moines, one in Sioux City—have called this morning. They want a report on the Senate farm hearings."

"So? Sinc loves to cover—"

"Sinc's out sick."

"And you want me to cover the hearings?"

Sylvia began pacing in front of her desk, tapping the pencil against the clipboard more rapidly. "I think this is a biggy for all our rural customers. The farm crisis is a major, major story out there. We'd sell a lot of spots if we wrote it up." Sylvia stopped pacing and switched gears. She gave Cynthia a playful nudge. "The Indiana stations would probably use it too, once they found out we covered. So your mama could hear you on the radio tonight."

Cynthia Matthews shifted her weight from one leg to another, determined to let the record show she was an unwilling victim.

"Also!" Sylvia chirped, holding up a finger, her eyes now

sparkling. "Also, Senator Frederick Barker of Iowa is holding the hearings."

Cynthia shrugged. "I gather that's why the Iowa stations are interested in having them covered."

"Yes, but, well . . ." Sylvia removed her bifocals. "I thought that might make you more interested in covering. I overheard you tell Jake the other day that you were interviewing Washington celebrities for a new free-lance story you were doing . . . something on 'human loss,' I think you said."

"But what does that have to do with Senator Barker?"

"His wife died just a few months ago."

Cynthia Matthews's large blue eyes snapped to attention. "Actually, Sylvia, that might work out! I could go up after the hearing and arrange an interview. It's really hard to set up interviews for this kind of story over the telephone."

Sylvia nodded. Cynthia wondered whether Sylvia had heard her tell Jake that too.

"Okay, then, sold! I'd be happy to cover the hearings."

Cynthia waited for a grateful response, but got no reaction at all. Sylvia was staring into space.

"Sylvia?"

"Hmm?"

"What is it?"

"What? Oh, nothing . . . nothing at all. It all works out perfectly. And who knows, it might be good for you to meet this Senator Barker anyway. He's a single man now, and he's supposed to be very nice."

"Sylvia, for God's sake, the body is barely cold, and he's old enough to be my father!"

"And what's the matter with older men? I thought that was the rage these days." Sylvia winked. "Might be a nice change of pace. Rev up your lackluster social life."

"Who said I had a lackluster social life?"

Sylvia beamed at Cynthia. "Who had to?"

Cynthia groaned and headed for the Capitol Radio conference room.

Sylvia's frown reappeared as soon as Cynthia left the room. She stared at the clipboard, then at the clock, and then nervously at Gardiner Weldy's door. She bent down over the clipboard and scribbled "Cynthia" in the margin next to "Senate Farm Hearings."

"Well," she mumbled to herself as she looked at the notation. "*Half* the job is done."

"Jed!"

"Good morning, Sam."

"Hi, Jed."

"Good morning, Susan."

"Good morning, Jed."

"Hey, Dick."

A tall, dark, broad-shouldered man in his thirties, Jed Farber walked jauntily down the law firm's second-floor corridor filled with a sense of accomplishment. He had managed to get to the office on time with the prized booty of his early-morning expedition packed away neatly in the attaché case he was carrying.

His pleasure increased at the sight at the end of the hall: a sleek, perfectly groomed black woman in her early fifties leaning over a pad on her desk and taking notes, a telephone receiver at her ear. He was on time, and, as usual, his very very efficient secretary, Yvonne Bailey, had come in early.

Yvonne finished the phone call just as he approached her desk.

"Good morning!" he said cheerfully, shuffling through the neatly organized stack of mail awaiting him.

"Good morning!" Yvonne smiled on reflex, but the grin faded as she surveyed Jed Farber. Yvonne's eyelids slid down to half mast and she began shaking her head. "Oh, Lord, look at you," she moaned, emitting a clucking sound. "Do you know what the temperature is out there this morning? When in the world are you gonna get a hat?"

The phone rang, and Yvonne picked it up, still shaking her head. "Good morning, Mr. Farber's office. Yes, Mrs. Farber, how are you this morning?"

Jed Farber put his finger over his mouth, pointed to the door next to her desk, and pantomimed a tiptoeing gesture, then beckoned to her to follow.

Yvonne smiled and nodded, translating the message.

He winked at her, walked into the office next to her desk, and shut the door.

"Well, he's in a meeting just now," Yvonne said, her pen poised over the pad before her. "Can I give him a message?" She began writing. "Mmm . . . yes . . . uh-huh." She wrote a few words and then put the pen down. "I can imagine." Restlessly, Yvonne played with one of the small gold picture frames on her desk. "My goodness, you must be." She put the picture frame down and looked at the clock.

"Yes, Mrs. Farber," she said into the telephone. "I certainly will." The crisp, breathy tone of her delivery contrasted with the irritated expression on Yvonne's face. "Yes, I promise. As soon as possible. Good-bye."

When she hung up the phone, Yvonne took a clean coffee mug out of her desk drawer, walked over to the office percolator, filled the mug with hot black coffee, grabbed her pad, and entered Jed Farber's office.

Jed had taken off his coat and was standing behind his desk with his back to her, staring out the window.

Yvonne placed the coffee cup down on his desk, and picked up her list. "Mr. Langman says the clients from Willamar are going to be in town next Tuesday. He wants to know if you're free for lunch."

"Tuesday lunch is fine."

"You do have that appointment with Mr. Bradley . . ."

"But not until three."

"You're right." She made a notation. "I'll tell Mr. Langman 'yes,' then. Let me see . . ." Her eyes moved down the list. "Milton Burmeyer called. He wanted to know whether you would be interested in participating in a D.C. Bar seminar on the new tax proposals—"

Jed turned away from the window and faced her. Yvonne stopped reading, gasped, and put her hand over her mouth. He was wearing a tight pair of blue plastic goggles. The small, circular eye cups were cutting into the flesh around his eyes, the tight white rubber strap flattening the sides of his face and driving a deep ridge into his thick dark hair. A frogman attired in a beautifully tailored navy-blue three-piece suit. "It depends on what's involved, where the seminar takes place," he said, maintaining his businesslike tone.

Yvonne collapsed giggling into the nearest chair.

"No, now seriously," Jed deadpanned. "I want your honest opinion. Are they me? Do they give me that special something all the women of Washington have been craving?"

"What in the world *are* they?"

"Goggles." He beamed, causing the ridges to indent further. "Swimming goggles. One size fits all!"

"Lord, what's gotten in to you?" Yvonne cackled, shaking her head.

"Actually, they're for my kids. They're both on swim teams." Jed winced as he pried the rubber straps off his head. "They say they have the most chlorinated eyes on the team, and I promised them I'd pick up some goggles. This morning was the last chance I figured I'd get before the weekend." He opened his attaché case and pulled out a small paper bag. "Here."

Yvonne took the bag, but gave him a wary look. "I don't *do* goggles."

"They're not goggles. And they're not for you, anyway. They're for your new grandson."

She pulled out an infant-size undershirt with "Redskins" written across the chest. "Oh, aren't you a sweetheart." She cooed. "That is just adorable!"

"That's just what Walt Friedman said."

"Who's Walt Friedman?"

"The man who finally consented to open his sports store early in response to my frantic banging on the door." Jed Farber sipped his coffee. "My schedule doesn't fit in real well with those of the area stores. I had to plead with him that the eyesight of two children was dependent upon his kindness."

"Oh, before I forget," Yvonne said, going back to her list. "Mrs. Farber wanted to know what time Friday you plan to—"

"Six o'clock."

Yvonne nodded. "I'll call back and let her know. Let me see . . ." She held up a card. "You told me to remind you about this—Lilah Ballustrom's party on January twenty-fourth, cocktails from seven to nine. Regrets only."

Jed groaned. "Okay, I'll take care of it." He looked at his watch. "Too early to chance a call. She's probably still home."

Yvonne blinked. "You lost me on that one."

"If I wait, I can avoid Lilah and regret to her answering machine."

"You don't want to go?"

"Not particularly. Besides, the twenty-fourth is Friday. I always save weekends for the kids."

"Weekend *nights* too? Lord, no wonder you come in here looking so sorry Monday mornings! There *are* baby-sitters, you know."

"Well, when you only have custody of your kids on weekends—"

"Lawyer all week, daddy all weekend." Yvonne sighed and slowly rolled her eyes to the ceiling. "Doesn't leave much time for being a *man!*"

"What is this?" he asked. "Early-morning advice to the lovelorn?"

"Look on the bright side. If you *go,* you don't have to worry about answering machines!"

"Sold!" Jed Farber scowled, shaking his head and entering the notation on his pocket calendar.

"Oh, I almost forgot. Mr. Selebri called to confirm. He's meeting you at the courthouse at ten A.M."

Jed Farber winced.

Yvonne frowned. "I thought you said this was just a routine pleading."

"It's not the pleading. It's the client," Farber sighed. "I go in to argue a simple discovery motion, but just spending a few minutes with Selebri is enough to make me feel as though I'm getting a gangster off on a narcotics rap." He looked up at her.

Yvonne put her hand over her mouth, but it didn't work. Suppressed laughter erupted through her fingers as she got up and headed toward the door.

"What?"

"That's nothing to how Selebri's gonna ·feel when he gets a look at you this morning." She giggled. "Hard to believe from those funny red circles around your eyes that 'one size fits all.'"

The Senate Agriculture Committee hearing room resembled a large posh dining room. Elaborate chandeliers hung at regular intervals over the huge table, which was "set" with microphones for the panel members. A fireplace and walls dotted with attractively framed pictures gave the room a feeling of intimacy unlike the larger, more institutional hearing rooms of Congress.

The grandeur evaporated quickly into general chaos at the far end of the room where photographers scrambled amid cramped heaps of video equipment, and reporters squeezed into the clutter of chairs assembled at the press table.

Senator Barker pounded the gavel, signifying the beginning of the hearing. The noise subsided. "A tragedy is taking place in the heartland of this country," the Senator began. "We are here this morning to look at the dimensions of that tragedy, and, hopefully, to find some solutions. We have reached a state of crisis. . . ."

Squinting through the TV lights, Cynthia Matthews cast her eyes about the room. It was theater, pure Washington theater: professional actors transmitting their message to an amateur audience out there in rural America. She looked around the press table at the "transmitters," the eager farm reporters busily underlining sentences in the testimony transcripts with magic markers.

Not all the big shots in the stellar cast were onstage. Two members of the committee had already been there, entered their remarks into the official record, and excused themselves to attend other hearings. A few other Senators were whispering on the sidelines with staff members.

In contrast, Senator Frederick Barker was actively orchestrating the proceedings from the head of the table, leaving no doubt in anyone's mind as to who had the lead part. The television lights picked up the white streaks in his dark brown hair. The large, square-shouldered Senator was a powerful presence, especially in contrast to his first witness, a Mr. Macintosh, a mousey little man with thick glasses.

"Senator, I've been with the Iowa Corn Association for decades, and I've never seen a year as bad as this one," Macintosh said without expression.

Cynthia had plugged her tape recorder into the committee room's sound system. She checked her meter. Perfect. For once, the system was working.

"In what way?" asked Senator Barker.

Macintosh elaborated, making it sound as though Iowa had been hit by a torrential storm, but it was raining corn instead of water. Cynthia marked down the reading on her tape recorder for one particularly dramatic sentence. The delivery was lacking, but the words were strong.

The setting, however, lent a false sense of importance to the event. Cynthia Matthews had heard the same words all her life. At home it was called "porch talk." In bad weather, her father and his friends would sit around in creaking rockers worrying about too little to sell. In good weather, the "porch talk" agonized over too much to sell. She couldn't remember a time of happy "porch talk." There was always a gripe, always too little or too much.

Cynthia looked around the austere surroundings and listened to the words reverberating off the walls of the room. Ashes to ashes and porch talk to porch talk, with one difference: Tonight's "Porch talk" will be brought to you on the radio by your little girl who escaped and found glamour in the nation's capital. Her attention returned to the chairman.

"Patrick Sommers and I go back a long way," Senator Barker was saying. "It's important to differentiate between person and policy." Barker smiled at his witness. "I feel real bad, Pat, that you are here today as a policy, not as a person."

Everyone around the table chortled, and the grilling of the Agriculture Undersecretary began.

Cynthia found herself fascinated by Barker. He was physically imposing, but it was his intellectual skills that came across most dramatically as he eased his witnesses through the paces, stressing the important facts when Macintosh slurred nervously over them, and summing up articulately whenever the long-winded Sommers ran on too long.

Checking her watch, Cynthia evaluated the obstacles between her and the Senator, and mentally charted a speedy route from the press table to the Senator's perch. She would rush up when the break came, to see about setting up an interview.

The more she watched Senator Frederick Barker in action, the more enthusiastic she became about interviewing him.

# · 2 ·

"Breasts," Brittany Spinnet announced as her teeth chiseled tiny ridges into the artichoke leaf she held in her hand. "The man has breasts. I simply cannot deal with a man with breasts."

"What is it with you and anatomical perfection?" growled Pamela Ricci, a heavily made-up, dark-haired woman laden with exotic jewelry. "It's how a man performs in bed that counts."

"Oh, God, the original earth woman!" giggled Brittany.

Cynthia Matthews's eyes wandered from Pamela, the interior decorator, to Brittany, the environmental lobbyist, and she wondered why, though they were ten years out of college, they always regressed to dormitory banter at these shared lunches.

"What do you think?" Brittany nudged Cynthia.

"I think he's a very thoughtful man." Cynthia shrugged, taking a sip of wine.

"Now we're hearing from the ultimate romantic!" Brittany stared at the ceiling. "How many years have I spent listening to Pamela Ricci panting in heat on one side of me and, on the other, Cynthia Matthews, entertaining elaborate fantasies of discovering true love! Reality has not changed anything for you two. You're still dreaming the way you did when we were all virginal Wellesley College freshmen!"

"And you?" Pamela scooped up a mound of sausage. "Have you changed? While we were dreaming virgins, you were walk-

21

ing around with a frown on your face, shaking your head and saying 'I don't know. I'll bet it hurts a lot when you do it.'"

"Well, I was right, wasn't I?"

Cynthia leaned forward and put her hand over Brittany's. "If it still hurts, honey, you're doing it wrong."

Pamela cracked up.

"Flab." Brittany shuddered. "From the tongue to the toes, the man is all flab. And what's more, he's 'handicapped,' as they say in the trade."

Cynthia gave her a perplexed look. "Handicapped?"

"Haven't you ever heard that expression? He shares custody of his kids. Handicapped men are a pain in the ass. If you want to see them on weekends, you have to play mommy to their offspring."

Cynthia just stared at her.

"How is his love-making?" Pamela buttered her roll.

"Too passionate. He's really the most emotional man I've ever slept with. Like sticky paper you want to pull off and get rid of." Brittany winced. "Do you know what he says when he comes? You won't believe this! 'Thank you!' she crooned in a high-pitched voice, breathing heavily. 'Oh, thank you. Thank you!'"

"Well, that's better than 'What time is it?'" Cynthia forked up a clump of spinach.

Pamela snickered. "Remember the guy from West Point Susie Rampol dated senior year? She said he always shouted 'Yes, sir!' during orgasm. Remember? She vowed the day he saluted, she'd leave him."

Brittany folded her delicate hands together in front of her on the table. "Well, at least I've learned something from this experience." She looked first at Pamela and then at Cynthia. "I simply cannot respect a man who does not take care of his body."

Cynthia made a face. "Britt, you're getting impossible."

"No, just selective."

"Name me a man, any man, who could really turn you on."

Brittany put down her fork slowly and looked Cynthia straight in the eye. "I'd take Rob Diamond."

The lettuce Cynthia had just swallowed formed a rigid lump in her throat. She washed it down with wine, but felt it lodging somewhere above her diaphram, its passage thwarted by the muscles that were suddenly contracting throughout her body. "Believe me, you can do better than that." She congratulated herself on the lighthearted tone of her delivery.

"Better? Silky golden hair? Azure eyes? A perfect body? What could be better?"

"A soul, for starters."

"I'll bet Rob Diamond didn't whine 'Thank you!' when he came."

Cynthia smiled with her lips only. "If he had deigned to stoop to words at all, he undoubtedly would have chosen 'You're welcome.'"

Pamela laughed, and Cynthia looked down to avoid her eyes, fearful of what her own might reveal.

"Now, there," Pamela lectured, pointing the butter knife at Brittany. "There's a classic example of a perfect body and a rotten everything else."

As the two argued Rob Diamond's pros and cons, Cynthia played with her food, wondering when she would stop reacting this way every time his name was mentioned, when she would stop entertaining childish fantasies about his rushing toward her across crowded rooms.

She swept three slices of swiss cheese to the center of the plate, topped them off with a sliver of bermuda onion, and stared at the collage she had created.

When she stopped perpetuating the myth, she decided. That's when it would get easier.

Not now, though. Not yet.

"Well, Cynthia certainly showed him," Brittany pulled out another artichoke leaf and turned to Cynthia. "I'd say you discarded him rather adroitly, exposing his illegalities in print for all to see!"

"Now, I'll drink to that." Pamela raised her glass toward Cynthia. "To the woman who managed to have the city's biggest catch fall in love with her, but, in the end, decided journalistic integrity was more important than bagging the big one!"

"To ultimate power!" chimed in Brittany, elevating her Perrier.

Cynthia looked from one to the other and then back at the

red and yellow collage on her plate. What easier audience could there be for the inevitable dismantling of the myth?

Once and for all, she decided. It had to be now.

"I have a toast." Cynthia raised her wine glass with a trembling hand. "To a major scoop."

Two sets of eyebrows and glasses were raised simultaneously.

"The one I am about to give to the two of you." She took a gulp of wine and put the glass back down. "It's not true about Rob Diamond."

"What's not true? We read the story you wrote. All of Washington read the story!"

"Oh, the article was true. It was just the folklore that went with it that wasn't, the part about his falling in love with me." There was a meaningful pause. "He didn't."

"But you dated for a long time. And everyone said . . ."

"Everyone *said*, that's right. Everyone, including Rob, insisted he was in love with me." She shrugged self-consciously. "And everyone lied, including Rob."

"Cyn, what the hell—" Pamela began.

Cynthia held up her hand. "The truth was I was approached by two people who felt the law firm that represented their family's interests had mishandled their trust funds, and they told me several other clients had similar suspicions. So I began checking it out for a possible story. The law firm in question was the one Rob was in."

"Yeah, yeah. We know all that!" Britt said.

"Well, I had begun checking into the law firm's accounts before I even met Rob." She ran her finger around the bottom of the wine glass. "I guess, in retrospect, that Rob knew that I was just a few steps away from finding out about him, that the complaint was correct and that he was one of the people who had done the mishandling."

"So what?" Brittany asked impatiently. "What does that have to do with—"

"So . . . So he came on very, very strong. He artfully transformed Reporter Matthews into Lover Matthews, for a few weeks, at least." She looked up, her lips rigid. "It was really very easy. Reporter Matthews is a pathetic pushover, and Lover-Boy Diamond is very convincing."

Pamela stared at her, absorbing the meaning.

Brittany refused to. "Did he admit, finally, that it was all a ruse?" she demanded.

"No, he—"

"Then maybe you're just reading motives into it. How do you know—"

"I know! Believe me, I know. I *should* have known all along." She chewed on her lip. "I think maybe deep down I did. I just liked being in love. Being loved by Mr. Great . . . I was, well, so flattered. It's humiliating, really. The vanity of it all."

She looked up at them suddenly. "You know what's really despicable? There were the facts, staring me in the face, proving his misconduct beyond a shadow of a doubt, and there I was, an experienced fact-finder, and I refused to believe the records for a while."

"What made you change?"

She sipped her wine. "I may be a hopeless romantic, but over the years I've become a seasoned reporter, and there was no way—even with my help—that Rob could put together an explanation strong enough to overcome the evidence." She laughed ruefully. "In the end, his legal argument essentially boiled down to 'I love you.'" Cynthia pushed her wine glass away and leaned back in her chair.

Brittany played with a piece of green pepper. "It's weird. You know, the rumors are you slept with him to get the story."

Cynthia's eyes grew wide. "That is the sickest part of all. We reached a kind of unspoken gentleman's agreement, making him the wounded lover, and me into the coldhearted journalist."

"Sounds like an intelligent face-saving plan to me," Brittany said quietly. "What's so sick about that?"

"That she'd be more comfortable coming off as a righteous bitch than a vain female taken for a ride by Mr. Debonair?" Pamela snarled. "I'd say that's sick!"

"Naaaw." Brittany sipped her Perrier slowly. "I'd say it's just Washington." She smiled at Cynthia. "Very, very Washington. Fits right in with the native dating customs."

Cynthia sat thinking for a while and then lifted her glass. "To new goals!"

Pamela turned on her wicked grin. "And new men!"

## · 3 ·

Later that afternoon, Cynthia sat in Capitol Radio's large workroom surrounded by the sounds of industrious reporters at deadline time.

Coworker Jake Weinstein, a short and compact man of thirty with a meticulously cropped black beard, pounded away on the typewriter at the desk facing Cynthia's.

Across the room, enveloped in smoke, forty-five-year-old Brian Mulroney took a long drag on the cigarette dangling from his mouth as he tapped out another sentence.

In the corner behind Brian, Suzie Pepper, a recent college graduate, was valiantly attempting to splice tape without disturbing her newly applied nail polish.

Looking around the room, Cynthia decided the scene would have made a good photographic display—a poster entitled "Hotshot Reporters at Work." She laughed a little. The truth was, no one took what he or she was doing very seriously. That was because no one in the room took Capitol Radio very seriously. For each staff member, Capitol Radio was "bread and butter"—the source of a stable paycheck that could be lived off en route to or from more serious projects.

Cynthia herself saw Capitol Radio as a solid job to hang on to until she felt confident enough about her free-lance work to do that full time.

Jake Weinstein was a professional musician, not yet "professional" enough to live off his music career. Suzie Pepper hoped the skills she was learning at Capitol Radio would enable her to get a job at a "real" radio station in the future. The absent Sinclair Cleaver—who called in sick as frequently as he reported for work—was already partially retired, splitting his time evenly between writing farm reports for Capitol Radio and relaxing at his farm outside of Washington.

And as for Brian Mulroney, tours of duty as a reporter in war zones around the world had yielded him an endless supply of anecdotes and the dissolution of two marriages. Faced with the economic strains of child support, he had opted for money over danger, Capitol Radio over UPI.

Cynthia smiled as she watched Brian. He was now working on a one-minute spot on a White House press handout that, she was certain, he would soon deliver to Capitol Radio subscribers with the same deep, throaty intonations and the same sense of drama that had characterized his past broadcasts from Beirut and Vietnam.

Sylvia Berg appeared in the doorway to the radio workroom. "Cynthia, Gardiner wants to talk to you," she announced. "He's upset about the farm hearing story you wrote."

Brian Mulroney stopped typing in midsentence. Jake Weinstein looked up aghast. Suzie Pepper pulled off her earphones. The sense of Capitol Radio's journalistic unimportance was imparted to the staff by its chief executive officer, who preferred afternoon-long lunches to office "busy work." Gardiner Weldy rarely looked at a story after it was written and recorded.

"*Talk* to me?" Cynthia gasped, hurrying toward the door. "I just assumed the story was a fait accompli! The requesting stations wanted it hours ago!"

Gardiner was sitting upright in his regal desk chair when she entered his office, a solemn expression on his face. About five feet nine inches tall, with a physique reminiscent of a spider, Gardiner Weldy had small, nondescript brown eyes, sallow skin, and a main of gray-black curls so meticulously assembled his employees joked that he slept each night in rollers.

But Gardiner also had pizzazz, and as he glared at Cynthia across his polished mahogany desk, attired in an expensive suit, his well-starched white shirt adorned with gleaming gold cufflinks, Gardiner Weldy came across as a distinguished editor-in-chief about to vent his wrath on a lesser professional.

"Three sound bites in one spot?" Gardiner cringed and put his hands to his head. "So many voices, my dear. *Too* many voices!" He sat back in his chair. "Confusion, that's what we have here."

Cynthia looked thoroughly perplexed. "But, Gardiner, we *always* use . . ."

"Now, I specifically instructed you at the morning meeting to go for the *pathos* in covering this story, Cynthia." He looked at her with forlorn eyes. "What happened to my pathos?"

"Pathos?" Cynthia gasped. "Christ, Gardiner, the story is filled with pathos! You have the commodity trade groups on one side howling in pain over surpluses without sales. You have the administration officials on the other side, tearing their hair out in frustration because the high value of the dollar is killing off exports. You have the compassionate, rural Senator, desperate to do something for the people back home . . ."

"Compassionate rural Senator?" Gardiner mocked, "My, my, you've been in this business too long to be sucked in like that, Cynthia!" He made clucking sounds. "I don't hear honest compassion. I hear a rallying cry for help for the Iowa farmer, which translates into an articulate call for votes from a man facing reelection in what I understand will be a difficult campaign. I mean," he said, clipping his words, "this doesn't sound to me like a news report. It sounds like a campaign promo for Senator Frederick Barker!"

Was the criticism justified? Shocked by her boss's rare attempt at editing, Cynthia began replaying the spot in her head.

"Take my advice," Gardiner went on softly, encouraged by her silence. "Rewrite the piece using the Macintosh and Somers sound bites, telling what it was that the Senator said, but leaving out his voice. You'll have a more honest news story."

"No," Cynthia said slowly, shaking her head. "That wouldn't be accurate, Gardiner. Really, the Senator was the central presence at the hearing."

Sylvia entered with a cup of coffee that she placed before Gardiner. "Uh, Gardiner, the Iowa stations I talked to *were* primarily interested in Barker," Sylvia said quietly as she neatly folded a napkin and set it down next to the coffee cup.

"Next time *I* will take the calls from Iowa!" Gardiner bellowed.

Cynthia jumped. Gardiner rarely raised his voice, and never, never spoke that way to Sylvia.

"I agree that it's not our job to promote anyone, Gardiner," Cynthia said in a conciliatory voice. "But at the same time, it is also not our job to censor—to keep Senator Barker's voice off the air just because he's articulate."

Gardiner looked uncomfortably from Sylvia to Cynthia. Then he sighed. "All right." He took the tape off his console and handed it to Sylvia. "Feed it as is."

"What do you make of that?" Cynthia whispered to Sylvia as she closed the door to Gardiner's office. "An attempt by Gardiner to show editorial interest?" She giggled playfully, but when she looked for a response, Sylvia had turned away.

Cynthia's cohorts stared at her attentively as she walked back into the workroom.

"It's a history-making event here at Capitol Radio," Brian Mulroney said, speaking into his fist as though it were a hot microphone and delivering the words in the breathy tones of an on-site news report. "The crowd is tense. None of the people I have interviewed here can recall another incident like this one, when Gardiner Weldy took time out from his busy social day to actually *read* a Capitol Radio spot, let alone balk at issuing it!"

Room-wide laughter erupted.

Oblivious to the joking, Cynthia walked over to her desk and sat down, a puzzled frown on her face.

Jed Farber groaned as he sat behind the wheel of his car. The traffic was moving slowly, bumper to bumper, with no end in sight, and to make matters worse, the car directly in front of his was slowing to a stop, miles away from the curb, no signal . . . nothing.

Leaning on his horn, and stepping on the gas, Jed Farber swerved around the stopped car, narrowly missing an automobile on his other side that was making a left-hand turn.

Rush-hour traffic. Asshole drivers.

Warmed by frustration, he flicked off the car radiator and loosened his scarf. He reminded himself he was in no hurry. Nothing was awaiting him but an empty apartment and a night of work. Still, his fingers played impatiently on the steering wheel.

He turned on the radio and listened to a report on an upturned truck on the Washington Beltway had halted traffic for miles in both directions.

His breathing slowed down. At least he was not on the Beltway.

His impatience. That was one of the long list of grievances Celeste Goldman had just spelled out for him over cocktails.

The light changed. As Jed lurched forward, braking quickly to avoid the car ahead of him, he awarded Celeste Goldman two points for accuracy.

Actually, Celeste had been on the nose all the way: He *was* impatient. He *was* intense. He *was* too involved with his children. That *did* ruin social opportunities on the weekend. He *was* emotionally cold and distant.

Well, to Celeste Goldman he was. Jed shifted uncomfortably. He frankly thought of himself as a very warm person, an incredibly loving person, in fact. That was certainly the reputation he had in the family, wasn't it? In his mind, he called his relatives to the witness stand one by one.

"No matter how busy Jed is, when you have a problem, he listens," his Uncle Hymie said, shaking his round bald head. "And another thing," Uncle Hymie went on, jabbing the air with his index finger as he pointed it at the judge. "If you call Jed Farber collect, he always accepts the charges."

"I remember during my emotional breakdown," his sister, Daphne, sighed, dabbing her eyes with a handkerchief as invisible weights pulled down the corners of her mouth. "There was only one person who was there for me all the time, day and night, listening, advising, consoling, giving me the strength to go on."

"You couldn't ask for a better son," his mother declared with the quiet conviction she usually reserved for her canasta group, a conviction that dared anyone to disagree.

Well, take that, Celeste Goldman.

No, now be fair. Be fair. He *had* been cold with Celeste . . . disinterested.

On the other hand, how else could a man be expected to respond to a woman who basically disliked his children? To a perfectly intelligent, attractive person with an interesting job who nonetheless spent half her life preoccupied with counting calories and age lines and the other half searching hysterically for "Mr. Right"?

"I'm thirty-five, Jed. I feel my biological time bomb ticking," she had said with a quivering voice—as though she had cancer or something!—"and I feel there is no future for the two of us." She had gazed down into her whiskey sour misty-eyed. "I—I just can't waste the time. I have to look elsewhere."

And what had he felt?

Nothing. Absolutely nothing. After almost six months of off-on dating, he had felt nothing.

Maybe she was right about his being "cold and distant."

The car ahead moved on. Jed followed, but this time at a more conventional pace.

As he stared with irritation at the long string of red tail lights lined up before him on Connecticut Avenue, Jed tried to figure out what it felt like to have a biological time bomb ticking inside you. It was a sensation that seemed to be common among the women he dated. More common than sexual arousal, certainly.

Sociological pap, all of it. Why hadn't they planned ahead if it was so damn important to them to reproduce? And wasn't it interesting that all these women dying to make babies before it was too late were bored at best when confronted by his two off-spring?

*Very* interesting!

He stared at the ceiling of his car to avoid the view of endless tail lights.

Well, farewell, Celeste. May you tick on somebody else for a while. Easy come, easy go. The truth was, he was losing little more than an excuse to go out to dinner and the theater during the week and well-meaning but dispassionate sex.

Suddenly his eyes lit up in response to the traffic ahead opening up, and in response to the rather ironic song that had just begun to pour forth on his car radio.

Stepping down on the gas, Jed sang along with the music: "Whatever happened to old-fashioned love/ The kind that would last through the years/ Through the trials/Through the smiles/Through the tears?"

He noted his voice had a caustic ring to it.

In her living room, later that night, Cynthia turned the stack of typewritten pages facedown on the desk, and viewed it with a look of total disgust. Prepackaged homiles from the mouths of

Washington's major-movers—that's what her freelance piece on "human loss" for *America Magazine* was turning out to be.

Perhaps the interview with Senator Barker would yield more substance.

The fact was, *American Magazine* did not *want* substance. They wanted a glitzy national survey premised on the absurd question "Tell me, Mr. Famous, how does it feel to lose a loved one?" They wanted exactly what she had got—polished quotes from the political elite, verbal press releases that ranged from sentimental to maudlin.

What was the problem, then? She had fulfilled her assignment, and she would be compensated for her efforts with a by-line in a national magazine and a formidable paycheck.

The problem was, the article underscored her own personal inability to deal with "human loss."

She stood up and began walking restlessly around her living room. "Tell me, Ms. Reporter, how does it feel to lose a loved one?"

She reached up and took the gold picture frame from its place on the high shelf of her bookcase. Gently, with the bottom of her big navy-blue sweatshirt, she swept away the dust that had gathered on the glass.

The picture showed Cynthia as a teenager sitting next to her father on the tractor. She was clowning at the camera, her head on her father's shoulder. What a ham.

He was smiling too, but you could tell he was a bit embarrassed by her antics, by her "carrying on." That's what he always called it—"carrying on." She heard him grunt the words with that funny mixture of irritation and affection he always used.

She lowered her eyelids a little as though the sun were shining, sucked in her cheeks slightly, and held her head up, imitating her father in the picture.

She was "his replica." That's what everyone said. While Jimmy, Georgine, and Sarah were short and dark like their mother, she was tall and fair and slim like her father. Jonathan was too, except that he had his mother's dark eyes. Cynthia was the only offspring with "Marshall Matthews blues"—the only real "replica."

In personality too. Or so the family lore went. "Stubborn,

just like your father," her mother used to grumble. "A playful devil, just like your father."

She stared at the man on the tractor. Stubborn, he was one stubborn ox, that was for sure. But a playful devil? Well, maybe in his youth. "Purposeful" was more the way she would have described him. A man with crops to tend to, who plodded ahead as forcefully and consistently as the tractor he rode.

Well, yes, but there were those funny sparkles he got in his eyes . . . The truth was, in later years, he had always sparkled when she was around. That's what her mother had said. "The light of his life," she had said.

"You were always his favorite," Georgine had sighed when they were all home for the funeral. And so she'd been. Oh, probably just because she was a girl and the youngest, and she looked like him. But it was true. She had always felt favored.

In trips home over the last fifteen years, when something was upsetting her—though she had never been able to communicate her angst to him, never tried, really—just sitting next to him on the porch swing, watching the sun go down, talking about little things, other things, she had always felt soothed.

The fact was, she had moved into another world, an interesting, stimulating world beyond Marshall Matthews's grasp, but she had never found the homespun love in this new world that she had had in his. She felt a knot in her throat and she yearned to explode it by crying, but the tears could not come.

"You need to cry," Georgine, the big sister, had instructed at the funeral. But there was no one to cry with—no one who could understand. Everyone she knew was either from her "old" world, or her "new" world.

Cynthia smiled as she ran her finger down the picture of the tall, wind-burnt figure of her favorite farmer. Oh, the irony of it. She, who had spent a childhood dreaming of driving that tractor miles and miles and miles and miles away to the promised land was now *in* that promised land, longing to be back on the tractor.

She had always known how deeply her father loved her. What she hadn't realized—until his death—was how very much she loved him back.

She smiled and placed the picture on a lower shelf where it was more visible.

\*　　\*　　\*

It was past midnight when Senator Frederick Barker unlocked the front door and entered his large Chevy Chase, Maryland, home. Automatically, his hand reached to his right for the switch in the hallway.

He winced as the bright lights illuminated the vast expanse of an absolutely immaculate living room. Every pillow on the sofas seemed carefully placed. The wooden floors glistened underneath the dust-free Oriental area rugs. The antique tables and cabinets oozed lemon oil. The brass lamps glistened.

The Senator's head bobbed up and down slowly as his eyes surveyed the room: "No one lives here anymore."

He whisked the lights off abruptly.

In the darkness, Barker fumbled his way around the familiar pieces of furniture, slowly navigating a route to the bar at a distant corner of the room.

He turned on the small table lamp next to the bar. His hand trembled slightly as he poured a healthy amount of scotch into a glass. He held the drink up, and toasted his reflection, still clad in hat and coat, in the mirror behind the bar. "To yet another evening dedicated to Thad Rankerman's campaign coffers!"

The eyes in the mirror lost all expression. Barker's jaw clenched. "The last one," he promised himself. "No more nights like this one . . . no more." He took a healthy slug and refilled the glass.

Turning around and facing the darkened living room, he hurled his hat on top of an armchair. He took off his gloves, and tossed each one on a different end table. He threw his coat over the back of the sofa. "Better," he grunted, surveying the layer of debris.

Grabbing his drink, he turned on a lamp and examined the pictures in frames on the table—the former inhabitants: three children in varying stages of development, his wife, Penny, in an evening gown at around the age of fifty.

He collapsed into an old armchair and sat very still for a while, listening to the silence.

Sixty years old. Sixty years and four months, to be exact. That made him—how did the demographers put it? "Young-old." That was it. At a kind of productive height, but embarking on a period of disintegration that would inevitably lead to his demise.

"Young-old!" He lifted his glass ceremoniously and took a healthy slug.

He felt "old-old"—an anachronism, a man who had already outlived his time, outlived his wife, outlived that stage of having a family noisily bustling around his house, outlived politics, at least *real* politics.

He thought back to his first successful campaign for Congress, and smiled a little. His daddy's old pickup truck. That's what had won the seat for him. Not his ideas, or his promises, but rather his old man's pickup truck.

He guzzled some scotch and grunted a little. Worked so well, he'd used one just like it for some of his campaigning when he had run for the Senate the first time. Enabled him to get to the people, and have them notice him—a gimmick.

Senator Barker's gray eyes turned dreamy for a while, but then they sobered. Well, you can't do that anymore, can you? Hell, no. Today, twenty-five different political polling consultants will tell you: Pickup trucks at best will reach one fiftieth of your general voting population, and less than one tenth of one percent of the occupational/ethnic sample you're having trouble with.

He drank some more.

What's more, those esteemed consultants will charge you an arm and a leg just for that tidbit of knowledge. Yes, they will. They'll also tell you that there aren't any good old down-home-folks voting in Iowa today.

Senator Barker's head wagged a little. No, sir. There's a whole new generation, one that can only be swayed by electronics. Whereas you could convince their forebears to vote for you by showing you were human—by pressing the flesh—these new voters demand a human touch that comes through headphones, through car radios, through the tube.

Ah, the almighty tube!

Oh, granted there are some in Iowa still old-fashioned enough to read their mail, but it costs a pretty penny just to have the consultants single them out and get their addresses.

And if you happen to be one of those unusual members of the Senate whose earnings are pretty well summed up by his Senate salary and his speaking engagements, you're an anachronism, an outdated man about to enter a campaign against a *new-wave politician*—an opponent who doesn't grow wheat or corn, like opponents in the old days, but who grows dollar bills instead, a filthy rich, immoral, rotten, low-level . . .

Barker closed his eyes and gulped his drink. This time, bless it, the liquor seemed to go right where he needed it, right to his head. The tension evaporated in a wave of giddiness.

Yes, it made perfect sense, didn't it? He had been forced to turn to *crime*! He snorted a laugh over that one. No doubt about it! He'd had to resort to unethical tactics to keep the *decent* man in the Senate! Well now, wasn't *that* a thigh-slapper?

Gradually, the gleam left his eyes. To be fair, he had probably been a little bit crazy at the time. He focused on a painting on the wall across the room, pleading his case. His wife was dying. That seemed to make him more desperate than ever to hold onto what he had left, to the *one* thing that had really *mattered* in his life.

He finished what remained in the glass and walked back to the bar for a refill. He stood there for a long time, drinking and yearning—suddenly—for companionship. Not, he admitted, the companionship of his biological family: his late wife, his grown and departed children. Rather, he longed for the companionship of the group that had always functioned as his real family, his sounding board in moments of strain—the attentive young aides, the inner circle of political cohorts.

Well, just like his wife, they were no more, could be no more. For the first time in his life, he had done something he could confide in no one. He had willingly, intentionally, committed an act that had isolated him from his ample supply of confidants and had included him in a fraternity he had always regarded with contempt.

He closed his eyes tightly, mourning the loss, accepting the facts: He who had always prided himself on abiding by a higher standard, had succumbed to the common denominator. He was now just like all the others, the weak ones he had always disdained . . . the ones, quite frankly, he still disdained.

Funny, wasn't it? How it had taken a transgression to make him realize he really believed the haughty rhetoric he had spouted all these years . . . the little lessons in ethics he had bestowed upon his staff.

He grunted. More than anything else, *that* undoubtedly made him an anachronism in modern American politics.

The eyes opened slowly, and, staring into the mirror, the cagey politician examined the bottom line: Was it the sin that was plaguing him, he asked the eyes, or was it something baser—the fact that it might not work?

Both.

The eyes staring back from the mirror were filled with self-loathing . . . and something more. Weariness. Battle fatigue. A need for escape, and not just from politics. From it all.

They frightened him, for they were not the eyes of a cover-up artist, a shrewd con man. No, he who had spent a lifetime deciphering the truths that lurked behind the babble knew only too well that these were the potentially suicidal eyes of a man who was becoming increasingly unable to bear the burden of his guilt in isolation, a man desperate to purge himself by confessing.

His body chilled. He was going to give himself away.

He took another sip and watched as his Adam's apple struggled with the liquor's passage much the way his mind was struggling with his burden. He was both desperate to protect himself, and desperate to rid himself of the weight by confessing.

But who was there to tell? Whom could he trust? Who knew him well enough and cared for him deeply enough to hear him out without either condemning or condoning . . . or exposing him for that matter? Who would understand the desperation that had motivated him? Who would be able to ease his mind by putting the deed into perspective: one minor impropriety in an otherwise honorable career?

And who . . . oh, God, *who* was smart enough to help him figure a way to get out of it intact?

There was only one possibility.

Senator Barker walked slowly over to the sofa, sat down, took the telephone off the end table, and put it in his lap. He stared at it for a while. Then he tapped out a number.

It was picked up after the first ring. "Hello?" Jed Farber's voice sounded groggy, as though he had been awakened. "Hello?"

Barker opened his mouth to speak, but then, his eyes staring off into space, he slowly put the receiver back on the telephone.

# · 4 ·

Cynthia Matthews fidgeted in her bed, awake before dawn Friday morning, still fretting over whether or not to go to Lilah Ballustrom's party.

She reminded herself she had a professional out. The interview she had set up with Senator Barker was scheduled for six o'clock that evening. She could always call Lilah Saturday and explain that the Senator had kept her too long for her to make the party.

She stared at the shadows on the ceiling in her bedroom. No, she decided finally. No more cowardliness. Face Rob. Face them all. Show up. Stare them down. And leave as quickly as possible.

With new resolve, she bounded out of bed, got dressed for work, and packed a party dress to take along with her to the office. Capitol Radio was halfway between Senator Barker's office and Lilah's house. She would definitely be able to make it to the party if she returned to Capitol Radio after the interview and changed there.

At six o'clock in the morning, she was all packed and ready to go.

"*Hasta luego.*" She heard the words in her head with a rural Maryland lilt.

Well, all right then! Determined to stay upbeat, she told herself the early hour gave her another project. She could check out the bus stop and find out whether the dilapidated van of Hispanic men was a daily occurrence.

She even prepared a little. With the help of her college English/Spanish dictionary, she wrote out a few questions in Spanish, and practiced saying them out loud—just in case the van *did* arrive, and there were some passengers left to interrogate after the driver drove off.

She was at the bus stop for less than five minutes when she heard the funny rumbling engine sound. Sure enough, there was the dilapidated green van on the horizon. Someone had fixed the broken headlight, she noticed.

She stepped back into the store doorway closest to the bus stop, determined to avoid the driver's eyesight this time.

As he had before, the driver hopped out, ran around, and opened the back door. But this time she heard a strange sound coming from inside the van. A squeal.

"EEEEEEEEE!"

And this time the driver did not have to urge the men to exit. They were scrambling out. They turned around and looked nervously into the van's interior once they made it to the pavement, then ran off into the darkness.

"EEEEEEEEE!" It was getting louder, closer to the back door.

"EEEEEEEEE!" The cry crackled the cold quiet of the streets as a heavy, curly-haired man crawled out of the van.

"EEEEEEEEE!"

The driver smacked the man on the chest with his fist, and the cries stopped suddenly, as though the man had been snapped out if it by the punch.

"You!" the driver said, putting a hand on each of the man's shoulders. "Don't come no more, hear?"

The man stared at him.

"No *trabaha* no more!" the driver yelled. "*Nada!* Ayn tee en day?"

In a stupor, the man plopped down on the curb.

The driver climbed back in the van and drove away.

Cynthia looked around. Again, the passengers had all dispersed, leaving the street totally silent. The man sat very still on the curb, his back to Cynthia.

Then another figure walked back toward the man, under the spotlight of the street lamp. Cynthia squinted. It was the teenage boy she had seen the last time—the one who had escorted 'Me Pablo!' away. The boy bent down and spoke softly to the man in Spanish. Cynthia could not make out the words, but from the way the boy was gesturing, she had the feeling he was saying, "Come on. Let's go."

Guillo. He called the man "Guillo."

She stood very still in the darkness of the store's doorway, trying to breathe soundlessly.

"Guillo" was not responding, and the boy was getting impatient. He stood for a while observing the man on the curb from different angles, as though looking for a physical explanation for his peculiar behavior. Finally, the boy sighed and began walking away.

"*Por favor!*" Cynthia shouted, emerging from the doorway quickly before the boy could escape, like the others, into the darkness.

He jumped a little.

She ran over to him and then looked at "Guillo." Tears were streaming from the man's eyes, carving dirt lines along his cheeks, but the eyes remained open, unblinking, expressionless.

"*Porque . . .*" She faltered. "*Porque es loco?*" she asked, pointing to Guillo and hoping the spontaneous question translated into "Why's he crazy?"

The boy just frowned and shrugged.

Time to switch to the prepared interrogatories. "*El carro va a traerla aqui a esta hora todas las mananas?*" she asked, taking pleasure in the expert way she had managed to roll the r's in "*carro*" and praying she had said: "Does the car bring you here every morning at this time?"

The boy nodded solemnly, like a child replying to a strict teacher. "*Si,*" he said, drawing the word out for several syllables.

"*De donde viene el carro?*" she asked, hoping he would tell her where the van came from.

The boy did something Cynthia had not anticipated: He broke into fluent Spanish. Pointing to the right over his shoulder, and then to the left, and then to the right again, he went on and on in an animated diatribe she could not understand, for what seemed to be a very long period of time. It was then that she realized she had spent a lot of time preparing the questions, no time at all contemplating how she would field the answers, in a tongue she had not conversed in since her senior year in college.

When he finished, she went on to her third question, realizing it was futile, that this whole project of hers had not been adequately thought out, but she ventured forth nonetheless.

*"Como puede llegar alle?"* How do you get there? she asked.

"Easy," his gestures told her: He shrugged and held his hands out palms up. Unfortunately, he then went on to words. So many words. Cynthia stared down at his round face with the broad, high cheekbones and the eyes shaped like half-moons, realizing that if she had really prepared for this, she would have brought a tape recorder, so she could translate the sentences some time later. She saw a bus emerging on the horizon, just over the boy's left shoulder, and she was terribly thankful. There would be other stories. She had obviously not thought this one out very clearly. She signaled to the bus driver to stop.

*"Gracias,"* she told the sweet, sincere boy as she ran to catch the bus.

"Perhaps you would be more comfortable if we conversed in your native tongue."

The words came from behind, delivered in flawless American English.

Cynthia stopped dead in her tracks. Slowly, she turned around to the source of the sentence.

It was a very different boy she faced this time: cocky, all-American, his tongue displayed prominently in his cheek, his hands shoved in his jean pockets. He was chuckling.

She waved the bus driver on.

"You really got a kick out of that, didn't you?" Cynthia snapped. "Letting me go on and on like an idiot!"

His eyes sparkled. "Yoooooo speeeeeek Spanitch wery well!" It was a perfect takeoff on "Pablo's" painfully crafted utterance two days before.

They both laughed. She held out her hand. "I'm Cynthia Matthews."

"I'm Carlos Ramirez." He shook her hand.

"Okay, Carlos, where *does* the van come from?"

"A factory. We work an overnight shift in a factory. The van picks us up here each night and brings us back each morning. The first fifteen people in line each night get to work."

A sweatshop? she wondered. An employer taking undue advantage of an impoverished work force! The other men certainly looked exhausted, debilitated. "Is the work hard?" she asked eagerly.

"Not at all!" He laughed a little. "We just put metal parts together and load them onto a truck."

The exploitation was financial, then. "What do you get paid?" she asked, frowning.

"Five dollars an hour." He practically shouted it. "That's almost two dollars above the minimum wage!"

It didn't make sense. "Why?" She said it to herself as much as to Carlos.

He frowned suspiciously. "Why do you want to know?"

"Just curious. I live in the neighborhood, and noticed you all the other morning when I was waiting for my bus. It just seemed a little strange, that's all." Her eyes wandered over to Guillo, who was now lying down on the curb, staring wide-eyed at the dark sky. "What's the matter with him?"

"I don't know." Carlos studied the man for a while. "I was wondering too. He just began screaming and crying in the van for no reason."

"He's been normal other times?"

"Normal!" Carlos snickered. "This is not a very normal group! They're all—" He stopped abruptly. His eyes narrowed as they stared at Cynthia. His jaw clenched.

"I'm *not* from Immigration, Carlos, if that's what you're worried about."

He kept staring at her, his mouth firmly shut.

She reached into her bag and pulled out a few press ID cards and handed them to him.

"A reporter." His concern eased only slightly.

"A neighbor . . . Just a person who's curious about why some of these men seem so strange."

He looked at her alertly. "In what way do you think they're strange?"

"Dazed. Crazed." She pointed at Guillo. "Hysterical."

He stared at Guillo.

She had a feeling Guillo's behavior had the boy concerned too. "Have any of the others behaved that way? Suddenly screaming?"

He looked away and shrugged uncomfortably.

They stood there in silence for a while. An impasse. Finally Cynthia pulled out her wallet and handed him one of her business cards. "If you get curious too, give me a call."

He said nothing, but he put the card in his pocket.


"Pamela called," Jake Weinstein yelled out as Cynthia returned to Capitol Radio from an assignment late that afternoon. "She said to tell you to keep your chin up and give them hell at Lilah's party tonight."

Cynthia dumped the stack of cassettes she was carrying onto the top of her desk and flopped down in the chair.

Jake's eyes roamed the empty workroom. "Would you look at this place?" he snickered. "Some news organization! Brian's started his weekend boozing. Sinc's off to his family farm. What would happen if a news story broke right now?"

"You're in Washington." Cynthia began labeling the tape cassettes. "News is civilized. Every respectable newsmaker knows nothing can happen late Friday afternoon and still get reported!"

Jake sat down at the tape console and plugged in a set of headphones. "And what if the House Majority Leader suddenly discovered—right now—that the President of the United States had secretly ordered the Air Force to drop bombs on Iran?"

Cynthia held out her arms. "You and me, Jake, we'd be here to get the word out to the hinterlands!"

"Yeah?" Jake stood up. "But you have to interview Senator Barker in less than an hour, and I have to head off to a big gig tonight as soon as I finish transcribing this tape."

The workroom door opened and Gardiner Weldy sauntered in.

"Gardiner!" Jake shouted. "Just when we needed you!"

"Needed me?" Gardiner asked. "How did you need me?" He oozed his way soundlessly across the room, his spidery walk propelling him forward. Cynthia found it an amusing contrast to Jake's jerky motions.

"We were worried that if a dramatic news story broke suddenly, there would be no one here to cover it." Jake explained. "I have to go get ready to perform at Quartos, and Cynthia has an interview in less than an hour."

Gardiner laughed. "Even Capitol Radio has to close up sometime. Have a good performance, Jake!"

Jake put on the headphones and began transcribing. To Cynthia's dismay, Gardiner Weldy settled down in a chair next to her desk, and turned to her expansively. "Is this a Capitol Radio interview or one of your free-lance endeavors?"

"A free-lance endeavor."

"Ahh, I'm so proud of your energy, Cynthia. We all are. It's remarkable how you manage to fulfill Capitol Radio's needs so capably and still find time to 'make your mark,' as they say, in broader journalistic circles."

Gardiner's smarmy praise triggered an instinctive desire in Cynthia to upchuck. But as she looked at the fatherly expression in his face, she remonstrated with herself. Wasn't it possible that every so often Gardiner Weldy was sincere?

"What's the subject matter this time?"

She played with her pen. "Human loss . . . well-known Washington personalities who have recently lost members of their families."

"Human loss?" Gardiner's brow wrinkled with empathy. "How very difficult that must be as an interview topic! Who is your subject for tonight?"

"Senator Frederick Barker." Recalling Gardiner's reaction to her news story on Barker, Cynthia feared a hostile response. But instead, Gardiner's expression became more compassionate. "Oh, yes of course," he mumbled softly, "I read it in the papers—his wife."

Cynthia nodded solemnly. They sat there sighing and nodding together, and Cynthia began to feel as though she and Gardiner were guests at some sort of wake. The image made her feel like giggling.

"And that sensationally bright-green knit outfit that is hanging out in the front closet—that is what you intend to wear to ease the bereavement of the senior Senator from Iowa?"

"No. Not at all. I have a cocktail party to go to tonight. I was planning to come back here after the interview, leave all my equipment, and change before taking off for the party."

"Ahh," Gardiner purred, nodding. "Cinderella shedding her workday encumberments and heading off to the ball."

"I promise I won't clutter up the office or anything. I thought I'd just come back tomorrow morning and retrieve—"

"Oh, my, don't worry about that! I want you to feel as comfortable in this office as you do in your own home!" Gardiner scrutinized Cynthia more carefully from across the desk. "You seem unusually tense." He tilted his head. "Is there something about this interview that concerns you?"

She felt her face get hot. "Not . . . not the interview. It's the party that's—"

"The *party*?" Gardiner's eyes teased. "You're concerned about going to a party?"

"No!" Cynthia was exasperated with herself for opening up this line of questioning. "Not at all. I'm fine."

They sat there awkwardly for a while. Finally, Gardiner looked at his watch and stood up. "I don't know what your concerns are about this party," he whispered to Cynthia. "But all I can say is—and this is from a male perspective—that slinky green number out there in the closet on your extraordinarily beautiful frame should guarantee you 'belle of the ball' status!"

Cynthia opened her mouth to respond, but by the time she thought of something to say, Gardiner was out of the room, the door closed behind him.

Jake's eyes moved from the door back to Cynthia. "A piece of advice, Cinderella," he sneered, stroking his dark beard malevolently. "Lock the bathroom door when you come back to change!"

Cynthia blinked. "What?"

Jake wiggled his bushy eyebrows. "Old Gardiner seemed unusually interested in your plans for the evening, if you ask me."

Cynthia looked at him sarcastically through lowered eyelids. "*Amazing* the things you manage to pick up with headphones on."

"Comes with the turf," he quipped, "being a crackerjack reporter."

"Pegging Gardiner as a sex-crazed male?" she snickered. "I'd have those crackerjack instincts checked out if I were you!"

"He's got something going, that's for sure." Jake squinted into space. After a while his eyes lit up. "Maybe it's not you. Maybe he wanted to know how much time he'd have before you got back. So *he* could try on that sensssssssaaaaationally bright green outfit that's hanging out in the hall closet!"

Cynthia laughed. "Isn't it time for you to leave for your gig?"

At the sound of a knock on his door, Senator Frederick Barker shoved the glass he was holding inside his right desk drawer, closed the drawer carefully, and leaned back in his chair. "Come in!"

"I won't ask if you're busy, because I *know* you're busy!" Jed Farber pranced in, slamming the door behind him. "Miranda says you have a reporter coming in twenty minutes." Farber grinned broadly. "But Miranda *also* says you might enjoy a little entertainment between now and then."

A barely discernible gleam appeared in Barker's eyes. "And you came all the way across town just to entertain me?"

"Well, I *would* have, had I known you had a twenty-minute vacancy, but as it happened, I was in the neighborhood anyway. A client of mine just testified before the Banking Committee." Jed Farber slipped into the chair in front of Barker's desk and really looked at the Senator for the first time. "Geez, Rick," Jed said softly, "you look exhausted."

Senator Barker stared at Jed and, with a deadpan expression on his face, asked, "Is that in the realm of 'entertaining'?"

They both laughed.

"How about a drink?" Barker asked, walking over to the cabinet in the corner.

"You got any wine?"

"Wine," the Senator grumbled. "Can't understand the appeal of wine. Tastes like apple cider gone bad, if you ask me."

"Only the kind *you* have!" Jed laughed. "Only when you let it sit there in the cabinet for weeks at a time, opened and waiting for me to come back."

Barker handed him a glass of wine and sat back down.

"I'm drinking alone?"

Barker opened the desk drawer, pulled out a glass, and set it on top of the desk.

Jed's eyes traveled from the drink to Barker, and then back again.

Barker stared Jed down. "What?"

"Oh, nothing. Just . . . well, it makes me wonder what you keep in the *left*-hand drawer!"

They both laughed and sipped their drinks. Jed looked around the room. How many hours had he spent in this room? How many late nights? Nothing had changed.

Suddenly he turned to Senator Barker. "Remember the night of the Vice Presidential nomination?"

The Senator laughed heartily. "The night *you* taught *me* naiveté!" he said.

"No," Jed protested. "You *were* under consideration! *The Washington Post* said so! *The New York Times* said so!"

Senator Barker hooted. "That's right, the only say-so we were missing was the President's!"

"That didn't stop Sam from rounding up the press," Jed laughed.

"Nor did it stop you from rounding up supporters," the Senator reminded him.

"And it didn't stop Hank from writing an acceptance speech."

"Best damn speech I ever didn't give!" They both chuckled. The Senator took a slow sip of his drink and leaned back in his chair. It was his turn to look around the room. His eyes slowly surveyed the chairs and the conference table, the couch, the flags, the pictures on the wall.

"I can see you all here," he said, "running around madly like the bunch of kids you were." He drank some more. "You know Hank just wrote a novel."

"Yes, I heard."

"It's a political novel, set in Washington."

"Any good?" asked Jed.

"First-rate." The Senator moved his head up and down in solemn pronouncement.

"Did you read it?"

"He sent me a copy."

"Did you read it?" Jed repeated.

The Senator looked embarrassed. "I *will* read it, soon as I have some time."

"If you didn't read it, how do you know it's first-rate?"

Senator Barker looked at Jed and then burst into laughter. It was the throaty sound Jed had come to know as the real laugh, subtly distinguishable from the political guffaw. "It said so on the jacket!"

They sat and drank quietly for a while, comfortable with one another and at home in the room.

"Dreams," the Senator said hoarsely.

Jed sat up in the chair and leaned forward, putting his elbows on the desk. "That one could still come true."

Senator Barker frowned and dismissed the idea with an impatient wave of his hand. "Too old." He sipped his drink.

"Too old to be President or Vice President?" Jed protested. "If anything, you're still too young."

"Too old for those kinds of dreams," the Senator said abruptly. "Too knowledgeable, maybe. Too cynical, too." He stared into space. "Sick of it all. Sick of what politics does to you."

"What does that mean?"

Senator Barker shrugged. "Jed, my boy, maybe it's time for new dreams."

"Like what?" Jed looked up with interest.

The Senator winced at his enthusiasm. "Oh, maybe getting out of here, I don't know."

"That's ridiculous! You're at the height of your political career! You're much closer to making that acceptance speech today than you were ten years ago!"

The Senator did not seem to be listening. He sat very still, holding his glass and staring down at the desktop. "I guess that's a little like locking the barn door, isn't it?

"What is?"

"Harboring new dreams now."

Jed waited.

"You know," Senator Barker sighed, "I don't think Penny ever even knew about the night of the Vice Presidency. I didn't crawl into bed that night until well after midnight, well after the dream had collapsed, and I didn't tell her. Probably never told her." He drank some scotch. "That's really pathetic," he muttered.

"What is?"

Senator Barker leaned back in his chair and stared at the ceiling. "The fact that I can't even remember if I told her." The Senator closed his eyes and took a deep breath. "The only reason I'm sure I went home is because home is where I always went when there were no more dreams." He opened his eyes and forced a smile. "Some bedmate, huh?"

"Well, you just—"

"Some husband," the Senator interrupted. "Some partner. Some father." He shook his head.

"Rick," Jed said softly, "this is a really difficult period for you, but as I've told you a million times before, you've just got to—"

"Why does death bring on the guilt?" The Senator stared into space. "If Penny were alive and healthy today, you know as well as I, I'd still be transgressing, still be glibly pursuing all the things that made me a rotten husband."

Jed played with his glass. "The finality, probably. As long as Penny was alive, you could tell yourself you'd change . . . take some time off *next* month." He looked up at Barker and smiled affectionately. "Hey, this is not something that is uniquely yours! We, neither of us, did particularly well as husbands!"

"Correction—neither of us did particularly well in *marriage*," Barker stormed. "Mine was my fault. Yours was *her* fault!"

"Oh, I'm sure not entirely . . ."

"Entirely!" Barker rattled his ice cubes. "Not only was Anna totally disinterested, but she was a shrew to boot!" He shook his head. "For the life of me, I'll never understand why you married her."

Jed stared into his wine glass.

Barker watched him for a while. "Or why that whole thing still haunts you so." He leaned forward suddenly. "Isn't it different, though, today?"

"Different? How?"

"With all these professional women walking around, I don't

know. I just figured today there was more of a chance to share dreams—men and women together."

"Well." Jed laughed uncomfortably. "That's what all the magazines and newspapers say, isn't it?"

"Damn, what I would have given if once, just once, I could have come home and told Penny about something I was working on and had her get excited about it. Or understand it. Or *want* to understand it." He drank some more.

Jed studied his friend with growing concern. He had never seen Barker drink like this. "Is it just Penny, Rick?"

"Huh?"

"I don't know. We've been over all this before. Many times. I just have a feeling tonight you've got more than Penny on your mind."

Barker's gray eyes brightened as they stared across his desk. Jed could feel the clouds lifting the way they always did when the two men shared an intimacy, when one suddenly realized, with pleasure, that the other knew him as well as he knew himself, knew exactly what he was thinking. For a moment he said nothing, gratified thoroughly by the look. "What, Rick? What is it you have on your mind?"

Barker closed his eyes and inhaled deeply, like a man suddenly relieved of a burden. "I . . . uh . . . I tried to call you the other night."

Jed thought for a moment, and then looked at the Senator askance. "Wednesday night?"

"Yes."

Jed grunted. "One-forty-six A.M. Wednesday night? Thursday morning to be exact? That was *you?*"

"Yup."

Jed laughed and threw his hands up in the air. "I should have known! Who else has a sleeping pattern completely out of sync with mine?" Then he frowned. "Why the hell did you hang up?"

Barker shrugged. "I realized I woke you up. Didn't want to keep you from getting your beauty sleep."

"Well, hell, once you woke me, it was a fait accompli! Believe me, I would have preferred talking to you to tossing and turning by myself for the remainder of the night! Why did you call?"

Barker checked Jed's glass, which was still full, picked up his own, and got up and walked over to the cabinet. "Something . . . Something I felt I could only tell you."

"Wait! I know!" Jed slapped his hand down on Barker's desk, and Barker looked over at him with interest. "Yes, of course! I thought of you as soon as I saw the headline in the paper Thursday morning!" Jed's face glowed. "They finally nabbed Senator Percy Langdon! Damn, I knew you'd be thrilled beyond belief, after all these years of watching the devious son-of-a-bitch's antics, waiting for the ax to fall!"

He looked over at Barker, suddenly suspicious. "Is it just possible you knew the whole thing was coming *before* that story broke? Hmm?"

Barker sighed uncomfortably and then cleared his throat. "Jed . . ."

Jed squinted at the Senator. "You had something to do with it, you old devil! No one's been tabulating Langdon's misconduct as thoroughly as you, all these years. You fed the investigators information! That's it, isn't it?"

Barker's eyes started to cloud over again.

"Hey, Rick, if you did, if you played any role whatsoever, surreptitious or otherwise, in nailing him for the seamy, un-ethical shit he's been, you should be feeling nothing but vindica-tion—unadulterated pride in your accomplishment!"

Barker squeezed his eyes shut. "No, Jed, no. I—"

"You always said his flagrant abuses gave the rest of the Sen-ate, the decent officeholders, a bad name! And you were right. Why should men of integrity like you share the spotlight with that rotten apple?"

His eyes down, Barker made his way back to his desk and collapsed in the chair. "I played no role whatsoever in my col-league's demise."

"Your colleague? Since when do you consider that scumbag your *colleague*, for God's sake?"

Barker looked up at him suddenly, and Jed felt chilled: a stranger's eyes.

"You have to go, Jed. That reporter is coming."

"But you haven't told me—"

Barker stood up abruptly, the way he always did when he

51

had determined an interview was over, and Jed obediently rose to his feet, realizing that this was the first time he had ever been issued the exit command in all their years of friendship.

He had been wrong, dreadfully wrong. He did not know how or why, but his misjudgment panicked him. His instincts told him he had failed his closest friend at a moment of need—great need. "Are you sure you should talk to a reporter right now?" Jed said it with concern.

"Why not?"

"You're . . . you're upset about something." Jed looked at the drink and then around the empty room. "Where's Bartholemew? Where's your press guy?"

"Home with their families, as they ought to be on a Friday night!" Barker stormed. "Where *you* ought to be. I can certainly handle an interview with a reporter for a feature story on my own!"

"What *is* it?" Jed asked softly. "You can tell me. We've always heard each other out."

"You hear what you want to hear, Jed. You've got selective hearing. Tonight, you seem to be more interested in talking. Anyway, you probably wouldn't hear the words even if I uttered them."

"Try me."

"Not enough time." Barker looked at his watch. "Another time." Barker walked around the desk and put his hand on Jed's shoulder, escorting him to the door. "I'll call you tomorrow."

Outside the Senator's office, Jed Farber paused at the elevator, and then changed his mind and headed for the stairs. He felt vaguely troubled as he walked slowly down the circular marble staircase to the ground floor.

Cynthia Matthews got out of the elevator and checked her watch. Six on the dot. She walked through the empty corridor looking for room numbers. She found the right one, and the big sign: SENATOR FREDERICK BARKER, IOWA.

The office was empty except for a middle-aged woman wearing a sweater, skirt, and sensible shoes who seemed to be expecting Cynthia and who went to the inner sanctum to tell the occupant she had come.

The woman was "of the mold." Cynthia pictured what she must have looked like in her youth—a skinny, gawky sweet secretary who put in extra hours developing a reputation for reliability and efficiency in the home office, slowly working her way up over the decades. She alone knew when the Senator was free for lunch and when his schedule was too tight, which of his offspring had a birthday that needed to be commemorated, when it was time to send his wife flowers for their anniversary, which constituents he would want to talk to immediately, which should be put off.

The woman probably had never married because she was married to her job, married to the man she served, much the way nuns are married to God, and she served him with a similar sense of mission and fulfillment.

Capitol Hill was filled with such women.

Cynthia stopped speculating about her as the indispensable one announced with an efficient smile: "He can see you now."

Cynthia went into the Senator's office.

Broad of shoulder, thick of gut, the Senator sported a loosened tie. His plentiful hair was tousled, his face bespectacled. He was probably going on the twelfth hour of his day.

The lined face broke into a grin as Cynthia entered, and he stood up. "Hello there, young lady," he said jauntily. "Sorry to make you come so late, but it's been a very, very long week." He beckoned to a chair on the other side of his desk, and Cynthia sat down.

She put her tape recorder on the desk between them. "As you know, Senator, this isn't a radio spot, but do you mind if I record it anyway?" she asked. "I feel more comfortable working from a tape."

"No problem." The Senator leaned back in his chair. "Hey, listen, I want to thank you. My Iowa office says the report you did on the hearings Wednesday was very nice."

Cynthia watched her fingers as they plugged in the microphone. "You sounded quite dynamic, Senator Barker."

"I figured I must have if they liked it!" he laughed. He gave Cynthia a perplexed look. "Refresh my memory. What exactly is it we're doing today?"

"*America Magazine* is doing a story on human loss. They've

asked me to interview prominent figures in Washington who have lost members of their families."

"Lost?" he sneered. "You mean like 'misplaced'?"

"Well, um, have family members who have recently passed—"

Senator Barker leaned forward. "Tell me, sweetheart," he whispered. "Does *America Magazine* have a problem saying the word 'died' or do you?"

Cynthia exploded into relieved laughter. *"America Magazine!"*

He patted her hand. It was like being stroked by a big soft friendly bear. "I'm glad to hear that. I'm sick of these damn euphemisms." He stood up. "Before we start, how about a drink?"

Cynthia hesitated. This was unusual.

"C'mon," he cajoled, walking over to a cabinet in the corner of the room. "It is cocktail time." He winked at her. "My brilliant insights will come through clearer, believe me."

She laughed. "Do you have any wine?" Senator Barker seemed to be wavering in front of the cabinet. She wondered how much he had already had to drink.

He winced. "Part of the wine generation, are you?" He poured her a glass of white wine and poured himself something yellowish-brown.

The wall was filled with pictures of Senator Barker and various luminaries. Cynthia's eyes passed from Kennedy to Johnson to Carter, watching the Senator age a little in each frame.

Her eyes caught another picture—this one on his desk—a family portrait. Senator Barker was seated next to a very attractive woman with tightly curled light brown hair. She had a towheaded little girl in her lap. The Senator—much leaner and darker haired than the present version—was holding a little boy. An older child—a blond girl about ten—was sitting between the two adults. They were all smiling, except for the little boy who looked as though the sun was in his eyes.

Cynthia compared the Senator Barker in the family portrait to the Senator Barkers in the wall hangings and judged the family picture to be the same vintage as the Kennedy era.

Bringing the two glasses back to his desk, he held hers up. "To brilliant insights!" he toasted as he handed it to her. His eyes followed Cynthia's to the portrait. "That's a little outdated," he said with a laugh. He pointed to the older girl. "She's about your age." He took a sip of his drink, and looked at Cynthia curiously. "Where are you from?"

"Ballard, Indiana."

He raised an eyebrow. "A farm girl?"

Cynthia felt her cheeks grow hot. "Does it still show?"

"Shucks, honey, I've been to Ballard! There aren't many other possibilities." He stared her down. "There's nothing wrong with being a farm girl." He tilted his head, just the way her father always did, his visage stern, daring her to disagree.

She cleared her throat. "Certainly not."

She felt the intensity of his glare diminish and noticed an indulgent, fatherly sparkle appear in his eyes. Again she had a sense of déjà vu—her own father, telling her his sternness had been a put-on.

The sparkle grew, lighting up the Senator's grave expression until he snorted a laugh. "It's okay, honey, probably the nicest place for a Ballard, Indiana, farm girl to be these days is in Washington, D.C., with a solid-paying job as a radio reporter!"

They both laughed. Cynthia turned on the tape recorder. "They say politicians are married to their careers. Does that—"

"Who says?" he interrupted playfully.

"Does that fact—that absorption in work in any way lessen the emptiness now?"

He picked up the microphone and leaned back in his chair, ready to roll.

"Well, yes, most certainly it does," he began jocularly. "I plead guilty to being a man with a big job and probably an even bigger ego." He grinned at Cynthia. "I think probably the very same characteristics that made me a less-than-perfect husband over the years now help, uh, ease my bereavement."

He leaned his head back against the top of the chair and began talking amiably to the ceiling. "Lord knows, I've got plenty to keep me busy these days. I've got several important pieces of legislation I'm determined to push through this session of Congress.

"Trade bill," he mumbled, shaking his head. "Gotta have a

trade bill. Gotta do something about this onslaught of imports that are driving Americans out of work, draining our manufacturing sector." He paused to take a sip of his drink.

"Senator Barker—"

"Bad, bad state of affairs," he went on, "especially in Iowa. The economic strains that have hit this nation so hard have created havoc in my home state! I've got farmers who can't sell! I've got manufacturing workers who have worked a lifetime for the same company and now suddenly find themselves laid-off." He rocked slowly back and forth in his swivel chair, his eyes opened wide in a forlorn daze. "Tough reelection campaign ahead," he mumbled. "Very, very tough campaign."

"Senator Barker, you—"

"The tax bill," he said, still rocking, his eyes now glazed. "We've got a new tax bill to write this session of Congress. We're going to—"

"You said before that words like 'lost' and 'passed away' are euphemisms," Cynthia broke in, determined to get the Senator back on track. "What is the appeal of euphemisms at a time like this?"

Barker's eyes snapped. "Euphemisms skirt the issue—any issue," he roared. "I'm an expert on euphemisms. Politicians are in the euphemism business! We're all schooled in—"

"Why do people need to resort to them in discussing death?"

The Senator gulped his drink. "If ever there was an issue— a subject—everyone wanted to skirt, to tiptoe around, instead of tackling head-on, it's death." He stared down into his glass, frowning. "The death of someone close . . . in my case, someone I lived with for forty years, is . . ." He shook his head slowly and swirled the drink around. "Is . . . is . . ."

"Terribly painful?"

"A unique kind of pain," he said slowly. "A pain on many levels. A pain on the 'no one is there to tend my home' level, the level of minor displacement, down to the, uh, down to the 'no one is there to share my dreams' level." The Senator stopped talking abruptly and drank some more, as though the words had suddenly caught in his throat and he needed the liquid to wash them down.

"All the way down to the guilt," he went on. "The bottom level of pain, the uninterrupted guilt."

Cynthia looked up alertly. "The guilt?"

"Guilt for all the things you never got to say, never got to do for her . . . guilt for all the things you did." Again, he was communicating with the ceiling. "So many things I did."

The bearlike body had become fragile, the booming voice a weak quiver. She, who had been getting platitude after platitude in her *America Magazine* interviews, was suddenly coming close to something else: real pain. It moved her and frightened her at the same time.

"Senator Barker," Cynthia began in her peppiest on-air voice, "I've been interviewing a lot of people lately who insist upon resorting to euphemisms, as you put it. Why are you opposed to them?"

That seemed to snap him back.

"Because I've lived a lifetime of euphemisms!" he bellowed, leaning forward and pounding the desk. "That's what public life is all about. And I've had it, quite frankly."

Cynthia laughed and stepped in again to change the mood. "You're tired of euphemisms?" she asked coquettishly, her eyes gleaming. "Or you're tired of public life?" She sat back, waiting for the denial.

"Both!"

She jumped.

"Oh, hell, this is a time of great—what do all the psychologists say? 'Transition.'" He got up and walked back to the liquor cabinet. "That's it—'a time of great transition.' Why not take it one step further? Why not move from public life to private life too? I've already gone from husband to widower." He poured himself a drink. "From philanderer to widower."

"This must be a very difficult period for you," Cynthia said softly.

"I love it!" he howled. "All you young psychoanalysts! Is that the expression of the day? 'Difficult period'?"

"Mrs. Barker was known and loved by many people," Cynthia went on quickly. "She was a political force of her own, an avid campaigner for you—"

"You *have* done your research!" the senator snapped as he returned to the desk, his glass refilled, and picked up the microphone. "She was an astute politician, a rallying force for countless charities, a lady of bountiful energy and charm, the woman behind the man, a credit to me, to her beautiful children, to Iowa and to this wonderful country of ours."

This time the words were totally devoid of expression.

"That's what you learned in your research, wasn't it?" His voice had a mean tinge to it.

Cynthia nodded, perplexed.

"Do you believe it?"

She nodded again.

"Well," he mumbled, "I did for a while back there too." He looked at the family portrait and drank some more.

"Let me elaborate." Senator Barker leaned back in his chair and held the microphone close to his lips.

"Penelope Barker hitched her wagon to what she thought would be a star, but what turned out to be a United States Senator, by definition a totally self-centered, self-indulgent breed." He looked at Cynthia. Her discomfort seemed to fuel him. "She lived a lonely, empty life as a result, raising three children as a single parent, seeking substance in hollow charity functions, and only enjoying the complete, rapt attention of her husband when she was comatose and hardly capable of participating in a meaningful exchange." He closed his eyes tight and sat there for a minute.

Cynthia squirmed, then stood up and smoothed her skirt. "Senator Barker, let's skip this interview. I don't think you're in—"

"I'm fine! About time I told the truth, stopped resorting to 'euphemisms,' as we both like to keep putting it!"

"I won't use what you just said about Mrs. Barker," Cynthia said abruptly.

"Why not?" He turned to her angrily. "It's the truth, goddamn it! Why are all you young people so hell bent on ignoring the truth? Why, you're a member of the truth-seeking Fourth Estate, aren't you?"

Not tonight she wasn't. Certainly not on behalf of *America Magazine*. This was not supposed to be an exposé. Commercial pap, that was what she was after.

At the moment, all Cynthia wanted to do was to retrieve her microphone and go home. But her subject showed no signs of relinquishing it. He sat there across the desk, clutching it, as if it were a gun and he were taunting Cynthia with threats of suicide.

Cynthia broke out in a sweat. That was exactly what was happening.

She stepped in to stop him. "Senator Barker," she began in a low, reportorial manner, "you are in the midst of a long and distinguished political career—"

"Hogwash!" He dismissed the statement with a wave of her own microphone. "More damned euphemisms! I'm on the verge of a difficult election that will probably wipe out my 'distinguished,' as you put it, career!"

She had never had an interview get so out of control. "Well, but you have a substantial record to fall back on—"

"Record? You naive idiots in the press think a record means something? You think years of work and preoccupation with being a good Senator, at the expense"—he waved the microphone at the family portrait—"of being a good anything else, you think that amounts to a hill of beans when you're up for reelection? Well, let me tell you something, my little farm girl, a solid record doesn't mean diddly. Records make past senators. Money makes future Senators."

"I would think that your past record would earn you an abundance of campaign contributors," she said, feeling like a child reciting from an American history textbook and realizing, once again, that she was only inciting him to disprove her.

"Would you really?" he howled. "Well, my dear, this may come as a shock," he whispered condescendingly across the desk. "In truth, *soiling* your record is what earns you an abundance of campaign contributions."

Cynthia felt a sudden spurt of adrenalin, a quickening of the heartbeat: reporter's instinct. She was about to get more than a feature piece on human loss. She leaned forward attentively. "Soiling your record?"

The Senator slammed his mouth shut and looked away quickly.

Damn. She'd lost it—whatever "it" was. Something. Something coming, something big. She switched gears, returning to the tactic that had started the Senator's outpouring: denial.

"Now, Senator Barker," she said in a little farm girl singsong, "I *have* done my homework, and I happen to know that you are a man on a level way above the record-soilers."

He closed his eyes and drank some more.

"A man of integrity—"

He turned on her, a vein at his temple bulging, a bull, ready to charge. "You know what you *want* to know! All of you! Naive young hero worshipers, writing my lines for me, listening only to your own words!"

"I'm not a hero worshiper. I just know—"

"The money's not in laws," Senator Barker hissed into her microphone. "The money's in loopholes. To the victor the spoils, and to the Senator the power to write in loopholes." He threw back his head and laughed, repeating the phrase.

"Loopholes?" She said it like a child discovering a new word.

"Tax loopholes!" he sneered. "Tiny little itty-bitty loopholes that mean millions to the right people, but aren't even noticeable in those big complicated tax laws, so tiny the muckraking idiots of the press don't even know they exist.

"No," he went on, muttering now to himself. "The press wants to know whether there's gonna be an investment tax credit. What's the rate of capital gains gonna be? How much will be set aside for IRAs?

"The press!" He shook his head with disgust. "'Will intangible drilling expenses be write-offs?'" he said in falsetto. "'How much will the rich man have to pay?'" he boomed in baritone.

"No one knows enough to ask the right questions! No one understands that it's the little things that mean a lot. The developers, the insurance companies, they know! And," he said, hurling the ceiling a wolflike smile, "what's more, they pay. One night of little promises means a sackful of PAC contributions!"

"No—"

"Have loopholes, will travel!" He shouted up to the ceiling. "All over the place! Jimmy Farnsworth, in Philly, he *loves* my little loopholes! Just like my buddy, Ralph Buddington, right here in Washington!" He turned around to Cynthia, his face flushed, his eyes menacing. "Let me tell you, sweetie, it takes a *mountain* of out-of-state money to win votes in Iowa these days!"

The energy dissipated and his head began bobbing up and down. "An anachronism . . ." he whispered. "Just . . . an anachronism."

Then he looked up, and this time his eyes seemed to focus, really seeing her for the first time in a while. His face hardened, and he hurled the microphone across the desk. He leaned back in his chair and closed his eyes.

"Senator Barker—"

"Get out of here," he said through taut lips, his eyes still closed.

Her hands trembling, Cynthia hastily packed up her equipment and walked out of Senator Barker's office, closing the door behind her. She smiled sweetly at the secretary in the reception area. As though nothing happened, she instructed herself, as though nothing happened.

As she paced back and forth waiting for the elevator, drenched in perspiration, she was filled with a peculiar fear that if she did not get out of the building quickly, she would be stopped, her evidence confiscated.

The elevator came. She got in and smiled at the other occupants as though nothing had happened. As though nothing had happened.

She raced down the steps outside the building and took a deep breath when she got to the sidewalk. And then another breath. Free at last. Free from the ugliness of the scene. Another breath. Free with her evidence.

She pulled her tape recorder out of her bag, rolled back the tape a short distance, and then pressed the Playback button. "Jimmy Farnsworth, in Philly," she heard Senator Barker's voice say clearly, "he *loves* my little loopholes!"

She stopped the tape, put the recorder back in her bag, and began walking down Capitol Hill.

She had it. She had it all clearly and unmistakably on tape. What she would do with what she had, that was another question, one for tomorrow. Not tonight. Too much already for tonight.

She reminded herself that there was an emerald-green outfit in Capitol Radio's closet awaiting her return.

As she walked toward her office, she found relief in the way the icy-cold air helped clear her head, cleansing it of the disturbing memories of the interview.

Lilah Ballustrom's party—the source of trepidation all week—now loomed before her as a welcome escape.

# · 5 ·

The interior of the Georgetown townhouse looked like a small fine-arts museum. The well-polished floors were topped with small Oriental rugs and surrounded with tastefully positioned potted plants. The furniture in the downstairs foyer, living room, and dining room area consisted largely of black leather and chrome pieces. The bleak abstract paintings on large canvases along the wall intensified the institutional feeling.

The "museum" was well filled. About seventy-five guests were sipping and munching, oohing over the spinach soufflé and silently estimating the calories of the baklava.

At the bar in the corner of the living room, the bottle of red wine quivered a little as Cynthia gingerly dipped its neck down into the top of the plastic "party" wine glass. The red liquid trickled out falteringly. When, finally, the glass filled up, Cynthia carefully stood the bottle back up in its place on the bar, gratified by the fact that her trembling hands had managed to accomplish the tricky maneuver without spilling a drop.

She stared at the dark redness and reaffirmed her oath: no thoughts of Senator Barker until she got home. She had come here for a purpose: to make a statement, to prove to herself that Rob Diamond was past history, and that what was past no longer hurt. She had come to demonstrate that not only to herself, but to Rob as well. When she accomplished that, she could go home. A giddy female gurgle erupted from the corner where Rob was standing. Cynthia almost spilled her wine.

She stared over into the distant corner and watched him holding forth before a large group of grateful men and women. He was standing directly under a bright, inset ceiling light that highlighted the white streaks in his blond hair and gave him an aura of splendor. His bronze tan underscored the pasty-winter complexions of those around him. His easygoing gestures were in sharp contrast to the stiffness of the rest of the crowd.

She regained her composure, raised her chin—as Pamie had instructed her—and lifted her wine glass in a silent toast: to Rob Diamond, Penultimate Horse's Ass.

No, she decided, not to him, but to us. To all of us: to the wife he cheated on long before the divorce; to the child he helped create, but long ago stopped visiting; to the law firm he cheated before and after they made him a partner; to the trusting clients whose money he usurped; to all the women who came before me and to the pathetic souls yet to come. A toast.

She took a sip from the glass and, feeling the liquid slide down her throat, waited for it to trickle out to the other parts of her anatomy and imbue them with the strength to go on.

It was not happening. Cynthia reminded herself that up close, the lines around Rob's eyes and mouth had a barely discernible dissipated look. But she was not up close. And from a distance, his perfect proportions and striking coloring made him look much younger than thirty-eight. Breathtaking. She had to admit, inhaling abruptly, that he was simply breathtaking.

She forced her eyes to move to other corners of the room.

The Undersecretary of Commerce for something or other was looking dolefully into the eyes of a member of the East Wing White House staff.

Senator Olson's administrative assistant was insisting that a deputy trade representative try the broiled brie almondine.

The staff director of the Congressional Committee on Education and Labor seemed to be arguing heatedly with a Deputy Assistant Secretary of Labor.

She knew many of the guests by name, but she preferred to delineate the familiar faces the way they thought of themselves: by their titles. This was, after all, a Washington party.

She looked up at the absolutely perfect fake antique beams on Lilah Ballustrom's brand-new townhouse's unusually high stucco ceiling, awed by the size and elaborate finishing of the resplendent hunks of oak that were, in fact, purely decorative.

Weren't the beams somewhat symbolic of the party guest list? How many of these resplendent people, Cynthia mused, could be removed and still have the United States Government—like the ceiling—remain perfectly intact?

She sipped her wine. Well, Lilah could be proud. She had assembled a stellar cast of Washington hopefuls: the over-thirty but mostly under-forty set, the "special assistants to" who planned on one day being *"the"* . . . journalists who expected you to comment on their latest series, young partners in prestigious law firms from whom subsequent administrations would select their advisers.

And who, Cynthia pondered as she took in the party guests, who was she? The pariah? The plunderer of the hero of this party? Only to those in the know.

A lesser pariah.

She felt very lesser. She wondered whether she would ever feel like more than an outsider in this group. Then she wondered whether she wanted to. Then she wondered when she could go home.

Cynthia left the bar and walked over to one of the food-laden tables. She bent down over a large platter of exotic hors d'oeuvres, pretending to inspect them. In fact, it was a stalling gesture. As her eyes scanned the food, her mind recaptured the view of herself she'd seen in Capitol Radio's bathroom mirror just before she'd left for the party.

She had looked good, she assured herself as her hand circled over the stuffed mushroom caps.

Exceptionally good, actually. Her blond hair—frequently flat and lusterless at this wintry time of the year—had glistened and fluffed under nicely at her shoulders. She had managed to apply eye makeup in a subtly dramatic way: accentuating the large size of her blue eyes, but stopping short of the "raccoon" look. The intensity of emotion caused by the interview with Senator Barker had flushed her cheeks with such radiant color she had hardly needed any blush-on.

The emerald knit outfit her sister, Georgine, had given her for Christmas had, for some inexplicable reason, managed to caress her body in just the right places, transforming her normally long, somewhat flat contours into rounded, sensual curves. The low-cut vee above the bust certainly promised the viewer more than Cynthia knew there was underneath.

She was, she told herself, every bit as round and succulent as that cherry tomato down there on the platter, stuffed with spiced cream cheese. And more colorful, too. The screaming green of the two-piece knit—"Your color!" Georgine had insisted—was certainly a dramatic contrast to her usual understated hues.

She picked up the knife and sliced off a sliver of pâté, convinced now that she looked sensational, but at the same time wondering why no one else was noticing.

Because the men at this party were inherently asexual, that's why! Power was the aphrodisiac here, titles the turn-on. This was, after all, a Washington party.

A spurt of communal laughter erupted from Rob Diamond's corner. She felt a trickle of perspiration slither from her right armpit down her rib cage to her waist.

She changed her mind about the pate.

Out in the foyer, hostess Lilah Ballustrom wrapped her arms limply around the shoulders of her newest arrival. "Jed!" she murmured, her upturned cheek paused in expectation.

Jed Farber bent down awkwardly, and the embrace missed. His mouth was suddenly nudged up against her earlobe, his nose smothered in a mass of her frizzy hair.

He gave her body a quick, self-conscious squeeze, and emitted a smacking sound. It worked. She released him majestically.

"Aren't you Christmasy!" Lilah cooed as he took off his coat, revealing a bright red crewneck sweater.

"Jesus," he grumbled as he looked around the room. "You didn't tell me 'subdued' was the theme of this party!"

"Oh, Jed, you're always so silly!"

"Are there any other colorful people here?"

Lilah thought for a moment. "One," she said mysteriously.

There was another knock at the door. "The bar is around to the left," Lilah trilled to Jed as she heeded the call.

Jed approached a glass table with an enormous salad bowl filled with fresh strawberries the size of golf balls. A short woman in a long black dress was examining the bowl intently.

Her moist, painted dark red lips caressed each other in slow motion as she gazed upon the crimson baubles.

The perfectly lacquered dark red fingernails circled the top of the bowl for a moment and then dove down, plucking up a strawberry by its leafy green base with the agility of a veteran sea gull.

The nails transferred the catch to a nearby silver bowl heaped with whipped cream. Round and round the strawberry was swirled, slowly, artfully, until it was completely covered with the snowy whiteness.

Taking care not to drop a morsel of cream, the nails carried the strawberry up to the moist red lips. They parted, and then clamped down abruptly, leaving a touch of white on the lips and a gaping wound in the strawberry. A tongue came out from between the lips and whisked away the cream.

"Hello, Eleanor," Jed said.

Startled by his voice, the woman looked up and smiled. There was a miniscule stain of red on her right top front tooth.

"Jed, can you imagine!" she exclaimed. "Fresh strawberries in January! I wonder where Lilah got them?"

"At Giant," he said.

"Giant—the supermarket?" she asked in shock. "I've never seen any like these in Giant!"

"They don't look like that in Giant," Jed said soberly. "You have to take them home and feed them."

"Feed them what?"

"Hormones," he whispered. He looked down at the bowl. "Estrogen, I'd guess."

"No! Estrogen?"

"Look," he said, pointing. "They all have breasts."

She started to bend down and look into the bowl more closely, but stopped. Her eyes returned to Jed. "You're kidding."

Jed nodded solemnly. "I'm kidding."

She smiled sheepishly, and then laughed a little. "I guess I'm a little obsessive about strawberries!" Eleanor said.

Now Jed laughed too. "A little." He started to ask Eleanor how things were going at the International Trade Commission, but when he opened his mouth, Eleanor's eyes had left him and returned to the bowl. Her fingers were poised again, ready to pounce.

Jed realized he had turned right, not left as his hostess had instructed. He turned around and headed for the bar.

In the Rob Diamond corner, the crowd was dispersing, the hero moving forward, toward the door.

Cynthia watched.

Rob seemed to carry a spotlight with him. As he moved, he was greeted by a path of upturned faces, and murmurs of "Rob." "Rob." "I'm so sorry." "Looking great, Rob." "Keep your spirits up, Rob."

He beamed and pressed the flesh like a candidate for office. At the door, he enveloped the hostess. "I warned you I'd have to leave early, Lilah." He sighed. "I really wish I didn't. Wonderful, wonderful party."

Lilah quivered a little in his embrace. "Chin up, Rob." The cliché was clothed in passion. She watched with longing as the door closed behind him. So did the rest of the crowd.

Cynthia closed her eyes, inhaled deeply, and slowly let the breath out.

"Hey, gorgeous!"

Cynthia whirled around to greet the heavyset man in a dark three-piece suit calling to her from behind, grateful at last to be acknowledged by someone, even a blowhard like Tom Blakely, Channel Eight's nightly newscaster.

Blakely squeezed Cynthia and turned to her the way he turned each night to the Channel Eight sports reporter. For a moment, she thought he was going to say, "Great game for the Redskins, wasn't it, Jack?"

He winked at her. "Great article in *Washington Magazine*, wasn't it, babe? Hear you really knocked the town's legal community on its ass with that one!"

Blakely's larger-than-life off-camera vocal tones caricatured his on-camera presence. The people standing close by turned around and eyed Cynthia coldly. Cynthia clenched her teeth and stared into her wine glass. "Hello, Tom."

"I tell everyone, 'Watch out for that Cynthia Matthews,'" Blakely boomed in his best broadcast voice, oblivious of Cynthia's discomfort. "That's your ultimate muckraker there! Don't be fooled by those innocent blue eyes!'"

"Hazel," Cynthia said, for some reason feeling the need to be contradictory. "They're hazel."

"See what I mean?" grinned Tom, nudging her. "You know all the facts!"

Over Tom Blakely's shoulder, Cynthia noticed a dark-haired man in a bright red crewneck sweater approaching the bar. She stared as Blakely went on with his monologue.

The man in the red sweater was tall and broad, and, well, a little awkward. Boyish. Unmanicured. Different. His angular features—the broad face, the large nose—were almost too strong, but the overall effect was dramatic, especially against his thick dark hair. It all gave him a kind of unconventional handsomeness.

Cynthia wondered who he was. As she watched, a woman in a maroon silk shirtwaist dress with a little bow tie at the neck tapped him on the shoulder.

"Suzanne!"

"It'll clash with your sweater," Suzanne warned, pointing to Jed's glass of red wine.

"I wouldn't want to drink anything that matched," Jed laughed.

Suzanne held up the plate of hors d'oeuvres she was carrying. "Have you tried the miniature quiche, Jed?"

"The what?"

"The miniature quiche."

"Please, Suzanne, you're talking to a man who has just been outclassed by a strawberry!"

"A what?"

Jed shut his eyes and waved his hand. "Forget it."

"Have you read the Pointsettar brief yet?"

"Suzanne, this is a party. Why don't we forget that we're attorneys?"

"Seriously, Jed, have you read it?"

"Can I refresh your drink?"

"Yes, thank you, but just some more Perrier, please."

"Just Perrier? Come on, Suzanne, it's a night for strawberries, for miniature quiche, for *amour* . . ."

Suzanne frowned and looked at her plate. "Which is the amour?"

Jed howled. He stopped abruptly when he realized she was examining her food in earnest.

"One Perrier coming up."

As Jed poured the drink, he looked up and spotted something very colorful across the room. It was a bright green knit outfit clinging to the shapely body of a tall blond woman he had never seen before.

The woman turned her head and a lock of hair fell down over one eye. Soft hair. Falling hair. Hair you could touch in a room of frizzed, lacquered, and sculptured looks. Color in a room of conscious understatement. A dress that revealed a body in a room of expensive fabrics that avoided curves. Damn, she looked just like that doll Lisa used to have. The one from the international collection. What was it? Miss England? No, Holland. That was it, Miss Holland.

Farber stared some more. An incredible face. Tiny bones. A delicate nose balanced by two pronounced but equally fragile-looking cheekbones. Smooth, smooth skin—or at least it looked that way. It was hard to be certain from such a distance.

And the eyes. Huge blue eyes. He squinted. Did they sparkle? You could tell a lot about a person by the sparkle.

Then he realized the eyes were staring back at him.

Testing, Jed smiled at her and tilted his head. She smiled back and tilted hers. Then a group of people moved in, blocking Jed's view.

When the group dispersed, Jed looked again. The woman in the green dress was gone. He walked over to a group of familiar faces—a White House staff member and two Justice Department lawyers—involved in a familiar topic of conversation: the new Attorney General. They welcomed Jed, but as they continued talking, his eyes darted around—searching.

Everyone seemed restless. While lip service was being paid around the room to aid for the Contras in Nicaragua and the constitutionality of the Gramm-Rudman tax plan, most of the participants were twisting their necks and looking for something that was proving elusive.

Lilah emerged from the kitchen with a new tray of hot canapés and thrust it on a table with a flourish.

"Lilah, you have outdone yourself!" gasped an economist standing nearby.

Lilah beamed. In her peripheral vision, she noticed a speck

of emerald green moving from the left side of the room to the right, and a speck of bright red moving from right to left.

Cynthia Matthews moved to the bar and poured herself another glass of red wine. Jed Farber moved up behind her.

"We're destined for each other," he declared.

She whirled around, startled. Her eyes sparkled when she saw who it was. "We are?"

"Look around the room. We're the only two islands of color in this massive ocean of drabs."

She looked around the room slowly, and then back at him. "Is this going to be an honest, open relationship?" she asked in mock seriousness.

"Completely." He mimicked her tone.

"Then I think it only fair that I admit the truth. It's my sister, not me."

"What do you mean?"

"My sister gave me this outfit." She sighed and looked up at him. "My inner core is really beige."

"Good news."

"Yes?"

"My inner core is gray. My mother gave me this sweater." She giggled.

"My mother and your sister will hit it off terrifically," he said.

They laughed together.

"Am I keeping you?" he asked, stepping aside.

"From what?"

He shrugged. "From rushing back to a stimulating conversation in another corner of the room?"

"That must be the one corner I hadn't tried!"

He tilted his head. "You don't find this a fascinating, awe-inspiring group?"

She shrugged. "I guess I just don't fit in."

He beamed and raised his wine glass in a toast. "I have been coming to Lilah's parties for years *hoping* to find someone who did not fit in!"

She laughed.

"Do you have a name?"

"Yes," she replied playfully. "Do you?"

He gazed at her, smiling. "Have you seen the strawberries in the other room?"

She nodded, her eyes never leaving his. "A bit bulbous."

"Have you tried the miniature quiche?"

"Do you think I should?"

"No," he declared.

"The food is certainly exotic," Cynthia admitted with respect.

"Ahh," he whispered. "But you must not eat any of it."

"Why not?"

"Lilah spent six months losing fifty pounds at a diet farm about five years ago," he hissed. "She returned svelte, but with a slight mental problem. She now believes that each calorie consumed by a guest somehow registers in her 'lost' column."

"Ahh . . . stretch marks on the brain!"

"Exactly!"

"Do you know Tom Blakely?" she asked, pointing to the other side of the room.

He looked. "Isn't he that pompous ass on local news?"

"Yes! Yes!"

"Do you know what *amour* means?" he asked.

Her eyes got misty. *"Oui."*

They stood staring at each other for a long time.

She held out her hand. "My name is Cynthia Matthews."

He took her hand and looked deeply into her eyes. "My name is Jed Farber, and you have the coldest hand I've ever touched."

"Would you believe I've been here for hours, and I'm just starting to thaw! I had to park blocks away," she groaned. "Georgetown."

"Yes, Georgetown," he commiserated, "where every inhabitant is equipped with three cars and no garage."

"Exactly."

"Are you an Indian chief?"

She looked up at him, confused this time. "No. Why?"

"Lilah always tries to get at least one of each at her parties and thus far I've met large numbers of doctors and lawyers."

She raised an eyebrow. "Obviously *you* are not an investigative reporter."

"Why?"

She stared him in the eye deadpan. "Indian chiefs have warm hands."

He returned the look. "Do you know that for a fact?"

Her eyes glistened. "You're a lawyer!"

"And you're a newshound!"

They clicked wine glasses.

Suddenly his entire expression changed. The smile evaporated, replaced by a look of shock, then a frown.

"What?"

"I know you."

"You know me?"

"I know *of* you," he corrected himself.

"How so?"

"Your byline. The lawyer exposé."

"Yes." She started to smile, but changed her mind as she noted the expression on his face. "You weren't in it."

"My friend, Rob Diamond, was."

An icy chill swept through her body, tensing her muscles. She looked away quickly. "He just left. You missed him."

"Your article will probably completely ruin his career."

"Not fair." Her eyes snapped back to his. "If his career is ruined, he did it himself. He dipped into a trust fund."

"He liked you," Jed said.

She shrugged. "I liked him too."

"But you betrayed him."

"I did *not* betray him." She clenched her jaw and looked at him defiantly. "He knew I was a reporter. He knew what I was doing. My job was to find the truth and report it."

"At any expense?"

She looked away. "I'm not happy if it ruined his career."

"It made yours."

Her face turned to stone. "That's melodramatic and unworthy of a logical legal mind." She thrust up her chin. "If the article was good for me professionally, it's because it showed I could do my job well. If it ruined his career, it was because it uncovered the truth. He may be a good friend of yours, but you know as well as I that he was guilty."

"He said you had deceptively sweet blue eyes."

"Hazel," she said, gulping her wine. "They're hazel."

He downed his glass and took a deep breath. "And where do you live in the nation's capital?" The voice was playful again, but the mood wasn't.

She brightened anyway. "Adams-Morgan. Do you know it?"

"Ahh." The tone was condescending. "That marvelous crosscultural environment just blocks from the White House. An integrated neighborhood, where yuppies meet yuppies."

"I—I don't think of myself as a yuppie . . ."

"Really? Then I suppose you're one of the Hispanics?"

"Actually, I'm black." She laughed at her joke. He didn't. Something in her seemed to snap with his rejection. Her jaw tightened. Her eyes turned to ice. "Where do you live?" she asked.

"Bethesda." He looked down at his glass.

"The suburbs?" she scoffed.

"The suburbs," he conceded. "I have to."

"Someone's forcing you?"

"No . . . Your type wouldn't understand."

"My type? What does that have to do with it? Tell the truth," she whispered. "You're a lawn addict?"

"No—"

"Well then, you like a challenge. An office that's hard to get to."

"Obviously, *you* have no children."

Bull's-eye. She shriveled. She looked down into her glass for a long time, then back up at him suddenly. "Do you have children?" she asked tenaciously.

"Yes." He smiled smugly. "That's why I live in the suburbs."

"Is your wife here?" She began looking around the room.

"No," he said uncomfortably. "We're divorced."

"But you have custody of the children?" she persisted.

"No," he gave in. "She has custody."

"Ahh, she has custody of the children, but you have custody of the neighborhood?"

"Yes," he said weakly.

"What's this, Jed," said a tall, thin man walking up. "You have custody of the neighborhood?" He laughed. "That's a good one." He nudged Cynthia. "My wife even got the neighborhood."

73

"Cynthia Matthews, Hank Samuels," Jed said, "I trust you two will excuse me." He pointed to Suzanne, who was standing a few yards away. "I have to discuss a brief."

Cynthia slowly ran her finger around and around the rim of her wine glass, staring into space. She heard sounds, and realized the man she had just been introduced to was talking to her. "Excuse me," she said, turning to the voice. "I really have to be getting home." She smiled curtly and headed for the door, where she complimented Lilah Ballustrom on a wonderful party.

# · 6 ·

The clock told him it was four A.M., and his mind told him four A.M. was just as bad as three A.M., which was just as bad as two A.M. or midnight, for that matter. Time would heal nothing. The nightmare was true, and the damage was irreversible.

He was not only guilty of misconduct. He was guilty of openly admitting that misconduct to a reporter with a live tape recorder. Worse. He had gone out of his way to do so. He—shrewd, calculating, veteran politician of the first order—had forced a reporter to listen to a detailed account of his wrongdoing.

He was insane, certifiably insane.

And that frightened him, troubled him even more, to tell the truth, than the devastation of his career: the fact that he could no longer count on himself. He had lost control over his own actions.

Frederick Barker groaned slightly and rolled over in bed. Back to oblivion. Please. Let the sleep come again and wipe it all out. Oh, please.

But the heaviness, the same heaviness that had, just hours before, anesthetized his mind and rendered his body immobile, was now arousing him, making his head throb and making his body feel chilled and overheated at the same time, until he could not tolerate lying in bed anymore.

The Senator sat up and fixed his feet firmly on the carpet beside his bed. He sat very still for a while, intentionally sidestepping the memories of the nightmare, trying instead to recall what happened afterward.

He had stayed at the office very late, long after his secretary, Miranda, had gone home, long after everyone but the cleaning crew had left. He had stayed there, closeted in his chamber, in a state of mourning . . . mourning the death of all that mattered.

He had sat at his desk for a long time, hoping everything would just go away, but the opposite had happened. It had all come back—not the gory details of the interview. Just the bottom line. That had set him pacing. Needing to vent his feelings through some sort of action, he had begun walking back and forth across the office, trying to clear his head, pausing every so often to look out the window at the Capitol building down the street, lit up in splendor against the darkened sky. That was the loss, the loss he was mourning, all that had ever mattered.

In an especially maudlin moment, he had contemplated taking his daddy's old shotgun and blowing away the useless mass of organs, blood, and flesh that was left—the rubble of the disaster—but all the time he was considering the logistics (Where was the gun? The ammunition? Did he still know how to fire it?) he was also getting on with his life—making himself a pot of coffee with Miranda's little percolator, and wearing a path across the office rug with his pacing. At some point, heaven knows when, he determined he was sober enough to make the journey to his home in Chevy Chase.

Then at home, he had spent an hour or two intentionally wiping out what little sobriety he had attained, drinking and drinking, finally allowing himself, in the privacy of his empty living room, to rant and sob and writhe and, yes, even scream out, discovering a pit, a depth lower than anything he had ever thought could exist, a mode of behavior that now, in the presence of a new day, made him cringe with discomfort.

That had been another man. Where had that other man come from?

Senator Barker stood up tentatively, and walked on rubbery legs to the bathroom, where, unwilling to turn on the light, he fumbled in the medicine chest for the aspirin. Ignoring the fact that his fingers were shaking, he popped two tablets into his mouth and downed them with water.

Grasping the banister tightly each step of the way, he went downstairs into the darkened living room and lowered himself slowly into the familiar large wing chair ("Daddy's" chair on family evenings, "the Senator's" chair during late-night staff meetings at his home).

He rested his head against the chair's high top. Outside lights shining through the bushes next to the window created shadows on the ceiling. He watched the shadows move.

He wanted a drink, but personal inhibitions forbade that. Drinking was a follow-up, not a precursor: a reward meted out at the close of business. It was a pleasure, permitted in excess only on rare occasions. In moments of adversity you were permitted to drink as much as you liked, but only in private and only at night. Once you went to sleep, it became "morning," and only alcoholics drank in the morning.

Granted, there had been a few lapses of late, but they had underscored the importance of the rule, hadn't they? The consequences had been catastrophic.

Time to return to the rule: Only alcoholics drank in the morning.

He was *not* an alcoholic.

In the shadows on the ceiling, he saw Everington Lablume, in his loose-fitting white summer suit, the billows of flesh below his jaw line quivering as the senior Senator from the state of South Carolina tried laboriously but unsuccessfully to make a point before his secretly snickering fellow legislators.

Old man Lablume. He saw him on the ceiling, but more forceful than the sight was the remembered smell of the man, the funny smell: a mixture of extra-sweet after-shave and pungent gin and vermouth. Senator Lablume's last term in the Senate had coincided with Frederick Barker's first.

Barker had arrived just in time for Everington Lablume's swan song. Back then Frederick Barker had been a driven young man, anxious to make his mark, to change the world, to make the United States Senate a productive body of aggressive, forward-thinking representatives of "The People." The demise of

Everington Lablume, a senile, saliva-dripping, verbose relic of the degenerate past, had seemed a damn good way to begin.

He had always considered Lablume an ineffectual, booze-ridden blowhard. Now, as he stared at the man on his ceiling, he wondered what had made Lablume start drinking. Fear of losing it all?

Everington Lablume was the alcoholic caricature. Three decades in the United States Congress had taught Frederick Barker alcoholics were not necessarily caricatures. Take Tom Connory, a brilliant tactician—provided you got to him in time each day—Elliot Livingsley, Chad Romney, Todd Snyder, Sam Leopole. . . .

On his ceiling, Frederick Barker saw the whole fraternity march forth, along with their embarrassing moments.

He was *not* one of them, would not *be* one of them. Not he. Why, he had never even been a heavy drinker until Penny's death.

Strange, how the death of the weaker half of the marriage partnership—the death of the dependent half—had somehow made the stronger half fall apart. Strange what a burden freedom had turned out to be. Liberated, at last, to live, eat, and sleep politics, he had not only lost interest—he had gone out of his way to kill his career.

So many things he had never realized. Like the fact that it was a godsend to be alone only when you lived with someone.

"Oh, Penny . . ." The sound of his own voice, quivering like that, startled him, upset him, confused him. When was the last time he had called out for her in a moment of need? He couldn't remember.

Were they right, then, the "condolence" people, when they kept telling him this was a "difficult time"? Lord knows, he had never before been a lot of the things he had turned into since Penny's death: a corrupt politician, a confessor, a hysterical, sobbing man, a pathetic, miserable, humiliating . . .

He sat there, staring at the imagined figures on his ceiling, and then closing his eyes, staring and then closing, drifting in and out of sleep, until he opened his eyes and daylight had wiped all the figures away.

The brightness coming through his windows hurt his eyes at first. And then, gradually, he felt it fueling him with energy. Life returning.

\*   \*   \*

*"Your father's a crook!" Rob Diamond snarled from under a spot-light. "Even your own father!"*

*"There, there," Lilah Ballstrom said, patting her hand. "There's nothing wrong with being a farm girl!"*

Her sleep disturbed by the dream, Cynthia Matthews turned in bed restlessly.

The picture. It was the family picture that had been on Senator Barker's desk, but now Cynthia was in it. It looked just like Senator Barker's ten-year-old daughter, but it wasn't. It was Cynthia at the age of ten, standing between her mother and her father.

The picture came alive and Cynthia looked up at Daddy and smiled. He looked like Senator Barker, but it was Daddy. Only he didn't smile back. He turned away from her and faced the audience.

"No more euphemisms," her daddy said. "I'm tired of using nice words. I want to tell you the truth!"

He reached over and poured himself a glass of yellowish-brown stuff. He poured it into a great big glass—one of her mother's good lemonade glasses. He filled the glass so full, Cynthia was afraid it would spill on her new sundress (the white one with yellow flowers on it that she had embroidered all by herself), but it didn't. Daddy gulped the liquid down real fast.

Cynthia felt her head get dizzy, as though she had drunk it herself. She tried to interrupt. Daddy was going to say something wrong. She had to stop him, but when she opened her mouth, nothing came out. Her head was spinning, and her voice had no sound.

Daddy was saying something terrible. She couldn't hear the words, but everyone was shocked.

Channel Eight's Tom Blakely gave his cameraman the "record!" signal, and the klieg lights went on, and the soundmen held out their long mike polls, and Daddy kept talking, talking, talking.

"Don't feel bad, hon, he never understood you," Brittany whispered.

She still couldn't hear what Daddy was saying, but she heard the sound of the lemonade glass when it splattered all over the front porch, and her mother cried, "My favorite glass!" and her father closed his eyes and said, "Get out of here."

Cynthia's body jerked, and she bolted upright in bed.

An anemic yellow ray filtered through the curtains in her bedroom. Her eyes focused. Her curtains. Her dresser. Her bedroom. Morning. It was Saturday morning.

Relieved, but still disturbed, she slumped back against the pillows, thinking about the dream, understanding it in ways she could not put into words. Then its details began evaporating. She let them go, lying very still, at first comforted by reality and then disappointed by it.

Reality was not so great either.

Her Siamese cat, Sapphire, hopped up on the bed and settled on Cynthia's pillow, offering a clear-cut choice: Get up, or inhale cat fur. Neither option seemed appealing. In fact, nothing seemed very appealing.

After a while, she got up. As she stood next to the bed and stretched, she felt a chill creep over her entire body. She shut the window and looked around the room for her bathrobe.

She found it on the floor at the foot of the bed. She put it on and tied it tightly around her, but still she shivered. Her eyes caught sight of something else: a lump of emerald green discarded into a heap on the bedroom floor.

Picking up the dress she had worn to the party, she hung it in the closet, and stood staring at it. Her eyes saw instead a broad-shouldered man in a bright red crewneck sweater telling her they were the two most colorful people at the party.

As her fingers caressed the dress on the hanger, she saw the playfulness in his eyes, the dimple in his chin that became more pronounced when he laughed.

Had there been a dimple? She saw one now.

Then the playful eyes became cold. She saw Jed Farber from behind now, walking away. She pushed the green dress back along the rod in her closet. Way back. She surrounded it with slacks and blouses and "dress-for-success" suits, erasing it from view.

"The ball's over, Cinderella," she reminded herself grimly, "and I wouldn't hold my breath waiting for someone to show up with a glass slipper."

She walked into the living room. A half-filled bottle of wine and an empty wine glass with red stains at its bottom and around its rim were standing on her desk, reminders of the time she had spent sitting there when she had returned from Lilah's party, sipping wine and staring blankly at the picture behind the desk, trying to sort things out, certain that sitting at her desk—the place where she always figured things out—she would somehow calmly be able to put all the strange pieces of Friday night together.

But it had not worked. The wine had just anesthetized her to the point where she had been able to forget all the pieces. She picked up the wine glass and bottle and carried them into her kitchen.

She prepared the coffee, put away the wine bottle, rinsed the glass, put it in the dishwasher, and declared Friday officially over. Saturday lay ahead. There was work to do, pieces to put together.

Senator Barker.

She poured some coffee into a mug and sipped it. She could feel it circulating, waking her system up.

Senator Barker.

She took another sip, and then another.

First things first. The Barker tape was still at Capitol Radio, along with the other equipment she had left at the office before leaving for Lilah's party.

She went to her room to get dressed.

Showered, clean-shaven, and attired in a sports shirt, beige button-down sweater, and brown slacks, Frederick Barker leaned back on his living-room sofa and laughed heartily into the telephone receiver he held in his hand. "Well, it *was* overreaction on your part," he drawled. "But I'm kinda touched by it, nonetheless. It's good to know you care."

"You're leveling with me?" Jed Farber persisted. "There was nothing—"

"Just a maudlin nouveau widower who'd had too much to drink turning on the person closest at hand, that's all. Guess I was a bit miffed at you for stealing my thunder about the Percy Langdon case . . ."

"How'd it go with the reporter?"

"Oh, fine. The subject was 'human loss—how it feels to have your wife die.' Needless to say, I was in rare form for *that* one!"

"Rick . . . about the booze—"

"Beat you to it! Decided myself in the early hours of this morning I was drinking too much. Almost called you to tell you," Barker laughed. "But it was four-fifty-seven, as you digital clock enthusiasts would note instantly, and, judging by the enthusiastic reception my last nocturnal call got, I decided to wait until now."

"Hey, you can call me any time—day, night, middle of the night. You know that."

The Senator's face sobered. "I know that, Jed. I've always known that—and, I might add, taken advantage of it frequently. What I haven't done is tell you—out loud—how very important it's been to me to know you're always there. Hell, you held the whole family together during Penny's—"

"No testimonials," Jed Farber interrupted. "No need for testimonials."

"All right, then," Barker said softly, "as long as you know." His eyes suddenly twinkled. "I hear the clamoring of noisy children in the background. What's Daddy got planned for today?"

"A horror movie."

Barker groaned. "Makes me glad I have grown children!"

When he hung up the phone, Senator Barker's eyes darted back to the list on the coffee table in front of him. He put a check next to "Jed" and examined the other items that were part of his carefully crafted strategy for controlling the damage. It was a solid game plan, not necessarily a foolproof one, to be sure, but damn good under the circumstances.

He looked at his watch impatiently. Still too early to call the others. His eyes traveled down the list, pausing at "Ralph Buddington." Had that been the only name he had given Cynthia Matthews? He knew he had given her a definite name. He had a feeling, in fact, he might have mentioned more than one, but so much of the tirade was a blur to him. He could see the blond hair across the desk, the pretty face, but even that vision was a little abstract.

There were certainly a *hell* of a lot of names he could have given her. A needle in a haystack, that's what he was searching for. He sat very still, feeling his brain cells ticking. Not coming up with any pearls of wisdom, he reminded himself ruefully, but at least ticking once again, and fueled with newfound energy. Senator Frederick Barker had reentered the ring determined to put up a fight for his reputation, for his Senate seat, for his life.

Perhaps it had to happen the way it had, he thought philosophically. Perhaps one had to hit rock bottom in order to get a second wind, a drive to scramble back up to the surface.

Perhaps. But wouldn't it have been a tad easier if he'd hit rock bottom with a less-thorough confession?

His eyes wandered back to the telephone and clouded. Item one of the game plan saddened him. He had never lied to Jed Farber before.

Cynthia Matthews needed to talk to someone, someone who would understand the "scoop" she had been handed by Senator Barker and help her decide how to handle it, someone who would understand, but could, at the same time, be trusted not to divulge the information. A soundproof sounding board, that's what she needed.

There was only one possibility: Christopher Channing. Chris had worked with Cynthia for years at Capitol Radio, had been her closest friend in Washington, and, more important, her professional confidant. What's more, Chris understood Congress better than she, since he was now a Capitol Hill correspondent for NBC.

"He said all that?" Channing gasped in disbelief over the telephone. "He just let it all out like that? A veteran like Barker?"

"Yup." Cynthia cradled the receiver in the crook of her neck and put the typewritten pages back in order. "I've been reading to you right from my transcript. Verbatim."

"What the hell did you do to get him started?"

"Very little." She leaned back in the kitchen chair. "The circumstances set him up for me. Too much liquor, depression, and guilt over his wife's death, and . . . oh, someone else, maybe."

"Someone else? What do you mean?"

She rubbed her eyes. "I don't know, just . . . listening to the recording this morning, it seemed that whenever he got really angry, he directed his rantings at me in the plural. 'You young people,' he kept saying." She skimmed the pages. "Here it is—'Why are all you young people so hell bent on ignoring the truth?' And here's another reference. 'All of you! Naive young hero worshippers writing my lines for me.'"

Cynthia stared into space. "I have a feeling I happened along at the right moment. Someone warmed him up for me." She sighed and closed her eyes. "Maybe I'm just trying to transform insanity into logic. The man was crazy, Chris, out of control."

"I'll say," Channing chuckled. "Lucky for you. You have the makings of a fantastic story there!"

"Just the makings," she sighed. "It'll take a whole lot of research to make it work."

"I don't get it, though. PAC funds—Political Action Committee funds—are limited to a five-thousand-dollar ceiling, aren't they? That's hardly a windfall."

"Five thousand dollars per *business*," Cynthia corrected. "That could add up to a mighty big haul if you get a commitment from the whole industry! I think that's what he was doing. The guy he mentioned—" She searched her notes. "'Ralph Buddington, right here in Washington,'" she read. "I'll bet he's some kind of lobbyist. Probably represents a group that has hundreds of members. If so, and this Buddington calls for PAC contributions from all his members, Buddington alone can bring in a sizable amount!"

"And the travel he alludes to?" Chris asked. "You figure that's to tap regional organizations with many members?"

"Exactly! Otherwise the trips aren't worth the airfare! Can you imagine how many real-estate developers in any one city in this country might be interested in his 'tiny little itty-bitty loopholes that mean millions to the right people'? There was another name he gave me—" Cynthia perused the transcript. "Here it is—'Jimmy Farnsworth, in Philly.' I bet he's a developer or something like that."

"What are you going to do?"

"Check around. Find out who the people he mentioned are. See whether I can find someone who can tell me where he's been traveling lately." Cynthia laughed a little. "And begin by asking you for a quick cram course on Congressional legislation. Specifically, the tax law into which Senator Barker wrote all those 'itty-bitty loopholes'!"

"It's not a tax law, not yet at least. It's just a tax bill. It's out of committee—the Senate Finance Committee has finished writing its version—but it hasn't been taken up for a vote by the whole Senate yet."

"So the Senate hasn't even approved it yet?" She sounded disappointed. "It has a long way to go before it's passed by both houses of Congress, then, doesn't it? Before it becomes law?"

"Yes, but that doesn't matter as far as you're concerned," Channing said. "Barker's on the Senate Finance Committee, so he's already written in his little loopholes. That's all you care about. What he wrote."

"And how do I go about finding that out?"

"You start by picking up a copy of the bill. The Senate Finance Committee has copies for the press. Then you find out what interests the names he gave you represent."

"Say this Jimmy Farnsworth is a real-estate developer," Cynthia interjected. "And I find someone in his organization who admits Barker made a deal. Then what do I do?"

"You go through the bill and single out the provisions that are good for developers, and find someone who can tell you whether Barker wrote in any of those provisions."

Cynthia frowned. "Who could tell me that?"

"Any Finance Committee staff worker who's been involved in the bill-writing process. Believe me, the staff people live the legislation, day and night, during the whole bill-writing phase. Those closest to it know exactly which Senators put in what." Channing paused. "I'll get you a name."

"Fantastic!" Cynthia heaved a sigh of relief.

"Cyn, aren't you wondering what Barker is doing today? You think he just drops something like that and forgets about it?"

"Frankly, I bet he doesn't even remember doing it!"

"Hah! I say you get a phone call and a plea for mercy!"

Cynthia shuddered. "Chris, you know the personalities on Capitol Hill better than I do. What is Senator Barker like?"

"A very powerful, pragmatic, intelligent, upstanding lawmaker." Chris Channing chuckled. "At least that's what I would have said, had we not had this conversation."

The phone rang as Cynthia was rereading the transcript in her living room. She got up to answer it, but then, remembering what Chris Channing had said about the possibility of Barker calling, she grabbed her tape recorder off her desk and took it into the kitchen with her.

"Hello."

"Is this Cynthia Matthews?"

The familiar sound of the voice jolted her system. She pressed the "record" button down, and nudged the microphone between her ear and the telephone receiver. "Yes, this is she."

"Ms. Matthews, this is Senator Barker calling. I'm sorry to bother you over the weekend, but I felt I owed you an apology, one that deserved to be delivered before Monday." It was the smooth, strong-voiced delivery of an experienced politician.

"Yes?"

"I suppose in the course of a lifetime, there comes a period for everyone when a series of misfortunes, bad luck, anxieties— whatever you want to call 'em—seem to come together, all at once, in a jolting way," he went on in a relaxed, conversational tone. "I'm afraid, entirely by accident, you happened along at just such a time for me."

"I understand . . ."

"Well, I can't say that I really expect you to understand," he interrupted. "I think my behavior last night was beyond understanding, to tell the truth, beyond anyone's comprehension, including my own. I'm just saying that you should not have been exposed—that's all—and I apologize for that."

Cynthia raised an eyebrow suspiciously. "You'd like me to forget it ever happened?"

She heard a funny growling sound on the other end that erupted into an amiable laugh. "That would be a pretty difficult task, now wouldn't it? No, my dear, I think that even a highly disciplined young lady like you would have trouble forgetting a scene like that one!" He grunted a little. "I must say I've forgotten an awful lot of it myself, but I suspect that's because my mind was so dulled by alcohol, I had little control over my ramblings in the first place."

Cynthia pressed the microphone against the receiver. "Would you like me to refresh your memory?" she asked, hoping to get either an admission or a denial.

"Lord, no!" he boomed good-naturedly. "This was not intended to stimulate a replay of last night!"

"What then? What *was* the purpose?"

There was a pause on the other end. She waited to see how he would phrase the request.

"Oh, I suppose just a phone call from a man who is proud of the three decades he's spent in public life, a man who considers excessive drinking abhorrent, who considers maudlin emotional outbursts equally distasteful, who had never engaged in either before, and who wants to apologize for the fact that— through no fault of your own—you were subjected to both last night."

"What was it about me that brought last night on?" she asked, hoping a new tact might ruffle his control over the conversation.

"Oh, sheer happenstance, that's all. You caught me at rock bottom, honey, and as a result, were turned into an innocent victim." He sighed a little. "Ironically, I think I have a lot to thank you for . . ."

The tone was suddenly softer, introspective. She leaned forward attentively. "*Thank* me?" she prodded.

"Maybe a person has to tumble all the way down to a nadir of sorts in order to realize he's there, and to start climbing out," Barker said slowly. "Last night did that for me. I awoke today with a new resolve. I guess I just called to tell you that, and to apologize for the unpleasantness I caused you."

"Do you—"

"And to assure you that the next time our paths cross, the circumstances will be more comfortable for both of us."

The summation. "Thank you." She gulped the words instinctively and immediately chastized herself.

"Thank you, my dear, for hearing me out."

When she opened her mouth, she realized he had hung up. *"Damn!"* She slammed the telephone down.

Senator Frederick Barker leaned back on the sofa in his living room, folded his hands together in his lap, and contemplated the telephone on his coffee table, as though he were looking for clues.

Well, the farm girl was a journalist, that was for sure. She had been waiting for him. Matter of fact, he'd bet she had even recorded the conversation. She was certainly trying to get him to put something more on the record.

He got a gleam in his eye. He had won the telephone conversation. No doubt about it. But had he won her over in the process? He knew full well the strategy was only a defensive tactic, a way of making it difficult for her to amass the proof. Would she try? And if she did, would she keep pushing when she came up against impasses?

Barker shrugged and scrutinized the telephone more carefully. The farm girl was a journalist. The question was: Which was the real Cynthia Matthews? Compassionate farm girl or tough journalist?

He did not like the answer he came up with.

"The death of someone close . . . in my case, someone I lived with for forty years, is—"

Cynthia pressed the "stop" button on her tape recorder, cutting off Senator Barker's voice, and rubbed the fingers of her right hand back and forth over her lips slowly. She closed her eyes and arched her back.

Getting up from the desk, she walked around her living room. She had done everything that could be done on a Saturday—all the preliminary work. Why not put the article aside and go on to something else?

Why not? She stood at the window and looked at the street lights gleaming in the darkness and realized it was no longer afternoon.

Why couldn't she stop? And why was she going back over the early part of the interview—over all those words that had nothing to do with the confession?

She sat down in an armchair and once again told herself that she had lucked into what could prove to be a sensational story.

Sapphire jumped into her lap. Cynthia let her hands sink into the cat's fur and admitted it: She felt depressed, not lucky.

Sapphire moved her body cozily around Cynthia's fingers, purring in the caress.

Perhaps it was the "lucked into" part. It was not a scoop that had resulted from tireless, brilliant investigative reporting. The information had come to her because she was fortunate enough to be in the right place at the right time.

Fortunate enough. She grunted. Did asking a man who had drugged himself with an excess of booze disturbingly provocative questions about the death of his wife constitute "good fortune" or "taking undue advantage"?

Cynthia rubbed her eyes and asked herself a more discomforting question: Was this a sensational political exposé, or was it the *real* story on human loss: the tale of a man so shattered and confused by the death of his wife that he had desperately sought to hang onto what was left in his life by stooping to do the despicable?

For the first time in a long and distinguished political career.

For the first time? Perhaps he had always—

Cynthia pushed Sapphire off her lap. She stood up and walked back to her desk. No, her gut instinct told her that it was the first time. His deranged manner told her that.

Idly, she pressed the Fast-Forward button on her tape machine, stopped the recorder, and then pressed Playback.

"Guilt for all the things you never got to say, never got to do for her." The voice was hoarse. "Guilt for all the things you did. So many things I did."

She stopped the tape recorder and shuddered.

She admitted it. She had liked the man. For some reason, he had touched her, in his gruff warmth he had reminded her of—

Cynthia went over to the bookcase and took down the picture of her father sitting next to her on the tractor. She stared at it for a long time. His daughter, Senator Barker had said, was "about your age." Had he opened up to her for that reason? Had his daughter been the "someone else," the other person she felt Barker was addressing?

She gazed at her father in the picture and felt terribly emotional and confused at the same time. He was getting all mixed up in her head with Senator Barker. Death did that. It hurt so, it made you crazy.

"The death of someone close . . ." She heard the Senator's voice on her tape.

Oh, the death of someone close.

She put the photo back on the bookcase, and knew a decision had been made. Not necessarily a rational one. No, a highly emotional one, to be sure, and probably the wrong decision, but she, who had led a thoroughly rational professional life up to this point, was certainly entitled to one highly emotional decision.

At her desk, she paused a moment, and then picked up all the papers—the lists, the notes, the transcript. She took the tape out of the recorder, walked all of the precious evidence into her bedroom, opened the top drawer of her dresser, and deposited them all way in the back underneath a stack of underpants.

"Senator Frederick Barker," she sighed, "for the moment, at least, your confession will go no further. Your secret is safe with me."

Alone in his living room, late that Saturday night, his stomach churning, Jed Farber leaned on his stereo cabinet, and pondered the peculiar passions of fatherhood.

He loved those two children slumbering in the extra bedroom, loved them more than life itself. That love created extraordinary highs and extraordinary lows. Today had, unfortunately, been a day of lows. He began to recount them to support his argument, but his stomach responded with painful cramps. No need to recall. What he needed instead was to regain perspective.

Perspective, ah yes, perspective. And to remember, always, that it was his profound desire to do the right thing that made him so acutely aware of having done the wrong thing, of having failed. That same desire would serve him well in the end. It had to.

Unconvinced, he repeated the conclusion: It had to. A father who cared so very deeply had to be a good father . . . in the end.

He sat down on his living-room sofa and opened a book, but after a while he looked up from the page and stared into space. He saw two large blue eyes staring back at him. The vision soothed him. They were so cool, so inviting, so merry that he even began smiling up at them. The hell with that bullshit about hazel. He knew blue eyes when he saw them, and hers had been the bluest eyes he had ever seen.

Gradually, the lines of his face hardened.

Is that what they had looked like to Rob Diamond? The blue eyes began to take on a new dimension—Mata Hari eyes.

Just one minute. Wasn't there some need for perspective here? The fact was, good old Rob Diamond, his friend of more than a decade, his drinking buddy and his fellow attorney, *had* been guilty of misconduct. No one knew that better than Jed, who had spent a lot of time looking for errors in the article in order to help Rob get off the hook.

Then why had he reacted to her that way last night?

The all-too-familiar ulcerous rumblings began starting up in his stomach. He pulled out a roll of antacids and popped a tablet into his mouth.

His focus returned to reality, to the debris that littered his living room. It looked as though a huge cloud had exploded, pouring out not rain, but children's possessions: sneakers, elementary-school textbooks, mismatched socks, sweatshirts and jeans with at least one arm or leg inside out.

Worse than the debris was what was underneath it: the modern sofa, the matching chairs, the well-appointed coffee tables, the thick, wall-to-wall carpeting, the well-placed but personality-less pictures on the wall.

Jed Farber felt on the verge of suffocation, a daddy with no mommy, a bull imprisoned in a delicate Danish Modern furniture display.

He closed his eyes and rubbed his stomach.

Something was missing. How about a grown-up, for starters? An adult to talk to.

He looked at his watch. Who called a woman at ten o'clock on a Saturday night? Ridiculous idea.

The ulcer pains got worse.

He walked into the kitchen and dialed the phone number he had scrawled on the piece of paper hours before. The phone was picked up on the second ring.

"Hello?"

"Hello . . . Cynthia?"

"Yes."

"This is Jed Farber. We met last night at—"

"Lilah's party."

"Lilah's party, right. I was the one who—"

"Hated me."

He paused. "Well, frankly, it was my impression that you returned the favor."

"Oh, and I suppose you're calling to rekindle the old flame?"

Jed shook his head. "Don't."

"Don't what?"

"You're about to do it again. I'm going to end up with custody of the neighborhood. I can feel it coming."

He heard laughter. "I'm sorry. Really, I'm sorry. I've just had a really bad day."

"*You've* had a bad day!"

"Look, I spent a good twelve hours working on a story I'm not going to do. Yes, I'd call that a bad day! What did you do?"

Jed closed his eyes. "I took my son to see *Dead Is the Flesh.*"

"Isn't that that really frightening horror movie?"

"Yup. He wanted to see it."

"How old is your son?"

"Seven. It was *his* idea."

"Wow," Cynthia gasped. "He must be one brave little boy. I know some adults who've seen it and they say—"

"He isn't brave."

"What do you mean?"

"I had to physically peel the pathetic little kid's hands off his eyes—and that was twenty minutes after he ran out crying. That was when we were in the car, four blocks from the movie theater!"

"Well, it *is* supposed to be very—"

"*He wanted to see it!*" Jed roared.

He heard an explosion of laughter on the other end. It subsided. "Sounds like you've had a bad day," she said softly.

So softly. Jed's head was swimming. "Fatherhood is a little intense."

"Is he your only child?"

Jed groaned. "Please, let's not get into that—"

"Come on," she cajoled. "Who else contributed to your day?"

"I have a lovely ten-year-old daughter. Her name is Lisa."

"Ten years old, eh? Going through a sensitive stage, perhaps?"

"Right."

"Hurt feelings? Lots of hurt feelings?"

"How did you know?"

"I have an eleven-year-old niece. I hate to tell you this, but it gets worse at eleven."

"Thanks a lot. I needed that."

"But they come back. Girls always come back to Daddy."

"What are you? Some kind of adolescence expert?"

"Nope. Just a daughter."

Jed laughed. "I actually called for a reason. To tell you that you are wrong. Your eyes are blue, not hazel."

"Not true! When they get angry, they get greener. They turn hazel. At least that's what my mother says."

"Then perhaps you weren't angry."

"I wasn't angry. *You* were angry. *You* walked away!"

Jed grinned. "The prosecution rests. Your eyes remained blue."

"Why did you walk away?"

"I hate to lose an argument."

"I won?"

"Hands down."

She sighed. "It was a Pyrrhic victory. I lost you."

"Want a second chance?"

"You didn't strike me as the type who gives second chances."

"Last night—no. But that was before a day of strenuous parenting. Are you free for brunch tomorrow?"

"Yes."

"I drop off at Sunday school at nine and pick up at noon. How about brunch at nine-fifteen?"

"Fine."

"Where do you want to go?"

"Why don't you just come over here?"

Jed took a deep breath. Yes, why not? Why not right now? "Where's 'here'?"

She gave him her address. He passed the street every day on his way to work.

"Jed?"

"Yes?"

"Do you . . . um . . . do you have a dimple in your chin?"

He shifted uncomfortably on the couch. "Yes."

"Good."

His face reddened. "Well, I'll see you tomorrow."

"Be careful," she warned him.

"Why?"

"The yuppies," she whispered into the telephone. "The neighborhood is crawling with yuppies."

"Bitch."

They both laughed.

# · 7 ·

At nine-thirty on Sunday morning, Jed
Farber arrived at Cynthia's apartment with a bag of croissants,
the Sunday papers, and a chip on his shoulder.

"I'm late, but I had no choice," he declared from her doorway, daring her to make an issue of it.

"I must be late too. I hadn't noticed the time." She beckoned
him in.

"I dressed down intentionally for the neighborhood," he
said gruffly, pointing to his sweater and jeans.

Cynthia hung his jacket up in the closet. "To tell the truth, I
find it awkward when people show up for brunch in tuxedos."

He handed her the brown bag.

"Mmm, croissants," she murmured, carrying it into the
kitchen. "That's perfect. I just have bagels."

"Highly significant, that." Jed followed her into the kitchen.

"Highly significant, what?"

"That I bring you croissants and you buy me bagels. Says
something about how we interpret each other."

She looked up at him wide-eyed. "It does?"

"Well, obviously you think of me as Jewish, and I think of
you as—"

"French?" Her eyebrows went up. "I'm not at all French. I'm
actually a person who loves bagels—especially the ones they have
at a new store that just opened around the corner—and who

serves her friends what she likes to eat herself." Gingerly, she placed the croissants with the bagels on a tray and put them in the oven. "I didn't think of you as Jewish. I thought of you as a possible friend." Her eyes twinkled. "Would you prefer to be Jewish?"

He stared at her awhile, and then laughed. It was a strange laugh—one that started as a slow, rumbling, internal sound and then grew until it erupted, dissipating the tension in his body. "You win. Again!"

"Do we have to keep winning and losing? It will absolutely ruin my appetite for both bagels and—"

"No!" They stared at each other. "I'm terrific at cooking sausages," he said very seriously, his eyes never leaving hers. "Would you like me to try working on that pan over there?"

She brightened and nodded.

As she made the eggs and he cooked the sausages, they talked about the headlines in the newspapers he had brought. The elections in the Philippines and the possible ouster of Ferdinand Marcos, the tragedy of the space shuttle explosion. The conversation was as animated and as personal as it was political, each trying to sound terribly clever, and, at the same time, evaluating the other's cleverness.

Jed finished the sausages before Cynthia finished the eggs, and wandered out of the kitchen, continuing the talk, but sounding somewhat distracted. He returned as she was putting the eggs on a platter.

He peered at her intently. "You have a beautiful apartment."

"Thank you!"

"And a very attractive cat."

She smiled.

"And bagels and croissants that are in the process of burning in your oven."

"Oh, my God!" she gasped, running to the oven. She took out the tray and scrutinized its contents. "Thank God, they're perfect."

"A little crisp."

"No." She looked at him sternly. "Perfect."

She put the bagels and croissants in a basket and handed

them to Jed. Picking up the platter containing the scrambled eggs and sausage, she led the way to the dining room.

"What's the 'I' for?" she asked as he followed her.

"What 'I'?"

"It says 'Jed I. Farber' in the phone book."

He groaned. "Hey, how about some congenial foreplay first! Let's not go right for the middle name!"

"Come on," she said as they sat at the dining-room table and she served the eggs and sausages. "Out with it."

"Issac."

"Isaac?"

"You heard me." He stared at her, defying her to react.

A muffled laugh erupted through her tightly closed lips.

"An insensitive response, if ever I saw one!"

"Well, it's just that . . . you just don't strike me as an 'Issac.' Besides, 'Jed' and 'Isaac' don't go together."

He dug into his eggs. "That's why. My mother named me 'Jed' because she'd heard the name in a musical and liked it. But she felt guilty because it wasn't a proper Jewish name. So she compensated." He made a face. "*More* than compensated."

"What musical? I can't think of a musical with a 'Jed' in it."

He waved her away. "Not important."

She put down her fork. "Come on. You've gone this far. What musical?"

"*Oklahoma!*"

"*Oklahoma!*" she howled. "That's 'Judd,' not 'Jed,' and he was the villain!"

His ears reddened. "Well, it appears that she wasn't listening very carefully." Jed began talking about his family—the liquor store his father had had in Brooklyn, the eccentricity of the huge assortment of aunts, uncles, and cousins who had played major roles—frequently intrusive ones—in his childhood. The more he talked, the more questions Cynthia asked, and the more he seemed to relax.

She was curious. She found him a very funny raconteur. But she asked the questions for other reasons as well. Although the Brooklyn he described bore no resemblance at all to Ballard, Indiana, the family stories were familiar ones. He, too, had chosen a very different world. He, too, had very fond feelings for the family he had left behind in the "other" world. But Jed Farber had managed, she decided, to bridge the gap: to look back with affection, with pride, with humor, and without self-consciousness. And she wanted to know how.

He ended with what he described as the "most recent source of angst—the great migration south," the transplantation of the entire Farber clan from a ten-block area in Brooklyn to a ten-block area in Miami.

As he detailed the traumas, the decisions of who got which apartment, what should be taken, what should be thrown out, and which of her daughters his deceased grandmother "would have wanted" to be the inheritor of the sterling silver tea service, Cynthia laughed so hard she had to wipe tears from her eyes.

"Your turn," he said finally.

"My turn?"

"Your sordid past. All of it!"

She tried to think of where to begin.

"No, wait a minute," he stopped her, grinning. "Let me guess." He leaned back in his chair and looked at her. "A Wellesley girl, eh? Okay. Your father's a corporate type. A lawyer? A doctor? No," he said, squinting in search of a clue. "A corporate type. A commuter.

"You grew up in the suburbs. Willow trees. Huge willow and oak trees with tire swings hanging on long ropes from their thick boughs, and all you kids—a big family, four or five kids—took turns on the tire swing."

He leaned forward, encouraged by the sparkle in her eyes. "Blond, wholesome, all-around kids. Your brothers were jocks—football players on the high-school team. No! Prep school, I bet."

Smugly, she buttered a bagel.

"Yes, prep school. You too! Saint Ann's or Mistress Goodbody's or something." He stared dreamily into space. "On vacations, you all came home to the big old house with millions of rooms, and there were group games and singing and touch football competitions with everyone killing each other to win, but"— he held up a finger—"always with good sportsmanship!"

Cynthia was happily devouring the bagel.

"I forgot the country club!" he yelled. "Country club dances and country club tennis matches—a competitive athletic bunch, all of you—freckled noses in the summer and ski trips in the winter, and maybe Jamaica for Christmas, but only after you all stopped believing in Santa Claus."

She stared dreamily into her orange juice.

He leaned forward. "Well, how right am I?"

She looked at him in amusement. "Five kids."

"And?"

She thought for a moment. "Freckled noses in the summer."

"That's it?" He looked at her suspiciously. "Come on . . ."

She sighed. "That's it, but—you've made my day."

"How?"

She thought as she munched an apple wedge. "Your description is definitely the image I've been trying to perpetuate all these years."

"What's the true story?"

She shrugged. "I am the youngest of five children born to Bess and Marshall Matthews in Ballard, Indiana. My father's no longer alive." She paused. How simple that made it: *no longer alive.* "He was a farmer, a good farmer, but not a rich one. The freckles came from summers in the fields!"

She played with the bagel. "Of the five of us, all graduated from Fallspoint High School. Two graduated from college—thanks to generous scholarships. All escaped the farm, and all but one escaped Ballard, Indiana. My brother Jimmy's still there." She tilted her head as she stared down at her plate. "He's running the local gas station/grocery store, and . . ." She nodded slowly. "And he's probably the most content of all of us." She had never thought of that before, but it was true.

"Actually, I like that better," he said softly. He frowned. "How could I have been so far off?"

She looked at him mischievously. "Your croissant-bagel complex."

"What's that?"

"Well, the 'me' that you described is not only not me, it isn't you either. It's one of those upper-crust-type families—the other side of the tracks to both of us."

"And why on earth would I want that?"

She sipped some orange juice. "Possibly because you like

me, and that makes you uncomfortable. So you want to make me less likable—one of 'those others' you can't trust."

He glared at her. "Have you been studying psychology?"

She broke out laughing. "Well, in a way. Let's just say I've spent a lot of years at the Washington dating game!"

"Any other symptoms of this desire of mine to alienate?"

"Friday night at Lilah's party. You made me into a first-class bitch for nothing more than doing my job!"

"Your job!"

"Haven't you ever represented an unsavory type? Aren't there parts of your work that would appear—"

"Sure, but I've never betrayed a client. That's something quite different!"

"Neither have I! Truth is my only client," she proclaimed grandiosely. "That's the inherent difference in our jobs." She smirked.

"Ahh, it must be gratifying to toil in such a lofty profession." He finished his eggs and chuckled. "You are a woman of many talents. You certainly rose to the occasion at Lilah's party, convincingly performing the bitchy role I had unfairly carved out for you. What method acting!"

"*You* walked away, you rat!"

"And you're bringing it all up now because you know that if I walked away again—now, after you fed me so well—I'd be a total ingrate?"

She grinned. "Damn straight. But now that I've got you, how can I get you to trust me?"

Silently he buttered his croissant.

"That's what I thought." She feigned despair. "You'll never trust me, and I'll always be afraid you'll walk away. We're doomed from the start."

"That's not all." He shook his head. "There's another stumbling block—your bedroom."

"My bedroom?" She raised a perplexed eyebrow.

"You'll have to repaint it. I can't handle purple bedrooms. As a matter of fact, I'm surprised at the broad Washington dating experience you've alluded to, given the color of that bedroom."

"What's wrong with purple?"

"To an insomniac, purple's a nightmare. I'd never be able to sleep."

"Are you an insomniac?"

He nodded.

"Gee—that's positively exotic!"

He moaned. "Only to people who have no trouble sleeping."

"How did you know it was purple?"

"I peeked while you were scrambling the eggs."

"Do you always check out the color scheme of women's bedrooms?"

His eyes warmed. "Only if I like the way they scramble eggs."

They sat very still, laughing and looking at each other.

Gradually, though, his eyes lost their light. Some new thought had occurred to him. Suddenly he blurted it out. "Did you have an affair with Rob?"

She practically dropped the coffeepot she had picked up. "Bagels and croissants, all over again!" she shouted. "Why—"

"I'm sorry." He looked more than sorry. He looked as though he, too, had been surprised by what he had asked. "I don't know what—"

"Why is it so important to you to drive a wedge, to put me on the other side? What is it with you?"

"I truly am sorry. I can't believe I even asked that question." Instinctively, he reached across the table for her hand. "You are completely right. That was unforgivable."

Her righteous fury subsided as she noted the concern in his eyes, and as she realized that she had not only avoided the question—she had made him misinterpret her answer. She saw a softness in his eyes as he held her hand she had not seen before, and it moved her. At that moment, she wanted to tell him the whole story. His eyes told her he would understand.

But the moment passed.

"Maybe I am just trying out the psychological role you've given me," he mused. Then he grinned. "I guess that means I like you."

"If that's 'like,' I'm in no hurry to repaint my bedroom."

He laughed with relief. They were back to playing games.

"Okay, you get one gauche question in return. Ask me anything you want."

"Why did you get a divorce?"

He winced.

"Did you do her wrong, or did she do you wrong, or did you grow apart?"

"I said one question!"

"I was trying to make it easier—multiple choice."

"We grew apart."

Cynthia beamed. "That usually means she did you wrong."

He stared at her with a strange expression she could not read, a mixture of 'My God, you're right' and 'You're absolutely insane.' She didn't care which it was. She liked the look.

"What is she like?"

"In one word?"

"Would you like another multiple choice?"

"No, dammit!" He thought for a moment. "Consumer," he said.

"*Fantastic* possibilities! Does she devour men?"

"Only if they're wearing expensive price tags. My sister, Daphne, describes my former wife as 'the kind of woman who shops enough to see the same dress reduced six times at Saks Fifth Avenue.'"

Cynthia giggled. "What—"

"No more! One question, that was the agreement." He studied her hand as he held it in his. "So here we are, the farm girl and the Brooklyn boy in the promised land, enjoying career opportunities unknown to our predecessors."

Cynthia laughed. "Where's the next generation going to go? Will Lisa and Timmy venture back to Brooklyn in search of their roots?"

"Naw." He kept playing with her hand, gently stroking it, examining it. "Because I'm such a devoted father, I have intentionally refrained from a lot of major accomplishments in order to leave them a ready supply of potential goals right here in Washington. They could make millions, for example. They could achieve fame." He wrapped his fingers around her hand and held it tighter. "I've left them another possibility," he said quietly. "Living happily ever after."

It sounded so very sad, the way he said it. Without thinking, she reached over and put her other hand over his.

He sat up abruptly and pulled his hand away. "So, what stories have you written other than that lawyer exposé?"

"Well, how's *that* for a nonsequitor!"

"A mood changer," he corrected her, raising his index finger. "Just a mood changer." His eyes teased. "It might be good for us to get all your career facts out in the open, anyway. I'm getting a little nervous about how many other friends of mine may have been brutalized by your appetite for truth."

She thought for a moment. "How about Police Officer Gregory Rhines?" she asked with a sparkle in her eye. "Was he a close friend?"

Jed shook his head. Then his eyes clicked in recognition. "I read that one! The rotten cop? That story in the weekend magazine section back in . . . when was it? November?"

"Late October." She nodded.

"Now, that was an appropriate subject! A lousy creep, if ever there was one!" Farber looked at her curiously. "How did you ever discover him in the first place?"

"I was coming out of a restaurant—just around the corner from here—one night with a bunch of friends. We walked out in time to see Officer Rhines make an arrest—and severely mangle this kid half his size in the process." Her eyes got larger. "Believe me, it was a scene that would have started any witness checking around!"

"What a perfect neighborhood for a reporter!" Jed shouted. "My God, girl, you live in a muckraker's dream world!"

She laughed, but her eyes seemed distracted, as though something had just occurred to her. She leaned across the table. "Listen, let me try one out on you." She played with her napkin. "It's probably nothing, but tell me what you think." She described the scenes she had witnessed at the van.

He listened carefully, then sighed and shook his head a little when she finished. "Naw . . ."

"But what about the crazy man? And he wasn't the only strange one, believe me. Plenty of the others looked deranged too!"

He shrugged. "Yeah, but that's probably just because they're down-and-outs, economic rock-bottom. Judging by the kid's fears that you might be from Immigration, I'd guess they're all illegal aliens."

"And why is someone going out of his way to hire illegal aliens? To pay them way above the minimum wage?"

"Just another softhearted American corporate mogul!" Jed laughed. "No," he said, sobering, "I'm sure there's something illicit about it. The employer probably saves a bundle by not having to pay social security, insurance, health benefits, that type of thing. But you have to ask yourself who's suffering as a result. Sounds as though the workers are getting better money than they would any place else, for what the kid told you was relatively easy work."

Cynthia nodded. "I guess you're right. It's just a feeling I got. I don't know, the guilty look on the driver's face . . ."

"Are your instincts *always* right?"

"Always!" she proclaimed haughtily, but she had trouble maintaining the look on her face. "You happen to be looking at the woman who single-handedly figured out that old man Bernes, in apartment three-oh-nine down the hall, murdered his wife and disposed of the body in the trash Dumpster behind the apartment!"

Jed gasped. "How did you figure *that* out?"

"Easy. Mrs. Bernes disappeared suddenly. Mr. Bernes was behaving, well, suspiciously. The trash people forgot to clean out the Dumpster for a few days, and it began giving off a dreadful odor . . ." She leaned across the table. "An odor the nurse, who lives in apartment four-ten, told me could *only* come from decomposing flesh."

He stared at her, startled.

"There was only one problem."

He looked at her suspiciously. "What was that?"

"Mrs. Bernes came back! Perfectly healthy!" She burst into giggles. "God, was I embarrassed! Suddenly seeing the lady walking merrily down the hall!"

He laughed along with her. She put her hand over her eyes. "I can't believe I actually owned up to that out loud," she groaned. "I never have before!"

Gently, he pulled her hand away from her eyes and held it

in his. He was looking at her with a mixture of amusement and affection that made her feel wonderful.

"Senator Barker? This is David Steele of the Steele Travel Agency. I was out of town yesterday, and I just received the message that you'd called."

"Why, I appreciate your taking the time on a Sunday to call me back, Mr. Steele," Barker boomed into the telephone. "I know you're accustomed to dealing with my secretary, Miranda, but I have a little problem I'd like to get settled before Monday."

"Certainly, Senator. Whatever can I do to help?"

Barker detected timidity on the other end of the line, the reverent response the title "Senator" frequently inspired, and for once it gave him great pleasure. "Oh, I've just gotten the word that there's a reporter snooping into my recent travel itineraries," Barker said amiably. "You know, Iowans are pretty provincial at times. They don't realize that a United States Senator has national as well as regional responsibilities. I've been told this reporter is hoping to use my travel record to prove that I've been neglecting the constituents back home, if you know what I mean."

"I see."

"I just wanted to ask you, as a favor to me, not to—"

"You don't have to ask, Senator Barker. And it isn't a favor. It goes with the business. I'd never give out any information whatsoever on a customer's account. Nor would anyone in my employ. To do so would mean violating a trust, the kind of trust a travel agency's business depends upon."

"I thought so, Mr. Steele," Barker drawled. "I know we've been using you for years because Miranda says you're the best in the business. I just wanted to make sure there would be no problem. And to warn you, perhaps, that someone might be prodding you."

"Would you like me to call you if that happens, Senator? If a reporter makes contact?"

"Why, that might be very helpful, Mr. Steele. Yes, if you don't mind, I'd certainly appreciate that."

Senator Barker hung up the phone and picked up the list

on his coffee table. He put a check next to "David Steele Travel Agency."

After Jed left, Cynthia finished her story on human loss for *America Magazine.* She decided to leave Senator Barker out completely. Then she set about doing her Sunday chores.

As she washed the brunch dishes, she thought about liquor stores in Brooklyn and crazy uncles and aunts with exotic names like "Sadie" and "Hymie." As she folded laundry, she daydreamed about a very tall, dark, square-shouldered man with a dimple in his chin and a boisterous, rough-sounding exterior that belied an inner softness.

She was on an absolute high, about to get ready for bed when there was a knock on her door.

She looked through the peephole in the door and felt even higher. "Just the man I needed to answer a burning question!" she shouted as she opened the door and faced Jed Farber. "Is Brooklyn part of New York City?"

He blinked and then stared at her in shock. "You really don't know?"

"Hey, don't knock *my* regionalism!" She put her hand on her hip. "Do you know where Ballard, Indiana, is?"

He gulped. "Uh, yes."

"Yes?"

He laughed. "Yes, Brooklyn is part of New York City."

She raised her chin. "Two hours' drive from Indianapolis."

"That's it?" he roared. "*That's* the pathetic way Ballard natives think of themselves? A tiny dot on the map, miles from that great cultural center, Indianapolis?"

"Nope. That's the way we have to explain it to foreigners. It's just down the road a ways from Notchit." She smirked. "If I'd told you that, would you have been able to visualize it?"

"Yeah." His eyes got dreamy. "Huge weeping willow trees. Tire swings hanging from the boughs—"

They both began laughing.

"Don't you even want to know why I'm here?" he asked. "Do *all* your Sunday brunch guests return, uninvited, for a nightcap?"

"Why are you here?"

"I've come to enter the ranks of reporterism," he proclaimed solemnly. "I was thinking—what goes up must come down."

"Huh?"

He tried again. "What comes in must go out."

He got another blank look.

"What returns from a factory in Maryland early in the morning must venture forth to that factory late the night before."

"The van!"

"Well, you're not quick, but you *do* catch on after a while," Jed laughed. "If they get off around six-thirty A.M., then I figure it must be almost time for the shift to begin. Why don't we see if the pickup place is the same as the drop-off place?"

"But just hours ago you put down the whole thing!" she protested. "You said it was probably nothing at all."

"Ah, but that was before I got hungry for some below-the-border food. I thought we could pick up a few tacos-to-go, and snack as we watch the developing world go to work!"

"You're crazy," she mumbled happily, pulling her coat out of the closet.

It was an unusually mild evening for late January, and crowds of people were on the streets of Adams-Morgan, wandering in and out of the stores and restaurants. Cynthia and Jed sat down on a bench across the street from the bus stop, unpacked their bags of carryout food, and began eating and talking. None of the van crowd had arrived.

After a while, Jed leaned over, cloak-and-daggerlike. "I hate to be the one to tell the reporter about her story," he whispered, "but I think the reconnoitering we anticipated has begun."

"How do you know?" she whispered back.

"Subjects fit prior description," he said with such a stiff poker face, his lips barely moved.

She turned and looked in the direction of the bus stop across the street. There were already seven men standing in a line, all looked Latin-American, all had torn jackets and wool hats pulled down practically to eye level. Some had lunchboxes. They stood close together, but there was no sense of camaraderie, no talk. On a street corner bustling with people and noise, the sullen lineup of little dark men stood out rather dramatically. Three others joined the line. One was the boy, Carlos Ramirez.

"Let's get closer," Cynthia said, standing up. "I want to be seen."

They crossed the street. Carlos Ramirez looked up attentively when she brushed by, but then looked away. She and Jed lingered behind the line, staring into a store window.

A tall, thin black man in a light jacket and no hat with a cigarette dangling from his mouth walked over and nudged a man in a red wool hat at the end of the line. "Hey, man, like, I'm looking for the place where you get the jobs."

The man in the red wool hat stared up at him, speechless.

"You know, the factory jobs?"

The man continued to stare.

The black man grabbed him by the collar. "Hey, you deaf or something? I asked you a question!"

The man in the red wool hat leaned over, tugged Carlos Ramirez on the sleeve, and pointed to the black man.

"Yes?" Carlos asked, turning around. "What is it?"

"I just asked a simple question," the black man shouted angrily. *"Is this the place you wait for the factory jobs?"*

"Yes, yes it is." Carlos pointed to the man in the red hat. "He's not deaf. He just doesn't understand English. But this is the right place, and you'll get to go. You're number thirteen in line and they take the first fifteen men."

A few others lined up. Still, there was no conversation.

"I really like those red pants in the corner," Jed whispered, pointing to a small pair of girls' running shorts in the store window display. "Didn't like 'em much ten minutes ago, but they really grow on you, know what I mean?"

She suppressed a laugh.

Finally, the big green van rumbled up, and the driver hopped out and opened the back door. *"Ola! Ola!"* he shouted.

Cynthia looked around. The crowded street scene was perfect camouflage. None of the pedestrians even seemed to notice.

As the group crawled into the back of the van, the driver began counting loudly in broken Spanish. *"Una, dua, tres, quarta, cinca . . ."*

"This is for the factory jobs, right?" the black man asked when it was his turn to climb in.

The driver frowned and stopped counting. "You American?"

"Yeah," the black man said, "I'm American."

The driver beckoned to the three men in line behind the black man and pushed them into the van. The three stumbled over Carlos Ramirez, who had stopped in the van doorway to hear the interchange between the driver and the black man.

The driver shook his head. "Sorry, buddy," he said to the black man. "I can't take you. My orders are no Americans."

Carlos Ramirez frowned, and then his eyes met Cynthia's. The driver slammed the back door, climbed in, and took off.

"What the fuck?" The black man just stood staring at the back of the van, rumbling down the street.

Cynthia went over to him. "Where did you hear about the factory jobs?" she asked.

He looked at her suspiciously and turned away. "Around," he said, walking off. "Just around."

She and Jed started heading toward her apartment. She looked up at him. "Well?"

"Carlos was the noncomitose one in the light-blue ski jacket," he said.

"Very good!"

"And Pablo, the one who called you a 'preety lady' the other day? He was the tall thin guy standing in line next to Carlos."

She looked up at him, surprised. "Right! How did you know that?"

"Easy. He leered at you when we walked by, but then backtracked quickly when he saw me." Jed grinned at her. "Oh, my supersleuth instincts are really getting good!" They walked some more. "But I'm not answering your *real* question, am I?"

"Nope."

He shook his head slowly. "I still don't think it's a story."

"But the driver—"

"Said no Americans, right. But that fits in perfectly with *my* scenario, that it's just mildly illicit. They want a work force that can't report them, that's all. I just don't think you have a serious crime. Somebody is giving a bunch of dregs solid pay and an easy night's work. Now, he might be doing it in ways that would please neither the Labor Department nor the Immigration Service, and that black man definitely has a valid discrimination complaint, but as I see it, writing it up as a story would probably only hurt the little guys. Deprive them of their earnings."

She sighed as they walked up her apartment steps. "You're probably right. It's funny, though. They looked quite different leaving for work than they looked coming home in the morning."

"How so?"

"Well, they were just sort of docile-looking tonight. The other times I saw them, several seemed in a peculiar kind of mad stupor." She pushed the elevator button for her floor. "And the man who went crazy? He wasn't there tonight."

"Well, you said he'd been given his walking papers."

"What did you think of the kid?" she asked. "Carlos Ramirez?"

Jed shook his head. "He doesn't fit in with the rest of them."

"And he seemed really surprised when the driver turned the black man away, didn't he? Suspicious . . ." She looked up at Jed. "Would you like to come in for that nightcap?" They were heading toward her door.

"I would, but I'm afraid I have to go home and pack. I've got a hearing in Detroit tomorrow." He sighed. "And a terrible week ahead. But!" He smiled at her brightly. "A silver lining at the end of the week! I am about to offer you the chance of a lifetime!"

"What?"

"Dinner with me Friday night. My former wife told me this afternoon her parents are coming for a visit, so she wants to keep the kids until Saturday."

"I accept!"

"Just like that?"

"Who am I to pass up the chance of a lifetime?"

They stood still, facing each other in front of her door. His eyes traveled from her eyes to her hair, to the features of her face, taking it all in, slowly, pleasurably, in a way that made her feel suddenly very beautiful.

Gently, he ran his fingers through her hair, and around to her neck. He lifted her chin and bent down and kissed her lips for a long time. When he backed away, he looked down at her longingly, as though he had not really wanted to stop. He stroked her cheek and smiled. "I'll call you."

Cynthia walked into her apartment still feeling the touch of his hands, seeing the sight of his face as it moved slowly, deliberately toward hers, tasting his lips caressing hers.

My God, a kiss. A real kiss, not a hurried one, nor a self-conscious one, nor a kiss that was a precursor to something else. But a deliberate kiss that was a beginning and an end in and of itself. A truly romantic kiss. A sign of affection. When was the last time she had had such a kiss? Back in her teens? She couldn't remember. But she felt just as giddy and excited as she imagined she had felt back then.

# · 8 ·

     "Out of the question!" Ed Bartholemew
bounded out of the chair he was sitting in at the conference table
in Senator Barker's office and began strutting around the room,
his hands shoved into the pockets of his gray suit pants, his soft,
dark blond hair rustling from his vehement head-shaking. "Out
of the question! He can't miss those hearings!"

     "Ed, we're talking important regional exposure," Thad
Rankerman argued, looking up from the itinerary in his hand.

     "No, we're talking Four-H Club. We're talking Shriners.
Face it, Thad, we're talking diddlies—diddlies at the expense of
major national news!"

     "It's the diddles who'll be going to the polls in November."

     "Exactly!" Bartholemew's eyes gleamed. "And they'll be vot-
ing for a United States Senator. That's what we have going for
us. We have the only candidate who's proven himself as a solid,
totally scrupulous, powerful United States Senator. A man from
back home who's made his mark for the people back home, and
achieved national celebrity status in the process. A man Iowans
can be proud of. An honest man—unlike the slimy, rich local
bastard he'll be running against. We've got the incumbent, Thad.
We've got to milk that!"

     "*Not* at the expense of regional exposure!"

     Bartholemew placed his hands on the conference table and
leaned across menacingly in Thad Rankerman's direction.

"What's killing Iowa farmers, Thad? What's killing Iowa factory workers? *Trade,* that's what! That's their single biggest gripe. And what have we going here? The biggest trade hearings this year! What's going to make the evening news in Iowa? Those hearings! And who's going to star on the evening news, articulately standing up for Iowa's farmers and workers at those hearings? Our candidate—Iowa's only *real* candidate—the incumbent, showing his people he's in Washington for them, doing his job when they need him!"

Rankerman's face reddened around his beard. "Trade's a big issue in every state. As I see it, you'll have a whole committee of grandstanding Senators at your hearings, all of them competing for a forty-second spotlight on the evening news, Ed. He'll have to be damn articulate to make sure he's the one who makes the spotlight!"

"He'll be articulate enough, believe me!"

"Could *he* register an opinion in here?" Senator Barker stormed from the head of the table. "Could the scrupulously honest, powerful incumbent enter into this fascinating discussion?"

"Rick, surely you understand the importance—"

"If you'll both be kind enough to shut up for a moment, I'll enlighten you with my down-home but at the same time stellar Senatorial wisdom!" Barker interjected.

Bartholemew sheepishly sat back down at the table. Rankerman cowered over his itinerary.

Barker put his bifocals on and examined the papers before him. "The trade hearings *are* important," the Senator said quietly. "Very, very important."

"Yes, and remember all the coverage you got last week from those farm hearings!" Bartholemew put in.

"He *held* those farm hearings!" Rankerman shouted. "They were *his* hearings. These are going to be full committee hearings. Everyone's gonna be coming out loudly against the trade deficit!"

Barker looked sternly at the two over the tops of his bifocals. Bartholemew and Rankerman stared down at the conference tabletop in silence.

"As I was saying," Barker went on, "the hearings are important, but there are three full days of hearings."

"But the last day is the culmination, the—"

"Yes, that it is," Barker interrupted. "However, there's no reason I can't culminate a little early, Ed, and still make both Thad's reception and his awards dinner." He grinned. "You're right, reporters are always looking for a spicey bite of oratory. But, frankly, it's been my experience that the sooner that bite comes, the better—kind of facilitates its placement on the evening news, if you know what I mean. I see no reason why I can't excuse myself before the noon break at Wednesday's hearings—to take care of 'some pressing business in Iowa'—and offer my 'articulate,' as you both put it, insights before all the others."

"Perfect!" Rankerman sighed gratefully as he made a notation on the sheet in front of him. "I'll count on you for Wednesday night, then."

"Okay," Bartholemew conceded, pushing back his chair. "That's a fair compromise." He began to leave, but then turned back. "Almost forgot," he said, handing Barker a piece of paper with four names on it. "These are all fairly new reporters to Washington who have requested in-depth interviews. Why don't you look them over and let Bob know what you think."

Barker nodded.

The two men began to leave.

"Thad," Senator Barker called out, "just one word before you catch your plane." He walked slowly across the room and stood looking out the office window beside his desk. Rankerman walked up behind him and waited.

"Uh, this contact of yours . . . the one you were telling me about last week, the one in our opponent's campaign?"

"Yeah?"

"Stay close to him for the next couple of weeks. Let me know if you pick up any vibes, any sense of . . . oh, elation, say, in our competitor's camp."

"Elation?" Rankerman asked. "About what?"

The Senator shook his head slowly. "Don't know. About anything. You tell me. Just stay close to him."

"Actually, uh, it's a *her*."

Barker turned around beaming. "Well, that should make it a more pleasant assignment!"

When Thad Rankerman left, Senator Barker continued staring out the window, looking at the view of the Capitol Building visible through the leafless wintry tree branches. It was a damn nice view, one he planned to savor as long as he could.

No matter what the Matthews girl did, Barker guessed Thad would hear nothing for a while. She was a reporter, not a politico. She would be checking her sources, rather than rushing to the opposing candidate's camp with her information. Still, it didn't hurt to keep tabs.

He perused the list of journalists Bartholemew had given him, walked over to his desk, and picked up the intercom. "Miranda, who is that young college intern you're always telling me about? The one you think is so smart? . . . Yes, that's the one, Bruce Abbott. Find him and send him in to see me, will you?"

Barker sat down at his desk and took out a clean piece of paper. On it, he copied over the names of the four reporters in his own handwriting, and added one more name: Cynthia Matthews.

"Come in," he shouted in response to the knock at his door.

A dark-haired, meticulously dressed, painfully thin young man walked eagerly into Senator Barker's office. "You wanted to see me, sir?"

"Yes, Bruce," Senator Barker said. "I have a little research project for you." He handed the boy the paper. "These, uh, five reporters have requested in-depth interviews. They're all relatively new to Washington, and we don't know much about them. I'd like you to round me up a sampling of articles each one has written. I believe you can find out by—"

"Oh, I know how, Senator! There's a computer retrieval system that enables you to get copies of articles just by programming in the reporter's byline. They showed us all how to use it last week!"

The boy's enthusiasm pleased the Senator, but fatigued him a little at the same time. "Well, then, go to it!" Barker grinned.

It was six-thirty A.M. Tuesday, closing time at the factory. In a rural section of Maryland, fifteen men straggled out of a brightly lit building into total darkness.

*"Vamos! Vamos!"* the van driver shouted. The exhortation created clouds of vapor in the icy air. *"Vamos,"* he continued,

ushering the bedraggled group into the back of the van. Carlos Ramirez crawled in next to his friend Pablo Rano.

When the van driver slammed the back door shut, Carlos leaned a little closer to Pablo. "So, you're rich again, my friend!" he teased in Spanish. The weekly job of unloading the tank truck at the back of the factory paid a higher hourly wage, and Pablo had got the coveted assignment that night.

"Uhh." Pablo dropped down on the floor of the van and sat very still. His mouth hung open. His gaze was fixed but expressionless.

As the van pulled away, some of the men began to doze, their heads wobbling in response to the bumpy ride.

Pablo continued to sit very still, his jaw slack, his eyes in a lifeless daze.

Carlos watched him with mounting concern. It was very un-Pablo-like behavior. Usually Pablo drove everyone crazy by talking all the way home in the van.

"Pablo . . ." Carlos tried again.

"Leave me alone!" Pablo screamed at him in Spanish. "Leave me alone! Shut the fuck up!"

Three of the dozing bodies shifted restlessly, but then went back to sleep. Carlos shut up. They rode on in silence for a while.

Suddenly there was an agonizing groan from the other end of the van. It came from a heavyset older man, whose curly black hair was laced with gray. Carlos knew only that the man was Guatemalan and that they called him "Francisco."

Francisco was slumped in the corner, sweating profusely. His breathing came in rapid gasps. The other riders stared.

Francisco groaned again, this time flailing his hands. He pulled himself up to the window, where his fingers worked frantically at sliding the window frame back.

No one moved.

Francisco finally got the window opened, and stuck his head out so far that only his lower body remained inside the car. The man's body heaved violently, pouring vomit out along the highway. Some of it splashed against the window, leaving large brown splotches on the pane. Again, he heaved. Again, the sickly, light brown substance splattered into the air, spreading more splotches on the windowpane.

Finally, Francisco slumped back onto the floor of the van, clutching his stomach. Drops of vomit slid off his chin and onto his shirt.

The rest of the van's riders looked away, down at their laps, at their hands. No one said a word.

The man rolled over onto his back, twisting and groaning, his legs pulled up to his chest.

Carlos reached into his lunch box, took out a napkin, and crawled to the back of the van. He wiped the vomit off Francisco's face and shirt with the napkin, but the smell was so awful, he feared he too would be sick. Carlos took a deep breath of the cold air blowing in through the opened window.

Francisco's hand kneaded his stomach frantically as he moaned. Carlos unzipped the top of Francisco's jacket, took off his own hat, and, using it as a cloth, gently wiped the sweat off Francisco's neck and face. He loosened Francisco's belt. Francisco gasped in relief.

"Francisco, what can I do to help you?" Carlos whispered nervously in Spanish.

The man closed his eyes tight and shook his head. Doubling up suddenly, he groaned loudly. The sound was high-pitched, a cry.

Carlos bent over Francisco's body and took his hand. The man squeezed Carlos's hand with his right hand as his left held his stomach and his body contracted violently in acute spasms of pain.

Panicked, Carlos Ramirez looked up at the others for help. Huddled together at the other end of the van, they all looked away.

Gradually, the spasms seemed to subside, and Francisco's shrill outcries turned into subdued moans.

At the drop-off point, Francisco managed to crawl out of the van, and then dropped down on the curb. The other riders ran off, and the van pulled away.

Carlos asked Francisco where he lived. It was just two blocks from the drop-off. "Come," Carlos said in Spanish, "I will help you get home."

With Carlos supporting him, the short, heavyset man, obviously in great discomfort, groped his way along the streets and then down the steps to his basement apartment.

The door was opened by a man in an undershirt and trousers. He led Carlos and Francisco into a dark room filled with other Hispanic men, some sitting, some sleeping in corners on the floor. Two men got up off a couch to make room. Francisco slumped down, still clutching his stomach. He opened his eyes and looked at Carlos.

*"Gracias,"* he whispered.

"You need a doctor," Carlos said in Spanish.

Francisco waved him away. "It goes away." He squeezed the Spanish words out. "The pain comes, but it goes also."

"For how long have you had this pain?" Carlos asked.

Francisco shook his head and closed his eyes. "Better already," he grunted, rubbing his stomach and doubling over into a ball on the couch. "Better already."

"He needs a doctor," Carlos said in Spanish to the man in the undershirt standing near him.

"And I need a million dollars!" The man laughed hoarsely. Everyone in the room laughed with him.

Christopher Channing had a perfect face. Every feature was exactly right. The eyes, perhaps, were a little on the large side, but that and the prominent dimples only seemed to make him more perfect. He was very smart, and an excellent reporter, but it was not his words that made increasing numbers of women tune in to his television news reports each evening.

Cynthia Matthews gaped at him from the doorway of the Burger Barn restaurant at noon on Wednesday. Sitting at the table, waiting for her to join him for lunch, he looked like an exquisite bronze statue, as perfectly crafted as a work of art, and as immobile as a statue.

Chris Channing's head was propped up by his right arm. His eyes were staring vacantly in her direction, but obviously, from their lack of response, not picking up any visual impulses.

She moved toward him, staying directly within what seemed to be his line of vision. She got no response. She kept walking. She stuck out her tongue. She crossed her eyes. She noted she was beginning to get strange looks from other tables, but still, nothing from Chris.

Finally, when she got to the table, she leaned over the empty chair he was facing, put her elbows down on the place setting, and, imitating his vacant look, stuck her face within one foot of his. She expected him to jump, but instead he just grinned recognition. "Hi."

"My God!" She pulled out the chair and sat down. "Your startle reflexes are in bad shape today!"

"Huh?" Now the smile became somewhat embarrassed. "I was just thinking. Uh . . ." He looked down at the menu. "I'm going to have the vegetarian burger. How about you?" He signaled a waitress.

"*That's* what you were thinking?" Cynthia handed the waitress her menu. "Two vegetarian burgers!" She turned back to Channing as the waitress left, examining him with some concern. His large blue eyes were darker than usual, more intense. "Chris, what is it?"

"Huh? Oh, sorry. I'm just lost in planning." He smiled sheepishly. "Lost in strategy."

"Planning for what?"

"I don't know. Maybe a free-lance story. Maybe just some fact-finding to satisfy me personally."

"What's the subject?"

Channing hesitated. Finally he looked up at her with discomfort. "Gardiner Weldy."

Cynthia flopped back in her chair. "Oh, no, not Gardiner again!" She groaned. "Chris, Chris, I thought working for someone else—being free of Gardiner Weldy—would stop your crazy obsession with doing him in!"

Channing sighed. "Okay, let's call it my obsession, an obsession that grew probably out of working for a man who is both incompetent and conniving, and who manages, by conniving, to get what he wants, while many of us competents don't."

"Come on now, that's *past* frustration, Chris! You got what you wanted. You're working exactly where you wanted to be working."

He nodded. "Right. So now I'm no longer vindictive. But I'm still, well, curious. I've always had this feeling that Gardiner is not what he appears to be." He looked up at her suddenly. "You know how he talks all the time about his old days working for the reputable Mott/Riley syndicate? Well, he never did."

Cynthia blinked. "What are you talking about?"

"Gardiner's only journalistic experience prior to Capitol Radio was working as Washington correspondent for a string of small-town New England dailies owned by his father-in-law."

"Well, a lot of people get jobs through family connections."

Channing sneered. "His career as a Washington correspondent was characterized by repeated journalistic transgressions—hyperbole, inaccuracy, misrepresentation—and culminated in one incident in which Gardiner actually tried to bribe a government official to say he had *not* been misquoted, when in fact, Gardiner *had* misquoted him."

Cynthia choked on the water she had just sipped and began coughing and giggling at the same time. "Stop! Stop! I can't take any more!"

Channing's eyes got darker, his jaw tightened. "I find this quite repugnant," he said tersely. "It really is *not* funny, Cynthia."

"Not funny?" she shrieked. "Attempting to bribe a public official to lie to your editor, I'd say that's pretty funny! Oh Chris," she said, wiping her eyes with her napkin as her gasps subsided, "the problem is, honey, you don't have an exposé. You have the makings of a sit-com!"

Channing glared. "What is it with you today? All this giddiness! I wanted a sounding board, not a—"

"Sorry. Really." She forced herself not to laugh. "Sorry. Go on." She put the napkin to her lips, anticipating future outbreaks.

"At any rate," Chris Channing sighed, obviously deflated, "when even this piddling local chain in the boondocks could no longer endure Gardiner's inaccuracies, his father-in-law paid him off in a large lump sum, which Gardiner used to set up Capitol Radio."

Cynthia eyed Channing sympathetically, and then looked down and played with the tablecloth for a while. "You have good gossip, honey," she said softly. "But you know as well as I you don't have an exposé there. Chris, we did not hire Gardiner. He hired us. He's paid us. He's the employer. You can't drag him into court for falsifying his résumé."

Chris sat thinking.

She shifted restlessly in her chair. "For heaven's sake, how long have you been working on this crusade?"

He turned on her. "Since I found out something else. He is not trying to run Capitol Radio as a reputable news outfit."

"Now, what is that supposed to mean?"

"Remember the profiles he had us all do on candidates during the last election? Democratic candidates only?"

"Yes?"

"Remember the series he had you do in November, on big labor's comeback? The one you had trouble doing because all your research indicated big labor was *not* making a comeback?"

"Sure do," Cynthia winced. "The one requested by those stations in the Midwest."

"No." Chris grinned. "In fact, sweetheart, that series was requested and paid for—amply—by a wealthy liberal politico in Michigan."

"What?"

"And the profiles were an attempt to convince the Democratic National Committee to fund subtle promotional spots that would be broadcast as news to our subscribers in the hinterlands. An attempt, by the way, that didn't work."

"Well, then . . ."

"And now he's feeling out a filthy-rich archconservative in—"

"For what? Why does he need extra money?"

"Because he is not only a rotten journalist. He is a rotten administrator too! He's been running Capitol Radio in the red for years now, taking home a healthy salary for himself, but not making it profitable."

"How can you be so sure!"

"I'm sure." Channing glared at her, his jaw fixed, and she was sure too. He turned the empty plate in front of him around and around. "I'll bring you more explicit proof next time." He leaned across the table. "Just answer one question. Do you agree that running what its subscribers and its employees think is a reputable news organization while all the time soliciting money from private-interest groups in return for promotional copy is just cause for an exposé?"

"Well . . . yes."

"Okay, then." He sat back in his chair. "Do me a favor. Keep your eyes open." He smiled and his manner slipped back into his usual warmth. "Trust me."

As the waitress arrived with their platters, Chris laughed good-naturedly. "The problem is that you're too preoccupied with *your* big story to listen to me talk about mine." He looked up and winked at her. "Well, your turn now. Out with it. What have you done about Senator Frederick Barker since I talked to you Saturday?"

Cynthia's appetite suddenly evaporated. She put her burger back down on her plate and played with her water glass. "I decided to hold off. Not to do anything right away."

Startled, Channing leaned across the table and lowered his voice. "A very powerful United States Senator has admitted—on tape—that he's been doling out tax breaks for campaign contributions, and you're thinking of sitting on it?"

"A very drunk Senator."

"So what?"

"A guilt-ridden, recently bereaved Senator."

"He called you! That's what it is. He called you Saturday and begged you—"

"He called, yes. But he didn't beg. He just apologized."

"And you fell for *that*?"

"No. No, that wasn't what made me decide to hold off." She played with her food.

"What, then?"

She looked into Channing's eyes. "I feel the confession was obtained at a time of great duress. The man was—well, filled with booze, riddled with emotions about the death of his wife . . ."

"You're a reporter, not a shrink."

Her eyes glared in outrage. "And the role of a reporter is to help someone commit suicide?"

"The role of a reporter is to uncover the facts—one way or another—and hold the crooks up to the spotlight."

"And gain fame in the process."

Channing threw his burger down on his plate. "Jesus, Cynthia, what's come over you?" he said in disbelief. "What's made the ultimate hard-nosed journalist suddenly turn to mush?"

"Mush? A man who has been a damn good member of Congress for thirty years is hovering on an emotional precipice, and you think it's mushy of me not to want to push him over?" She played with her food. "Chris," she said softly, "I have a favor to ask of you."

He waited.

"I know that not exposing this confession is sacrilege, but I can't do it. Not right now, at least. Not unless something else comes up, some additional piece of information gleaned under different circumstances."

"And you want me to give you some sort of journalistic dispensation?" he snarled. "You want me to assure you that you can step blithely over what has to be the best press handout in this town for a long time?"

She looked at him lovingly, tilted her head, and smiled sweetly. "Yes, Chris, that's exactly what I want you to do."

Channing growled. He shook his head. He looked at her with disgust. But after a while, begrudgingly, he gave in. Putting down his burger, he raised his hands as if making an official pronouncement. "I hereby give thee journalistic dispensation. And free Senator Barker in the process."

"See," she teased. "Isn't it more fulfilling to be a good friend than an accomplice?"

He pointed his finger at her. "No! I expect you to be both on this Gardiner thing!"

"Done," she said lightly, picking up her food. "I promise."

He looked at her curiously. "What is it?"

"What?"

"You're so different today, lighthearted about things you would normally take so seriously. You're . . . distracted."

She shrugged and went back to her food.

"Come on, no secrets. That's always been our creed. What is it?" He stared some more. "Are you in love or something?"

"Naw."

"Rob returneth?"

"No! God, no!"

"Then what?"

"Oh, I just started dating someone. Well, just one date and a lot of phone calls thus far, but he seems very . . . It's just fun."

"Christ, you're actually blushing. You of all people! Like a schoolgirl!"

She shot him a hostile look, but her face got redder.

"Who?"

She fidgeted with her fork and looked up at Channing nervously. "His name is Jed Farber."

"Jed Farber, who used to work on the Hill? Senate-side?"

"Yes, I think he said he did, actually." She took another bite. "He's in private practice now." She looked up at Chris brightly. "Did you know him when you were covering the Hill for Capitol Radio?"

Channing's eyes turned cold. "This date—this single date—did it occur before or after you decided not to do the story on Barker?" he asked angrily.

Cynthia frowned, confused. "After."

"Are you certain?" The tone was frigid.

"Chris? What?"

"Did you tell Jed Farber about Barker's confession?"

"No, of course not. You're the only one I've told. What does he have to do with Barker?"

Channing stared at her in disbelief. "You don't know, do you?" His eyes darted around the room. "I can't believe that you don't even know."

"Know what?" Now she was shouting. "Damn it, Chris, know what?"

"Know the name of the man who worked for years as Senator Barker's legislative assistant, who became legal counsel to the Senate Tax Subcommittee at Barker's request, the man who happens to be Senator Frederick Barker's closest friend to this day."

Her eyes were now opened wide, staring at Christopher Channing in terror. "Who?" she asked softly, but by then she did not need to hear his answer.

# · 9 ·

The phone was ringing when Cynthia walked into her apartment from work that night. She ran to pick up the extension in the kitchen.

"Hello?" There was no sound on the other end, and she was about to hang up, certain whoever it was had decided no one was home.

"Hello." The voice was tentative. "Is, uh, is this Cynthia Matthews?"

"Yes?"

"This is Carlos Ramirez. I don't know if you remember—"

"Yes, I do." She pressed the receiver to her ear. Carlos had used the business card she had given him! He had called! "At the bus stop the other morning. I remember who you are. What can I do for you, Carlos?"

"I would like to talk to you a little about the factory."

"Yes?"

"You said the other morning that you were curious about the work. I, uh . . . well, some things have happened that have made me curious too."

"You mean the black man Sunday night?" she asked quickly. "The one the driver refused to take because he was American?"

"Not . . . not just that. Other things too."

Her curiosity was now zooming to great heights. She tried to sound casual. "Well, would you like to come over and discuss them with me?"

"Yes, but I can't tonight. I was wondering, would you be free tomorrow? Thursday? I could do it any time from late afternoon until the time I have to report for work."

They made a date for seven P.M. the next evening at Cynthia's apartment.

Her mind was ticking along at high speed when she hung up. Yes, her intuition *had* been right! Something *was* peculiar. She began conjuring up major headlines, an exquisite scoop.

Then, as she always did, she switched gears. Probably nothing. Just a bright young opportunist deciding to capitalize on the interest of some crazy American lady. Would he show up with a gang of Latin-American toughies and vandalize her apartment? Suddenly, she wondered why, in God's name, she had given him her address.

But, she admitted finally, none of this had anything to do with what was *really* on her mind.

She took off her coat, poured herself a glass of wine, and walked with it into her living room. She sat down on the sofa and reviewed the facts she had been mulling over and over in her head since her lunch with Chris Channing earlier in the day, since the gnawing suspicion had begun.

One: She had decided to put the Barker story aside *before* Jed Farber had actively entered her life. Two: Jed Farber had never so much as mentioned Senator Barker to her—on Sunday, or in all the long nocturnal phone conversations they had had since Sunday.

Why, then, did she have the terrible feeling Jed had moved in on her expressly at the command of Senator Barker? To watch her, to make sure the Senator's confession went no farther?

Because it was a rather remarkable coincidence, wasn't it, that Jed Farber had just happened into her life immediately after his buddy, Frederick Barker, had incriminated himself on her tape recorder?

And not just happened in, but actively *pursued* her, on Saturday night, and then at brunch on Sunday, and then again Sunday night, and then again Monday night on the telephone from Detroit, and then again Tuesday night—adroitly working his way into her heart—totally mesmerizing her with her charm and his attention.

Just like—

She gulped the red wine, and she saw Rob Diamond, swooping down on her in his law firm's reception area. ("So *this* is the captivatingly beautiful reporter I've been hearing so much about!")

Was it all happening again? Another Rob Diamond, this one with dark hair?

No. This man had none of Diamond's smoothness, none of the suave coolness, none of the airs. That was one of the things she had loved about Jed from the beginning, his emotional transparency, his inability to be "cool."

Jed Farber was *real*. More than real. He was—well—wonderful.

So wonderful.

Too wonderful.

She closed her eyes and took a deep breath. When was she going to learn? When were the years of social experience in Washington going to add up instructively the way the years of professional experience had: in acquired skill? When would she learn that when a man was too good to be true, he was just that! And there was something wrong!

Angrily, she pulled the Washington, D.C., telephone book off the shelf on the side of her desk and looked through the business section for "Ralph Buddington," one of the names Senator Barker had given her in the course of the interview.

She copied down the number, picked up her telephone, and tapped it out. On the second ring, she heard a click and then the fuzzy sound of static: an answering machine message about to begin. Sure enough. "You have reached the American Insurance Association," a woman's voice began. "Our office hours are nine A.M. to five-thirty P.M. Monday through Friday. If you would like to leave a message, please give your name, the time and date."

Cynthia hung up. The American Insurance Association. A Washington lobby, she bet, an organization made up of hundreds of insurance companies coast to coast, each of whom had been called upon to contribute to the Senatorial campaign of Senator Frederick Barker.

She picked up the enormous envelope she had carried home from work with her. It contained a copy of the version of the tax bill recently approved by the Senate Finance Committee. She had gone to pick it up immediately after her lunch with Chris Channing.

As she turned the pages of the voluminous document, her eyes picked up bits and pieces of portentous, complicated language. Gibberish. Hundreds of pages written almost entirely in words that were foreign to her.

She despaired—not over the task itself, but at her impetus for taking it on. She took another sip of wine and proclaimed her resolve: If, in fact, Jed Farber's attentions were designed to make certain his best friend's career remained in tact, she would nail Senator Frederick Barker with every ounce of energy she had in her.

Four hours later, Cynthia lay in bed staring at the ceiling, picturing paragraph after paragraph of tax code swimming around in her head on huge waves of red wine.

The telephone rang. "Hello?"

"Good news."

It was the villain of the evening, and yet the sound of his voice pleased her. She snuggled back under the covers. "What?"

"I'm still alive!"

"That's it?"

"Isn't that enough? For God's sake, haven't you been worried sick all night?"

"Worried about . . . oh!" Cynthia sat up abruptly. "I completely forgot! Tonight was your dinner with your client, the gangster!"

"Correction—Theodore Selebri is *not* my client. Not definitely." Jed Farber sighed. "And I think he's probably more gauche than gangster."

"His hit men didn't have the restaurant surrounded?"

"Damn, you're starting to talk like me. I thought I was the neurotic one."

Cynthia leaned back against the pillows and smiled. "When did you get home?"

"I'm not home."

"Where are you?"

"At Mama Rosa's Motel."

"What?"

"Come now," he chortled. "A well-traveled woman like you? Don't tell me you have never heard of Mama Rosa's Motel!"

"*The* Mama Rosa's Motel?"

"You guessed it!" His voice was booming. "On the outskirts of Baltimore, conveniently located right next to Mama Rosa's Restaurant!"

"Jed, you sound strange."

A throaty, rumbling laugh built up to a peak and then subsided. "You are quick. You are sharp. You must be one crackerjack reporter."

"You are drunk!"

"Just as I said!" he hooted. "One crackerjack reporter!"

"Why are you drunk?" she asked sternly.

"Ted Selebri is a bit of a boor, but let me tell you, the man has fantastic taste when it comes to wine."

"So you let him get you looped?"

"Looped." He began laughing again. "Sloshed to the gills, guzzling the red stuff at ole Mama Rosa's Restaurant."

"Why are you at Mama Rosa's Motel?"

"You happen to be speaking to a major contributor to MADD."

"Mad?"

"An acronym—stands for Mothers Against Drunk Driving. Now, I ask you, how would it look on the obit page? 'Jed Farber, major contributor to MADD, died last night thoroughly sloshed behind the wheel of his car.'"

The rigid lines on Cynthia's face eased into a smile. "Only you—"

"Only me? Everyone gets sloshed! I thought it was supposed to be the American way . . ."

"No," she laughed. "Only you would have the presence of mind, when sloshed, to check into a motel."

He groaned. "Neurotic, huh?"

"Not neurotic. Responsible."

"Naw, neurotic. Responsible would be if I made the decision after becoming inebriated in a fit of reckless abandon. In truth, I made the decision after the first sip of wine. Damn, it was good. And sitting across the table from Selebri, I knew I had nothing else going for me tonight."

"Why did you eat way out there?"

"His choice. Wanted me to meet him on his turf, I guess."

"What was his turf like?"

"A modern, nondescript Italian restaurant with plastic flowers, fake pine paneling, and the best damn calimari I've had since my last real Italian meal in Brooklyn, out-of-this-world linguine with clam sauce, and well—" He began laughing again. "I guess I've already mentioned the wine."

"What was his purpose?"

"To entice me, he said, to become his attorney. The man has a manufacturing plant in Baltimore, and about seven others around the country. He says the Baltimore plant is about to make it big, since all of its competitors are no longer in business."

"When did he shoot them?"

"*Exactly* my question! Oh, phrased in a more subtle way. I asked what put them out of business. I thought the use of 'what' and not 'who' was rather ingenious."

"Must have been uttered after only one bottle," she said drily. "What was his answer?"

"'Couldn't compete'!"

"He shot them."

Jed laughed. "He even brought me a handout. I am now reaching into my pocket, and pulling out a sample of the wondrous things that Mr. Cost-Competitive himself manages to produce so competitively."

She heard a funny tapping sound, a metallic bouncing. "What's that noise?"

"Shit, they're all rolling off the night table. Damn."

"I take it he doesn't produce trucks."

"Godamn, you wouldn't believe it. They're falling all over the place. Wait a minute, let me . . . jeez, what a mess." The sound of metallic bouncing intensified.

"Jed," Cynthia giggled. "Maybe you should go to sleep."

"Not with visions of Selebri! No, not that! Tell me about your day. Give me something more pleasant to sleep on."

She thought for a moment. "Carlos Ramirez called. The boy from the van? He says he, too, has become curious about the job at the factory. He's coming over tomorrow night to share his curiosities with me."

"Do you think that's safe?" Jed suddenly sounded sober. "Entertaining him alone at your apartment?"

"Oh, he's just a boy." She sighed, Jed's concern eradicating her own. "I'm sure it's safe."

"Sounds to me as though you're taking unnecessary chances because you're desperate—a free-lance writer with no stories on the horizon!"

She giggled. "Jed, go to sleep."

"Well, you said yourself, you spent all day Saturday working on a story you're not going to do."

The Barker connection again. She bit her lip, appalled at the fact that she had completely forgotten her "realistic appraisal of Jed Farber" as soon as she heard his voice.

"Are you sure you should be entertaining the kid all by yourself?"

"I'll be fine. Sounds to me as though it's *you* we should be worried about. Heaven only knows what lingers in the corridors at Mama Rosa's!"

"Promise me that if the autopsy indicates the calimari did it, you'll finger Selebri."

"Will do."

Jed sighed. "I wish it were Friday night."

"Because you're afraid of dying tonight?"

"Well, partly." He sighed again. "But only partly."

Jed hung up the telephone and began picking up the small silver balls that had fallen all over the floor of his motel room.

"Ted Selebri," he said, imitating his client, Selebri's, dental delivery. "Duh best damn ball-bearing manufactooruh in duh whole Mid-Atlantic Region. Duh *only* ball-bearing manufactooruh in duh whole Mid-Atlantic Region!"

He squinted at the wastepaper basket over in the corner of the room, appraised the distance, and began tossing the ball bearings into the basket one by one. "She loves me. She loves me not. She loves me. She loves me not. She loves me. . . ."

Carlos Ramirez arrived the next night at seven P.M. on the dot, but he was very different from what Cynthia had been expecting. She realized, as he sauntered in and took off his jacket, how much the way she thought of him had to do with the circumstances of their prior encounters. He had been just one in a sea of small, dark Hispanic bodies.

He was about five-feet-five inches tall, Cynthia guessed, a good three inches shorter than she, but with broad shoulders and an athletic frame. Seated in her living room, in a white, button-down shirt, a navy-blue crew-neck sweater, and a very preppy pair of jeans, he came across as a rather self-assured American teenager.

Carlos was not an inner-city immigrant child reverently seeking the counsel of an older, more knowledgeable American. He was a slightly arrogant boy-man, looking for collaboration in what he felt could be a mutually beneficial arrangement.

"You told me you were curious," he began. "Well, I'm getting real curious too." He flashed her a smile. "The difference is, your being a reporter and all, I figured maybe you've got ways of getting your curiosity satisfied." He shrugged. "I guess I'd like to know some answers."

"What is it you want to know?" Cynthia asked.

"What makes them crazy!" He held his hands out palms up. "I'm working with a bunch of loonies, see? There's a core of guys who show up every night, and I swear, half of them come back nutty after every shift. Some act like they're drugged out. Others are crying and whining like babies."

Cynthia frowned. "You're saying they're not like that at all when they leave for work?"

"Well, it's hard to tell with some of them. It's a kind of weird group to begin with. But, yes, in general, the ones who've become crazy seemed okay when we lined up to go to work." He lit a cigarette. She hopped up to get him an ashtray.

"It didn't really get to me until Tuesday morning, coming home in the van," he called out after her. "Pablo Rano, this other guy, he's from El Salvador like me, and he's the one who told me about the job. Pablo and I, we just started working at the factory a month ago, and, well, we've been noticing the others and kind of laughing at them a little. 'Crazy spirits fly in the factory'—that's how some of the men explain the weird behavior. Well, Pablo and I don't believe in crazy spirits, so we thought that was kind of funny."

Cynthia put an ashtray down on the coffee table in front of him. "What happened Tuesday morning?"

"Pablo went crazy too!" Ramirez's dark brown eyes opened wide. "He sat there in the van in a daze, and got real angry when I tried to talk to him, snarling, fussy. And when I told him about it later—when he showed up for work that night—he didn't remember any of it."

Carlos took a long drag on his cigarette. "Something else happened in the van coming back Tuesday too. One of the older guys, Francisco is his name, he suddenly got real sick—throwing up with bad stomach cramps, that kind of thing. He was a mess. Couldn't even stand up by himself. Heck, I had to practically carry him home!" He looked up at Cynthia suddenly. "Then the night comes, and who's standing there happily on line by the bus stop, taking a few last sips from his liquor pint before heading for work? Francisco!"

He moved forward on the sofa. "What I want to find out is if they are all crazy and sick to begin with, or is something out there making them crazy? I mean, I like the money and the hours, but I don't want to go crazy."

"What exactly do they do in the factory?"

"Pablo and I just load crates on the outside. That's the lowest-paying job, and we've got it because we're the newest ones to work there. But from what I've seen, the inside work is real easy. They just take these parts, press them together with machines, wash them off, dry them, and give 'em to us to load onto the truck." He shrugged. "The place is very clean. In fact, it smells like some kind of disinfectant, as though they keep it washed down all the time."

Cynthia perked up. "A disinfectant? Something with an odor? Maybe that's it. Maybe they're inhaling something."

"Naaaw," Carlos laughed. "My mother's a cleaning woman, and it smells just like the stuff she uses. She cleans two apartments a day, five days a week, and *she* doesn't seem crazy."

"What is the name of the company?" Cynthia asked.

"No name. We get paid in cash at the end of each shift, and there's no name on the factory, no name on anything. I've checked."

She raised an eyebrow. "Now, *that's* unusual."

Carlos shook his head as he put out his cigarette. "Not really. I mean, this is no up-and-up enterprise going here. That's for sure. For one thing, all the workers are illegal. None of them have papers."

"Well, then, that's a story in itself!"

"That's no story," he snickered. "You live in this neighborhood, and you think that's unusual? It's common practice! Believe me, the whole economy of Adams-Morgan is based on

133

stuff like that—employers hiring illegals under funny circumstances, and the authorities looking the other way."

"No . . ."

"Who do you think staffs all the restaurants? Hey, look, I've been working in restaurants here since I was thirteen years old— too young to work legally—and that's the way things operate!"

She felt like an aged innocent being coached by a condescending, slick, young know-it-all, and it irked her. "Well, then, why are you concerned?" she asked irritably.

"I'm not like the rest of them." He sat up in the chair, raising his chin. "I have a future. I don't want to take any chances working someplace that could make me crazy."

Not only arrogant, but a snob to boot. "Then why don't you just quit?" She was losing interest in the whole project.

He lost some of his hauteur. "It's good money, good hours. I can work there and still work at Rico's Restaurant on weekends. It's . . . it's a good job for me while I'm waiting."

"Waiting? For what?"

"For the papers to come through—the green card."

"So you're illegal too!"

"No!" That made him angry. "What do you think? I'm like them? Me and my mother, we're legal—legal, but just, uh, impermanent."

"What does that mean?"

The dark eyes flashed. "It means, if you have connections and hardship—the hardship, in my case, being a father who was an innocent victim, murdered in crossfire in El Salvador six years ago—they let you into the United States, let you break your neck to earn enough money to pay rent and food, let you learn English and graduate from high school and feel like you're an American. But then they tell you you're not one yet, can't be one yet. Oh, you don't have to *leave* or anything, but you're not allowed to go on to college either. You—"

"That can't be true." She'd had enough of this. "If you are a graduate of an American high school, surely you could—"

"No college without papers! Hey, I am an expert on that, believe me!" He lit another cigarette. Cynthia noted his fingers were trembling slightly. "Oh, you can lie. Like my cousin, Frankie. He just said he was Puerto Rican on the form, and he's now at the University of the District of Columbia. But, well, I figure, like, what if they clamp down? You know? What if he graduates and all and then they say, 'You lied. None of this counts.'"

He took a long drag on the cigarette. "Besides. I am *not* Puerto Rican, don't want to be. I'm . . . American, really. An American with El Salvadoran ancestry."

She wondered whether she was being conned. She vowed to check. "What high school did you graduate from?"

"Woodrow Wilson, last year, class of eighty-five." He looked her straight in the eye. "Check, why don't you?"

She nodded curtly. "Where is this factory?"

Some of his self-assuredness dissipated. "I don't know." He shifted a little in the chair. "I know how to get there, but, as I said, there is no address. The van just takes us and brings us back each night." He looked up at her eagerly. "I could show you. Take you there. The factory is closed on Saturday, and I don't have to be at work at the restaurant until late afternoon. If you are willing—"

She was willing, less enthusiastic than she had been before this interview, but still willing. She stood up. "Why don't you meet me here around eleven Saturday morning? We'll drive there in my car. In the meantime," she said, walking him to the door, "talk to the men in the van. See what you can find out about their lives, their backgrounds."

"*Talk* to them?" The idea obviously seemed somewhat demeaning to the self-proclaimed aristocrat. "Most of them can barely talk!"

"Try anyway," Cynthia instructed.

From Capitol Radio Friday morning, Cynthia called the admissions office of the University of the District of Columbia. To her surprise, she discovered that, without papers, a graduate of an American high school was prohibited from going on to college. Ironically, an El Salvadoran who stayed in El Salvador had a better chance of getting into an American university—as a foreign student—than an El Salvadoran in the United States without papers.

She called Woodrow Wilson High School. A "Carlos Ramirez" had, indeed, graduated in the class of 1985. In the top quarter of the class, to be exact.

# · 10 ·

The restaurant Jed had chosen for their Friday-night dinner had Cynthia's favorite ambience: It was intimate and quiet and candlelit and very French, with fresh-cut flowers on each table.

She was certain, by the color, shape, presentation, and aroma of the food, that she was devouring gourmet fare prepared to perfection. It was, however, an intellectual evaluation. Her taste buds were not working. Nor were her suspicions. Her week-long anguish over the dark side of Jed Farber had melted away, along with her taste buds, in a dreamy cloud that was transforming "Senator Barker's spy" into the most exciting dinner companion she had ever had. All of her concentration was on their conversation.

They had not even got around to ordering dinner until an hour after they sat down. Now, their meal completed and the bill paid, they were still talking, oblivious to the fact that the restaurant was emptying and the waiters were waiting restlessly to clean up.

Cynthia felt so relaxed she began regaling Jed with family stories and anecdotes of life in Ballard that had not surfaced in her mind for years. Warmed by the presence of her brothers and sisters—if only in funny recollections—by his interest, by how handsomely the white collar of his shirt contrasted with the darkness of his suit and hair in the flickering candlelight, Cynthia wanted the evening to go on forever.

"Are you telling me," Jed asked, leaning forward, "that I am dining with the first female president of the Junior Four-H Club of Poller County?"

Cynthia bowed her head reverently. "For two years' standing."

"Damn!"

She leaned back in her chair and looked at him. "Okay, now your turn."

"Well, Four-H clubs weren't real big in Brooklyn!"

"So what were you?"

He thought for a while and then looked up, a little embarrassed. "The 'scholar.'"

"Was that an elected office?"

"Selected, not elected. Selected for me at birth." He sat back in his chair. "You have to realize I was the third child, born to my parents at a time when my mother was sure she was too old to have any more children—ten years younger than number two—and the first son."

"I smell sexism!"

"Ahh, traditional Jewish sexism! The worst kind. Just ask my sisters! My mother was convinced that I was a gift from God, and I was treated as such, amply fed, nurtured, adored, and revered—and not only by my parents, but by all the aunts and uncles as well. My father was the firstborn son of eight Farbers. So the mantle of the firstborn son of the firstborn son fell on my shoulders." He leaned forward, his eyes gleaming. "Do you hate me yet?"

"It is getting more and more tempting."

"My childhood consisted primarily of my being waited on and supplied with all the books the public library had to offer."

"What did you do in return?"

"Fulfilled the task, of course. Behaved like a genius both academically and socially. By the time I was fifteen, I had skipped three grades, made no friends, and was a pathetically anemic freshman at Columbia."

Cynthia's eyes clouded sympathetically. "Weren't you lonely?"

"I should have been, I guess, but I lived surrounded by cousins, all of whom treated me like God's gift. It wasn't a half-bad existence."

"But then wasn't it difficult for you to be in college when you were so young? Didn't you feel out of it?"

Jed shrugged. "Not in the library, and that's where I spent four solid years. I graduated with a full scholarship to Harvard Law School at nineteen—and still no friends."

He played with his wine glass, his eyes becoming more sober. "That was the beginning, I guess. That was my entry into the real world. Here I was, living away from home for the first time, dating girls for the first time, and without any of the social skills other people my age had developed over time."

"So, what happened?"

Jed grunted, his eyes still down. "So, I married the first girl who showed an interest in me. She was very beautiful, and I was terribly flattered."

Cynthia waited for more. He looked up at her for a while, and then looked away. "Oh, I admit my childhood was strange, psychologically speaking. 'Sick' I guess you could call it. Living in this isolated world of intrusive aunts and uncles and cousins, never dealing with the outside world." He smiled. "But that's the vision of hindsight. The hindsight that comes from hundreds of hours of psychotherapy at great cost."

Her eyes got larger. "Are you still in therapy?"

"I never was." Jed's eyes twinkled. "My sister, Daphne, went through therapy. So, I got it all secondhand. 'A bargain,' as my mother would say."

He pointed his finger at Cynthia. "Now, my sister Daphne says—or at least Daphne's shrink says—that my problem is an overwhelming acceptance, a blind adoration, of my family. Potentially very destructive!"

"And how does that manifest itself?"

He thought for a while. "Oh, I've probably transferred some of it to the next generation. I'm sure I'm too involved in my kids, obsessed, you could probably say." He played with the candle. "I was probably more devastated by getting a divorce than most people are. 'Too damn intense,'" he growled, as though imitating someone. He grinned up at her. "That's what Rick Barker always says."

Her body chilled. "Rick Barker?"

Jed blinked at her in disbelief. "I've never mentioned him to you, have I?"

"No." She studied his eyes, trying to see if he was looking for signals in hers.

"Frederick Barker, the Senator from Iowa? I worked for him when I first came to Washington. We've stayed very close." Jed laughed and shook his head. "God, I can't believe it! The man is a mixture of father, mentor, and best friend to me, and in all these conversations and phone calls you and I have had, somehow his name never even came up!"

"Hard to believe," Cynthia murmured, watching him.

"I guess it's hard to cover your whole life in just a couple of days!" He shrugged. "Well, anyway, Rick's always yelling at me to loosen up in my relationships, to stop worrying all the time. Mostly he says it when he thinks I'm worrying too much about him."

She wanted to wipe out this intrusion, to change the subject—quickly—and recapture the mood of the evening. "Doesn't everyone do that?" she asked gently. "Worry about people they care about?"

"Not as aggressively as I do!" His face became serious as he stared at the candle. "I tend to get a little overinvolved, I guess. Take things harder than other people as a result. My father died seven full years ago, and I was absolutely devastated." He drank some wine. "Still am, at times."

"Why can't that be a virtue? Why must it be a liability?" Cynthia leaned across the table toward him. "What you're telling me is that you love too much? What is that line in *Othello*? 'He loved not wisely, but too well.'"

Jed broke out laughing. "Well, there you go! Look where it got poor Othello! Luckily Shakespeare has never crossed my sister's path, or Othello would be another name in Daphne's 'for examples.'"

Cynthia looked at him affectionately. "I feel the same way about my family. But it's very unfashionable these days." She played with the candle. "I miss them a lot. I think we all miss each other. It . . . it was a difficult choice—deciding to leave home. It didn't seem to be when we all made it. But as we've gotten older, I think it's been difficult for all of us."

She kept playing with the candle. "I was devastated by my father's death, too. Although, to be honest, I mean, to be fair . . . well, the fact is, as my friend Brittany says, he never understood me. For the last fifteen years, we lived in two very different worlds, and he never had the least idea of what mine entailed."

Jed leaned forward on his elbows. His eyes were so very dark, so comforting. "But he loved you. You told me yourself that he saved all your report cards, all your letters, all the 'Cynthia memorabilia.' You were his special treat, from what you said, his indulgence. What the hell difference does it make whether or not he fully understood the intricacies of your life as long as he loved you?"

She looked up at Jed suddenly. "None," she declared emphatically. "Absolutely none!" She felt a warm wetness creeping into her eyes.

Jed reached across the table and took her hand. He looked at it and smiled. "You know, my father never read a book in his life—only the *New York Daily News*. But when I moved to Washington, he bought *The New York Times* every Sunday, and labored through the Book Review Section to find a book he could send his son—the 'reader.' Then he'd buy the book and send it to me."

Jed groaned. "Most of them were these strange esoteric treatises. I think he figured if he didn't understand it, I'd like it. Godawful stuff. And each one came to me with a clump of sweaty dollar bills stuck somewhere in the middle, attached to a note that read: 'So, listen, Sonny, don't spend all your time reading. Have some fun!'" Jed smiled sadly as he shook his head. "How is that for misunderstanding?"

When he looked up, Cynthia was laughing, but there were tears streaming down her face.

Jed looked at her with alarm. "I'm sorry. Did I say something that—"

"No. No." Cynthia shook her head, still smiling and still crying. "It's just that . . . I guess I feel a little as though we had the same father."

"The same father! Big gruff Sam Farber with his Yiddish jokes and his big belly and his inner-city wino clientele, and Marshall Matthews, the lanky, monosyllabic farmer?"

She kept laughing and crying. "In the important ways— yes."

Jed squeezed her hand in both of his, but watched her tears

with mounting anxiety. "Hey, what do you say we let them reclaim their table?"

He put his arm around her as they walked to the door. "Cynthia," he asked slowly, "how long ago did your father die?"

"Just a month."

He tightened his grip. "A month? I had no idea! You made it sound like something that had happened years ago. Why, you're still in the midst of it."

She tried very hard to stop crying, but the concern in his voice made the tears come even faster. "I'm sorry," she whispered as she cried. "I feel so silly. I don't know why I . . . this is the first time I've really cried about it."

He turned her around to face him, and lifted her head up until she was looking into his eyes. "The first time? Why?"

The tears were spilling down her cheeks in profusion. "I don't know. I—I think maybe this was the first time I found myself with someone who could understand."

He pulled her close to him and wrapped his arms around her. He held her tightly as she cried, kissing the top of her head.

The maître d' shifted from foot to foot, holding their coats, but they were oblivious.

Jed Farber awoke, but then changed his mind. He closed his eyes, and he languished in the delicious and unusual feeling of total relaxation. He was becalmed.

His lips smiled.

And sated. God, he felt sated.

He inhaled the perfumey smell of the blond hair that was brushing against his nose and mouth, perfectly willing to stay that way forever—becalmed, sated, inhaling.

But his head was waking up. He had to admit it, he was thinking.

When was the last time he had spent a night like this? Talking and laughing and touching and making love . . . and then talking and laughing and touching and making love . . . and then . . .

Hell, when was the *first* time?

His muscles suddenly tensed. His mind snapped to attention. Since when did he refer to screwing as "making love"?

He opened his eyes, his forehead in a frown. How could he feel so acutely close to someone so foreign? This Aryan specimen who had been president of the Junior Four-H Club? Face it, she was the ultimate shiksa—what his mother would call "a regular Farrah Fawcett"—the forbidden fruit he was supposed to either reject because it was forbidden, or crave for the same reason.

He had never craved one. To tell the truth, he had never really thought about it much. But he had rarely slept with one, and certainly never got this entangled.

How entangled? Two dates, for Christ's sake!

Entangled.

How could this Aryan creature make him so hungry for her—mentally as well as physically? How could this woman from another planet get his jokes and return them so adroitly? How could she create this crazy urge in him to know more and more about her? How could she be so much fun?

And how the hell could she make him feel this relaxed? No one had ever made him feel so at ease, so at peace.

He closed his eyes and inhaled deeply. He was drifting back to perfumed peace. One night. Why ask so many questions? One little night.

Oh, but what a night. With his eyes still closed, he kissed the top of her head and hugged her.

He felt a return hug. They lay there very still for a while.

"If last night was an example of your insomnia," she said drily, "I don't think it's insurmountable." Her head had not moved. The voice was coming from below.

He laughed and hugged her again.

She kissed his chest and then his neck and then his chin and then his nose. She looked him in the eyes and smiled, running her hand down his face to the dimple in his chin. Remembering that she had said she loved it, he tried to make the dimple more pronounced. They both laughed at the attempt.

"You have to pick up your kids."

"Not yet."

"All that talk about being compulsive," she sighed, smoothing down his hair. "Look how loose you are."

"Mmm." He kissed her eyes slowly, first one, then the other.

"Sure you won't be late?"

"Sure." He nibbled on her earlobe. "I said I'd be there at eleven-thirty. It takes twenty minutes to get from here to your place, twenty-five minutes from there to the kids." He continued nibbling. "Figure a half-hour for breakfast here first, fifteen minutes each for showers, which means we can relax for roughly seven minutes fifty seconds." He nibbled on her earlobe some more.

"How come?"

"It's nine-oh-seven."

She sat up. "You knew? You sat here lusting after my earlobes, all the time acutely aware it was nine-oh-seven."

"No." He grinned and pulled her back down. "I started lusting after your earlobes at eight-fifty-seven."

"I don't believe in digital clocks," she mumbled into his neck. It tickled.

"I warned you," he laughed, flinching from the tickle, "I am a digital clock person."

"You never told me that. I would have left immediately."

"You should have deduced that," he said, back at her earlobe. "I told you I was a tense, neurotic, wound-up, ulcer-ridden, anxious—"

"You certainly don't make love like one."

He took her face in his hands, hungry for the blue eyes that were so huge, so placid. He leaned back against the pillow to get distance, and he looked at her, just stared at her, contented.

Without makeup, the eyelashes were blond—soft, sandy beaches around the blue seas of her eyes.

He watched with fascination as his fingers moved down her thin nose to its tip, marveling at the graceful way the nose turned up at the end. His hands caressed her face like a sculptor, pleased by the results of his fine chiseling: the dramatic placement of the high cheekbones, the delicateness of the mouth.

She moved her face back and forth slowly, responding to his caress like a kitten being petted, and kissed his fingers as they ran along her lips.

"What are you thinking?" she asked playfully.

The question snapped him back to reality, and since the honest answer mortified him, he said, "I'm wondering what you are going to do today."

The cool eyes told him she knew that was not what he had been thinking.

He pretended not to notice. "We could have an additional forty-five minutes of bed time if you were willing to spend the day with me and the kids."

She smiled. "It's tempting, but—"

"It's a fantastic opportunity," he said, yawning and stretching. "A swim meet. I've never been to one before, but they say the heat from the indoor pool revitalizes your skin, that sitting for hours waiting for your kid's event heightens your patience. The Saturday swim meet—a new addition on our venue—will be followed by an old favorite. The traditional Saturday night bedtime argument over whether or not the children have to go to Sunday school tomorrow."

Her eyes glistened a little, as though she had just been offered a free trip to Paris, and was both touched by the invitation and deeply disappointed that she could not accept. She moved her hand down along the inside of his outstretched arm and rubbed his chest gently. "I think I'd better go home. I told you, I promised Carlos Ramirez I'd go to see the factory with him today." Her eyes moved back up to his. They were serious, imploring. "I really would like to spend a Saturday like that some other time, though."

He felt a flutter, a tingle deep inside, and was unsure whether it was a reaction to her fingers, which felt so good moving down his body, or the fact that the statement sounded completely sincere.

"I'd like that too," he whispered. He cleared his throat, trying to regain control. "We have some extra time. I explained I might be a little late, just in case . . . just in case—" He smiled. "This happened."

"You what?" She looked at him with shock. "How did you know I wouldn't insist on going home last night after the restaurant?"

He shrugged. "I didn't. I guess I hoped you wouldn't."

She pulled away from him. "Do you always orchestrate things this way?" she demanded angrily. "Do you always manipulate—"

"No." He cut her off, pulling her back to him. "No, never."

She resisted the pull. "Then why did you do it this time?"

"I thought about last night all week." He wondered why he was admitting such things to her.

"Oh, Jed, so did I." She crawled back into his arms. She kissed him. Then they kissed again, longer, and he felt it starting all over again.

But she sat up abruptly. "Do you do this often?"

He burst out laughing. "All the time. All the time!" He turned her over on her back in the bed and pinned her down.

"No, what I meant was—"

"What you meant was—" He kissed her, feeling in control again, and relieved by that. "What you meant was, you wanted me to tell you you were special, a 'once-in-a-lifetime,' which is a ridiculous request, given your age and my age and our assumed number of romantic liaisons. I mean, be sensible." He felt good. He felt sensible.

She just stared at him, and her eyes seemed to get larger, sadder, until he could stand it no longer. They were drowning him, discarding his verbal garbage, sucking out the truth.

"I thought about last night all week," he said finally, in a hoarse voice, "and I never dreamed it would be . . ."

He never finished because her lips were on his, telling him that he didn't need to finish, that she was already three paragraphs ahead of him.

# · 11 ·

"This one's mine," Cynthia said, pointing to the battered 1979 Plymouth parked around the corner from her apartment house.

"This one?" Carlos Ramirez was obviously disappointed. He spent the first fifteen minutes of their trip to the factory giving Cynthia a dissertation on the pros and cons of some of the newer, sportier models available on the U.S. automobile market.

"Do you have a car?" she asked as he completed an analysis of the high-velocity potential of the Mazda RX-7.

He grinned broadly. "Not yet."

He then launched into another dissertation designed to enlighten his driver. This one was cultural: an analysis of the national differences that existed in Latin America—which countries produced the largest number of lazy people, which countries created criminals, which had the most corrupt rulers. Miraculously, El Salvador emerged as the best. "In general, El Salvadorans are the hard workers," Carlos summed up. "We are known as the 'New Yorkers' of Latin America—fast-moving, aggressive, driven. Know what I mean?"

"Have you ever been to New York?" Cynthia asked.

He grinned broadly. "Not yet."

Cynthia broke out laughing. "I take it El Salvadorans are the talkers of Latin America too!"

"I *have* been going on a lot, haven't I?" The cockiness faded,

146

but only a little. "See, I haven't had a chance to talk in English for a long time. Most of my friends are away at school, and with my family, I speak Spanish all the time."

Cynthia frowned. "Are you more comfortable speaking English?"

"It's not that. I'm just used to talking about different kinds of things in English. It's like my social language. When I talk Spanish, I talk like a son, a nephew, a cousin."

"Does your mother speak English?"

"Well, she's learning. She's a teacher, see? But she can't get as job here as a teacher without learning English." He reached into his pocket and waved a plastic card in Cynthia's direction. "I almost forgot. I brought this for you."

"What's that?" she asked, looking from the highway to the card and then back again.

"My student ID from high school." He placed it on the dashboard. "Proof that I am who I am, and not one of *them*, not like the others in the van."

The snobbish arrogance again. "What is the matter with *them*?" Cynthia snapped. "Why is it so important to you to prove you're superior to the other workers in the van?"

Carlos stared out the front window, thinking. "You know that bag lady who always stands on the corner of Eighteenth and Columbia Road?" he asked. "The real fat lady with red hair who's always dressed kind of like a little girl? The crazy one who just stands there all the time and says—"

"'Happy day!'" Cynthia giggled, "'Happy, happy day!'"

"That's the one!" Carlos turned to her. "Say you moved to El Salvador, and the crazy lady did too, and the El Salvadorans pointed to you all the time, saying, 'There are those two American women!' How would you feel? Wouldn't you want to make sure they understood there was a difference?"

"But they would know after a while. Just by—"

"Did *you* know that day when you asked me those questions in Spanish?"

"I know now," Cynthia said. "You don't have to keep telling me."

"I guess it's the job," he said slowly. "See, I come from a very proud family. My father was headmaster of the school in our village in El Salvador, as was his father before him. For generations, my family was respected. You know? When we came here, my mother said, 'You are better than the others, but no one knows that. You have to start from scratch, all over again, to prove yourself!' So I did! I worked hard in school, got all kinds of awards, even." He shrugged. "Now I am back to scratch, all over again."

"But you don't have to work at jobs like the ones you're working at," Cynthia said. "You have a high-school diploma—not college, maybe, but certainly, with a high-school diploma you could find something—"

"No. I prefer to wait. The papers could come any day. Looking for a different job would be like saying there is nothing to wait for."

The logic escaped Cynthia, but the catch in his voice did not. She decided to go on to something else. "Did you try interviewing the men? Asking them questions?"

"A little." He waved her away. "They—they really have nothing to say."

"Carlos, you *are* different from the men in the van," Cynthia said slowly. "You are intelligent, educated, clever enough to be a detective—to think of questions that would get them to open up—and astute enough to read between the lines, and find out even more than their words alone could tell you."

He frowned, thinking.

"Heck, look at it as extra stimulation in a job that is obviously beneath you! We've got a mystery here—right? People acting crazy. One way to find out why is to understand them better."

"Yes . . ." He nodded slowly. His eyes brightened. "I like that. I could—" He looked out the window for the first time in a while. "Oh, hey. We passed it!"

"Passed it?" Cynthia stepped on the brake and looked around. They were only thirty minutes from downtown Washington, but in a completely rural area. *"Here?"*

"Well, back there a little."

Cynthia pulled her car up to the place Carlos indicated, got out, and stood by the roadside staring in disbelief, her mouth open. *"That's* the factory?"

Carlos nodded. "Yup. That's it."

Cynthia shook her head as her eyes wandered over the grassy hills and huge old trees that surrounded the building, making it practically invisible from the road.

The "factory" was, in fact, a big old barn, no different from the other structures that dotted the countryside around it, just a few miles off the main highway.

The temperature was below freezing, but the sun was bright, and from the road the rambling old structure had a sleepy, bucolic look to it. Its weathered wood seemed to be crying for a "Mail Pouch Tobacco" sign.

She was shocked. The image of the dazed, dead-eyed little Hispanic men trickling out of the van in the darkness of night seemed so out of sync with the rustic simplicity of the setting. Her eyes darted up the grassy hill and around the barn. No signs. No name. Not even a parking lot. There was no access from the main road—no indication that anyone had been inside that old barn in years.

"The big green van drops you off right here?" Cynthia asked.

"Yes, and then we walk up."

Together, Cynthia and Carlos hiked from the road up over the grassy slope to the building. Cynthia noticed a barely discernible footpath on the frozen grass.

"This is where I load the crates," Carlos said when they got to the front of the barn. "They pull the truck up right here to the front door."

Cynthia frowned. "Where does the truck come from?"

"The back of the barn. I'll show you."

They walked around to the back of the barn. There was no driveway, but the grass was flattened and, in a few places, Cynthia could discern tire tracks.

"See, they unload the parts from the truck here at the beginning of the shift," Carlos explained. "Then the men who work inside the factory put them together. And then, when they're finished, I reload them onto the same truck."

"And there is absolutely no name on the truck?"

"Absolutely no name." He said it with conviction. "Believe me, I've looked and looked."

Cynthia whirled around. "Where does the truck come from? How does it get here in the first place?"

Carlos shrugged. "I don't know. It's always here when we arrive for work."

Cynthia looked down at the ground and followed the flattened grass. The tire tracks went to a point by a clump of trees a few yards off and then seemed to branch out in several different paths, to the left and to the right, all across grass and under trees.

The two of them walked along one route of flattened grass for what Cynthia gauged to be about a quarter of a mile, and hit a dirt road.

She looked around. The other paths of flattened grass, the ones that had meandered off in different directions, seemed to end up at the same place.

"Look over there!" Carlos shouted, pointing. At the end of the road on their right stood an old, dilapidated, white building that, Cynthia mused, had it been in Adams-Morgan, would doubtlessly have a sign in front of it broadcasting its imminent transformation into "Luxury Condominiums." In this neighborhood, however, it could only qualify as a broken-down house. All its window panes were knocked out, its exterior walls in varying stages of decay.

"What do you think that is?" Carlos whispered.

"Where there's a barn, there's a house." Cynthia reasoned, "That must have been it. Part of an old farm, maybe." She looked down the dirt driveway to her left. "I bet that ends up at the main road," she told Carlos. "That must be how they get the truck in and out. What I *don't* understand is why they settle for such indirect access. It certainly wouldn't cost much to just build a dirt road directly up to the barn from the front . . . unless," she mumbled, "unless they don't want anyone to know they're using the barn."

She turned to Carlos. His eyes were fixed on the eerie old house. The frightened look on his face chilled her.

"Let's get out of here, Carlos."

"Okay with me!"

They ran back to the car.

*　　*　　*

"Here's what we got from *that* polling sample," the consultant said, whacking another chart down on the table in the study of Senator Barker's Chevy Chase home. Barker and his campaign aides gazed at the results.

Oh, poor Iowa, Barker thought, his eyes moving from chart to chart of the tiresome presentation. Iowa had been given a series of electroencephalograms. All those wires and suction cups had been stuck to the state's communal head, so Iowa's brain waves could be recorded and interpreted by hordes of eager "political doctors," like this one. The experts then passed on the results—for a tidy sum—to politicians like himself, who were expected to quickly alter their own beliefs to match those oozing out of the electorate's brain matter.

What ever happened to leadership? Senator Barker wanted to growl. (It was replaced by *follow*ship, he informed himself silently. Do whatever they want, or whatever the consultants have determined it is they want.) Ridiculous.

Barker leaned forward abruptly. "Meaning what, Tom?" he asked the consultant.

The Senator settled back in his chair again, complimenting himself on his timing and delivery. The interjection had convinced everyone he was paying close attention, and he had even managed to flatter the consultant by calling him by his first name.

Damned if he knew what the pompous ass's last name was. Damned if he cared. Damned if he was even going to listen to the response his interjection had triggered.

To tell the truth, this whole presentation reminded him of the way Penny used to go on and on explaining to him where she was seating guests at one of their dinner parties and why. The only difference was Penny didn't charge for wasting his time.

The telephone rang, and Senator Barker's eyes traveled to the extension in the corner of the room: a most welcome respite. "Keep going, Tom," he said, giving the consultant a good-old-fellow clump on the back. "I just want to grab this."

He walked over and plopped down in the leather chair next

to the telephone, hoping for a long conversation. "On the contrary," the consultant went on, "the numbers here show . . ."

"Hello?"

"Good morning, Mr. Senator! Ralph Buddington, here!"

Senator Barker sat up, suddenly both attentive and concerned. He had called Buddington right after the Cynthia Matthews interview and warned the man that he had "heard a reporter was checking around," asking questions about what Barker had put into the tax bill and why. Buddington had assured Barker he would make certain "his people" opened up to no one, and would let the Senator know if there were any problems.

Did the phone call mean there *was* a problem?

"Why, now, what a nice surprise," Barker crooned. "How are you this morning, Ralph?" The Senator's eyes moved to the other side of the room, checking the men, who were perusing a new chart.

"Why, I'm just fine, Mr. Senator. Are you, uh, free to talk?"

"Well, I have some staff people here with me, but I'm sure they won't mind if I take a few minutes out. What is it, Ralph?"

"I took care of that little matter, as I told you I would, and I just wanted to report back."

"Uh-huh. Everyone's been informed?"

"More than that, Senator. Everyone's adamant—completely behind you on this one. But that's really last week's news," Buddington chortled. "I just wanted to let you know I called my people back yesterday, just to check on whether there had been any activity, if you know what I mean."

"Yes?"

"None whatsoever. No calls, no questions, no reporters' inquiries of any kind."

"Well, isn't that good news, Ralph? I suppose it was just a false alarm. I certainly appreciate the call." Senator Barker hung up the phone smiling, with a warm spot in his heart for compassionate farm girls.

At his children's swim meet, Jed spent most of his mental energy translating the highs and the lows of the day into funny future anecdotes for Cynthia, and rehashing the dreamy recollections of Friday night.

It was only on the ride home that he began to feel uneasy. Instead of recalling happy memories, he started tabulating the relationship in quantitative terms. In just one week, he had seen the woman twice and called her eight times. If Friday night and Saturday morning were counted as two different times, and if the "no answers" were included in the data, it came to three dates and fifteen phone calls in less than one week.

It was a record that signified reckless abandon, and Jed Farber was a man vehemently *against* reckless abandon.

By the time he and his children reached his apartment, his manner had changed completely. Instead of plodding through activities, lost in thoughts of Cynthia, he was throwing himself into action to rub out the memories. He and Timmy and Lisa labored together with unusual intensity over the spaghetti sauce for dinner. Accustomed to their father's strict adherence to bedtime hours, the children were surprised when he suggested they try "one more game of Monopoly" less than fifteen minutes before "lights out."

By the time the children were put down, his ulcer was acting up. His stomach tightened some more at the sight of the telephone. He turned on the television set instead, tuned in the Capitols' hockey game, and settled back on the sofa.

On the television screen, the Ranger goalie took his stick and smashed it into one of the Caps' star players as he skated past at the mouth of the goal, and the entire Caps team began crowding menacingly around the Rangers' goalie.

"We're gonna see a fight!" the announcer boomed out against the roar of the crowd of spectators. "We're in for a big one!" The noise reached a crescendo.

At the other end of the living room, Jed Farber's eyes glazed over, picturing a very different brawl, one he had participated in seven years before.

It hadn't started out as a brawl. It had started out as yet another quiet evening in the life of the Farber family.

Jed had come home from work late, after the children were asleep, and Anna had greeted him at the door of their beautiful home—a compromise house: not as expensive as she had wanted, but more expensive than he had wanted—with a kiss and a "How was your day?"

It was summer. He remembered the pleasant feeling of

stepping from the humid heat outside into the cool air conditioning, the pleasure of seeing Anna's delicate, tanned body in a bright yellow blouse and a pair of snug-fitting white pants. As usual, she was immaculate, and so was the house. All the toys were put aside in neat little piles, the furniture was dust-free and sparkling.

An American scene: "Daddy-the-wage-earner" was returning home to "Mommy-the-perfect-housewife."

But tonight Daddy was coming home with some baggage—a potential bomb, to be exact. That's why he had worked late, intentionally staying at the office until he knew the children would be fast asleep.

In his mind, he had already dismissed the matter as a fake bomb, slander conveyed by a sick lady. And as he followed Anna into the kitchen, where she had kept dinner warm for him, comforted by the familiar smell of her perfume and the coziness of the house, he finally diffused the bomb: Nancy Seegram was a crazy bitch and the story she had told him was a lie.

He ate his dinner as Anna jabbered on about her day—a day at the neighborhood pool. Lisa was on the verge of learning how to swim—all by herself! And Timmy, the rotund nine-month-old, had napped for almost two hours after his morning in the sun.

Jed remembered how he had hated to break the mood. It had all suddenly seemed so silly. But he believed in total honesty, and, when he finished his dinner, he cleared his throat and began.

"Nancy Seegram called me at the office today."

"Really?" Anna said. "What did she want?"

"She wanted . . . uh, she told me . . ." He looked down at the table, at the empty plate and the green flowery place mat spread neatly beneath it. "She called to announce that you and Bernard were having an affair. Have been, she said, for three months now."

Anna stared at him intently as he spoke, her face emotionless, but fascinated, as though she were listening to a favorite soap opera. Then she picked up his plate and sighed as she took it to the sink.

For a moment, he interpreted it as a sign of pity for poor,

crazy Nancy Seegram. But then, as she watched the water run in the sink, Anna said quietly, "I guess it was just a matter of time before you found out."

Sitting silently now on his living-room sofa, Jed vividly recaptured the feeling of that moment—the sense that something very heavy had bashed him in the chest and knocked the wind out. "Found out?" he had gasped. "It's true?"

Anna sighed that little sigh of hers, with a graceful tilt of her head, and continued rinsing the dish. "Yes, it's true."

"What do you mean, it's true?" he yelled, jumping up and pacing the floor. "You've been screwing around with Bernard Seegram for months?" The idea was laughable. This was Anna. Anna, his bride. Anna the mommy. Anna who, throughout their marriage, had exhibited very little appetite for things sexual. She had found it all, well, "messy." Anna the adulteress? "Impossible!" he shouted.

Carefully, Anna put the dish in the dishwasher. She opened the door of the counter under the sink, took out a dish towel, and began wiping the water off her hands.

Slow motion. His whole body was in turmoil and she was moving in slow motion. "Why?" He screamed it so loudly that she jumped.

She took a deep breath and put the fingertips of her right hand to her forehead. It was a gesture she used often when he was loud. It said: Please, Jed, I can't take that tone of voice.

"Jed," she said, very calmly. "Please sit down. We've got to discuss this like two adults."

He sat down at the kitchen table like a robot, his heavy breaths coming as loudly as rumbling ocean waves, but quicker, much quicker.

She sat down opposite him. She took another deep breath and began. Staring him straight in the eye, she told him that she and Bernard were in love, and had been, actually, since they first met, since the two couples had first begun socializing. Surely he must have realized that she and Bernard were, well, the "same type of people," just as he and Nancy were the "same type of people."

As she went on and on, enumerating the many interests she shared with Bernard and the many he shared with Nancy, he felt his head pounding so hard he had trouble hearing all the words. She sounded as if she had spent hours in front of the mirror, practicing her delivery, and her gestures and facial expressions. He felt as if he were paralyzed, sitting there in a stupor, staring at this beautiful tiny princess with long, polished nails and precision-coiffed, jet-black shiny hair who was telling him in a singsong voice a story of a romantic love affair much the way a girl would tell her best friend.

The sense of disbelief turned into a frantic need to make her stop, to turn it off. He pounded his fist down on the table.

"Jed, don't be difficult."

"Difficult?" he roared. "My wife—the mother of my children—is sitting across the table telling me she's been having an affair with a horse's ass—"

"I thought we could discuss this as mature adults."

"Mature adults don't do these kinds of things! Mature adults don't climb into bed with their best friend's husband—the father of their daughter's playmate—and then calmly—"

"Oh, yes, they do." She smiled—actually smiled! "Jed," she said, shaking her head. "Jed, you are so old-fashioned . . . so rigid, so out of it. People today are finding new freedoms."

"Like adultery?" he screamed. "Shit, Anna, that's old enough to have made it into the Ten Commandments! I wouldn't exactly call it a new-wave discovery!"

"No." Her eyes hardened. "I mean like realizing you made a mistake and getting out of it instead of living with it for the rest of your life."

"We're talking about divorce now, right? That's your big new freedom?"

She looked down at the table, considering. "Divorce without stigma is, yes."

"Divorce without stigma? That's what, the modern-day follow-up to love-without-marriage? Or sex-without-love? Divorce-without-stigma means you get a divorce and I don't feel bad?"

"Well . . ."

"Does it mean you get a divorce and the kids don't notice?"

"Oh, Jed . . ."

"What then? That you get a divorce, but we keep living together like nothing ever happened?"

"Stop it!" she shouted. Then she caught herself and calmed down again. "You are not going to do this to me," she said, smiling at him again. "You do this all the time. You bulldoze me with words, with your sarcasm, with your cleverness. Not tonight." She clasped her hands together in her lap and sat up straighter in her chair as though posing for a formal picture. "Tonight I am controlling the conversation, and it will be calm, reasoned, and productive as a result."

"Productive? What does that mean? We decide who gets what?" He threw back his head and howled, enjoying the knowledge that this was exactly what she did not want him to do. "I love it! Let's see now, I definitely want their Mercedes! You get Bernard and the Buick and I get Nancy and the Seegrams' Mercedes! No, better yet! I'll give Nancy to you and Bernard, and I'll get the Mercedes and keep the kids!" He howled again. But the last word of the sentence got to him and he sobered up. His kids. His babies. Was this really happening?

Suddenly his whole demeanor changed. "What about the children?"

She shrugged. "They're little. By the time they're old enough to understand, they'll be used to it. You know, divorce is no big deal anymore. Everyone's getting divorced."

He couldn't believe it. It was the same tone of voice she used to exonerate herself from an expensive purchase—"Everyone's wearing navy this year."

"Everyone's miserable, so we should be? You want to deprive my children of a family because it's the fad?"

"What family?" she hissed. "How can you call it a family when the parents hate each other?"

"I love you!" He didn't think before he said it. He didn't have to think. It was a fact—a "forever" he had never thought to question.

"You don't love me," she said through clenched teeth. "You love your children. You love your Senator. You love your stupid relatives. You don't love me. You've never loved me."

He thought he did. Ten minutes ago, he thought he did. But maybe he hadn't thought. Everything was whirling around in his head. "You don't love me?" His voice squeaked.

"No." She looked him right in the eye.

"You love Bernard?" He felt hot, wet tears falling down his face. "You love that effete asshole?"

"He's not—"

"An ass! An effete, prissy, affected ass!"

"He's a better man than you'll ever be!"

"No," Jed said, momentarily calmed by the sudden realization of what was really happening. "Not better, just richer. A filthy-rich asshole. That's what it is, isn't it? All this fancy talk, this romance! You're about as romantic as a stone."

"Not with him."

His body flashed heat. He felt it flaring out to his face, to his fingers. "Oh, sure. I see his appeal. If anyone could fuck you without messing up your hair, Bernard could."

"Really, Jed."

"Does he want to marry you?"

"Yes!" Her eyes gleamed victoriously.

"Do you have it in writing?" he sneered. "You'd better! Because, let me tell you, baby, you get nothing from just *screwing* a rich asshole—no designer dresses, no fancy cars, no diamonds! You get nothing but dirty!"

"Even you," she gasped. "Even you have never spoken this vilely before. How dare you—"

"How dare I? Where the hell do *you* come off 'how daring' me?"

She stared at him coldly as he paced. "I hate you. I hate your loud voice and I hate your lack of taste and I hate your willingness to live like a pauper and I hate your awful, vulgar family, and I hate your stupid jokes." She said the words as though she were reciting a grocery list.

Her lack of emotion moved him to ever-greater heights of passion. He paced, and as he paced, the passion turned to rage. He could feel the anger rumbling inside of him, growing. Tears were streaming from his eyes, but he was suddenly his Uncle Abie's nephew, and like Uncle Abie, the Farber family brawler, Jed was now ready to punch. "I want to kill you!" he groaned as he moved toward her. She screamed and ducked her head.

But he wasn't Uncle Abie. He couldn't hit another person. He never had. The punch was as foreign to him as adultery.

In a stupor, he walked out of the kitchen. He couldn't see

through the tears. He bumped into a dining-room chair and knocked it over.

"Don't you hurt my furniture!" she screeched from the kitchen. For the first time all night she sounded upset.

Then it hit him. That was all she cared about. Not him, not them, not forever after, not in sickness and in health, not watching the babies grow. Just the "things." The material evidence of their union.

"Your precious fucking furniture!" he howled. He picked up the delicate chair and slammed it down on the vintage antique table. Wooden pieces fell all over the place.

"No, no!" she screamed, running into the dining room.

Her reaction pushed him over the brink. He had finally found a way to hurt her. He walked over to the hutch where she kept the good Rosenthal china and began smashing plates on the table, one by one.

She collapsed on the chair sobbing.

He stared at her and he stared at the debris and he cried, cried with noises, this time, childlike noises of pain. The sound scared him.

Then he walked out the door, got into the car, and drove off, his vision completely blurred by tears, and so out of his mind that he instinctively turned on the windshield wiper for a clearer view.

To this day, he had no idea exactly where he had driven, or where he had stopped to buy the booze. Or why he had bought it. Had he thought that was what you were supposed to do under the circumstances? He just knew that after driving a while, he had checked into a motel with a bottle of bourbon. He remembered the taste of the first gulp. Awful. He hated bourbon. Maybe that's why he'd bought it.

And the second gulp. And the third. A night of pacing and pouring and thinking . . . thinking . . .

This couldn't be happening to him . . . to the same man who just last Saturday took Lisa to the zoo? Oh Lisa, his Lisa, what would happen to Lisa? He'd fallen on the bed, racked by sobs.

And then he drank. And then he paced. It went on all night. God, what a night. A night he would never forget, although everything had become blurrier and blurrier as the bourbon took hold. He paced, and he paced, and each time the anger and the sorrow blew up to the point where he could not take it anymore, he squeezed it out of his body in convulsive sobs.

Had she always hated him? He had been so flattered by her adoration—that beautiful little thing at the junior college in Boston who was so awed by his brilliance. Had it been his brilliance, or his Harvard degree and the hopes of a moneyed future? Had he disappointed her? Sure, she had pressured him to leave Capitol Hill and take a job with a law firm, and he had promised he would—later.

Had she been unable to wait? How could "later" be too long when you had pledged yourself to go the distance?

Was it possible that she never loved him? Just saw him as a ticket to a loftier level of living than her family's?

How many times had he gone over it all?

Now, impatiently, Jed got off the sofa and turned off the hockey game. He was doing more than reliving their fight. He was bringing up all the never-answered questions that had plagued him for seven years.

He went into the kitchen and poured himself a glass of wine. He had no idea how or under what condition he had fallen asleep that night seven years ago. All he knew was that he had awakened the next day with a terrible headache and another kind of pain that told him it had not been a dream.

Out of habit, he had called the office to tell them he wouldn't be in. The next thing he knew, he was speaking to the Senator.

"Where the hell are you?"

"I—I've had problems. I—"

"I know," Senator Barker had said. Jed could still hear the change in his voice—the gruffness softening. "Where are you?"

In a stupor, Jed read the name of the motel off a book of matches in the ashtray next to the bed.

"Stay there," the Senator ordered. "Do you hear me, Jed? I want you to stay right there."

"Why?"

"I'm coming."

"Why?"

"Promise me you'll stay put."

It was a promise Jed had had no trouble keeping. He felt paralyzed.

The next thing he knew, there was a knock on the door. In a fog, he had got up to let in Senator Barker.

Anna had called the office and left a terse message: She had taken the children to New York, to her parents. She would accept no calls from Jed. Jed would be contacted shortly by her attorney.

Senator Barker insisted on accompanying Jed back to the house. When they got there, the mess had been cleaned up. Anna, the perfect housewife. The pieces of the dining-room chair were stacked neatly in a corner. There was a note on the vestibule bearing essentially the same message transmitted to the office, with one addendum: "We will not return until you have moved your things out of the house."

Jed read the words impassively, but when he passed one of Lisa's dolls in the living room, he picked it up, clutched it to him, and slumped down on the sofa. Senator Barker sat down next to him and held him as he wept.

That was the last time he had ever cried.

Jed sipped his wine as he walked back into the living room. After a night like that, he guessed, there were no tears left.

He stared at the painting on his wall and counted the ironies. Number one: Their breakup had triggered a joyous reunion in the Seegram household. Number two: The financial strains of breaking up had forced them each to do what the other had always requested—Jed had had to leave the Senate for a more lucrative job with a law firm, and Anna had had to begin her career as an interior decorator.

Number three: Seven and a half years later, he still had no answers. He had nothing but the nagging suspicion that he had never been loved. That, and a hardened determination never to let himself be so innocent again, never so vulnerable.

Jed turned around and stared at the telephone in the corner of his living room. He would never be so vulnerable again.

# · 12 ·

Cynthia awoke Sunday morning to a chilling breeze rustling the curtains of her bedroom window, and a more chilling fact: Jed had not called.

She picked up the phone, hoping it was out of order. She slammed it down when she heard a dial tone.

Son-of-a-bitch.

The digital clock flashed seven A.M. She put on a sweat suit and went out for a run.

The air was cold and moist, the sky gray. As Cynthia gazed at the hostile silver heavens, she imagined her father's voice uttering the official pronouncement: "Snow's comin.'"

She took a deep breath, let it out, and then jogged into its vapor and beyond, down the street, around the corner, running by old brownstones and apartment houses and stores and benches, all of which seemed to be imitating the heavens' color scheme. Gray. Everything was cold and gray. Life was cold and gray.

She had talked too much. That was it. As her feet pounded the pavement, all her words repeated on her, all the hackneyed things she had said. Words, words, words! She gagged on them now, humiliated.

And then, later . . . Oh, God, later. She almost tripped on the pavement.

Later she had committed the cardinal sin—not by sleeping

with him, but by making love, really making love. Losing all sense of self-protection, she had told him with her body, with every move and gesture, that she was in love with him.

She turned around and headed home. Time to put an end to it. Too late to rewrite Friday night, but plenty of time to stop this infantile longing. No more. She picked up her pace, flying, it seemed, through the city streets. The hell with him.

At nine-fifteen, Cynthia was immaculate—doused with perfume, rinsed with mouthwash—and pacing the floor, acutely aware that "Sunday school" was about to begin.

She read *at* the Sunday papers, devouring long paragraphs with her eyes only, oblivious to their substance. Only the newspaper print left a lasting impression, sending her to the kitchen sink at regular intervals to wash her hands.

Her Siamese cat, Sapphire, roamed the living room in a state of agitation, mirroring her owner.

At twelve-thirty, staring sadly out the window, Cynthia admitted reality: Sunday school was over and Marshall Matthews's prediction had come true. Snow was pouring down from the sky.

Well, it was Sunday, and there was work to be done. She straightened. She vacuumed. And finally, with grim resolve, she dragged all her dirty clothes down to the laundry room in the basement, and sat staring at the clothes as they spun around in the washer and dryer as though the machines' windows were television screens.

She hauled the clean clothes back upstairs to her apartment.

Purposefully, she folded, her lips taut, her hands precise, creasing all the clothes in the right places, placing them in appropriate piles.

Yes, it was just one missed phone call. No, who was she kidding? When Jed Farber said he'd "call you tonight," he called.

He was a man she had studied like no other man, watching for signals, hearing all the words.

Something had happened. As she put the laundry in her dresser, she vowed she would find out what.

There was a knock on the door.

She opened it. Jed stood before her, his navy-blue ski parka and gloves dripping in the hall. His cheeks and nose were raw red, his hair sprinkled with snowflakes. There was a growl on his face. She noted, however, it was a fake growl.

"You've been out of your apartment!" he accused from the doorway.

"Guilty!" She stepped aside to let him in, hastily dismissing, in her ecstasy, all the vows, all the questions. Who cared? He was here. He was real.

"Do you know how long it took me to find a parking space?" he grumbled, walking brusquely past her into the living room. "Hours! It had to be hours! As it was, I ended up parking in Connecticut." He turned to her in deadpan. "The state, not the street."

She smiled. He was pretending nothing had happened since Saturday morning too. "Not guilty on that count. There are two thousand three hundred twelve parking spaces in this neighborhood. My car is only occupying one."

"Where is it?" He moved toward her menacingly. He grabbed the cowl of her sweater. "Tell me, dammit! I want that parking space!"

She laughed and he laughed too. He let go of the sweater, and tried putting the cowl back in shape. She looked down with amusement as he kept trying to fold it, to flatten it, and the cowl would not comply. Clumsy boy hands trying to do a girl's job. She fixed it for him.

He sniffed and looked at her curiously. "What shampoo do you use?" The voice was totally different this time. "It always smells so good."

"Can you smell it now? From there?"

He grinned. "No, not clearly."

She moved closer to him and he put his arms around her and kissed the top of her head. "Better. Much better. It's coming through loud and clear." He laughed and the reverberations tickled. "You are getting totally soaked at this very moment," he whispered into her ear. "The cold wetness is creeping from my jacket through your nice dry white sweater, sending chills throughout your body, but you are afraid it would be impolite to mention that fact."

She giggled and backed away. "Can I take your coat?"

He gave it to her and popped something into his mouth.

She frowned. "What was that?"

"An antacid pill."

"Was it something I said, or just the pleasure of my company?"

He grinned. "Neither. I'm an addict." He walked back toward the fireplace in her living room. "Actually I'm just shifting gears. I always leave my children with a hug, a kiss, and an antacid tablet. How about if I build us a fire?"

"Wonderful!" She hung his coat up over the tub in the bathroom. "How was Sunday school?" she called in. She could hear him moving logs from the woodpile to the fireplace.

"A little more involving than I would have liked," he said. "It was Parents' Day. We all participated in the classroom activity. I starred in Timmy's class. They were acting out Purim, and let me tell you, I am one terrific Hamen!"

"Hamen?"

"He's the villain of the story of Purim. That's all you have to know."

"How come?"

"Because that's all I remembered, and I was outstanding."

She walked back into the living room, and he turned around from the fireplace, his shoulders pulled up to ear level, one higher than the other, his face in a grotesque mask, his hands curled like claws.

Cynthia began laughing. "You look like a combination of Dracula and Richard the Third!"

With exaggerated physical relief, he fell out of character. "That's the beauty of villains. They all look alike. A good Hamen is a good Dracula is a good Richard."

She sat down on the floor, watching as he built the fire. "And the swim meet?" She handed him a book of matches.

"Six hours in an atmosphere reminiscent of Washington in August," he groaned, shaking his head. "Fortunately, the kids handled it better than I did. They did really well." He lit the match and moved back next to her on the floor. "How was the factory?"

She told him about the rustic barn.

He listened alertly, frowning as she described the driveway

that offered indirect access. "Did the barn have any windows?" he asked when she finished.

"Yes, now that you mention it, little windows around the sides at the very top, near the ceiling. Whoever turned it into a factory must have added those. Barns don't have windows."

"All the way around?" Jed asked intently. "Think now, were there windows on all four sides of the barn?"

She thought for a while, and then looked up at him. "No! Only on three sides! Not in the front!" Her eyes lit up. "I get it."

Jed nodded. "Nothing showing from the road."

"Yes! No lights at night when the shift is working!" She shuddered. "It's a little creepy."

"Obviously an entrepreneur who doesn't want a whole lot of publicity," Jed mumbled.

They both stared into the fire. "I told Carlos I was going to take an afternoon off this week and see if I could find out who owned the property," she said. "Isn't there a county clerk's office out there or something like that where I could find out?"

"Yes, and that's an excellent idea." He grinned at her. "And how was Carlos? Still arrogant?"

"Well, precocious." She smiled. "The truth is, I like him. Except, I thought teenagers were supposed to be silent and truculent. This one can't stop talking!"

"Oh, he's probably an only child of adoring Latino parents, encouraged to sparkle all the time."

"No, he told me in the car coming home he has two older sisters, married and living in Miami." She looked over at Jed slyly. "But then, he's the firstborn son, of the firstborn son. The prodigy of the family! I guess that explains it."

Jed raised an eyebrow. "Hmm, I'm beginning to like the kid too!"

She laughed, but sobered as she stared into the fire. "Is it difficult to find out who owns a plot of land?"

"No, not at all. It's really a simple procedure— Damn!" He jumped up. "I forgot! I left my stuff outside in the corridor!" He headed for the door and returned carrying an attaché case and an overnight bag. "I figured if I'd carried these in, you would have been sure I was moving in and have a fit. Accuse me of, what was it? 'Orchestrating' things again? 'Manipulating'?"

"What are they for? Are you going out of town?" she asked good-naturedly.

"Naw . . ." He sat back down next to her. "Just with the snow, uh, it's supposed to really pile up tonight. I wanted to make sure I could get to my office tomorrow morning. Hey— would you like to go for a walk later? It's really spectacular out."

"Yes!" She felt terribly happy, warmed by the fire, by his presence. Gradually, however, the words penetrated. She turned to him. "What does that mean? 'Make sure you could get to work tomorrow'?"

"I thought I'd, uh, stay downtown."

"Downtown?"

"Yeah. You know. In a hotel."

"Oh, really?" She raised an eyebrow.

"Yes." He looked at her uncomfortably. "Really."

"What hotel?"

"The Shoreham, dammit. I thought I'd stay at the Shoreham!"

She looked at him in wide-eyed innocence. "The Shoreham?"

"You don't believe me."

She squinted. "Do you have a reservation? Surely you— planner-aheader that you are—must have realized that the Shoreham gets very booked up with conventions."

"Yes."

"Yes, what? You have a reservation?"

"Y-yes."

She stared at him, still squinting.

"You don't believe me."

"I could check," she said.

"You really don't believe me! You think I came down here planning to move in for the night—thinking you would ask me to spend the night. You honestly don't believe me!"

She stared at him as he shifted uncomfortably. Then she got up and walked into the kitchen. She looked up the Shoreham Hotel in the phone book and dialed the number. She looked back into the living room. He was shifting around nervously in front of the fire.

"Omni Shoreham Hotel, good evening."

"Hello, I wondered if you could help me. Do you have a reservation this evening for a Jed Farber? First name J-E-D, second name F-A-R-B-E-R."

"Thank you, ma'am. One moment, I'll check."

Cynthia glared through the doorway as the muzak poured out of the receiver. He had not moved.

"Hello, ma'am?"

"Yes?"

"I show a reservation for a 'Jed I. Farber' for tonight."

Cynthia looked back into the living room. Jed was doubled over with laughter, rolling around on the floor, celebrating, no doubt, the ingenious way he had managed to pull it all off. She felt her face get hot.

"Ma'am?"

"Yes, that's it," Cynthia snapped into the phone. "Uh, just a moment," she said to the operator sweetly.

"Yes, ma'am?"

She looked back into the living room. "Cancel it."

# · 13 ·

It was "morning meeting" time at Capitol Radio. Cynthia had been assigned the day's top story—the Senate Trade Hearings—and the rest of the staff was gathered around the long conference table waiting patiently as Gardiner Weldy urged assignments upon them.

Well, not "patiently," so much as "hostilely," Cynthia noted wryly. In truth, only sweet-faced Suzie Pepper seemed enthusiastic. At the foot of the table, opposite Gardiner, Sylvia Berg was bent over a pad, dutifully noting down each assignment as Gardiner pronounced it. Her secretary's pose, however, was undermined by a raised eyebrow and tightly drawn lips: Sylvia Berg's mask of disapproval.

A study in passive aggression, Brian Mulroney sat next to Cynthia puffing away feverishly on his third cigarette of the morning. Knowing how the meticulous Gardiner hated smoke, Brian concentrated each morning on filling the conference room with as much of it as possible.

And across the table, furious about the assignment he had just received, Jake Weinstein jerked about restlessly in his chair, his bearded face bearing the sneer of a malevolent Jewish leprechaun ready to pounce. He pounced. "Rudolph Rettinger is a right-wing evangelist!" Jake exploded. "What *possible* newsworthiness is there in my covering his speech?"

"I'm sure you'll find some, Jake," Gardiner Weldy crooned,

his eyes floating lightly over Jake's, intentionally not registering Weinstein's fury. "Try to figure out the man's mass appeal, Jake. That's what our listeners want to know!"

"*What* mass appeal?" Jake squealed. "The guy's a lunatic!"

"Oh, my, my," Gardiner laughed, picking up his papers and heading for the door. "Go with an open mind! Think like a reporter!"

Jake jumped up, kicked his chair back into place, and stormed out of the room after Gardiner.

"Sylvia," Cynthia began as they walked out into the hallway together, "weren't today's assignments awfully—"

Sylvia Berg held up her hands, closed her eyes, and shook her head resolutely. "Don't ask me. I just work here."

Cynthia thought of one person who would be extremely interested in the proceedings of this morning meeting . . . but then remembered Chris Channing had told her he would be out of town until Wednesday. She plopped down in her desk chair and watched silently as Jake Weinstein threw microphones, cable wires, and other supplies into his canvas bag, preparing to leave. "Asshole!" Weinstein mumbled under his breath. "The guy's an A-one asshole!"

Brian Mulroney laughed.

Cynthia turned to Jake. "Do you think you could put your Mad Max act aside for one moment and take a larger look at what's happening here?" She turned to Brian. "I'd like your opinion too."

"What do you mean?" Jake kept packing his gear.

"Well, there was that news briefing this morning about how the President's new budget will affect the government's entitlement programs." She looked from one to the other. "Now, *that's* an important story for our Florida audiences, down there in social security land. For Arizona stations too, right?"

"Right."

"And there was that Interior Department report on toxic chemical contamination on wildlife preserves—perfect for the western stations, right?"

"Right."

"Then *why*, instead of those stories, was Jake assigned to cover a speech by Rudolph Rettinger, and why was Suzie assigned to cover the Right-to-Life demonstration?"

"It's the anniversary of the big Supreme Court decision on abortion," Suzie piped up. "That's why."

"*Last* week was the anniversary," Cynthia snapped. "And the President addressed the group, both of which made it appropriately newsworthy, and we covered it." She shot Suzie a look. "I know, because I covered it! Why cover a small rally one week later when there is no other side to report? Why give an open mike to the Right-to-Lifers?"

They all seemed thoroughly disinterested.

"Don't you see a political thread to the assignments Gardiner's been giving out lately?" Cynthia pressed. "A leaning to the political right, to be exact?"

"Oh, Cynthia," Suzie laughed. "You're being silly."

"He's an asshole," stormed Jake, walking out with his gear. "That's the one consistency!"

Cynthia turned to Brian. "Haven't you noticed lately—"

The phone on Cynthia's desk buzzed, signifying an incoming call. She watched as Brian yawned, and gave up. "Cynthia Matthews," she announced, picking up the telephone.

"Hi. It's Carlos Ramirez. My mother said you called?"

"Yes, Carlos!" Cynthia leaned back in her chair.

"Sorry I wasn't home," he said, "but I got in later than usual. I was busy playing top-notch reporter, just like you told me to." He laughed a little. "I was, well, *trying* to interview the men."

"Good for you! What did you find out?"

"Mostly that they're really afraid to open up. It's like they think I'm from Immigration or something! But one guy said he'd meet me at McDonald's tonight before the shift. It's Francisco—the one I helped home that day after he got sick? Guess he figures he owes me."

"Good. Milk the debt for all you can." Cynthia played with the telephone cord. "Listen, Carlos, I talked to an occupational health expert last night. That's someone who specializes in workplace hazards. I told him about the work process in the factory— what you told me. He said you should find out what they're washing those parts in."

"I only saw it from a distance. I just figured it was water, you know? Hot water?"

Cynthia sat up. "It's heated? You didn't tell me that."

"Yeah, it looked like it was heated. It kind of bubbled."

"See what you can find out. If it's a chemical, the occupational health hazard expert said, that could explain a lot. It might be that the men are inhaling the fumes and that's what's getting to them."

"Naw . . . I don't think that's it," Carlos said slowly. "The night I watched, they were all wearing masks over their faces—you know, to protect them."

"You didn't tell me that either!" Cynthia gasped. "See what I mean about how important it is to be an astute observer? Look at all you missed!"

"You really think that stuff is important?" he asked incredulously.

"I have no idea. But it could be. Any little fact could be important. You've got to get as many facts as you can."

"Yeah, I guess you're right."

"Carlos, I'm taking tomorrow afternoon off. I'm going to go out to the county clerk's office in Maryland to find out who owns the property the factory is on. I'll call you when I get home. Have some more information for me!" It was an order.

Senator Barker's legislative assistant Ed Bartholemew was waiting in the Senate Finance Committee anteroom when Barker arrived for the first day of the trade hearings. "Standing room only," he whispered in the Senator's ear. "Not even that! There are loads of angry reporters who couldn't get seats milling around out in the hall, relegated to watching the proceedings on a monitor! Biggest press turnout of the year!"

"Check with Dan about the statistics I wanted," Barker said sotto voce. "They weren't finished when I left the office." He paused at the Senators' entrance to the hearing room and listened for a moment. The chairman was finishing up his introductory remarks. Barker looked at his watch. "I'm gonna need those statistics in about twenty minutes, Ed."

Bartholemew nodded and ran off.

Senator Barker took his seat among the other Finance Committee members at the large, raised, horseshoe-shaped podium in the front of the room. About fifteen photographers were crawling around on the floor between the podium and the witness table snapping pictures. On either side of the witness table, the klieg lights were on, the network cameras poised to roll.

Barker squinted through the lights. Bartholemew had not exaggerated. The press tables were packed, and people were standing in the aisles in the spectator section. What's more, the splendid Senatorial podium—normally dotted with name plates and empty chairs—was fully occupied.

Poker-faced, Senator Barker scanned his colleagues' dark suits and somber expressions. Hail, hail, the gang's all here, ready to do battle with the United States' soaring trade deficit in a grandstand play dedicated to the folks back home. Why, even Senator Pritchards had shown up, a feat in itself!

His tongue ran along the inside of his cheek as he noted the inordinately large number of Asian faces at the press table. Well, that said it all, didn't it? The Japanese had even amassed a journalistic surplus! Not only had the Japanese press corps shown up in force, but they had obviously been the early birds, managing to beat out the American reporters for the limited seating at the hearing-room press tables!

Yes, sir. Barker silently bet that the "loads of angry reporters" Bartholemew had described standing outside in the halls were all American . . . getting a firsthand taste of what it was like to be outclassed in international competition! (He also bet that fact would not show up in one written account of the proceedings.)

His eyes caught a speck of shiny flaxen hair among the dark heads at one press table. He looked more closely.

She was wearing a light blue sweater, one, he guessed, that matched those baby-blue eyes of hers. He couldn't see the eyes clearly. They were focused on the notepad in front of her, on which she was writing. But there was something about the coloring and the posture that made him certain it was Cynthia Matthews.

Through the glare of lights she came across much the way she had through the blur of booze that night in his office: a tall, slender, attractive combination of blond hair and pastel-colored clothes, in a conscientious, determined pose. Obviously, *she* had gotten to the press table early enough to steal a seat from the Japanese.

The sight of the all-too-familiar black tape recorder on the tabletop in front of her jolted him, but only momentarily. Recalling Ralph Buddington's phone call, Senator Barker watched her for a while, feeling a kind of tenderness mixed with gratitude. If she were doing a story on him, he would have gotten feedback by now.

Well, thank the Lord if he'd had to open up that way, he'd done it to a reporter kind enough not to rush out and win herself a hotshot byline at his expense. He sighed. Apparently not all the members of the Fourth Estate were vultures.

"These numbers are exacting a human toll across this country of ours, Mr. Chairman," the Senator from Rhode Island went on. "In my own state, I've seen . . ."

As Barker's eyes scanned the podium, he forecast the predictable diatribe that would go on before the first witness even got to open his mouth. His colleague from Pennsylvania would bemoan steel plant closings in his home state. His colleague from Michigan would groan about auto plant closings.

He looked at his watch and relaxed. He wouldn't need those statistics for about an hour.

At the press table, Cynthia Matthews took the completed cassette out of her tape recorder and replaced it with a new one. The high-flung, flamboyant oratory she was recording might not have any impact on the soaring U.S. trade deficit, but it would certainly have a beneficial impact on Capitol Radio's deficit.

Capitol Radio's radio station customers were interested in news from Washington, especially news from Washington with a regional twist. And she had—on one cassette alone—Senators from seven different states translating the national news into regional chaos—plant closings in Pennsylvania, in Michigan. . . .

When the hearings broke for lunch, she would race back to the office and give Sylvia her list of Senatorial sound bites. Sylvia would then start the phone calls ("We have a news story on the trade hearings, pegged on what *your* Senator says. . . . Would you be interested?"). Cynthia would write and record a "wraparound"—a general report on the hearings that could fit each of the sound bites. Then she would cut and splice the tape and, by the end of the afternoon, Capitol Radio would have made a lot of sales, and Cynthia's voice would be heard in two-minute spots on little radio stations all over the country.

She listened for a while as the first witness—a negotiator

from the trade representative's office—concluded his dull prepared statement. She sighed. More sound and fury, signifying nothing.

Absentmindedly, her eyes roamed to the podium, to the gray-streaked brown hair and bearlike physique of the committee's "minority chairman." The sight made her stomach queasy once again, and she looked away quickly. She had been sitting quietly in this overpacked room for almost two hours now, oblivious to the crowds scrambling around her, consumed with an awareness of just one other presence in the room: Senator Barker.

She had decided not to follow up on the Barker interview out of compassion for the man. However, once she had made the decision, her estimation of Senator Barker had switched from thinking of him as a tragic, emotionally battered lawmaker to regarding him as a crook getting away scot-free.

He certainly didn't look the least bit tragic up there on the podium this morning, did he? On the contrary, the man was the picture of Senatorial splendor! She was beginning to feel she had tossed journalistic responsibility to the winds by not showing him up for the corrupt politician he was!

The words of the trade negotiator traveled from her ear to her pen, unprocessed by her mind. Her mind was preoccupied with Senator Barker, moving from journalistic guilt about not following up on his confession, to . . . to . . .

Was it possible she was sharing her life, her innermost thoughts, her *bed* with the Senator's messenger? Jed had said nothing to make her suspicious, but he didn't have to say anything to further the cause. Just being there with her all the time was a way of making certain she was not working on a story about Barker.

No.

No, what? No, it was not possible? Or no, she couldn't bear the possibility?

From what Jed said, he and the Senator talked all the time. Surely the subject of the interview had to have come up. Or perhaps Barker had not told Jed, preferring, instead, to monitor her behavior on his own, casually, in telephone chitchat, without Jed's even realizing it.

Of course, she could tell Jed and bring the whole thing out into the open. But who would bear the brunt? She would! For withholding the information in the first place, and then for knocking his mentor off that pedestal. She knew very well who had seniority in Jed Farber's feelings!

In her lap, Cynthia's left hand clenched into a fist involuntarily.

One thing was certain. She hated Frederick Barker, hated him for putting her in an untenable position: She was either falling in love with a man whose attentions were fabricated, or withholding information from the man she loved, actively "covering up" like a criminal while the crooked Senator maintained his status as a reputable lawmaker and Jed Farber's idol.

Talk about ironies!

The committee chairman turned the microphone over to his "distinguished colleague from Iowa," and Senator Barker began cross-examining the administration's trade negotiator.

"Mr. Johnson, I want to thank you for participating in these hearings under the circumstances." Barker said it in the manner of a host welcoming a guest who had overcome great obstacles to make the party. "Why, I understand you just got off a plane from Tokyo."

The trade negotiator sighed and gave Barker a weary look. "Yes, Senator, just two hours ago, to be exact."

"My, my, my . . ." Barker looked around the panel. "Most of us up here are accustomed to jet lag, but I'd venture jet lag from Tokyo—halfway around the world—is the worst. And I sympathize with you, Mr. Johnson. How long have you been doing this? Trekking back and forth?"

"Me personally? Oh, for about four years, Senator."

"And roughly how many trips have you made back and forth in that time, would you estimate?"

"Oh . . . well . . . I guess about thirty. Maybe more." The trade negotiator's tone grew wary.

"Thirty trips!" Senator Barker gasped and looked around the podium. "Here, we've all been bemoaning the toll the trade deficit has taken on our own regional constituencies," he drawled amiably. "Perhaps, gentlemen, it's time to look at the bright side—the boon to our airline industry from having the President's trade negotiators commute to Tokyo!"

For the first time since the hearing began there was laughter. Cynthia did not laugh. She sensed a sudden change in the air. Up to this point, the hearings had been characterized by bipartisan commiseration, with Senators from both parties speaking out loudly and passionately about the pain the trade imbalance was causing the folks back home. Frederick Barker, the Democratic leader of the committee, was about to take on the Republican President's trade policy.

"What are some of the issues that have caused you people to fly back and forth to Tokyo so much, Mr. Johnson?" Barker went on in his smooth, good-old-boy tones. "What trade accomplishments have resulted from logging all those miles?"

Johnson reeled off a long and comprehensive list: auto export accords, voluntary steel restraints, semiconductors, coal, textiles. . . .

"Well, now, that is a mighty impressive agenda," Senator Barker exclaimed when he finished. "But I'm afraid I'm all confused. Take coal, for example. Didn't Japan agree back in nineteen eighty-three to maintain import levels of U.S. coal, to increase them, even, if they stepped up their steel production?"

"Well, yes, Senator. That was part of the joint—"

"Then how come, Mr. Johnson, Japan's importing less than half as much of our coal today as it did in eighty-three, despite the fact that Japan's steel production is up, and despite the fact, I might add, that Japan has managed to hold on to a healthy one-quarter share of *our* steel market?"

"Well, Senator—"

"And take automobiles, Mr. Johnson. Wouldn't you say the twenty-five percent drop in value the dollar has recently undergone against the Japanese yen would give American carmakers a better chance to compete with the Japanese, on the basis of price?"

"Yes, it should."

"Why, then, Mr. Johnson—"

The cameramen were getting hysterical commands from their correspondents: "Roll! Roll!" The newspaper photographers were shifting back and forth—from the Senator, who was getting louder and angrier, to the uncomfortable witness before him.

"And now, let's take a look at these semiconductors, Mr. Johnson."

There was a spurt of excitement throughout the room. At the table around Cynthia, the reporters who had been yawning and whispering cynically throughout the proceedings were now scribbling furiously on their notepads.

"Our" trade problem was being articulately transformed into a Republican fiasco.

That would be the lead for the newspaper journalists, the live clip for the TV networks and radio: a catchy array of facts, preceded by a skillful buildup and then cleverly orchestrated by a consummate politician.

"Is it too much jet lag from all these trips, Mr. Johnson? Is *that* why our negotiators keep losing out?"

The room erupted in guffaws.

Laughter reverberated from inside the shower curtain wrapped around the tub in Cynthia's bathroom, and steam poured over the top, condensing on the room's ceiling and floor and misting up the mirror.

Sapphire pulled herself up from her spot in the corner, sniffed the air, and, as though sensing things would get worse before they got better, the cat pawed haughtily out of the room, in search of a drier, calmer environment.

"If you like my shampoo so much," Cynthia teased, "why don't you try some?"

Jed turned down the bottle she offered and poured some of his own shampoo on his hair. "I like to smell you, not smell *like* you."

Cynthia stepped under the shower nozzle. "Oh," she groaned in ecstasy, rinsing the shampoo from her hair, "don't you just love the way it feels, the liquidy warmth pouring down all over you?"

"Uh-huh." Jed gazed down, entranced by the way the water was spilling over the delicate lines of her upturned face, propelling the shampoo bubbles down to the roundness and crevices of her body. Instinctively, his hands reached out, wanting to feel what it was like to slither down her skin along with the suds.

"I'm so glad you like really hot showers too." Her eyes stayed closed.

"Mmm." His hands changed direction and began massaging her scalp, helping her work the lather out. The heat, the vapor, the water, the wonderful all-American face—he had the giddy feeling they were standing alone and naked in the middle of one of her father's cornfields in the midst of a sweltering July downpour.

"I know what you're thinking," she said.

"Yeah? What?"

"You're thinking I'm hogging all the water."

"Yup," he laughed, bending down and kissing her chin, "*exactly* what I was thinking."

"Okay," she sighed, stepping out from under the spray and pushing him in. "Your turn."

He squeezed his eyes shut as the water and shampoo cascaded over them. "It's lonely under here all by myself."

Cynthia picked up a bar of soap and began lathering her body. "Two can fit?"

"Definitely." Jed picked up a bar of soap with one hand and beckoned her with the other. "Piece of cake."

She stepped under the nozzle with him. "Piece of cake?"

"That's my son's favorite expression." He wrapped his arms around her. "I think the translation is somewhere along the lines of 'no sweat.'" He pulled her close and kissed her until the waves of water made them both gasp for air, and move, giggling out of the water's spray.

He watched his hands as they began soaping her neck and her breasts.

"What's the derivative?" She rubbed her soap bar along his chest, then out to his shoulders, and then in circles around his stomach.

"God knows!"

She flicked a drop of water off the tip of his nose with the tip of hers and closed her eyes, enjoying the feeling of her hands sliding around his body, his hands on hers. "Piece of cake," she murmured softly.

He pulled her closer. Slowly, he moved his bar of soap along her shoulder blades, and down her back along her spine.

"Mmm," she murmured, undulating her sudsy front back and forth against his as she soaped his back. "This is my favorite part."

"Mine too."

They stood that way for a while, enveloped in the warm cloud of steam, the water pouring down from above, their eyes closed, their bodies sliding slowly back and forth against each other.

"I have a confession to make," she whispered in his ear.

"What's that?"

"I've never done this before."

"Done what?"

"Taken a shower with someone."

"We did it yesterday."

"No, I mean before yesterday."

"Really?"

"Yes, I . . . I don't know." She played with his earlobe. "I guess the idea just never came up." Her soapy hands moved to massage the back of his neck.

He turned his head slowly from side to side in response to the massage. "Do you like it?"

"Mmm, I like it. A lot."

He held her tighter.

She wrapped her arms around his shoulders and rubbed her cheek against his. Then her eyes opened. She stared alertly at the wall over his left shoulder, her forehead creasing. "I can't really think of anyone I would have done it with. It's . . . well, it's different from sleeping with someone, even. It's more . . . more . . ."

"Intimate."

"Mmm," she sighed happily and closed her eyes again, pressing her body against his. "More intimate."

Then her eyes reopened. "Did you and your wife take showers together?"

Jed let go of her abruptly and burst out laughing. "Hardly!" he shouted, walking back under the pouring water. "Mostly, during the course of my marriage, I took cold showers, and always alone!"

Cynthia reached under the torrent of water, and ran her fingers along the hair on his chest. "Well, then, who have you taken showers with?"

He tried to open his eyes, but the water was pouring down

over them too hard, and he gave up. "Do you really want an answer to a question like that?"

"No." She looked away and quickly began rinsing off her own body. "Definitely not. No. Not at all."

He stepped out from under the spray and whisked the extra water off his face. He gazed down at her.

She avoided his eyes at first, but then she looked up at them, into them, studying them, finally, reading them. Her expression changed from embarrassment to suspicion, and then from suspicion to certainty. "Hah!"

"What."

"You've never taken a shower with anyone before either!"

He laughed and playfully pushed her back under the nozzle.

He stood very still watching the water gush over her hair, and slither down along her soft curves. When he stepped back under the spray, his lips met hers hungrily.

# · 14 ·

"Hey, how's my favorite attorney doing?"

Jed smiled, warmed by the familiar boom coming from the telephone. "Why, it's Mr. Trade Hearings himself!"

"Come on now . . ."

"You looked damn good on CBS again last night!"

"Frankly, I preferred NBC," Senator Barker quipped. "But I gather you didn't call just to personally give me my Neilson rating. What's up?"

"I just wanted to tell you I got a letter from Buzzy."

"My son knows how to write?"

"Now, cut that out!"

"No, I'm pleased, Jed. Very, very pleased. Frankly, I thought the boy's communication skills were limited to making collect long-distance telephone calls."

"Come on, Rick, it was a really nice letter. I think he's sort of found himself in this new job."

"Thanks to you," Barker grumbled. "Thanks to you for finding him the job in the first place!"

"Now, that happens to be exactly what *he* said, only to be honest, Buzzy was a hell of a lot more articulate about it than you!" Jed played with the stationery on the desk in front of him. "It's a very thoughtful letter, Rick. Very sensitive. A kind of re-examination of his life, an itemization of a new agenda, a new determination, I think, to improve himself, to grow up."

"Says something, doesn't it? The fact that he chose to share these thoughts with you and not with his father?"

"No, Rick. My guess is he chose to share them with you *through* me. He knew damn well that I'd call you as soon as I got the letter." Jed leaned back in his chair and put his feet up on the desk. "I called to tell you about the letter, but also for another reason. How would you like to celebrate the end of three sensational days of trade hearings by having dinner tonight? I want to show you the letter and . . . uh . . . something else too."

"Damn, Jed, I'd love to. Fact is, I've got a three-thirty plane out of here to Des Moines. I'm addressing a godawful fundrais—"

"Shit."

"Listen, you can show me the letter when—"

"Uh, yeah, fine. It's just, well, it isn't just the letter. I wanted to, um, introduce you to someone too."

"Who?"

"A woman I'm seeing."

There was a pause, followed by a Barkeresque chortle.

"And just what is *that* supposed to mean?"

"Interesting, very interesting is all," Barker boomed. "This just has to be the first time in—how many years have I known you?—the first time that you've had a woman you actually wanted me to meet!"

"Not true. You've met a whole lot of—"

"*Met.* That's the operative word here. 'Met.' Bumped into, maybe, because we happened to be at the same function at the same time. Happenstance, in every case. Oh, for good reason, I'd say. I could understand your unwillingness to parade most of them before me. Forgive my bluntness, Jed, but you'll have to agree they were a pretty sorry lot, all of them!" Barker chortled again. "The fact that this is someone you *want* me to meet—"

"Well, we'll do it another time," Jed parried.

"Not so fast, boy! Not so fast! This one has to be someone special. What's her name?"

Jed sidestepped, suddenly not willing to reveal anything more. "You'll like her," he said. "We'll just do it next week if you're busy tonight. Hey, listen," he switched abruptly, "since we can't enjoy your company tonight, how about if we at least feast on your culinary specialty? What's the recipe?"

"For my chili?"

"What else? You know as well as I you are capable of concocting exactly two meals—chili and cold cereal. The latter I can figure out for myself."

"This *is* a change for you!"

"What?"

"You never dated a woman before strong enough to handle my chili! I like her already!" Barker teased.

Jed laughed. "Okay, then tell me how to make it."

"Be happy to. But, uh, first, um, before I forget. Do you think you could . . ."

"I am, even right now as we speak, putting Buzzy's letter in an envelope addressed to your home in Chevy Chase."

"Hell, how did you know?"

"Years of training. A good legislative assistant knows how to anticipate where his gruff-speaking but softhearted boss's interests really lie."

"Legislative assistant!" Barker scoffed. "Jed, you're a hell of a lot more to me—and to Buzzy, for that matter—than a former legislative assistant! Christ, do I have to spell out how important—"

"Nope. Just give me the recipe. And keep it hot—like the lady."

Wednesday evening, an exhausted Cynthia Matthews trudged down the hall to her apartment. When she got to the door, she reflexively fumbled in her purse for her keys. Then she remembered. Her face brightened and she knocked on the door.

"YEEEEEEEEES?" bellowed a deep male voice on the other side of the door.

"It's me!"

"WHOOOOOOOOO?"

Cynthia looked around the empty corridor self-consciously. "Shh!" she whispered into the door's crack. "Open the door!"

"See how uncomfortable it is standing out there, waiting for someone to let you in?"

She put her hands on her hips and glared at the peephole in the door. "I will never again give you the key to my apartment!"

"You won't have to." The deep voice was now laughing. "I had an extra one made."

"You what!" Cynthia smacked her purse against the door.

"You would call that assertive, huh? Downright ballsy?" He laughed malevolently.

"Yes!" she said in a controlled voice, gritting her teeth and talking to the door as though it were a person. "You could have asked me!"

"Well, look at it this way, if we each had our own key, you would have been able to let yourself in."

She was now making angry faces at the door. "Is that what this is? A lesson?"

"Naw, I just happened to pass a locksmith." His voice turned apologetic. "If you'd rather I didn't have one, I'll just throw it out."

"Jed, open the door."

"You really feel strongly about it, don't you? That settles it. Wait right there and I'll go throw it out."

"Jed! Open the door this instant!" She banged.

The door opened, revealing a large Jed Farber with a small delicate white apron tied around his middle. His shirt sleeves were rolled up, and the apron's petite, ruffled bib seemed to be struggling to span the distance across his chest. "Welcome home, dear," he chimed in falsetto. "How was your day?"

Cynthia took one look at him and began laughing. "My mother sent me that apron. I can't decide if it looks worse on you or on me!"

"Hey," he said soberly. "Don't criticize. Dinner is almost done."

He put his arms around her as she moved closer.

"You're impossible," Cynthia groaned into his left shoulder.

"You can have the new key," he whispered, hugging her. "I had them make it purple . . . the same shade as your bedroom."

Cynthia pushed him away and walked past him, shaking her head. She hung her coat up in the closet as Jed retreated into the kitchen. "Sit down and relax!" he yelled in. "I'll be right there."

Cynthia plopped down on the sofa. She sniffed. "You *did* make dinner!" She sniffed again. "What is it?"

"I figured I should make dinner," Jed continued cheerfully

from the kitchen. "I mean, it was the least I could do. You know, I never make the bed."

She blinked. "What?"

"I was thinking about it on the subway this morning. Do you realize you always make the bed? Every morning, when I get out of the shower, you've made the bed. Not that I would make it. As a rule, I don't make beds, don't really believe in making beds. But still, you've borne all the bed-making responsibility."

Cynthia smiled. "What else did you think about on the subway?"

A wicked gurgle erupted in the kitchen.

"What is it?" Cynthia repeated. "What form of hot and spicey are we eating?"

"Chili."

"You're on! Is this an old recipe from your childhood in the Barrio?"

"Worse," Jed yelled in. "It's Iowan chili!"

On the sofa in the living room, Cynthia stiffened. Barker.

"It's Rick Barker's famous recipe," Jed explained. "I called him today to see if he could go out for dinner with us tonight, but he was going out of town. He gave me the recipe and a rain check."

"Jed, did you tell him who the other half of the 'us' was?"

"Well, he knows I'm seeing someone I want him to meet."

She leaned forward. "Does he know my name?"

"No, not yet. Why?"

Cynthia ran her fingers along the sofa cushion. "Cynthia Matthews might not be a big name in this town, but let me tell you, in Iowa, they listen to me a lot." She tried to say the words with the bravado they merited, but her throat was so parched the delivery was slightly scratchy.

"Well, then, I'll be sure to name-drop you next time!" Jed walked into the living room carrying two glasses of wine. "Mmm, it even smells hot, doesn't it?" He handed Cynthia a glass. "I absolutely love hot, spicey food." He sat down next to her on the sofa. "Ever had Jewish food?"

"Well, some. I don't know. What do you consider 'Jewish food'?"

Jed stretched his legs out and fell back in a semiprone position on the sofa, his eyes closed. He lay very still and slowly opened one eye. "You know it's Jewish if it doesn't crunch. Nothing prepared in my mother's kitchen has ever crunched. Carrots lie limp on the plate. Celery is soggy. Beans droop. And by the time they are served, they are all roughly the same color, grayish-greenish." He put his hand over his heart. "You are looking at the son of the all-time champion of Jewish cuisine," he groaned. "Oh, God, my mother's pot roast . . ."

"Dead?"

"And deadly." He rolled his eyes up to the ceiling, so only the whites showed, closed one, and lowered the other eyelid halfway. He let all the muscles in his face go limp, lolled his tongue, and whimpered slightly.

Cynthia howled. "What on earth are you doing?"

"Acting out my mother's pot roast." He barely moved his lips.

"Did she make it often?"

He sat up. "Only for special occasions. Like every time I got a good report card, every time I came home from law school for vacation, every lousy birthday, all my life. It became known as 'Jed's favorite,' and a family tradition as a result. I still have nightmares. When you say 'birthday' to me, instead of seeing a chocolate cake and candles, I see my mother beaming as she carries out a platter of the most pathetic, exhausted hunk of meat—" He turned to Cynthia abruptly. "Who's Christopher Channing?"

Cynthia did a double take. "What was it about Jewish cooking that made you—"

"Not Jewish cooking. It was the 'hunk' part. I almost forgot. He called before you got home." Jed looked at her suspiciously. "He has a deep, mellifluous voice that reeks of testosterone."

"What did he want?"

"'Nothing special,'" Jed said in a breathy baritone. "Just call him, when you have time." Jed looked at her menacingly. "You take one step toward that phone and you're—"

Her eyes sparkled. "Pot roast?"

"Who is he? He seemed to know exactly who I was!"

Smugly, she drank some wine. "I think you're jealous."

"Curious. Just curious."

She laughed. "He's an old friend. We used to work together at Capitol Radio." She leaned toward Jed. "He is very happily married to a friend of mine that I introduced him to."

"Okay." He took a sip of his wine and settled back. "I'm ready."

"For what?"

"For a report on your accomplishments at the county record keeper's this afternoon?"

"You're on!" Cynthia reached over and pulled a notepad out of her purse. "Our camouflaged factory is in block seven-twenty-three, lot six, in case you care. I took that morsel of information, just as you instructed, and went to the deed book.

"Now, that was the high point of the day—not, I'm afraid, because of what I uncovered, but just because it's fascinating. A history of property sales with names and dates. Somehow, it made the old barn come alive. The first recorded sale was in nineteen-oh-two.

"Then," she went on, looking down at her notes, "we go through six other deals—five sales, one mortgage foreclosure—until . . ."—she ran her finger down the list—"nineteen eighty-four, when it was bought from Girard Wisolocki by the F. C. Corporation."

Jed frowned. "The what?"

"My reaction exactly!" Cynthia shrugged. "It just said the 'F. C. Corporation, a Netherlands/Antilles Corporation.'"

Jed groaned. "An offshore company."

"But what does that mean? Why is a Dutch company using fifteen illegal immigrants in the United States to perform some . . . some process?"

Jed sat still thinking. "You don't know it's a Dutch company. It could be an American company hiding behind a foreign name. Was there any address for 'F. C. Corporation'?"

"Yes. A bank in Antilles. I wrote it down."

Jed turned to her. "Maybe Wisolocki—the guy who sold the land—knows more."

Cynthia looked back down at her notepad. "I tried that. I found a Wisolocki in the county phone book—a Helen, though, not a Girard. She turned out to be a cousin of the man who sold the land. Her cousin is retired in a trailer park in Florida. But she gave

me the name of the real-estate firm that handled the transaction."
She turned the page of her notepad. "Willaman Company. I called
them. The agent that handled the deal is no longer with the firm.
They had an address—tax bills are sent to the same address—a
bank in Antilles." She put down her notebook. "That's it."

Jed was shaking his head. "Sure sounds shadey to me."

"Do we have enough chili to invite Carlos Ramirez over for
dinner?" Cynthia asked. "I told him I'd let him know what I
found out."

"Hell, when I cook, I really cook!" Jed laughed. "We have
enough chili to feed the whole van!"

Carlos Ramirez arrived bursting with energy. He smiled as
Cynthia introduced him to Jed, but it was a distracted smile. All
the time he was cordially pumping Jed's hand, he was jabbering
away to Cynthia. He had done what she'd suggested, and he had
done some really interesting results, *very* interesting results!

"You know, for the first time since I got out of high school,
I've been using my mind!" he announced as they sat down at the
dinner table. "And it's incredible. I realize now I was getting
kind of mentally dulled out, know what I mean?"

Cynthia opened her mouth to speak as Jed ladled out the
chili, but Carlos went on, oblivious. "First of all, you were right.
It *is* a chemical."

Jed looked up. "What's a chemical?"

"The liquid. The hot liquid at the factory they wash the
parts in. Francisco—he's chief washer—he says it's a hot chemical. No one knows the name, but all the guys who work around it
have to use thick rubber gloves for protection."

Cynthia frowned, shaking her head. "That makes it a whole
different ball game, Carlos. That means—"

"Wait, there's more!" He swooshed the spoon around excitedly in the bowl of chili in front of him. "Remember how I told
you that Pablo—the guy who works with me loading the parts—
that Pablo went bananas one night too? Remember I said that up
until that time Pablo had been completely normal, like me?"

"Yes?"

"Well, like I said, I started thinking." Carlos pushed his chair
back, as though preparing for a presentation. "What, I asked

myself, was different that night? What did Pablo do that was different? And it came to me, just like that! The night he went crazy, Pablo had been given the assignment of loading the tank."

Cynthia shook her head, confused. "What does that mean?"

"This tank-truck comes every week to the back of the factory— the truck, I realize, has to be bringing in the chemical—and someone gets chosen to unload the stuff in it into the factory pipes. It's a real easy job. You just attach this nozzle from the truck to a receptacle. It's kind of like putting gas in your car. Anyway, the night Pablo got the job was the night he became dazed, irritable, you know— spaced out—when he got back into the van?"

Jed looked up at Cynthia sternly over his chili. "Did you know all this?"

"No, I—"

"No, see, no one knew it really, because I wasn't thinking!" Carlos went on, "I mean, there it all was, in front of me, and I just stood there, a dimwit like all the others." He turned from Cynthia to Jed. "You know, I read an article once about how you have to exercise your mind, just like your body, or it all turns to mush. Well, I think with this job and the other one—the one at the restaurant—my mind was beginning to disintegrate." He shook his head and scooped up a spoonful of chili. "Man, I'm glad you made me start thinking again."

As Carlos swallowed the chili, he immediately began coughing. His eyes teared. He drank some water, but the coughing continued. "Very hot chili!" he said to Jed in a choked voice.

"Try some lettuce," Jed suggested, pointing to the salad bowl. "Lettuce usually works."

Carlos took some lettuce, and some more water, and gradually the coughing subsided.

"Don't you eat a lot of hot food?" Jed asked.

"Mexicans do, El Salvadorans, not so much. This," Carlos gasped, pointing to the bowl, "this is Mexican."

"Actually, it's Iowan," Cynthia said brightly.

"You know, this might be a good time to tell Carlos what *your* mind-expanding research has yielded," Jed sang out across the table to Cynthia. "You might not get a chance, once he stops choking on his food!"

Carlos laughed a little sheepishly. Cynthia told him about

her trip to the county clerk's office, and Jed explained his suspicions about the name of the company.

"Why hide ownership?" Carlos asked.

"Probably because they are doing something pretty damn illegal!" Jed said.

"Wow! This gets better all the time!" Carlos turned to Cynthia, his dark eyes sparkling. "This could be a really big story for you after all, don't you think?"

Cynthia nodded. "Could be."

Jed stirred his chili around, thinking. "Hey, I don't want to ruin the fun, but I think you have a responsibility to report this place to the government."

Carlos gasped. "The government?"

Jed nodded. "The labor department has an agency—the Occupational Safety and Health Administration, or 'OSHA' as it's called—that has rules for safety in the work place, including what precautions must be taken if the workers are dealing with chemicals."

"But we don't know for certain—" Carlos protested.

"We know enough to know something's wrong. Hell, that's what you two are all excited about, isn't it? The chance we may have some sort of chemical bomb here? Some life-threatening impropriety? Isn't that the stuff big stories are made of?"

"What would this 'OSHA' do if you reported the factory?" Carlos asked Jed.

"Check it out."

"After perhaps warning the owner first," Cynthia said, looking pointedly at Jed.

"Cynthia . . ."

"No, really. There have been stories of OSHA inspectors on the take." She stared Jed down. "Isn't it just possible someone in the local office has *already* been paid off?"

"Possible," Jed admitted.

"And, even if not," Carlos broke in. "If they inspected, they would turn all the workers over to Immigration, wouldn't they?"

"Possibly," Jed conceded.

Carlos sighed. "So then the workers lose two ways. They lose their high wages, and they get into trouble at the same time. Perhaps they lose any chance to earn money."

"If the place is really dangerous," Jed pointed out, "doing that might save their lives."

Carlos looked up at Jed and laughed. "What lives? You don't understand. I've been interviewing these guys. They have no real lives. For them, earning that pay—sending money home—that's it, man. That is their whole life!" He looked from one to the other, shaking his head. "You just wouldn't believe it. Most of these guys can't even read. None can speak English. They came here in car trunks, most of 'em. They have no idea, even, where they are. 'Have you seen the Capitol building?' I ask them. 'The what?' they say. They live on streets and in flophouses, biding their time until they can report to work, to get the money, to send back to Latin America. It's unbelievable, really." He turned to Jed. "And now you want to end the only thing they have going for them!"

"The kid thinks he's some kind of Peace Corps volunteer. He's fascinated by the customs of the subculture!" Jed said to Cynthia, then he turned to Carlos. "Look, *you* have a life, don't you? *You* want to keep going? To have a future?"

"Of course."

"Well, then, don't you think you should worry about yourself and what might happen to you if these suspicions are confirmed?"

Carlos's eyes flashed at Jed. "I'm at the end of the line, far from the chemical. I have no signs of craziness!" He swallowed. "I'm willing to take a chance. To keep going—for the story."

"You're eighteen years old. You feel indestructible. But, for Chrissakes, Carlos, this isn't journalism school we're talking about!" Jed stormed. "This is a possibly lethal situation." He looked up at Cynthia for support. She looked away, and his anger intensified. "Is this normal for you?" he asked her across the table. "Do you usually go to such lengths, take such chances with other people's lives, just to get your bloody story?"

"But we don't know for sure—"

"But you have to be hoping for the worst!" Jed shouted. "Otherwise you wouldn't be interested!"

"It's just . . ." Carlos stared down at the tablecloth. "It's just that for the first time since high school, I'm thinking again."

"Well, enjoy it while you can." Jed sneered. "Too many powerful whiffs of whatever that chemical is, and your thinking days may be numbered."

"I don't work near the chemical!"

Cynthia looked nervously at Jed. "You admitted, Jed, that an OSHA official could be on the take already. How about if we compromise. We try to get as much proof as quickly as possible, to make a case—if, in fact, there is a case to be made—before reporting the place."

"And how do you go about doing that?"

"Carlos," Cynthia said after thinking for a while, "do you think you could you sneak out a sample of that chemical?"

"I could try." Carlos frowned. "You mean just scoop some up in a jar and bring it home?"

"Right. Just make sure it has a tight-sealing lid," Cynthia cautioned. "And for heaven's sake, don't put it in your lunch box! We'll take it to a commercial lab or something and get it analyzed."

Jed looked across at her, his irritation suddenly transformed into admiration. "Good for you," he said softly. "I hadn't thought of that. That's a very smart idea. That way we'll know for sure, and have proof too, if, in fact, it is a dangerous chemical."

Carlos looked at his watch and jumped up. It was time to leave for work.

"I'm sorry," Jed said softly, when Cynthia walked back to the table. "I came down pretty hard on you."

She shrugged.

"You're angry."

"Well, hurt. A little. I'm really *not* this coldhearted, blood-sucking reporter you seem to want to make me into. I wouldn't take a chance with someone's life. I just think in this case . . ."

"Okay, okay! My bagel/croissant complex surfacing again! What can I say?"

"Don't say anything." She passed Jed her empty bowl and grinned. "Just serve me some more chili."

"You want more?" Jed asked in disbelief. "Carlos barely touched his." He grunted. "The kid was clearly more frightened by the chili than the chemical!"

"It's all regional." She laughed. "A Latin-American just doesn't have the stomach to handle Midwestern chili." Cynthia played with her wine glass for a while and then looked up at Jed. "I freed up my schedule for Saturday." She spoke shyly. "I'd really like to do something with the three of you. If you still want to."

"Sure. Sure, I do. Lisa and Timmy are both primed for it." He seemed suddenly restless. Cynthia decided she was imagining it.

"You know," she began with excitement, "I thought maybe tomorrow night we could—"

"No plans!" Jed began shoveling chili into his mouth. From his tone, she knew she had not been imagining it. "Let's not . . . I should probably just go back to my apartment and, you know"— he laughed self-consciously—"clean out the cobwebs before I bring Lisa and Timmy back Friday night."

"I'll come too! I can help!"

"No. I mean . . . well, maybe. We'll see. Let's not plan. Why do you always want to plan?"

She felt as though she had been slapped in the face.

He ate some more. "Maybe we should separate a little before, well, you know."

She nodded, but she did not know. One step forward, one step back. He had made himself an extra key to her apartment, but at the same time was making plans for leaving. Why was she nodding? "Before what?" she asked finally. It took her a while to get up the courage.

He shrugged. "Before we get sick of each other."

"Are you getting sick of me?" She felt foolish as soon as she'd blurted it out. Not only foolish, vulnerable.

"No. Don't be ridiculous. Not at all. No."

His eyes exuded sincerity, but she was not convinced. She looked away, trying to make sense of these sudden radical fluctuations—the steps forward and then backward.

She sipped her wine, and reminded herself that the backward steps always came at the high moments. After a wonderful night, and during a cozy breakfast Jed would suddenly announce he might not be able to make it back to her apartment that night.

Yet he always came in the end, she reminded herself. But was he just being kind? Was he getting sick of her?

He stirred his chili. "It's . . . it's . . ."

She leaned forward. "It's what?"

He gave her an irritated look. "Why do you always want me to put things into words?"

A lawyer accusing her of always wanting to put things into

words! She saw the humor, but she felt something quite different. She felt rejection.

"Good news," Jed called out to her later, as he carried the chili pot into the kitchen. "There's enough left over for dinner tomorrow night!"

Cynthia kept her eyes on the dishes she was rinsing in the sink. She wondered whether there was enough for dinner for one or dinner for two. She decided not to ask.

# · 15 ·

Lisa Farber's head was turned completely away from the three of them. All Cynthia could see was short dark hair curling under slightly where it hit the zipped-up collar of her ski jacket. All Lisa could see was a blank wall approximately six inches from her nose.

"Where the hell is our lunch?" Jed growled, looking around for the waitress. "We've been here for hours."

In truth, it only seemed like hours. Cynthia tried to think of something upbeat to say to ease the tension around the table, especially Jed's. She was dying for Jed, who had tried so hard to make it all work, but whose attempts seemed to trigger emotional land mines that kept exploding on him. "Saturday morning with the kids" had turned out to be a comedy of errors, and was ending up a very black comedy indeed.

Cynthia looked at Timmy's frozen face, at the back of Lisa's head, at Jed's expression of unmitigated agony, and she felt paralyzed. She could not think of a thing to say.

She saw the waitress approaching with their lunch platters and prayed food might turn the tide.

The platters were served in total silence.

"Lisa, your lunch is here!" Jed called out.

"Not hungry," Lisa replied without moving her head.

"Lisa," Jed said through clenched teeth, "I said your food is here."

"And I said," Lisa retorted, imitating his tone as she stared at the wall, "that I am not hungry."

Jed tightened his fist, and opened his mouth. In reflex, Cynthia reached out across the table and put her hand on his fist. He looked up at her and, heeding the expression in her eyes, shut his mouth. The muscle in his jaw tightened as he ground his teeth.

Timmy's frightened brown eyes moved from Cynthia to Jed as he popped a wad of french fried potatoes into his mouth.

"Goddamn it, Timmy, use a fork!" Jed shouted.

Timmy jumped involuntarily. He put his hands in his lap and bent his head down forlornly over his food.

Jed looked at Cynthia. "I forgot to ask the waitress where your coffee was."

"It's okay," Cynthia said brightly. "I don't really need—"

"You wanted coffee. You'll *get* coffee!" Jed yelled. He stood up and threw his napkin on the table. "I'm going to the men's room," he announced. "I'll order your coffee on my way."

As he sauntered off, the table's occupants thawed somewhat. Lisa turned away from the wall. Timmy looked up.

"Lisa," Cynthia said softly, "you must be roasting. Why don't you take off your ski jacket?"

"Why?" Lisa's huge dark eyes raged. "Then I'll expose my undershirt!"

Cynthia smiled, suppressing laughter. "He was kidding, I think. Don't you?"

"Well, if he was, it wasn't funny," Lisa announced. Begrudgingly she removed her ski jacket, revealing a blue turtleneck sweater over which she was wearing a large white jersey that looked like an undershirt meant for a much larger person. It had the store name BENNETON written in bold letters across the chest.

"It *does* look like an undershirt!" Timmy giggled.

Lisa gave her brother a look that could kill.

"The problem is, you and your father are males," Cynthia said. "You guys don't know anything about female fashion."

Timmy grinned broadly as though he had just received the ultimate compliment.

"That," Cynthia said, pointing to Lisa's shirt, but trying not to look at it in order to deliver the line with conviction, "that is an ultimate fashion statement."

Timmy grinned. "Dad said it looked like an undershirt with someone else's name on it."

"'Benneton' is a very hip name." Cynthia tried to sound as though she meant it.

Lisa picked up a french fry. "It sure cost more than an undershirt."

"Don't tell him how much it cost!" Timmy wailed. "He'll kill us all!"

Cynthia laughed and picked up her hamburger. "You know, Lisa, when I was a little older than you, miniskirts were the 'in' thing."

"What's a miniskirt?" Timmy asked.

"A very, very short skirt—one that stops about halfway down your thigh."

"Wow!"

"Anyway, I lived in a small town, and they didn't have much in the way of fashion, so I sent away for a pattern and bought the material, and I cut and sewed and made myself the most incredibly gorgeous miniskirt you ever saw." Cynthia stared off dreamily. "It was red corduroy." She turned to Lisa. "You know what my father said when I put it on to wear to the school football dance?"

Lisa shook her head.

"'No daughter of mine's leaving this house dolled up like a cheap, half-naked tart!'" Cynthia remembered him bellowing. She shook her head. "Can you imagine how I felt?"

Lisa gasped. "What did you do?"

"Well, I don't know what my immediate reaction was, but I do know that I spent the rest of the night crying in my room, and I missed the dance."

"How come?" Timmy asked.

"Because he said I couldn't wear it, and I said then I wouldn't go!"

"Did you hate him?" Timmy asked eagerly.

"That night—you bet I did!"

Lisa looked at Cynthia with both sympathy and approval.

"When did you stop?" Timmy asked.

"Oh, pretty soon. Because I really loved him anyway, and he just didn't understand that miniskirts were the style. He thought it looked strange, and he wanted me to look great." She shrugged. "I guess because he loved me too."

Lisa looked away and said nothing.

Damn, Cynthia thought, I blew it with the ending. Not subtle enough.

Timmy looked at Lisa. "You're just upset because you fell on your butt!" he giggled.

Lisa glared at him.

"Well, you only fell because you were trying to show off," Timmy whined. "Dad's right! A pavement's no place for a cartwheel!"

Cynthia's heart sank as she noticed Lisa's head turning back to the wall. "Aren't we all trying to show off?" she asked, desperate to stop Lisa's withdrawal.

They both looked at her. It had worked. Now where was she going to go with it? Honesty, she decided. That was all that was left. She swallowed hard. Her throat was dry. "I am," she confessed uncomfortably. "I've heard so much about the two of you, and I know how crazy your father is about you . . . I—I wanted to show off so you'd think I was great."

Timmy frowned in contemplation. "You haven't showed off. You've hardly said anything."

"I know," Cynthia said, wondering how she could possibly be saying this. "I was going to be clever and funny, but I've been too nervous."

Timmy cocked his head to one side. "Nervous about meeting us?" He seemed to like the idea.

"Nervous about whether you would like me."

For the first time all morning, Cynthia saw a softness in Lisa's eyes. "Oh, you don't have to be nervous," Lisa whispered. The softness vanished. "Dad's certainly not nervous!"

Cynthia's eyes opened wide. "No? You don't think so?"

Lisa considered the possibility.

"Does he usually behave this way?" Cynthia asked.

"Well, he can be a real grouch," Lisa conceded, "but never like this."

"Have you ever seen *him* eat french fries with a fork?" Cynthia asked Timmy.

"No!" Timmy whined righteously. "That's what I was thinkin' when he yelled at me!"

"What's he nervous about?" Lisa asked.

Cynthia took a bite of her hamburger. "I think he wants us to like each other, and, well, everything's gone wrong. First the car broke down, then the roller-skating rink was closed for repairs—"

"Then the cartwheel!" Timmy piped up.

"And the more things went wrong," Cynthia went on quickly, "the more tense we all got."

"And the more he yelled!" Lisa reminded her.

Cynthia looked deeply into Lisa's big, dark brown eyes, noting the fiery sparks, desperate to transform them into compassion. "He's so nervous," Cynthia said softly. "He wants to show you off. He wants me to see how special you two really are, and he can't figure out how to make it happen. The harder he tries, the harder we all try, the more messed up it seems to get."

Lisa's anger seemed to subside. Cynthia saw her eyes grow sympathetic, or at least she thought she did. Perhaps it was just wishful thinking.

Lisa looked away and played with her hamburger bun.

Cynthia looked up in time to see Jed walking back to the table. His jaw was still clenched, his body stiff, and he was rubbing his stomach. "He's nervous," Cynthia mumbled, giving it one last try. "He's so nervous."

"Did you get your coffee?" he asked irritably as he sat down.

"Yup," Cynthia said gaily. "I finished it already!"

Lisa and Timmy giggled.

Jed looked in Lisa's direction and appeared relieved to see her face. "Lisa," he said, clearing his throat, "I was teasing about the, uh, shirt. It looks real nice."

"Daddy." Lisa waited until his eyes met hers. "Daddy, we've all decided to try to relax a little."

"Yeah?" Jed's eyes roamed hopefully around the table. "Good idea!"

"Hey, Dad?" Timmy chirped, gazing down into his father's platter. "You gonna eat those fries with a fork?"

Jed broke into laughter and shook his head.

"Didn't think so!" Timmy grinned, reaching down to his own plate and plucking up a french fry with his fingers.

Francisco Lopez thought he was forty-five years old. He was not sure. His mother had always tried to make him a little older than he was, to give his birth legitimacy. But he was sure he had been born more than a year after his father's death. So, yes, he figured that would make him about forty-five, but it was not important.

Having Cynthia interview Francisco had been Carlos's idea. He said of all the men in the van, Francisco was the most articulate and the most interesting. Now, sitting across her living-room coffee table from Mr. Lopez, Cynthia was beginning to comprehend how thoroughly inarticulate the others must be, if this one was the prize.

The acrid stench of the unfiltered cigarettes Francisco was chain-smoking were giving her a terrible headache, and a half-hour into the interview, she had got nothing but abstract answers to the two simplest questions on her long list: age and place of birth.

"How many children does he have?" she asked.

Carlos translated the question and Francisco went through what seemed to be a very difficult process of tabulation.

Cynthia looked at him. He was a tiny man—tiny in height, but thick in girth. Swollen, Cynthia decided. He looked swollen. His eyes were tiny slivers surrounded by soft fleshy eyelids above and bags below. His short fingers seemed almost crippled in their movement by the excess of flesh. There was also a strange flakiness to the skin on his hands, as though his fingers were in a chronic state of peeling. He had no wrists. And he was breathing with difficulty.

"Eleven children," Carlos translated. "He has eleven children."

"How old is the youngest?" Cynthia asked.

Carlos translated the question and Cynthia saw Francisco's expression change completely. The cockiness vanished. The man's breaths came quicker. Francisco looked down at his cigarette and said nothing for a while. Then, when he began to speak, the words were faltering, tentative. Cynthia leaned forward to hear Carlos's translation.

"'I do not know for certain. I met a man from my village here a few weeks ago, and he told me I had a new baby—less than one year old.'"

It took a few seconds for the gist of the statement to register on Cynthia. Francisco had not been home for more than two years. "I'm sorry," she said compassionately. "You must be very upset."

When Carlos finished translating, Francisco snorted a laugh, and said something.

"'Either that or I have a very long pecker!'" Carlos translated.

The solemn expression on Cynthia's face cracked. "Why did he leave Guatemala?"

"He says he had to," Carlos reported back. "He was a wanted man."

"Why?"

"For his union activities," Carlos reported. "He says he joined a trade union at the plant he was working at, and then suddenly one night they started killing the union leaders."

"Who killed them?" Cynthia asked. "Did they find the murderers?"

Francisco laughed. "'No one was looking,'" Carlos translated. "'It was us they were looking for—the other union sympathizers. That's why I had to leave—and quickly. I heard the police were looking for me.'"

"How did you leave?"

Francisco shrugged. Carlos translated. "'I left.'"

"But how?" Cynthia turned to Carlos. "How did he manage to get to the United States?"

Carlos asked Francisco. Francisco stared at the smoke rising from his cigarette for a long time. Finally he spoke, his eyes still down.

Carlos translated. "'I was lucky. There was a Guatemalan who looked something like me who had a visa for the United States. He had been living in the United States, but he was visiting in Guatemala.'"

Cynthia frowned. "He *gave* you his visa?"

The translation came back: "'In a way . . .'"

Cynthia leaned forward. "How did he get the man's visa?" she asked Carlos. Carlos translated.

Francisco shifted uncomfortably on the sofa. Finally he looked up at Cynthia—looked her straight in the eye for the first time all night. He clenched his jaw.

*"Lo mate."*

Cynthia did not know the words, but somehow she knew what he had said before Carlos gasped the translation. "He killed him!"

Cynthia sat speechless.

Carlos now leaned forward, furiously spewing out his own questions in Spanish. The two men screamed back and forth for a while and then the conversation calmed down. Carlos stood up and began walking around the room, visibly shaken. Francisco kept firing away in Spanish to Carlos.

"What, Carlos?" Cynthia asked as she stared at Francisco. "What is he saying?"

Carlos kept walking. "He says he did not kill the man for the visa. He killed the man because the man was going to turn him in, because he was desperate, desperate to live because if he died, the money would die, and his family would die. He says feeding his family is the only thing that he lives for, and he will kill again, any time he has to, if it means feeding his family."

"Is it possible," Cynthia asked Carlos, "that he was wanted by the police because he was a murderer, and not because of the union?"

Still pacing, Carlos translated the question. Holding his head high, Francisco stared at Cynthia as he answered.

"He says that in Guatemala, belonging to a union is a crime. Murder is not."

Cynthia and Francisco sat staring at each other. After a while, Carlos sat back down at the table.

Cynthia asked more questions. For one and a half years, Francisco's life in Washington had involved moving from flophouse to flophouse, and working what could only be called the periphery of the U.S. job market.

He had scraped fish, washed restaurant dishes by hand for twelve hours nonstop, pimped for two young Latin hookers who had run out on him, scrubbed floors, and recycled leftover food in one neighborhood restaurant Cynthia vowed to remove from her list of possible eating places. He had gathered empty beer cans for a return of five cents on the pound, and labored at very low levels in an assortment of construction, carpeting, floor-finishing, painting, and window-pane companies.

Then one year ago, good fortune had come in the form of the chemical vat job at the factory. It provided good money for easy work, and the chance to obtain the only thing that mattered to him: the money order purchased at the local liquor store that he sent promptly back to Guatemala. Success had come to Francisco Lopez.

"Does he hear from his family?" Cynthia asked. "Do they write regularly?"

Carlos asked. "'Why should they write?' he says. 'I cannot read.'"

"What does he do for pleasure?"

Pleasure? Francisco seemed confused. Carlos rephrased the question. It took two more rephrasings before there was an answer. "'Well, until this job, I was working two, sometimes three jobs a day, and had time for nothing but work and sleep. Now I have time, but not much. And I don't feel like doing much.'"

"Why?"

"'Lately, I have not felt too good,'" Carlos translated.

"Since when?" Cynthia asked.

"He says for a few months now," Carlos reported back.

"In what way?"

Carlos asked. Francisco mumbled a few things and then shook his head.

"'I eat little,' he says. 'But I get fat, fat in the joints of my fingers and legs, even. I am always now sick in my stomach, and very, very tired, always very tired, and yet unable to sleep.'"

Francisco tugged Carlos's arm and added something. He laughed loudly.

"He says it's sort of funny. For years he yearned for sleep but had no time. Now he has time, but cannot sleep."

After Carlos and Francisco left, Cynthia sat very still in her living room, staring into space, going over and over the interview. She did not replay it from her tape recorder. She did not need to.

\*   \*   \*

The presence of Jed in Cynthia's life brightened everything. She was on a high. For the first time she had found someone she wanted to wake up with every morning and go to sleep with every night, someone she enjoyed sitting around talking to for hours on end. She was abandoning her old protective reflexes, and doing so intentionally.

Sometime over the weekend, Jed had apparently stopped thinking and permitted himself the luxury of behaving impulsively. It took a herculean effort, but yielded readily apparent results: breakfast with him while his children were at Sunday school, then lunch and the afternoon with Lisa and Timmy. After he dropped off his children at their mother's house Sunday night, he returned to Cynthia's, with a suitcase.

While they never seemed to stop talking when they were together, certain subjects were off-limits: Nothing was said about the suitcase, for instance. Nothing was said about the escalation in their relationship. Cynthia sensed that Jed was trying not to notice what he was doing, and she did not want to do anything to make him notice. She who prided herself on her independence, now delighted in needing him—for advice, for commiseration, for comfort, for laughter.

Sunday night was followed by Monday night, and at breakfast Tuesday, Jed even went so far as to make plans, suggesting he and Cynthia take in a concert that night. He had an appointment with his "gangster" client, Ted Selebri, at Selebri's factory in Baltimore early in the morning, but, he told Cynthia, he was certain he would be back in Washington early that afternoon.

Cynthia had lunch on Tuesday with Mary Boynton, a long-winded public relations honcho who regularly tried to interest Cynthia in doing stories on her clients. Usually Cynthia found the sessions with Mary tedious and predictable, but this time she found herself actually jotting down a story idea or two.

As she left Mary Boynton and walked down Connecticut Avenue toward the subway stop at Farragut Square, she ignored the icy air, and focused instead on the yellow glow that was flickering down from the sky. Sunshine, glorious sunshine. She turned her face up toward the warmth.

Suddenly, she felt a heavy hand thud on her shoulder.

Startled, she whirled around, and then gasped in relief. "Chris!"

"That'll teach you not to walk around with your head in the clouds!" Chris Channing chuckled. He was wearing a dark gray overcoat with the collar pulled up. "Where are you going?"

"To the subway. Back to work. I just had lunch with Mary Boynton."

Channing took Cynthia's arm and led her to a bench at the edge of Farragut Square. "Come sit for a moment. I tried calling you, but it's a little hard to get through with that Jed character fielding all your calls!" He pulled her down on the bench beside him.

"That was last week," Cynthia corrected him. "And by the time I called you back, you had gone out of town on assignment again. Here I've been monitoring Gardiner's assignments, just as you asked me to, and when I try to report back, you're traveling!" She told him about the right-wing slant Capitol Radio reports had taken recently. He was not surprised. She had a funny feeling he had known without her telling him. When she finished, the sun was behind a cloud, and she was getting cold. "All right," she groaned, thrusting her hands into her pockets, "is the new backer a conservative? What have you found out?" She wanted to speed up the conversation.

Chris made a face. "Too much."

"What do you mean?" she asked, shivering and burrowing deeper into her coat.

"Well, Gardiner *has* found a rich conservative backer. The latest Capitol Radio phone bill shows repeated calls by Gardiner to this person starting in December, then intensifying in January. Sometime late in January, around the week beginning January twenty-seventh, the tables turned. Gardiner began getting calls from this person, and receiving all kinds of mailings."

Cynthia wiggled her toes. Her feet were beginning to feel like solid chunks of ice in her boots. She suddenly put together what Chris had said and his lack of surprise over her report. "Sylvia!" she shouted. "You've got to have Sylvia helping on this!"

"Don't be silly."

"Where else would you get a Capitol Radio phone bill? Who else would know about incoming calls and letters?"

"Sources aren't important," Chris snapped. "What's important is that it appears Gardiner isn't soliciting funds for Capitol Radio from this guy, he's soliciting a job for himself."

"How do you know that?"

"He and his wife went out to Ames, Iowa, last weekend—where the new benefactor lives—to look at houses. Gardiner's wife is looking for a job at the university there. I know, at least, that she's sent out a resumé."

Cynthia felt the February chill penetrating her entire body. Her lips began to chatter.

Chris went on, oblivious. "Anyway, it looks bad for both of us. You may be out of a job, and I have no story. If Gardiner were compromising a news outfit to make a buck, that would be a story. But taking a new job?" He shrugged.

"Who is the guy?" Cynthia asked through her shivers.

Chris winked at her. "See if you can guess by your assignments. I'm still hoping Gardiner will come through for me, and tamper with operations enough to give me a journalistic excuse to do him in."

Cynthia was disturbed by the facts, but she was so cold, she couldn't sit any longer. She stood up shuddering. "I'm freezing!"

Channing stared at her in shock. "You do look absolutely frozen," he said apologetically. He reached over and began rubbing her arms and back as she stood immobile before him. "Has the blood completely stopped flowing in your extremities, or does it just seem that way?" He took her gloved hand. "Is anything still alive in there?"

"Don't worry about me. If my fingers've died, I'll just dictate from now on."

They both giggled, and Chris gave her a hug. When he let go, she straightened his coat collar, which had got rumpled.

"We don't want NBC's ultimate sex symbol looking frazzled here." She paused for a moment and looked at him seriously. "What am I going to do if Gardiner closes Capitol Radio?"

"Frankly, I'm not worried about you," he said brusquely.

Cynthia gave him a hurt look.

"Hey, no, you're misreading me. How many times have I told you that for someone with your talent, Capitol Radio was a waste of time? You should either be free-lancing full-time, or working for an outfit worthy of you. This could give you the push you've needed. And my guess is that once forced to leave the security blanket of the regular paycheck, your adrenaline would really flow and you'd take off."

His dark blue eyes were intense, his face dead serious. He looked rather adorable puffing away so earnestly about her virtues. She kissed him on the cheek. "Let's continue this discussion later—preferably in a heated room!" She smiled at him affectionately and hurried toward the metro.

# · 16 ·

Ted Selebri had asked Jed to come out and see his Synco plant in Baltimore as a learning experience, a "physical introduction to the ball-bearing business," the man had called it.

Jed decided it had been very physical indeed. Visual, really. His head whirled with visions of discs holding little silver balls as they meandered down assembly lines: double-row bearings, self-aligning bearings, bearings, bearings, bearings. . . .

Damned if he could tell the difference.

As Jed drove back from the plant, he was disquieted by the fact that Selebri seemed to be less than certain himself. The "factory tour" had been vintage Selebri—more show than savvy. There were big pats on the back for foremen ("My main man, here!"), but despite the boisterous shows of camaraderie, Jed had noted that Selebri had trouble with many of his "main men's" names, and seemed equally hazy on some of the factory procedures.

Second generation, Jed growled to himself. Obviously, while Selebri's father had been toiling away in the factory, Ted Selebri had been out studying fine wines. The result was a chief executive officer with drive but without smarts.

Selebri waxed poetic about "cost cutting," but the only change he had made in the plant since his father had died two years ago had been to create a posh suite of executive offices. He talked incessantly about his determination to go "high tech" but was abstract at best when pushed for specifics.

He was the same way when asked about what kind of legal help he wanted. "Nothing yet," the man had replied. "I'll call you when I need you."

Well, Jed decided, he was in no hurry to answer his telephone.

He didn't like Selebri. He didn't like the man's old-world, tough-guy technique, and he didn't like his hollow, new-world jargon. Something inside told Jed that if, indeed, mankind was on the verge of building a better ball bearing, it was *not* going to be done at Synco. He also suspected Selebri's Mid-Atlantic monopoly had been acquired through low blows, not high tech.

As he got closer to his office, Jed hit a traffic backup at the busy intersection on Connecticut Avenue. He lectured himself for not remembering to turn off before he got to K Street. Too much thinking.

Resigning himself to at least temporary immobility, Jed relaxed and looked out the side window of his car. He saw a very familiar figure in a blue down coat standing at the edge of Farragut Square. He blinked. Yes, it was unmistakably Cynthia. A few strands of blond hair were blowing over her eyes. The tip of her nose was bright red. Jed smiled affectionately. It always got that way when she was out in the cold for a long time.

She was talking to a man who had his back to Jed. As Jed watched, the man bent over Cynthia, rubbing her arms, hugging her, in a way. Well, not really hugging.

Jed's throat went dry. Yes. It was hugging. What else could you call a hug?

The man stopped and Cynthia reached up and straightened the collar of the man's coat. The way she did it, the gesture was kind of personal.

Jed sat very still in his car, mesmerized by the blue eyes that were now opened wide, hurt, almost, staring up just the way they stared up at him, but they were not staring at him. They were focused on some stranger.

All Jed could see was light brown hair and a thick, masculine neck. But that was enough. It was, quite frankly, entirely too much.

Then her eyes got sunny, happy-looking, lighting up the way only Cynthia's eyes lit up. Something the son-of-a-bitch had said had made her happy. Who the hell was he? Then she leaned over and kissed the son-of-a-bitch on the cheek. Actually kissed him. Jed had trouble breathing.

Vaguely, in the back of his mind, Jed heard noise, but he was lost in the scene he had witnessed. The noise got louder, angry car horns were sounding off behind him. He realized the light had changed, and he was holding up traffic. Automatically, he switched his car into gear and moved on. His body was throbbing.

The lunchtime travelers had already come and gone, leaving the subway practically empty by the time Cynthia got on. Cynthia knew she was late, but she also knew it didn't matter. She had finished writing and recording the news story before she left for lunch, and the feature piece was an "evergreen," a story with no time constraints. She could always finish it tomorrow morning if there wasn't enough time today.

"No rush," Gardiner had said.

Seated next to the metro door, Cynthia was overwhelmed by a sense of "no rush." She stared at a teenager across the aisle for a while, mentally making him older, with dark hair and a dimple in his chin. It was only when the boy looked up self-consciously that she realized she had been smiling at him.

She leaned back in the seat and stared at the ceiling, feeling the metro's rumbling movement, vaguely aware of the anonymous bodies filing in and out at each stop, and she tried to think of another time in her life when she had felt so content, so happy to be who she was and where she was, satisfied it was today, rather than yearning for either yesterday or tomorrow.

Today, then tonight, then tomorrow morning. She wanted to have it all go slowly, so she could savor each part of it. She felt so unprecedentedly content.

"Hey, isn't this your stop?"

The deep male voice coming from the doorway jolted her.

She whirled around and looked through the metro window at the sign on the platform. It was her stop.

After she scrambled out of her seat, the familiar voice in the doorway registered.

No.

Her eyes snapped to attention.

Yes!

She gaped open-mouthed at the tall man with blond hair and a tanned face who was standing firmly in the train's entry to keep the doors from closing before she could get out.

How long, she wondered, had he been standing right there next to her? The object of her former fantasies had turned into reality, and she had been completely oblivious!

"Oh, thanks," she gasped as she sped past him. "Really, thanks!"

He walked out after her and followed her to the escalator.

"I can't believe I was so out of it I almost missed my stop," she mumbled over her right shoulder.

"I swear, at one point you looked right at me and didn't register who I was," he told her. "I was beginning to wonder if it was really you. Your mind was a million miles away!"

"That it was!"

"How've you been?" She was climbing the escalator and he was moving quickly to keep up with her.

"Great. I've been just great."

She stepped off the escalator and turned around to face him, at first astounded by the fact that she felt nothing, and then astounded by the fact that she had ever felt anything. She chalked it up to a lack of experience. Rob Diamond had entered her life at a time when she had not realized there was someone in the world as wonderful as Jed Farber.

The "golden boy" now had a decidedly bland look about him. "Thanks, Rob. I mean it! I'd probably be halfway to New Carrollton by now if it hadn't been for you!"

She waved "good-bye," and hurried off down the sidewalk.

"B. J.," she mused happily. Her life would forever be divided into two segments, "Before Jed" and "After Jed."

"Jed's daughter, Lisa, called," Sylvia Berg trilled out, waving a pink telephone message slip in Cynthia's direction when she walked into the office. "Lisa said she checked and you were right. Her father's birthday is February twenty-second."

Cynthia always wondered why Sylvia even bothered writing down messages when the woman committed them to memory so easily. But she smiled affectionately at Sylvia, warmed by the probability that Sylvia was Channing's coconspirator.

"Planning a little birthday party for Jed?" Sylvia snooped, sensing an entrée in Cynthia's smile.

"I don't know. Maybe. I did mention the possibility to Lisa last weekend." Cynthia hung up her coat. "Lisa says they've never celebrated his birthday. She didn't even know when it was."

"So, how did you find out?"

Cynthia laughed. "I saw it on his driver's license."

Sylvia perused the calendar on her desk. "That's the Sunday after this." She clasped her hands together on the desk in front of her. "I have an idea! How would you like to celebrate Jed's birthday at our cabin in West Virginia? Herb's always grumbling that no one ever uses it anymore, now that the boys are grown. It's right on a pond—a beautiful retreat this time of year."

"Well, Sylvia, that's very kind of you, but—"

"Such a lovely man, Jed, and, you said yourself, he's never had anyone celebrate his birthday. The cabin's only a two-hour drive from Washington, so you could leave Friday night and come back Sunday." Sylvia beamed. "A nice family weekend. A big birthday surprise."

"Well, it sounds—"

"Four bedrooms." Sylvia winked. "Very proper."

Cynthia started to protest, but stopped herself, suddenly realizing her resistance was a reflex response to Sylvia's meddling, a reflex that had no place in this discussion. This was a truly wonderful offer. Who cared if it was prompted by Sylvia Berg's overdeveloped matchmaking instincts?

The idea of a weekend—just the four of them—at a cabin in West Virginia, celebrating Jed's birthday . . .

"Well, thank you!" This time she said it with greater enthusiasm. "I'll talk to Jed about it." Cynthia headed toward the workroom and then turned around. "Really. Thanks, Sylvia!"

Cynthia was sitting at her desk dreamily contemplating a whole weekend in West Virginia when her telephone buzzed.

"Hello?"

"Cynthia?"

"Jed, are you back from the wilds of Baltimore?"

"I'm back. Sylvia said you just got back too. Where were you?"

Cynthia groaned. "Lunch. A little dull."

"Really? Who'd you have lunch with?"

"Mary Boynton. Do you know her? She has a big public relations firm and Gardiner thought it would be 'good to resume contact.'" She laughed at her imitation of Gardiner. There was a stillness on the other end of the line. "Jed, are you there?"

"Yes, I'm here. So you, uh, had lunch with Mary Boynton—just with her?"

"Yup."

"No one else?"

"Believe me, that was enough! How did your meeting go?"

"Okay—nothing special."

"Do you still want to try to get tickets for that concert tonight?"

"No, uh, that's why I called. I have to work late."

"Oh." Cynthia paused, the air suddenly knocked out of her. "Jed, is everything all right? You sound funny."

"Yeah . . . yeah. I guess it's just all the work I have to do."

"Well, I'll be there waiting when you finish!"

"I might, uh, might not be able to make it. I may have to work really late."

"I'll wait. No matter how late." She stopped, chilled by his silence. "It's easier to just come to my place than going all the way out to Bethesda, isn't it?"

"Well, maybe. I'll see. But, uh, don't wait up for me."

"Jed?"

"Yes?"

"What is it?"

"Nothing. Forget it."

Cynthia hung up the phone, trying not to remember that Jed had told her over breakfast he had a light workday ahead.

Jake Weinstein flashed a sardonic grin at Cynthia and plunged across his desk into her line of vision. "Hey, look on the bright side," Jake chirped. "Most women have to marry a man to make him want to stay at the office all night!"

One step forward, one step back. From high to low. From the possibility of a weekend in West Virginia to the possibility of not seeing him at all. Why did she always feel so devastated when he did this?

And why did he do it?

Work was Jed Farber's form of escape, and throughout Tuesday afternoon and evening he escaped, channeling his mental energy into legal matters, dulling the disturbing impulses from the other parts of his brain.

But even with work, every so often the other impulses haunted him. When he finished the brief and turned to his correspondence, when he put away one file and switched to another, he saw those wonderful azure eyes moving facilely from sadness to pleasure, sparkling in laughter. He saw her straightening the coat collar, softly, gently, with affection. He saw her looking up at that man the very same way she looked at him, and he could not stand it.

At about ten o'clock, he ran out of work, and he felt frightened, backed into a corner. He had no choice now. He had to think.

He walked aimlessly over to his office window and stared down below at the practically empty city streets.

Be practical. Why would she cheat on him? She wasn't married to him. No strings.

No strings? Hadn't he forced himself upon her, moving into her apartment, moving like an impetuous boor into her life, thoughtlessly taking up every second of her life, certain—without even asking—that she wanted what he wanted.

Why else would she have lied? He did not know Mary Boynton, had, in fact, never heard of a woman named Mary Boynton, but he knew full well that was *not* a Mary Boynton he had seen with Cynthia in Farragut Square.

He watched a car chug its way up the street, but it wasn't that that held his attention. It was an overwhelming sense of déjà vu.

With Anna he had been naive and blindly trusting. With Cynthia he had been neither. No, Cynthia was something else—a pursuit of pleasure. For a moment, he allowed himself to contemplate the pleasure. But only for a moment.

He had been equally blind, he reminded himself. In both cases, he had been foolish enough to believe that what he felt was mutual. What did it take, he asked the car waiting patiently at the stoplight, for him to realize that someone he desired might not find him equally desirable? He felt replaceable, eminently replaceable. And boorish. And foolish. He closed his eyes, unable to share the feeling even with the anonymous car waiting at the stoplight. So foolish.

He put on his coat. Home to Bethesda. He left his office and got into his car. He headed home, home to think, home to sleep. That was what he needed, a good night's sleep.

But the truth was, the only place he got a good night's sleep was in bed next to Cynthia, touching Cynthia, sensing her there with him under the comforter. He turned off at her street, refusing to admit to himself what he was doing.

As he walked down the hall to her apartment, he was faced with a dilemma. He had a key. But breaking into a woman's apartment at this hour of the night . . .

Instead he knocked softly. No answer. He started to use his key, but thought again of the man in Farragut Square. What if he were to walk in on something? He knocked again. Still no answer.

So what if he walked in on something? All the better! Have it out—out in the open! He opened the door angrily.

The silence snuffed his rage. Sapphire greeted him with that ridiculous mixture of a meow and a snarl that was her signature. There was a light on in the living room.

He tiptoed in. Cynthia was asleep in her blue bathrobe on the sofa, an opened book pressed under the left side of her face, her hair and skin and velour robe creating an aura of softness, a bundle of softness. His wrath dissipated into tenderness. He tiptoed over, bent down, and kissed her. She shook her head and sat up, still out of it.

"Hi. I must have fallen asleep. What time is it?" The book had left a ridge in her left cheek. She stretched and yawned, unknowingly mirroring Sapphire, who was doing the same thing over in the corner.

"Almost midnight. I'm sorry it's so late. I just got inundated with work." Even he was beginning to believe it.

She stood up and blinked at him, coming to. "Are you hungry?" She put her arms around his neck. "Do you want something to eat?"

He held her tightly, lost in the smell of her, soothed by her softness and her sleepiness. "No, I'm fine. Let's go to sleep."

She was lying in bed when he got in and her skin felt so warm against the coldness of his. She cuddled up next to him and put her head on his chest. "You're cold," she murmured, wrapping her warm feet around his cold ones, her arms around his waist. "So cold."

He felt his body thaw, his muscles begin to relax, but his eyes were darting madly in and out of the shadows of her ceiling.

"Cynthia?"

"Mmm?" She kissed his chest.

"Tell me what you did today."

"What I did today," she mumbled, and began drifting off to sleep.

"Cynthia."

She jumped a little. "What I did today?" She rolled over on her back. "Well, I went to work—"

"Start with lunch."

"Lunch. Lunch with Mary Boynton. Mmm . . . I told you about lunch."

"And then?"

"And then . . ." She yawned. "Oh, that was fun. When I was walking away from the restaurant, I bumped into Chris Channing." She rolled over on her side and put her head back on his chest. "You know—he's my friend at NBC. The one who called the other night?"

"Uh-huh."

"Well, we sat and talked for a long time in Farragut Square." She groaned. "Too long. I practically froze."

"About what?"

She sighed. "Oh, Chris's trying to work up this case against Gardiner. He hates Gardiner. And he keeps filling me in on all the details. It's—" She rubbed her face back and forth in the hair on his chest. "It's too complicated to explain now. Too sleepy. Tell you tomorrow." She yawned. "I love Chris. You will too. Maybe we'll have him and Carol over some time."

"Carol?"

"His wife. I told you. She's the one I introduced him to." She yawned again. "I love Carol . . . and the baby. They have the cutest baby. Louisa. Her name is Louisa." She nestled her head under his chin. "I'm her godmother."

Jed stared at the ceiling, silently begging forgiveness.

"And then I finished the script on the textile bill write-up." She yawned. "And then . . . oh . . . I don't know. I came home. Lilah Ballustrom called."

"What about?"

"To remind us about her party for that Scandinavian artist tomorrow night. I said you were working late tonight, but we both planned on going. And then Carlos came by. He left a chemical sample. It's in the kitchen. Should I have put it in the refrigerator?"

"No." He stroked her hair.

"Mmm. Good. I was afraid if I did we might drink it or something." She rubbed her face back and forth on his chest, like a child enjoying the comfort. "And then I read my book . . ."

She drifted off. He felt her body loosen completely, melting against his. But then he discerned a tensing. "Jed?"

"Yes."

"Sylvia—at work—wondered . . . Um, well, she asked me whether we'd like to take Lisa and Timmy and spend the weekend after next at her cabin in West Virginia?"

"How come?"

"She said her husband's upset because no one uses it anymore, now that their boys are grown."

He closed his eyes and brushed his fingers lightly along the lines of her face, the cheekbone, the nose, the lips, picturing what he was touching, soothed by the image. "Would you like to go?"

"She says it's beautiful. Right on a pond. Only two hours' drive from Washington. Four bedrooms."

Jed laughed, his eyes still closed. "Would you like to go?"

He felt her eyelashes flutter. "Only if you—"

He wrapped his arms around her tighter. "I think it sounds wonderful."

"I'll tell her 'yes' then, tomorrow."

He kissed the top of her head. "I'll tell her, too, when I call."

She relaxed again, and he felt himself drifting off with her, loosening, relaxing, breathing slowly in rhythm with her breaths. He admonished himself for being so stupid, and he delighted in the fact that it had been just that—stupidity—but as he felt himself dropping off into a deep sleep, he had a strange feeling of uneasiness. Something in the foundation had been weakened.

# · 17 ·

Carlos Ramirez lived around the corner from Cynthia in a small, sparsely furnished, and meticulously neat basement apartment he shared with his mother. The apartment consisted of a kitchen, living room, bedroom, and bathroom. Mrs. Ramirez slept in the bedroom, Carlos on a studio couch that also functioned as a sofa in the living room.

On Wednesday afternoon, Carlos opened his eyes to a stream of gray light coming in the living-room window, which offered a sidewalk-level view of the outdoors. As his eyes focused, he saw six small feet in galoshes walk slowly across the window frame. A tattered schoolbag hung down practically to ground level next to one of the boots. Carlos lay still watching. Sure enough, another batch of children's outerwear sauntered past. He frowned. If school was out, he had overslept.

He looked at his watch. He had. It was three-thirty. He closed his eyes and tried to remember what day it was. How could a person be expected to keep track when he went to work one day and came home the next, when he went to sleep and woke up on the same day?

His eyelids felt heavy. He had not been able to sleep much. He closed his eyes, and it came back to him again—the feeling of the heavy body leaning on his, the muffled moans of pain and discomfort, and Carlos knew right away why he had had trouble sleeping.

For the fourth work night in a row, Francisco had been too sick to make it home from the drop-off point on his own. For the fourth time, Carlos had helped. It was getting worse each night, this sickness, and it scared Carlos. He was not used to seeing people suffer.

"The pain comes, but it also goes." That had become Francisco's daily send-off, the words he uttered as he waved Carlos away each morning after they had managed to make it to Francisco's flophouse. "Go," Francisco had ordered that morning, pulling a pint bottle of booze out of the paper bag he always carried with him and unscrewing the top. "Better tomorrow. Always better tomorrow."

Well, it was tomorrow. Carlos climbed out of bed and took a shower. He came back to the living room, dressed, and made his bed, neatly spreading the brown corduroy studio cover over it as a finishing touch. He went into the kitchen. There was a note from his mother in Spanish on the stove. As always.

"Leftover sausage and rice in refrigerator," today's communication read. "Also, I made you soup. It is in the pot on the stove. Hot soup is good for a cold day."

Hot soup is good for a cold day.

Carlos turned on the burner under the pot, took the sausage and rice dish out of the refrigerator, and put it in the oven to warm. He opened the morning paper his mother had left for him on the table. Usually an avid newspaper reader, today Carlos stared at the front page for a long time, his eyes not really focusing.

He stood up abruptly. He ladled out a portion of soup into his plastic thermos. He wrapped the rice dish in aluminum foil and put both in his lunch box, adding a soup spoon and some napkins. He put on his coat and began to go outside, but stopped and walked over to a corner of the living room and picked up a comforter. Then he left.

It was beginning to snow when he arrived at Francisco's place. Carlos knocked and received what he had come to know as the customary welcome: First a hand pulled the frayed curtain that covered the door window slightly to the side. An eye peered out suspiciously. Then the door was opened brusquely by a man who walked away as soon as Carlos walked in. It was a different man each time.

Carlos squinted from the darkness and the smoke. The room reeked of cigarettes, liquor, and urine. He looked in the corner where he had left Francisco and his eyes made out a round, immobile lump in the center of the mattress.

"Hey, Lopez!" an anonymous voice called out in Spanish from across the room. "Wake up! Your nursemaid is here!" Two other men laughed coarsely. A few slumbering bodies on mattresses shifted positions, their sleep jarred by the noise.

Francisco did not move. He was lying flat on his back, just as Carlos had left him that morning—fully dressed in a zipped-up winter jacket, work pants, and shoes. Francisco's eyes were closed, his mouth open, the fingers of his right hand were wrapped loosely around the top of the now-empty liquor bottle.

Carlos sat down on the floor next to the mattress. Francisco's breath was coming in short, labored gasps. "Francisco?" Carlos whispered. He leaned closer. "Francisco?"

Francisco's eyelids fluttered and then opened. He looked confused at first, but then Carlos's face seemed to register. "Time for work?" he asked. With great difficulty, he pulled himself up.

"No, no," Carlos said, gently urging him back down. "It is just late afternoon. Wednesday afternoon. How do you feel?"

Francisco lay on his side and bent at the waist, hugging himself. "Cold," he whispered. "So cold."

Carlos wrapped the comforter he had brought around Francisco. Francisco clutched it tightly to him, pulling it up around his neck and ears. "Oh, yes. Better," he gasped. "So cold." His head nodded back and forth and then gradually his whole body followed the movement. Carlos realized he was trembling.

"Francisco, I've brought you some hot soup, but you'll need to sit up to drink it."

Obediently, Francisco pulled himself up, but when he reached a sitting position, he swayed and groaned. He lay back down, shaking his head and shivering.

Carlos took out the thermos and the spoon. "Here," Carlos said. "I'll feed you." He put a little bit of soup in the spoon and put it to Francisco's lips. Francisco swallowed and sighed as it went down. "Good," Francisco whispered. "Hot soup." He looked at Carlos. "Where did you get it?"

Carlos smiled sheepishly. "My mother made it."

Francisco raised a bushy eyebrow suspiciously. "For me?"

"Well, for a cold day," Carlos said. He fed Francisco another spoonful. Some missed and drizzled down the side of Francisco's face. Carlos wiped it away with a napkin. Then he gave Francisco some more.

Francisco looked up at him gratefully. Carlos stared back at Francisco with alarm. The man's skin was a strange yellow color, and so were the whites of his eyes.

The snow that had been falling lightly in the afternoon took on greater and greater force as day wore on. By evening, the forecasters were predicting a "record fall." Cynthia urged Jed to leave Lilah Ballustrom's party early, insisting that her snowtireless car would never make it home if they lingered.

Late that night, Jed lay sprawled out facedown on Cynthia's bed, clad only in his shorts. In her bathrobe, Cynthia leaned over Jed's large frame, administering a back rub.

Her hands formed two circles as the tips of her fingers went round and round the base at the back of his neck, round and round, slowly, gently, firmly.

Jed groaned and moved his head from side to side.

"Was that agony or ecstasy?"

"Ecstasy," he grunted. "Pure relief."

She smiled, and her hands continued their circular motions. She could feel his muscles loosening, the tension dissipating. After a while, she spread her fingers out along his shoulders, enjoying the sensuous feel of his flesh, kneading, stroking, back and forth, back and forth. His body swayed rhythmically in response to her hands, and the monotonous tempo soothed her, too. He moaned with pleasure.

"How could you tell?" he asked after a while.

"Tell what?"

"That my ulcer was acting up."

Cynthia looked up at the ceiling, thinking. Her hands kept kneading. "I don't know, just the way you looked when I walked into Lilah's party."

"Looked how? Disheveled?"

"Disheveled in an immaculate three-piece suit? Hardly!"

"What, then?"

Her hands moved down to his shoulder blades. "Tense, I guess. You looked very tense."

"Tense!" Jed roared. "Hell, I was the life of the party! I was standing there entertaining four people! In case you failed to notice, Steve Barnum was howling uproariously at the dry, impeccable delivery of my witticisms, and everyone knows ole Barnum has not so much as cracked a smile in three years. I was being very funny!"

"Too funny." Her fingers worked their way under and around his shoulder blades. "You were trying too hard."

"Oh . . ." he whispered. "Oh, that feels good. So good."

"Here?" She pressed her fingers down harder.

"Mmm . . . mmm . . ." He moved his shoulders up and down slowly. "So you mean I looked like an uptight basket case?"

"No, not a bit. Not to the others. It was subtle. White knuckles!" she said. "That was it! It was the white knuckles!"

"What the hell does that mean?"

"You were holding your drink so tightly your knuckles were white."

He groaned. "Great."

She laughed. "As I said, it was not readily apparent."

"But apparent enough for you to decide to rescue me by making a lame excuse about the snow and your car so we could leave the party." He moaned softly as she pressed the heels of her hands into his lower back.

"Well, I just thought . . ."

He growled. "You think I'm incapable of leaving a party with my own lame excuse if I want to?"

She smiled and kept pressing. "No."

"You think I need some Florence Nightingale to carry me off to her apartment and nurse me back to health, administering ulcer medication and plying me with the blandest goddamn dinner I've ever eaten?"

She giggled as she moved her hands up and down on either side of his spine.

"And I suppose this back rub is your idea of the final touch, the pièce de résistance?"

She lifted her hands from his back.

"Oh, don't stop," he whimpered. "Please don't stop."

She laughed and kissed him on the back of the neck and continued massaging. His muscles were completely relaxed now, his body at rest.

"Cynthia?" he whispered.

"What?"

"I guess what I'm saying so graciously is 'thank you.'"

"I know."

He rolled over on his back and looked at her, just looked at her. He frowned. "Why are you so good to me?"

She frowned back, mirroring him. "Why do you sound so suspicious when you ask that?"

He opened his eyes wide. "Do I?" he asked apologetically. "I don't mean to. Really." He closed his eyes and took a deep breath. "Oh, God, you have no idea how much better I feel. Relief. Such incredible relief." His eyes still closed, he beckoned her with his hands. "Come. Come closer. The finishing touch."

She lay down next to him on the bed. He put his arms around her and gently pushed her head down on his chest. He stroked her hair and sighed contentedly.

"What caused it?" she asked.

"I thought you were so good at reading between the lines."

"You have to give me the lines," she said, playing with the dimple in his chin. "What did you do today?"

He yawned. "Well, first of all, I overslept. We overslept. Remember?"

"Uh-huh."

"So I ran out of here without breakfast, dropped Carlos's chemical off at my friend's lab—" He opened his eyes. "They said they should be able to tell us what the chemical is sometime tomorrow."

Cynthia nodded.

Jed closed his eyes again. "Then I grabbed a danish at the office, and just barely had time to go over my papers before court."

"Uh-huh." She ran her hand down the side of his face. He smiled, his eyes still closed, and rubbed his cheek against her hand.

"Then I spent the morning arguing what I knew was a losing motion in front of the meanest goddamned judge on the bench—Herbert Greiner—breaking my ass for two hours, and all for naught. He ruled against me."

"Uh-huh."

He yawned again. "Then I had lunch with my ex-wife, followed by an argument with one of my partners about how to handle a case we're working on. Then I found out the secretaries were too swamped to get to the papers I needed typed by end-of-business today. So, furious, I left the office, only to discover it had started to snow. It took me about three-quarters of an hour to get a cab to the party."

"That's it?"

"That's it. The road to white knuckles."

She cocked her head. "You want my diagnosis of the cause of your ulcer attack?"

"Yup."

"Lunch with your ex-wife."

He opened his eyes and stared at her in disbelief. "Damn you."

"Am I right?"

"Let's go to sleep."

"I'm right!" she shouted victoriously.

He looked at the clock. "It's midnight, for Christ's sake! Let's go to sleep."

They pulled the blanket back, took off their clothes, and climbed under the covers.

He wrapped his arms around her. "You're freezing cold." He kissed her cheek. "All for my back rub." He kissed her on the mouth, and then again, more passionately.

"Why did having lunch with her upset you so?" Cynthia asked when he stopped.

"Not now," he whispered, moving to kiss her again.

She backed away. "Why not?"

He lay his head down on the pillow, facing hers. "Because you've made me feel absolutely wonderful, and I want to enjoy that feeling right now, alone with you. The last thing I need is my ex-wife here in bed with us." He kissed her nose. It was the closest he could get to her lips.

"An ulcer comes from suppressed feelings," Cynthia said.

"If you examine them—admit them—maybe it won't happen next time."

He rolled over on his back and grunted, staring at the ceiling. "She called the meeting to discuss putting the kids in private school."

"Why?"

"That's what I said, only louder and more irritably. They're doing fine in school and they happen to be enrolled in one of the best public school systems in the country."

"Why does she want them in private school, then?"

"Oh, status, essentially. Anna has spend a lifetime in search of status." He yawned. "Well, it's still elusive. I said no."

"Then what was the problem?"

"Not now." He wriggled under the covers. "Not now."

Cynthia folded her arms over her chest, her lips drawn into a taut line.

He gave in. "Oh, hell, she's . . . just a problem for me." He stared at the ceiling for a while and rubbed his nose. "Have you ever had lunch with an immaculately beautiful iceberg? It's goddamned discomforting! She sits across from me, this chilled package of perfection, eating nothing, drinking nothing—Anna never had much of an appetite for anything, including me—a little doll with shiny black hair and perfectly applied makeup, attired in a designer dress, oozing composure, oozing coldness."

He grunted. "And I find myself gorging and drinking and going on and on at the mouth just to compensate." He shrugged and turned to Cynthia, trying to crawl back into her. "No more," he whispered, kissing her eyes. "Please, no more. Just us, now. Just us."

"Did you ever love her?"

"Oh, hell, I don't know." He rolled over again on his back in exasperation. "I suppose so. Certainly I thought so. I was just young and naive." He yawned. "I was completely caught up in the whole thing—the two of us forever, making babies, watching them grow, aging together, loving forever—the constancy of coupledom!"

He laughed caustically. "She wasn't. It's as simple as that." Jed yawned again. "I suppose that's what bothers me. She's a reminder that the only thing I ever wanted in life can never be. Never. That life just isn't that simple." He closed his eyes.

Cynthia felt a chill trickle through her veins. Her muscles began jumping to attention, tightening up, one by one. Her heart pounded.

What did that mean, "can never be"? That Anna was all he wanted? Was that what had upset him? His unrequited love for his former wife? She felt her cheeks get hot.

Cynthia stared at the ceiling for a long time, trying to muster the courage to ask. Finally, she took a deep breath and opened her mouth. "Do you . . . do you still love her?" Her voice squeaked a little.

There was no answer.

She turned to look at him. He was sound asleep, the picture of relaxation, lying on his back breathing in a heavy, even tempo.

Cynthia stared back at the ceiling, horribly awake now and thoroughly miserable, unable to think of anything but Anna, Anna the iceberg, Anna the tiny, raven-haired jewel of perfection.

She tried to sleep, but every single part of her body was taut and vibrating. She tossed and turned for more than an hour, while the "insomniac" beside her slumbered on, unperturbed. At long last, she drifted off, yearning to be the kind of woman who kept men awake nights, who drove them to the depths of despair and fostered ulcers, the kind of woman Jed Farber would love . . . forever.

Twenty minutes after she fell asleep, the phone rang. They both jumped. Jed, who was sleeping beside it, grabbed for it.

"Hello?"

Cynthia squinted, trying to read his face to figure out who it was.

"No, no don't worry. You were right to call. Have you called an ambulance?" Jed listened. "I understand," he said softly. "Now just try to keep calm. Where are you?" He sat up. "A pen!" he whispered to Cynthia. She pulled herself up and reached for one.

On a newspaper next to the bed, Jed scrawled an address. "We'll be right there. No, I have a car. We'll be right there."

He hung up the phone and scrambled out of bed. "It was Carlos," he said, grabbing his suit pants off the chair. "Francisco is sick. Very sick."

\*    \*    \*

The snow had piled up and the removal crews had compounded the problem, heaping the snow plowed from the city streets upon the cars parked at the curbs, including Jed's.

Frantically, Cynthia and Jed shoveled the car out of the embankment and then cajoled it out of the parking space. Slowly, the snow-decked vehicle lumbered its way to the address Jed had written down.

Carlos was pacing outside when they got there. Jed and Carlos ran into the building as Cynthia continued scraping the car. The two men emerged carrying a body that looked lifeless and frozen. They lay Francisco down in the backseat, draped in a comforter, and Carlos climbed in next to him.

"Is he breathing?" Jed asked as they took off for the hospital.

"He's breathing, but badly. He's kind of gasping for breath," Carlos cried out. "I don't know what to do!"

"Just hold him. Maybe raise the top part of his body a little, loosen his collar, to make it easier for him to breathe," Jed said. "It's important to stay calm. Remember, we'll be at the hospital soon. They'll know what to do."

Cynthia leaned over the front seat and helped Carlos unzip the top of Francisco's coat and settle him. His breath had a strange fruitlike odor. But he was breathing.

Cynthia turned around and faced forward, terrified the breathing would stop, wishing she had taken that emergency first-aid course she had seen advertised, vowing to take it the next time it was given, vowing to do anything if they could just get this man to the hospital in time. She knew there was nothing she could do to make time slow down and the car go faster, and that made her even more frantic.

She watched Jed, wondering how he could remain so calm. With total concentration, he was commandeering the car down the roads, calmly maneuvering it in and out of snow piles, trying a new direction when he hit a skid, unperturbed when the tires screeched in rebellion.

Restless movement and anxious sighs emanated from the backseat. Jed sneaked glances in the rearview mirror. "You're doing fine, Carlos," Jed said in a voice of authority. "As long as he's breathing, there's nothing we have to do. If he stops breathing, tell me. Keep reminding yourself that we're taking him to a place where people will know better than we what to do. We'll be there soon."

Cynthia looked out the window. "You're going to Capitol Hill!"

Jed nodded. "To D.C. General."

"But isn't George Washington Hospital closer?"

"D.C. General is a city hospital. They can't turn anyone away—even illegal aliens who can't pay."

"George Washington can?"

"Not technically, but yes, I think so. If they deem his condition to be stable, they can have him moved." He lowered his voice and put his hand on hers. "See if you can keep Carlos talking. I think that will calm him down."

"How long have you been with Francisco today, Carlos?"

"Since this afternoon. He was . . . oh, jeez, he seemed really sick when we came home from work this morning, so when I woke up, I went over to his place to see if he was any better. I brought him some soup."

"Did he eat?"

"A little of the soup—yes. But then he seemed to get worse. I was going crazy. I wanted to get a doctor, but every time I suggested it, he'd say, 'No! No!' Then he just, like, went unconscious. At first I thought he was sleeping. Then, when I couldn't wake him, I told the men at his place I had to go call an ambulance. They went bananas. Said they would throw him out in the cold if I left, and there was no phone there. They were afraid that if an ambulance came, so would Immigration. That's all they think of, immigration."

"What did you do?" Cynthia asked.

"Finally, I couldn't stand it any longer." Carlos shook his head. "I was going crazy, really crazy. I told them I was calling friends, people who would not report them. I told them if he was not there and alive when I got back, I was turning them all in to the police. That's all I could figure out to do. I'm sorry to—"

"You did the right thing." They both said it at the same time.

Jed pulled into the hospital emergency entrance and

jumped out of the car. He and Carlos carried Francisco in, where two attendants rushed him off in a stretcher.

The nurse gave Carlos and Cynthia a form to fill out while Jed went to park the car. Cynthia filled in the first blank—"Name: Francisco Lopez"—and handed it back to the nurse. "That's all we know," Cynthia said. "He is from the neighborhood, no fixed address or relations that we know of."

It was three o'clock in the morning, but the emergency room was packed. She and Carlos sat down. A man across from them with a gash in his head was vomiting phelgm into a paper bag. A child of about three was stretched out listlessly on a woman's lap, the child's eyes opened but not seeing. Cynthia wondered if the child was conscious.

An obese black woman clutched her abdomen and rocked back and forth on a small chair, every so often crying out in anguish. A small Asian man held a bloody handkerchief up to the side of his head. There were twitching people, moaning people, and some who looked as though they were already dead, just propped up in seats.

Cynthia patted Carlos's arm, comforting him out of her need to be comforted. "Did Francisco think he was sick—seriously sick?"

Carlos swallowed and stared down at the floor. It was, Cynthia realized, the only safe place left in the room to stare. "I think he thought he was dying," Carlos said slowly. "I think he's thought so for a while."

"Did he say that to you?"

"No, but I think that's why he kept going to work all the time and sending off all his money. He hasn't bought food in two weeks—only liquor. I've been feeding him, bringing extra food to the job each night. I think he was determined to work as long as he could." Carlos stared for a while. "This is all hindsight, though. I didn't realize he felt that way until today."

"What happened today?"

Carlos unzipped his jacket and pulled out a brown paper bag. "He gave me this."

"What is it?"

Carlos shrugged. "All his important possessions, I guess. The other guys in the van tease him because he never lets the bag out of his sight—always keeps it zipped up inside his jacket. They said even in the heat of summer, he kept it inside his shirt—always." Carlos shook the bag and smiled. "It's a little deflated right now because he drank his last pint of liquor. That was the only thing I ever saw him take out of it." Carlos put the bag back inside his jacket.

"You want to open it?"

"No," Carlos said. "It's his."

Cynthia was touched. "You like him a lot, don't you?"

Carlos thought about the question and his eyes became very serious. "Yes, and no," he said. "I've been real curious about him. I've felt sorry for him because he's been so sick. I admired his stamina, that's for sure, and his determination to send money back to Guatemala all the time." He shrugged and smiled a little. "He has a great sense of humor that I like, too."

"Then what don't you like?"

"He was really sick after work yesterday, but he's been in generally bad shape for several days now. I've been kind of helping him home after each shift. Well, Monday, as I was practically carrying him down Eighteenth Street at seven in the morning, he stopped suddenly and snarled at me. 'Why are you doing this?' he yelled. And I said, 'Because I am your friend.' And he turned to me and he said, 'Friend? I would not do it for you!'"

Carlos laughed. "Later I started thinking about it, and you know what? He was right! Francisco would *not* have done it for me!"

"Oh, but you're wrong! I'm sure he would! After all, he liked you. He gave you his possessions."

Carlos shook his head. "That's 'trust,' not 'like.' The guy thought he was going to die, but just in case he didn't, he wanted his bag back and he trusted me more than the other people he knew." Carlos laughed. "And if you'd met some of his roommates, you'd know that was no big competition to win, believe me!"

Carlos stared down at his hands. "This whole experience— one of the things it's taught me is that liking is a luxury," he said slowly. "Kindness, friendship, those are all luxuries too, see? The men in the van—including Francisco—they have lives with no room for luxuries."

Jed walked into the emergency room. "Have they told you anything?" he asked.

Cynthia and Carlos shook their heads mutely.

Jed walked up to the nurse's stand, asked some questions, and returned. "They said they've heard nothing. They'll tell us as soon as they do."

"Here," Carlos said, standing up. "Take my seat. I'm going to go outside and have a cigarette."

As Carlos walked out, Cynthia noticed Jed's clothes for the first time. He was wearing his three-piece suit, a white shirt, and his dress overcoat—the clothes that had been closest to the bed—all of which were now saturated with snow and thoroughly rumpled. He had the look of a high-class hobo.

"Do you know what I had to go through to find a parking space!" he snapped as he plopped down beside Cynthia. "I couldn't believe it! I mean blocks and blocks—"

Cynthia burst out laughing, and her laughter got louder and louder.

"Everyone is staring," Jed whispered irritably. "Would you please tell me what is so funny?"

"You! You're hysterical about a parking spot?"

"Well, *you* go out there and try—"

"You who have dismantled snow drifts with your bare hands this evening, who have risen mightily to what only could be called an impossible situation, you who have been the only source of calm and reason in a scenario that drove me and Carlos to the verge of hysteria—now, *you* are practically undone by a lack of parking spaces!"

Jed looked down at his hands. "Emergencies are easy," he mumbled sheepishly. "It's just the rest of life I have trouble with."

"Do you know how to do pulmonary resuscitation? If Francisco had stopped breathing in the car, could you—"

"Yeah. Yeah, I know how."

She kissed him on the cheek. "I'm so glad. I just wish I'd known that in the car. I could have relaxed and enjoyed the scenery!"

"What would you have done if I hadn't been there?" Jed asked.

She looked at him, suddenly totally deflated, terrified. "Wished you were there!"

He looked at her for a long time. "Now, under cross-examination I'll plead extenuating circumstances or perhaps even deny having said what I'm going to say, and," he said, looking around the room, "you'd be hard pressed to gather any witnesses here. And in fact, that might very well be why I'm saying it here and now, but—" He looked at her and grinned broadly. "I love you."

She stared at him in shock.

"You probably think it was the back rub that did it," Jed said soberly. "The 'geisha girl' routine, the psychoanalysis. And that might have had some influence. But the truth is there are different people for different stages of life, and there is no one else I would rather be in the waiting room of D.C. General Hospital with at four in the morning."

"There is no one else I *would* be in the waiting room of D.C. General Hospital with at four in the morning!" she replied. "I love you too."

He put his arm around her and hugged her. "Well, I guess that's a kind of foundation for love, what do you think?"

Cynthia shook her head and leaned back against Jed's shoulder. "You're insane," she said happily.

A young man in a white coat walked into the waiting room. "The Lopez family?" he called out. He looked down at the papers on the clipboard he was carrying. "Francisco Lopez?"

Cynthia and Jed stood up and Carlos walked back in from the doorway.

"He's in a coma," the doctor whispered to the three of them. "We've taken a blood sample and should get the results within the hour. We suspect kidney and liver dysfunction. He's badly jaundiced and he bled abnormally when we took the blood sample. Plus"—the doctor shook his head—"he seems to have bruises all over his body. Those are all usually signs of liver disease."

"What would cause the disease?" Cynthia asked.

"Alcohol could," the doctor said. "Is he a heavy drinker?" Carlos looked down at the floor and shrugged.

"What makes you suspect kidney problems too?" Jed asked.

"His body is badly swollen, and he's deeply comatose. He doesn't even respond to painful stimuli."

Cynthia cringed, wondering how one administered "painful stimuli."

"We're going to hook him up to a dialysis machine," the doctor said. "We'll let you know, but it doesn't look good."

They nodded and sat back down. The euphoria of having delivered Francisco to the hospital on time vanished, replaced by the realization that the heroics were probably all in vain.

Staring down at her hands, Cynthia allowed herself to accept an even worse fact: No doubt the best thing that could happen to Francisco at this stage was a speedy death. She looked up at Carlos. He was staring into space.

Jed put his hand on the boy's shoulder. "Carlos, there was nothing more you could have done. That kind of destruction takes a long, long time to develop. You happened on the scene only recently."

"I know," Carlos said, understanding, but not seeming to feel any better. He went out to have another cigarette.

A woman walked in dragging a bleeding child and screaming something in Spanish. Cynthia buried her face in Jed's coat. He held her.

They sat that way for a long time. The bleeding child was taken away. The vomiting man fell asleep. One by one the others in the waiting room were called and followed the nurse through the doors. New people, in varying states of distress, came in to replace them. Carlos came back and sat down in an empty seat.

The young doctor kept coming out, whispering to people, and then returning to the closed doors. Finally he emerged and walked in their direction. He was shaking his head.

"We lost him," he said. "The blood test revealed severe liver damage, but it was the kidneys that actually caused his death. His high potassium levels caused his heart to stop."

Jed frowned. "Potassium?"

"High potassium levels caused by the kidneys' inability to excrete potassium."

All of them nodded, not knowing what it meant, but knowing all they needed to know: the bottom line.

"What happens now?" Cynthia asked.

The doctor looked down at the paper. "There are no relatives?"

"No."

"Well, any patient who dies within twenty-four hours of entering the hospital automatically goes to the medical examiner's office. They then determine whether an autopsy is necessary."

"Would an autopsy show more than liver disease?" Cynthia asked. "Could it show a cause?"

"It could. They could test for alcoholism, for example."

"For a chemical?"

The doctor nodded. "I guess so." He wrote down a number on a slip of paper. "This is the medical examiner's office," he said.

The sun was coming up as they climbed over snowdrifts to the car, its early morning light beginning to melt the havoc below. The three of them shoveled the car out and climbed in.

"Carlos, I took that chemical sample you got to a lab," Jed said after driving for a while. He looked at Carlos in his rearview window. "They said they should know what it is some time this afternoon. Why don't we all get some sleep and then go find out?"

Carlos and Cynthia nodded.

Cynthia turned around. Carlos had emptied the contents of Francisco's brown paper bag out onto the backseat.

"What was in it?"

Carlos picked up the contents one by one, itemizing. "A lock of black hair wrapped in cellophane," he said, examining it. "Soft hair. A baby's hair, maybe." He put it back into the bag. "A religious medal," he said, holding up a round, gold-colored piece. He picked up an old, brittle-looking piece of paper and unfolded it. "A letter," Carlos said, reading. "It's from someone who is writing on behalf of his wife—a friend. I guess she couldn't write." His eyes traveled down the page.

"What does it say?"

"More money," Carlos mumbled, reading. "'*Mas mas mas*' . . . That's all it says." Slowly he folded the paper up and put it back in the bag. "A key," he said, lifting one off the backseat. "To his place, I guess." He picked up a tattered piece of cardboard, with an address on it in Guatemala. "This must be where he sent the money orders," he said, showing Cynthia. The letters were printed in an awkward, childlike scrawl. "He could barely write," Carlos whispered.

He looked down on the backseat. All that was left were

coins. Carlos counted. "Three dollars ninety-five cents," he said. "Just enough to buy one more pint of his regular brew at the liquor store." He put the money back in the bag.

Jed pulled up in front of Carlos's apartment. When Jed and Cynthia turned around, Carlos was clutching the bag in the backseat. There were tears running down his face. He looked up at them and quickly wiped the wetness away with his hand. He opened the car door.

Cynthia put her hand on his arm. "Carlos, it hurts to witness death, and it hurts to witness a life that did not have much in it. But the ability to feel that sadness for someone else is a luxury. We're lucky to have luxuries, even when they hurt. You taught me that."

Trying to force a smile, he looked at her. She had tears too.

# · 18 ·

Cynthia watched Jed sway back and forth in her kitchen as he talked on the telephone. "Uh-huh. Uh-huh." A damp lock of hair drooped down over his bloodshot eyes. His thoroughly crumpled white shirt sagged out of his thoroughly crumpled pants.

He hung up the phone. "Carbon tetrachloride."

"What does that mean?"

Jed stared through eyes that seemed unable to focus. "Damned if I know." He took the receiver off the hook again and handed it to her. "Your turn. I'll be in bed."

The government had shut down due to the snowfall, and many private establishments had followed the federal lead. Cynthia and Jed had dutifully tried to inform their offices they would not be at work, only to discover both Capitol Radio and Jed's law firm were closed. Cynthia called several of the occupational health specialists she had interviewed before she found one in his office. Then she called the medical examiner's number they had got at the hospital and requested that Francisco Lopez's body be checked for traces of carbon tetrachloride.

"Ross Leonard will see us at four this afternoon." Cynthia announced to Jed as she set the alarm clock next to the bed. "I called Carlos and told him."

She heard a muffled response from under the comforter.

\* \* \*

Ross Leonard turned out to be a short bald man in his fifties with an enormous paunch and an equally exaggerated dramatic flair.

"Carbon tetrachloride?" he gasped, pacing around his office and shaking his head.

"Carbon tetrachloride!" He hurled out the words in disgust, and dropped into the chair behind his desk.

He looked up at his audience. "I didn't think anyone was using carbon tet anymore!"

"Mr. Leonard, you have to start at the beginning with us," Cynthia said, turning on her tape recorder. "We know absolutely nothing about this chemical except its name. What exactly is carbon tetrachloride?"

Ross Leonard leaned back in his chair and rubbed his eyes. "Carbon tetrachloride is a nonflammable solvent that's used for degreasing, dry cleaning, sometimes in fire extinguishers, too. Or I should say 'was used.' The restrictions on its use are so cumbersome that they amount to a virtual economic ban. In the United States, the government's tolerance levels for worker exposure are so low that nobody can afford to use it anymore. Not legally, anyway, because to use it legally, you have to set up incredibly elaborate—and expensive—protection systems." He threw his hands up in the air. "Good God, it's one of the few chemicals the United Nations has pinpointed for eradication!"

"Why?"

"Because it's damned lethal, that's why!" Leonard shouted.

"Wait a minute." Cynthia held up her hand. "Let's deal in specifics." She turned to Carlos. "Why don't you describe the factory procedure to Mr. Leonard?"

Carlos gave a rough outline of the assembly-line process. He told Leonard that two sets of industrial parts were brought into the factory, put together by men operating machines at the top of the line, and then sent down to a heated chemical vat, where they were rinsed. After being drip-dried, he said, the finished cylinders were loaded into crates and onto the back of a truck.

When Carlos finished, Cynthia turned to Leonard. "Now, in that scenario, what are they using the carbon tetrachloride for?"

"To degrease," Leonard said with certainty. "The machinery that puts the parts together gets 'em oiled up, so they need to degrease them before they use them, and carbon tetrachloride is one powerful degreaser, let me tell you! The same characteristics that make it dangerous make it highly effective."

Leonard leaned forward angrily. "Of course, while it's degreasing those parts, it's also having a rather devastating effect on the workers in that plant. It's destroying their livers, their kidneys, their brain cells, their lungs too, for that matter!" Leonard was breathing heavily.

Cynthia pointed a finger at Leonard. "Explain to me how. Go back to Carlos's description and tell me specifically how those workers are vulnerable."

"Well, first of all, if you use carbon tetrachloride in an open system like that, it's dangerous. The workers are inhaling it."

"They all wear masks," Carlos protested. "They use rubber gloves."

Leonard shook his head emphatically. "No good. Minimum protection. Not even. You've got a heated, volatile bath there. They're inhaling the stuff, masks or not. They may wear rubber gloves, but how many times do they reach in without them? Without thinking? Or how often does the chemical get inside the gloves? And it probably gets on their clothes too, and once it's there, it keeps working. The dermal exposure keeps going on as long as they keep the clothes on."

Carlos closed his eyes, picturing the same work pants in the van, night after night, never washed, rarely even removed.

"What does dermal exposure do?" Cynthia asked.

Leonard sighed. "As I said, carbon tet is a degreaser. Essentially it degreases the skin too, defats it, eats away at the lipid layer, which is the skin's protective barrier."

Cynthia leaned forward. "What are the symptoms? What does that do to the skin?"

"Little that's visible. It creates a dryness, a peeling."

"A peeling?" Cynthia recalled Francisco's hands, the dry, flaking skin. She looked at Carlos. He lowered his eyes to the floor.

"Yes, a peeling. But the important thing that's happening," Leonard went on, "is not visible. Once the lipid level is destroyed, the chemical gets absorbed into the blood stream. There are three levels of chemical exposure. Inhalation, ingestion, and dermal. It sounds like you've got two out of three here. They're inhaling it and taking it in dermally."

"And it kills the liver and kidneys?" Jed asked.

"Slowly. In chronic exposure, yes. The liver is a large organ, and it can undergo a lot of damage before any effects are noticeable. But when the effects *are* noticeable—jaundice, fatigue, nausea—it's often too late. Same with the kidneys." Leonard thought for a while. "The neuropsychiatric effects would be observable more quickly. They could be temporary too—the result of inhaling a powerful whiff."

"How do they manifest themselves?" Cynthia asked.

"Erratic behavior."

"Acting crazy," Carlos mumbled, seeing Pablo in a stupor the night he filled the factory tank with new supplies.

"Exactly!" Leonard proclaimed. "Acting crazy—highly emotional at times, spacey at others!"

Carlos put his hands over his eyes.

It was dark outside by the time they left Ross Leonard's office. The three of them sat in silence in Jed's car, their mood mirroring the stark coldness of the snow-crusted streets.

Finally Jed turned to Cynthia. "I think you have to go to OSHA now. This sounds like terrible stuff. It's got to be stopped."

She sat thinking for a while. "He said 'chronic exposure,'" Cynthia reminded Jed. "Just one more night or two wouldn't make much of a difference in terms of the workers, would it?"

"No, probably not. But what could you accomplish in that time?"

"I don't know. I'd really like to find out first who owns the chemical company. Maybe I'm unfairly sceptical about the government's capabilities, but I'm afraid once OSHA goes in, there might be no way of finding out."

"And how could you find out?"

She looked up, hopeful. "Maybe by seeing if there's a name on the chemical truck? By following it, if need be, after it makes a delivery." Cynthia turned around to Carlos in the backseat. "When are the deliveries made?"

"Tuesday nights."

She turned back around. "Oh, it's only Thursday," she said in resignation. "That's too long to wait."

They drove on.

"Why are you so sure it's a chemical company?" Jed asked.

"It has to be," Cynthia said. "Who else could be supplying the stuff?"

"Leonard didn't say the chemical was illegal," Jed said slowly. "He said it was 'restricted.' That means the chemical company's distribution of it is questionable, perhaps, but not illegal, necessarily."

Cynthia whirled around. "What is this, 'questionable, perhaps, not illegal, necessarily'? You're beginning to talk like a lawyer! What are you saying?"

Jed laughed. "I'm not saying, I'm asking. What makes you so sure it's the supplier of the chemical who's the culprit?"

"Who else could it be?"

"Well, I never heard Carlos describe the process until just now in Leonard's office. But from what you said, Carlos, it sounds like the chemical is being used to do something to industrial parts. To degrease them, that's what Leonard said, right?"

"Right."

"Where do they come from?" Jed asked.

Carlos shrugged. "A truck delivers them to the back of the factory."

"Where do they go in the end?"

"The same truck. It reloads them at the front of the factory."

Jed turned and looked at Cynthia.

"You mean it's the parts-maker," she gasped. "He's the one who—"

Jed nodded. "Who is using the chemical for an industrial process to bypass expensive safety precautions. It sure sounds to me as though he would be the one to gain."

Cynthia shuddered. "That is really creepy."

"Creepy? Hell, it gives us a project!" Jed turned to Carlos. "What time does the shift end, Carlos?"

"Six-thirty."

"The three of us, the three great supersleuths, should go

out there early tomorrow morning," Jed continued, "and follow the truck to see where it takes the parts! Carlos," Jed yelled over his shoulder into the backseat, "what exactly are the parts?"

"Ball bearings," Carlos replied.

Jed's head began spinning. His body started sending out alternating flashes of hot and cold, which chilled him and made him perspire at the same time.

Ball bearings. Oh, God. Ball bearings.

Jed stared straight ahead, fiercely trying to concentrate. He swallowed, and only when he was sure he could utter the words without a hint of disequilibrium did he open his mouth. "Are you sure they are ball bearings, Carlos?"

"Yes. Little silver balls? They come in and we stamp them into cylinders at the top of the line. Then they go through the bath and are dried, and we load them onto trucks. That's what you call them, isn't it? Ball bearings? They're used for motion—in machines and in engines for motion."

"Yes, that sounds like ball bearings," Cynthia said. She turned to Jed. "Right, Jed?"

Jed nodded.

"I wonder how many ball-bearing makers there are around here," Cynthia mused.

Jed glued his eyes to the road ahead, knowing all too well exactly how many ball-bearing manufacturers there were left in the Mid-Atlantic region. In his head, he heard all the little ball bearings falling off the night table at Mama Rosa's Motel—pling, pling, pling—and he was certain that in just a matter of seconds, Cynthia would remember hearing them too. Had he told her? Had he been specific that night? He could remember only his drunken state.

"You passed Carlos's apartment!" Cynthia shouted.

Jed did a screeching "U" turn and pulled the car up to the curb.

"What time do you want to leave tomorrow morning?" Carlos asked as he opened the car door.

Cynthia turned to Jed for the answer. "I'd think four-forty-five, just to be sure," Jed said, trying to sound like the executive, the man in control, the man whose brilliant insight had fostered the plan, but feeling instead like a fugitive desperate to separate himself as soon as possible from the other two.

"Pick you up then," Cynthia told Carlos as he slammed the door shut. Jed did another "U" turn and drove to Cynthia's. He pulled up next to where they had parked her car the night before, jammed on the brakes, and turned off the ignition.

"Why are you stopping here?" she asked.

"We're going to switch cars." He grabbed a window scraper from the floor of the backseat and scrambled out of his car.

"Jed?" Cynthia got out and stood on the side of the road, watching as Jed began scraping snow off her car at a feverish pace.

"You're better off driving my car tomorrow morning with Carlos!" he yelled, breathless from his frenetic activity. "Your car would never make it."

"*I'm* better off?" Cynthia looked at him in confusion. "But I thought we were all—"

"Not *we*. You." He began working on the rear window. "You and Carlos. I can't make it."

Her mouth dropped open. She stared at him as he hopped from window to window like a madman. "Jed," she said sternly, "*you* were the one who came up with the idea in the first place! You—"

"I forgot. I have to be in court. I can't make it. You and Carlos can go out together." He raced over to the other side of the car and began scraping, his eyes avoiding hers. "You'll do fine without me. Hell, it's *your* story!"

Her eyes opened wide in hurt.

"That ought to do the job," he panted, surveying his work. "Here." He held out his car keys. "Give me yours."

In a daze, she reached into her purse and pulled out her car keys.

He got in and turned on the ignition. "Pull my car up a little so I can get out," he instructed. "Then you can take the space."

"But aren't you going to spend the night?"

"Can't." He slammed the door shut.

Obediently, she pulled his car forward. He pulled hers out of the parking space and then sped off down the street.

\*   \*   \*

"Jed couldn't make it," Cynthia announced briskly when she picked Carlos up the next morning. "He had a complication with work."

"Was *that* what it was?" Carlos asked.

"What what was?"

"He was upset about something in the car coming home last night. I could tell."

"Really?" Cynthia shot him a look. "How could you tell?"

"Reporter instincts!" Carlos howled gleefully. "Man, I'm telling you, they're all turned on now! I am one perceptive hombre!"

Cynthia stared coldly at the road ahead, anxiously replaying the scene coming home in the car, searching for something to explain Jed's sudden exit.

"You look terrible," Carlos said softly. "Like you didn't sleep at all last night."

"Hey, cut the reporter instincts," she snapped. "We'll have a better use for them soon."

Carlos shriveled up in the seat next to her. "Um . . . I have a question," he said after they'd driven in silence for a while. "Say we follow the truck. What proof do we have that the same truck took the parts from the factory to the other destination?"

"Well, we're both witnesses. We can both state that we followed the truck, saw it move from one location to the other."

Carlos frowned. "Is that enough proof?"

"Probably," Cynthia laughed. "But just in case . . ." She pulled a camera out of the purse on the seat next to her and held it up.

"We take pictures?"

"Yup. Ideally, we take one picture of the truck before it leaves—of its license plate—and then another picture when it gets to wherever it's going."

"All right!" Carlos leaned back in the seat and shut his eyes.

The freezing temperatures had hardened the snow overnight, and it crunched under the wheels of Jed's car as it sped along the highway.

"Plenty of time," Carlos mumbled after a while. "My—uh—

reporter instincts tell me you're a little nervous and driving too fast."

Cynthia turned to look at him. His eyes were still shut but he was smiling smugly.

When they finally pulled up in front of the barn, Cynthia turned off her headlights. The sky was still black, and all that was visible was thick white snow flowing evenly along the rambling hills surrounding the structure. Light was pouring out an opened door at ground level.

"See the truck?" Carlos pointed to the top of the hill.

Cynthia squinted, waiting for her eyes to get used to the darkness. "Yes," she said hesitantly, making out a large dark object near the light. Gradually it came into focus. "Yes!" she said. She grabbed her camera and opened the car door.

Carlos grabbed her arm. "No! Let me do it!"

She shook her head. "What if they see you?"

"What if they see you?"

"They know you. They don't know me. I'll—I'll just act like a dumb blonde or something." She started to step out.

"But you have no boots!"

As he said that, Cynthia felt her feet sink into ankle-high snow. She had worn heels, planning on going right to work afterward. The fact that she, who wore dress boots to work on most winter days, had chosen high-heels this morning said something about her general mental state, something she refused to examine. She got back into the car. "Lend me your boots."

With reluctance, Carlos took off his boots. "Are you sure? I swear, I could do it easily. I know the terrain."

"No." Cynthia slipped off her shoes and stepped into Carlos's heavy footwear. She got out of the car. "Don't worry. I'll be fine!"

She took one step and fell. Splat. She felt the icy wetness penetrating all the crevices between her coat and boots, between her sleeves and her gloves, above the coat collar at her neck. She scrambled up before Carlos had time to get out of the car and ran up the hill.

She paused on the small plateau and decided to try a more circuitous route. She ran under the trees up the side until she got to the top, on the same level as the truck, but far to the left.

She was breathing heavily, more from terror than from the strenuousness of her trek.

She watched. The truck was backed up to the factory door, and no one was there. She started to run for it, but stopped. She looked at the crates piled on the back of the truck. How frequently did someone come out with a crate?

She should have asked Carlos! Loading the truck was his job! What was the matter with her this morning?

She looked at her watch. Five-fifty-eight. She waited. Five-fifty-nine. No movement. Nothing. Maybe she was wasting precious time. Six o'clock. Still nothing. Had they finished loading? Six-oh-one. She wished she had a dog she could be walking in case someone saw her.

A small shadowy figure came out of the factory. She looked at her watch: six-oh-two. He loaded a crate onto the truck. Five-fifty-eight to six-oh-two. She had at least four minutes. The shadowy figure took a breath of air, stretched, and headed back to the barn.

As soon as his feet crossed the threshold, she was off, lens cap off.

She clogged across the snow in Carlos's heavy boots, her camera poised, thinking of nothing, nothing but getting there. When she made it, without stopping, she snapped a picture. The flash worked! She couldn't believe it! Fueled by that high, she paused, placed herself so her lens caught both the license plate and the barn door, and snapped again. Ecstatic, she turned around and headed first to the trees, then down to the car.

Carlos was crossing himself when she climbed in.

"I didn't know you were religious!"

"I'm not!"

They both giggled in relief. "Now where?" she asked him. She was still on a high.

"The truck heads that way." He pointed. "Toward the highway. If we wait down the road a little, we'll be less noticeable."

They parked about half a mile down the road, near the highway, and waited.

"After we get the information this morning, what will you do?" Carlos asked. "Write an article? Go to the authorities?"

"Both."

He nodded, frowning.

"What's the matter?"

"Well, that's good, but a little sad too. On the one hand, we expose the factory owner for what he is—a creep taking chances with other people's lives—and we make sure there are no more victims, no more Franciscos. But on the other hand, we close the factory and stop the money coming in that feeds all the families."

"Not necessarily," Cynthia said. "We just force the workers to come up with ways to earn the money without endangering their lives."

"Believe me, most of those guys don't care!"

"If they knew the facts—really knew the facts—don't you think they would choose to live?"

Carlos chewed on a fingernail. "I stayed up real late last night, tossing and turning, trying to answer that question. And you know what I came up with? No! They'd choose to keep working in the factory for good money as long as they could!"

Cynthia sighed and leaned back in the front seat, thinking.

"But!" Carlos held up his hand victoriously. "I came up with another answer as well: If they really feel that way, then they have to be protected. It's the role of a good government—a democracy—to make sure that no employer disobeys laws and risks workers' lives to make a little extra money, right? And it's the role of citizens in a democracy, like us, to make sure the government does its job!" Carlos stared out the front window grinning. "At least, that's what Mr. Richmond would say."

"Who's Mr. Richmond?"

"The teacher I had for American history."

"Well, were Mr. Richmond's teachings an effective sleeping pill?" Cynthia laughed. "Did you to stop tossing and turning and get some sleep?"

Carlos's face clouded. "No. Not until, uh, not until I came up with something else."

"Really? What was that?"

"Things feel different to different people," Carlos said slowly. He turned to Cynthia. "I mean, like, chocolate might taste fantastic to me, but just sort of good to you. But we both bite into a candy bar and say, 'This is delicious.' Know what I mean?"

"You've lost me."

"There's no way of telling, just from the words we use, the expressions, whether things taste the same to both of us."

Cynthia shook her head, confused as to where this was leading.

"Same with feelings," Carlos went on quickly. "Say you tell me you have a headache. Now, I get terrible headaches, so I really feel awful for you. But it just might be that your head doesn't really hurt that much when you have a headache."

"Oh, Carlos," Cynthia murmured. She saw the connection now.

"It's just impossible to judge accurately what another person is feeling," Carlos continued. "It's real easy to overreact, to think things are worse than they really are!"

"Francisco's pain," Cynthia said softly.

Carlos swallowed hard and began nodding his head rapidly.

"Maybe it didn't hurt him as much as you thought it did."

"Yeah. Oh jeez, I hope it didn't!" His voice cracked and his chest began heaving. "And, well, there's more than that," he went on quickly. "Take pleasure. Maybe, well, his life seemed so miserable to me. But you can't tell how something really feels to another person. There had to be pleasures for him, don't you think? Things he did he liked—like sending those regular money orders home." He looked up at Cynthia hopefully. "That was a real accomplishment, right? I figure that was his equivalent of, say, my graduating from college. His goal. I mean, he must have felt really proud about that!"

Cynthia felt her throat constricting. She nodded and smiled at Carlos.

They heard the sound of a truck rattling up behind them. "That's it," Carlos said, looking over his shoulder. "That's the one."

Cynthia turned on the ignition and slowly pulled away from the curb. The truck turned left, onto the highway, and kept plodding along at a slow speed for several miles.

"I've never done this before," Cynthia said nervously. "You'll have to bear with me. I don't know how to follow someone without being noticed."

"You can begin by turning off your headlights," Carlos whispered, a gleam in his eyes. "It's daylight and we're the only car on the road with headlights."

Cynthia groaned and turned off her lights.

"They're turning off," Carlos warned after a few miles. "They turned on the signal."

Cynthia followed. There were several cars on the road, so she did not feel conspicuous. They went around a clover leaf and onto another highway. Cynthia and Carlos stared tensely ahead without talking as the truck plodded on and on, mile after mile. Just as Cynthia began entertaining nightmares of ending up in Florida two days later, the truck signaled another turn.

This time it pulled off the highway, turned right, drove down the road a few yards, and turned left into an industrial complex.

"Synco," Carlos said, reading the sign. "That was the name, 'Synco.' They're coming to a gate," he said, craning his neck to see. "What will we do at the gate?"

The truck pulled up and stopped. A man came out of the gate house, which had a big "Synco" sign on it, and walked to the truck.

Cynthia put the car in park, jumped out, and snapped another picture of the license, this time next to the corporate insignia on the gate. Victorious, she jumped into the car.

The truck pulled in and the man closed the gate behind it. For the first time, he noticed Cynthia and Carlos.

"What do we do now?" Carlos asked in panic.

Cynthia smiled. "This part is easy. 'Piece of cake,' as Jed's son would say."

She pulled up to the gate. "Could you please help me?" she asked breathlessly. "We are so lost, you wouldn't believe it. How do we get back on the main highway to Washington?"

The guard gave them directions, and they pulled out. "Piece of cake!" Carlos hooted, slapping his thigh.

They were just about two miles from the factory when Carlos heard Cynthia inhale sharply. He looked out the window, following Cynthia's eyes. "Mama Rosa's Restaurant and Motel," he said, reading the small sign next to two nondescript buildings in the small shopping center on their right. He looked back at Cynthia curiously.

She kept driving.

# · 19 ·

Sylvia Berg greeted Cynthia in the Capitol Radio reception area with a suspicious tilt of her head. "Jed called."

Cynthia's felt her body warm up. "He did? When?"

"Hours ago. A funny message." Sylvia peered down at the slip through her bifocals. "He's going to be tied up in meetings all morning, but he said that if you didn't make it in by ten, I should call his secretary and leave a message to that effect." Sylvia raised an eyebrow. "He sounded worried about you."

"Worried about you. . ." The words fell over Cynthia like golden rays of sunshine. Worried. Oh, he was worried. She smiled a little as she hung up her coat. When she turned around, she noticed Sylvia was looking at her alertly, awaiting an explanation.

"Oh . . . um . . . my car!" Cynthia explained, "He was probably worried because I've been having all sorts of trouble with my car!"

Sylvia stared her down. "That's all? Everything's okay?"

"Fine, Sylvia," Cynthia laughed. She looked at the clock. "I'm still on for covering that late-morning news conference on oil import taxes?"

"Yup." Sylvia went back to her desk work.

Pleased to find all the other reporters out of the office, Cynthia sat down at her desk and picked up the phone. A call to

OSHA revealed that all Maryland complaints were handled at the state office in Baltimore. She called Baltimore and made an appointment for early Monday morning.

Then she called the D.C. medical examiner's office. Traces of carbon tetrachloride were found throughout Francisco Lopez's body, she was told, enough to cite the chemical as a "possible" cause of death. However, because the liver and the kidneys were large organs that took a lot of abuse before falling apart, there was not enough to cite carbon tetrachloride as *the* cause.

Dammit.

When she hung up, she thought back to the view of Mama Rosa's Restaurant, right there, just a few blocks from the plant. A coincidence? Or a connection she had missed? Had Jed figured out from something Carlos said in the car last night that that "gangster" client of his—what was the guy's name? Sell-arbee? something like that—was involved in the illicit chemical factory?

Jed had been worried, Sylvia said.

Cynthia's visage hardened. Worried about what, exactly? Her safety on the icy highways in the predawn darkness? Or something more sinister? Worried because he had tipped off his client?

She grabbed the phone, called Baltimore information, and got the telephone number for Synco. She dialed it. "Yes, I'd like the name of the president of your company."

She bit her lip. Her hand trembled a little as she reached for a pen. "Could you spell that for me?" She stared down at the letters on the pad in front of her: "Theodore Selebri." She started to hang up, but then stopped. There was only one way to find out. She swallowed. "Could you connect me with his office?"

Her brain snapped along plotting strategy. This had to be handled the right way. The purpose was to figure out whether he had been warned without setting off any alarms of her own. "Mr. Selebri, please . . . Cynthia Matthews. I'm a reporter calling from Washington."

Her pen tapped nervously on the pad in front of her. Would he take the call?

If he does, play innocent, she instructed herself, and listen, above all, *listen* to the tone of voice, to the—

"Mr. Selebri? Hello," she said cheerfully. "My name is Cynthia Matthews. I'm a free-lance reporter and I'm thinking about doing a story on improvements in some of the older manufacturing industries in the Washington–Baltimore area. I wondered if I could ask you some questions about Synco."

Why, she certainly could! For twenty minutes, Theodore Selebri talked nonstop, explaining the plant's history, how he had inherited it from his father in 1984, and how, thanks to forward-thinking and cost-cutting, he had managed to put all his competitors out of business.

He was surprisingly indefinite on the specifics of this cost-cutting, as he was on his plans to "move into more high-tech operations."

Cynthia hung up the telephone, certain he had not been forewarned. She scanned the voluminous Selebri quotes she had written down. Her eyes stopped abruptly at one line in the middle of the page. "We're moving forward, going top-of-the-line in everything," it said, "from engineering to legal expertise."

She stared straight ahead. What the hell was Selebri's top-of-the-line lawyer up to?

"I take it everything went smoothly this morning," Jed said crisply when he called late that afternoon.

"Yes."

"Great." He moved on quickly to the business at hand: How about if he made his Friday night pickup of the kids in her car, and then they all got together for a movie and pizza?

"Fine."

The next three days proceeded along that course: personal intimacy, but a professional stand-off. Jed asked nothing about her trip to the factory—thereby convincing her he had made the connection between the plant and his client—and she asked nothing about his legal agenda.

She had one moment of paranoia. When the four of them were giggling at Timmy's antics at the roller-skating rink Saturday afternoon, Cynthia began wondering whether Jed might be using the distraction of "family fun" as a stalling tactic, to give his client time to cover up his tracks.

But that was just one moment, brought about, she decided

later, by the fact that she had been enjoying herself so thoroughly. Indeed, she realized, more peculiar than the significant omissions in their conversation was the fact that the omissions did not seem to matter that much.

Instinctively, they each fell back into the Cynthia-and-Jed relationship that had become so comfortable for them both: the frenetic, happy pace of "parenting" with Timmy and Lisa, the usual lengthy, yearning telephone call from Jed after the kids went to sleep Saturday night.

As a matter of fact, as they sat up reading under the covers of Cynthia's bed Sunday morning, the sections of the Sunday paper in a heap between them, she found herself wondering whether it would be that terrible to be married to a Russian spy, if everything else in the relationship worked.

"Have you ever thought about how bizarre our weekend schedule is becoming?" Jed asked, turning the page of the newspaper.

"Mmm."

"No, I'm serious. Saturday has become the day of good-clean-fun-with-the-kids. And then, praise the Lord, comes Sunday school." He cackled wickedly. "Sunday school and debauchery!" He moved closer and nibbled on Cynthia's shoulder. "It's all become a kind of sacrilegious takeoff for me. I mean, the Ten Commandments, Moses on the Mount, the tribes of Abraham, all have taken on exotic, sexual connotations!

"I miss you all Saturday night, and then Lisa whines Sunday morning, 'I can't find my Hebrew homework,' and I get an erection. I get into my straight, upright suburban vehicle, drop my two little religious scholars and their textbooks off at temple, and begin breathing heavily. By the time I get to your front door, I'm transformed into a sex fiend, ready to rape you in the vestibule!"

Cynthia chuckled. "So far you've always managed to make it to the bedroom." She looked at him, taking in the contrast between his large, hairy, masculine frame and the delicate lavender floral print of the quilt he'd pulled up to chest level. "I swear," she laughed, "you look like the wolf dressed up as Little Red Riding Hood's grandmother!"

"You guessed it," he hissed, pinning her on her back menacingly. "Don't trust me for a minute!" He kissed her on the neck.

"Are we going to continue our weekend tradition?" she asked, playing with his hair. "A soup dinner Sunday night?"

She felt his body tense slightly. He sat up. "Uh, I don't think I can come back tonight after I drop the kids off." He went back to the newspaper.

"Why not?" She watched him for signals.

"Huh? Oh, jeez, I'm really swamped with work."

"You're not too swamped to be lying here right now, reading the paper!"

"This is different!" he bellowed. "This is Sunday school!"

"And you're what? Born again?"

"In my own way, yes." He laughed, kissing her forehead. "But, starting tonight . . . uh . . . This is going to be a major work-week for me."

"Me too." She said it significantly. He did not seem to hear. "What are you working on?"

"Nothing I can go into. It's really complicated." He turned the page.

An unusual statement from the man who liked to "try out" his cases on her, acting out both sides. She stared at him. So that was the agenda? He was going to break his neck saving Selebri while she broke hers trying to nail him!

May the best man win? Her jaw clenched involuntarily.

She worked at calming down. That's the way it was supposed to be, she told herself. Everyone's entitled to legal counsel.

She studied Jed again, seeing him this time not as her lover, but as the opposition. She planned on settling the whole thing with one quick trip to the Maryland OSHA office Monday morning. What had he plotted that would keep him busy for five workdays? "You really figure this case or whatever will keep you busy all week?"

He ran his hand along the side of her face gently. "Come on now, just one week." He winked at her. "We have next weekend in West Virginia to look forward to."

She stared at the newspaper, wondering whether she would be able to enjoy spending the weekend at Sylvia's cabin with a man who had got Francisco's murderer off the hook.

"Looks like this new bill they're putting together on the Hill is going to mean major tax reform," Jed mumbled after a while.

Tax reform—Barker's confession. Cynthia's eyes rolled up to the ceiling. Great. Now she had a corrupt Senator in her bed along with the operator of an illicit chemical factory. She turned on Jed. "Just what exactly does that mean? 'Major tax reform'?"

He shrugged. "Major changes in the whole tax system. Progressive changes, it appears."

"No tax loopholes?"

Jed looked up from the paper and laughed. "Well, less loopholes, maybe, but believe me, as long as there is a Congress, there will be loopholes!"

"Aren't loopholes illegal?"

"They're not pure," he chuckled. "But I'm afraid loopholes are as American as apple pie. Loopholes are what you get for the boys back home." He winked at her. "As their representative in Congress."

"What about, if, say, you write loopholes for boys in other states . . . boys who pay you money to write loopholes?"

He sobered. "That's bad."

"Illegal?"

"Depends on the hows and whats. Highly unethical for sure." He yawned and began concentrating on a different article. Cynthia went back to her section.

"The farmers in the Midwest are in an uproar," Jed announced, turning the page. "The nineteen eighty-five Farm Law doesn't seem to be playing well in the Ballards of the country." He read some more and then put the paper down. "Wonder how I'd play in Ballard," he mused. He folded his hands across his chest. "Can't you just see the reaction? Native-born, corn-fed Cynthia Matthews brings back her boyfriend—a Semite from Brooklyn?"

"I'm afraid the only reaction would be 'Who is Cynthia Matthews?'" Cynthia snickered. "It's been quite a while since Ballard was my home base!"

"Okay then, your family." He nudged her. "Come on, they'd be more than a bit upset if you came home with me."

"Why?"

"Come off it! Your bringing home a Jew?"

She seemed confused. "If they liked you, it wouldn't make any difference."

"Don't give me that." He leaned back against the bedframe. "Has any Matthews besides you ever dated a Jew?"

"Yup. My sister, Georgine."

He warmed up. "Yeah? And what was the reaction?"

Cynthia thought for a moment. "My father felt he was 'promising'—that was my father's euphemism for 'able to earn a better-than-average living.' My mother thought he was strong. 'Just what the whole family's been looking for,' she said, 'someone who can control Georgine!'"

"But she broke up with him anyway."

"No! Quite the contrary! She married him!"

Jed sat upright. "Phil is Jewish?"

"Yup."

Jed looked at her angrily. "How come you never mentioned that?"

"I don't know." She seemed confused by his reaction. "I guess it didn't come up. I didn't think about it. I told you Phil was a lawyer and that he had a wonderfully drole sense of humor, and that I was crazy about him, and that Georgine and Phil's daughter is—"

"Leaving out the most important fact!"

She blinked. "For me, his other characteristics were more important."

"Come off it!"

She tilted her head. "Your Jewishness—you think that's your basic trait? The essence of your being?"

"I think it must make you feel very different from me!"

She ran her fingers against the back of his hand. "Well, yes, I guess so, but not in any sort of alienating sense—more in an attracting way. I love the things you are that I'm not. It makes you more interesting, really. We're alike in all the important ways. We laugh at the same things, have the same values. What is the word? 'Click,' that's it. We click." Her eyes melted. "Your 'Jewishness' is a very endearing part of you." She leaned over and kissed the tip of his nose playfully. "We seem to have the same ability to enjoy the Sabbath, no matter what our religions."

He pulled away. "Sunday is *not* the Jewish Sabbath," he snarled. "Saturday is."

She looked at him, startled. "What are you telling me? That you feel estranged from me because I'm not Jewish?"

"No. God, no!" He turned to her, his eyes darker in their seriousness. "You know that isn't it at all. That's ridiculous."

She took a deep breath. "I think you're right," she said resolutely. "It's something else."

He groaned. "I smell the hot breath of psychoanalysis."

"For some reason I don't understand, you keep expecting me to reject you."

"Yup, I was right. The shrink emerges."

"You keep waiting for me to do it, expecting it, almost wanting it."

"That's insane!"

"I hope so," she said.

The secretary at the front desk of the Maryland OSHA office pointed mutely to a stack of complaint forms on the table. The man in the first cubicle was more articulate. He told Cynthia the first step in all OSHA procedures was to fill out a complaint form.

His supervisor was involved in a meeting. Cynthia said she would wait. It proved to be just the first of a big series of waits.

Slowly and tediously throughout Monday morning, Cynthia worked her way from cubicle to cubicle to office to office, peeling off the elaborate layers of bureaucracy in her determination: This was an emergency. She would fill out a complaint only after being given assurances that this would be treated as an emergency.

Clearly, she was a nuisance.

Slightly before noon, an irritated-looking man led Cynthia into the office of a short, rotund woman of about fifty-five who was animatedly firing off words into the telephone receiver she held between her chin and her collarbone as she used her hands to filter through stacks of papers. The woman looked up over her bifocals, smiled at Cynthia, and beckoned to a seat on the other side of her desk—all without losing one beat in her telephone delivery. The man who had brought Cynthia in left hurriedly with what seemed to be relief.

The office, Cynthia decided, was about as institutional as you could get. A fluorescent light glared down from the ceiling with one of its three light bulbs blown out. A government calendar was taped up on one of the stark cement walls, an industrial poster containing information about how to report safety-code violations ("FILL OUT A COMPLAINT!") on the other. Dark green venetian blinds pulled up to half-mast sagged across the single dirt-encrusted window, offering a view of a dingy interior courtyard and other equally depressing-looking office windows across the way.

The government-issue plastic nameplate on the desk in front of the woman on the phone read: "Mrs. Patricia Furillo." The desk was in a state of critical overflow, strewn with stacks and stacks of papers, a half-eaten salami sandwich, and an ashtray too full to bear the burden of one more extinguished butt.

As Patricia Furillo went on and on, screaming into the phone one minute "How can you tell me that?" and then oozing out a "You're a doll, an absolute doll!" the next, Cynthia's spirits began to rise. This was the highest metabolism she had encountered all morning.

"So!" Mrs. Furillo said as she hung up the phone and shoved the papers she had been holding into a manilla folder. "Another troublemaker, huh?"

Cynthia opened her mouth to speak.

"They always send me the troublemakers," Mrs. Furillo chortled. "It's okay. I'm a troublemaker too." She picked up the filled ashtray and emptied it in the wastebasket. "What's the problem?" she asked, lighting another cigarette.

Cynthia met the woman's eyes and took a deep breath. "A Baltimore manufacturer is farming out an industrial procedure from his factory to a clandestine barn in rural Maryland, where a team of fifteen immigrant workers working an overnight shift from ten to six is regularly exposed to carbon tetrachloride without adequate protection. I want you to stop it."

Well, Cynthia decided, all the practice had at least made her delivery succinct. She leaned forward, waiting for another put-off, ready to pounce.

Mrs. Furillo leaned forward too. "What's your role in this?" she asked firmly.

"I'm a reporter. One of the workers came to me."

"How do you know the chemical is carbon tet?"

"A worker sneaked out a sample. We had it tested." Cynthia reached into her purse and pulled out a slip of paper. She handed it to Mrs. Furillo. "That's the name and telephone number of the chemist who did the testing."

Mrs. Furillo took the paper but did not look at it. "What is the name of the company?"

"There is no name on the barn, no name on the finished product," Cynthia said. "No payroll, I suspect. The workers are paid off each night in cash."

Mrs. Furillo sat back in her chair and took another drag on her cigarette.

"A worker who had the longest and closest exposure to the chemical died last Thursday at D.C. General Hospital of liver and kidney dysfunction. The autopsy revealed traces of carbon tetrachloride throughout his system." Cynthia reached into her purse and pulled out another slip of paper. "That's the name and telephone number of the man in the D.C. medical examiner's office who is familiar with the autopsy."

Mrs. Furillo looked at the paper. "Who is Francisco Lopez?"

"The worker who died," Cynthia said. "Now, I've been told by the people here that OSHA has to inform the employer, and that OSHA does not do night inspec—"

"Bullshit!" Mrs. Furillo picked up the phone and dialed the medical examiner's number. Cynthia listened as Mrs. Furillo asked questions. It sounded as though she was getting essentially the same report Cynthia had got.

Cynthia wished she had brought Carlos with her to further document the case. "I have a witness," she said when Patricia Furillo hung up the phone. "Someone who has been working in the factory. I could call him—"

Mrs. Furillo waved her away. "Not necessary. Not if we have something like a coroner's report and a lab's verification." She took the paper with the laboratory number on it and dialed it.

When she finished talking to the man at the chemical laboratory, she strummed her fingers on the desktop impatiently. "You know the location of this barn?"

Cynthia nodded.

"We'll send out a team tonight."

Cynthia's eyes lit up. "You can do that?"

"Of course we can!" Mrs. Furillo snapped. "This sounds like an emergency!"

"Do you have to inform the employer first?" Cynthia asked, realizing she was now spouting the bureaucratic jargon she had been listening to all morning.

"Not in a situation like this. Who is there to inform anyway?"

"What if they don't let you in?"

"Oh, they'll let us in. We have the right of entry under law, and if they refuse us, we have the right to go to court to get entry." Mrs. Furillo took off her glasses and rubbed her eyes. "Are you familiar with the work process in the barn?"

"Yes."

"I'm going to round up some hygienists," Mrs. Furillo said. "In a case like this—a situation of possible chemical exposure— we need certified industrial hygienists, not safety inspectors. You can tell them what you know of the process, and they'll know what to take with them for monitoring and testing."

"Um . . ." Cynthia played with her purse. "The workers are . . . most of them are illegal aliens. Would your people have to report them to Immigration?"

Mrs. Furillo stabbed out her cigarette and shook her head. "We don't ask if they're legal or illegal," she said. "That's not our job. A worker is a worker and we treat him as such. Most of the time for witness statements we don't even ask for a social security number. That's not of interest to us."

Cynthia wanted to kiss her. "If it's as bad as it looks, what happens?"

"We close it down. We fine the employer."

"But what if you can't track the employer down?"

"Sweetheart, we'll find him. Don't worry about that."

Cynthia decided to keep Synco to herself, but made a mental note to check back with Mrs. Furillo to make sure they had singled out the same employer.

"Now, you have to realize," Mrs. Furillo was saying, "we're just going to test tonight. If the situation seems real bad, we'll close down the site immediately, but we won't have the results of the blood tests for a few days."

"Fine. I understand."

Mrs. Furillo picked up the phone. "I'm going to call the hygienist." She paused and cocked her head at Cynthia. "Do me one little favor, will you, honey?"

"What?"

Mrs. Furillo pulled a paper out of her top drawer. "Fill out a complaint form."

"You bet I will!" Cynthia shouted, taking out a pen.

Senator Frederick Barker sat down at his desk and began going through the large stack of telephone message slips that had built up during the time he'd been out of town, quickly reading the name of each caller, and then turning the slips face-down in one of two piles.

Bob Smart.

Lila Frank.

Stephanie Roberts.

Jimmy Farnsworth.

Sam Clem—

His head jerked up. He stared at the empty chair across his desk, seeing her sitting in it, the blur of blond hair and blue eyes, the tape recorder on the desk in front of her, and it came back to him, now, his own voice blurting it out.

*"Jimmy Farnsworth in Philly . . ."*

That was the name he had remembered telling her, but had been unable to recall the next day. Yes, god*damn* it to hell, that had been the name!

He retrieved the phone slip. No message, just "You were called by Jimmy Farnsworth of the Philadelphia Development Association." Senator Barker looked at his desk calendar. The message was three days old.

He picked up the telephone and buzzed. "Miranda, get Jimmy Farnsworth at the Philadelphia Development Association for me, will you, dear?"

He hung up and began strumming his fingers impatiently on the desktop. All the old anxieties were suddenly back. Here he had thought that interview was dead and gone. In fact, had been certain it was.

Hold on, hold on, he instructed himself. The phone call was probably about something else. Had he heard of any other repercussions from the interview with Cynthia Matthews? Not a one in all these weeks. He felt his breathing slow down.

Probably nothing out of the ordinary. Still, now that he remembered Farnsworth had been the name, it couldn't hurt to say something.

His phone buzzed.

"Hello."

"Hello, Senator."

"Hey, Jim. Sorry to take so long getting back to you, but I just got back from a couple of days in Iowa. What can I do for you? Is there some problem?"

"Well, not really a problem, Senator. Something just came up that I thought you should know about."

"And what's that?"

"Well, we've had a reporter here . . ." Farnsworth's voice got lower. "Not a local Philadelphia reporter. One from out-of-state. Asking all kinds of questions."

Barker's fist clenched. "Really?" he asked lightly. "What kinds of questions?"

"About you—your trips to Philadelphia, who you met with here and for what purpose, what's in your tax bill that helps our real-estate interests, that kind of thing."

"Now, that's mighty complimentary of you, Jimmy," the Senator drawled. "But there are nineteen other Senators on the Finance Committee down here that'd be awful miffed at the idea that this is *my* tax bill!"

"I'm just quoting the reporter, Senator. The reporter seemed to think there was a direct connection, and had a very clear idea about which provisions you placed in the tax bill and how those provisions would, uh, well, *could* help out the Philadelphia Development Association."

Senator Barker's face grew grim. "And what did you say, Jim?"

"Nothing. Nothing at all. Just that I was frankly confused and surprised by the suggestion. 'Some things are good for us in the bill, some aren't,' I said, 'and I have no idea which provisions were Senator Barker's doing.'"

"Uh-huh."

"But, well, I found out that the reporter has a list of all the other Association members. What bothers me is, I don't know what my members are gonna do. Do you follow me, Senator?"

"Well, don't worry about it, Jim." Senator Barker's casual delivery did not match his taut visage. "It's probably nothing."

"Senator, I thought maybe you might want the reporter's name and address. I've got it written down right here."

Senator Barker stared at the empty chair on the other side of the desk, once again picturing her sitting there, infuriated by the vision. He bit his lower lip. "Naw, Jimmy. No need."

As soon as he hung up, Barker picked up the intercom. "Miranda, get me David Steele at the Steele Travel Agency, please."

He sat thinking. What ever happened to the report he had had the young college intern do for him? The one where he had added Cynthia Matthews's name to that list of reporters? He had passed on the information the boy had amassed about the other four reporters, but had been careful to keep the stuff on Cynthia Matthews. He hadn't bothered to read it since nothing further had happened.

He pulled out the side drawer of his desk and began fumbling through the papers.

Nothing's ever where you want it when you want it.

Aha!

He pulled out the report he was looking for just as Miranda buzzed him back. "David Steele's on line seven."

"Hello, Mr. Steele."

"Good morning, Senator Barker. How are you today?"

"Just fine. Listen, I was wondering . . . did that reporter we talked about ever make contact with you?"

"No, Senator. I would have called you if he had."

Barker smiled, and his body relaxed considerably. "Well, I've been traveling a lot, and I wasn't sure. Thank you, Mr. Steele. That's good news."

More relaxed now, the Senator settled back in his chair and pulled out intern Bruce Abbott's report on Cynthia Matthews. "Of the five reporters, Cynthia Matthews does not fit in," Abbott had written. "It is difficult to understand why she would have requested an in-depth interview, because most of her articles are nonpolitical and exposés rather than features. This is a reporter who seems to delight in uncovering misconduct."

Oh, what does a naive college student know, Barker thought to calm himself. He pulled out the sample of Cynthia Matthews's articles Abbott had attached, and began reading through them.

By the time he finished, his estimate of Abbott's overview had grown immeasurably, as had his discomfort. Ms. Cynthia Matthews was certainly an accomplished journalist. What's more, judging from her past offerings, it was damn hard to believe the farm girl had really sought him out that night just for input for a flighty story on "human loss." Scandal was more her cup of tea.

His phone buzzed again. "Yes, Miranda?"

"It's David Steele back on line seven."

Barker frowned and picked up the telephone. "Mr. Steele?"

"Uh, Senator Barker, I have an apology to make. After we talked, I checked with some of my employees, just to be certain. It is company policy that any unusual requests come directly to me, so I had just assumed—"

"And what did you find out, Mr. Steele?" Barker leaned forward in his chair. "Was there an inquiry?"

"Yes, Senator. More than a week ago. The employee who took the call was unaware of the policy. He's new here, and he—"

"What did he do? The employee?"

"Oh, he refused to answer any questions about itineraries! You don't have to worry about that, Senator! *That* is a very high priority here. It's just, well, if he had informed me, I would have called you immediately."

"No problem, Mr. Steele," Barker said cordially. "Thank you for calling back."

The Senator took a deep breath, and sat very still in his chair, clenching and unclenching his right hand. Well, how's that for a false sense of security? He began breathing faster. So the farm girl was cagey, rather than compassionate, eh? Plotting his demise even as she covered his trade hearings?

Barker picked up the Cynthia Matthews's articles and hurled them into the trash can beside his desk.

From what Farnsworth said, it sounded as though she had done her homework very thoroughly. He stood up abruptly, and headed for the door. No harm in checking a little.

The stout, middle-aged woman at the reception desk looked up as he walked into the room and did a double take. "Why, Senator Barker!"

"Hello, Mary. I was told Mary Burrows was the person who could answer a little question I have." He winked at the woman. "Didn't surprise me in the least. Mary Burrows knows all the answers."

She laughed and blushed a little. "What was the question?"

"I wanted to check on whether a reporter who's coming to see me tonight has done his homework—whether he's read the Senate Finance Committee version of the tax bill, the way he said he would before our interview."

Mary Burrows looked up at him happily, the way staff workers looked when they could fulfill a Senator's request. In this case, Senator Barker realized thankfully, she did not even consider the fact that the request was a little preposterous. (Since when did a Senator check up to make sure a reporter was prepared?) Ahh, blessed are those who serve.

"Well, I can tell you if he's picked up a copy." Mary Burrows reached into a folder and pulled out a list. "The first printing was short, so we're only giving them out to one reporter per publication, until we get some more in."

"So I heard."

She handed Barker a list. "Those are all the reporters who have picked up copies."

Senator Barker's eyes roamed down the page. He felt his pulse quicken when he got to the notation, "Cynthia Matthews, Capitol Radio," but he kept right on reading, careful to keep his face devoid of all expression.

He noted, as he scanned, that, with the exception of Cynthia Matthews, most of those who had sought copies were financial reporters. That made sense. A complicated piece of tax legislation in its preliminary stages had appeal only for those who specialized in business.

And, of course, for those anxious to hang Senator Barker.

"Nope. His name's not here." Barker smiled as he handed the list back to Mary Burrows and headed for the door.

"My, you sure have generated a lot of interest in this bill, Senator Barker," Mary Burrows clucked.

"Hmm?" Barker turned around. "How's that?"

"I heard one of the young people on the staff complaining the other day about a session with a reporter that dragged on and on. He said the reporter kept him on the phone for a full hour, and every single provision the reporter asked about was one that had been inserted by you, Senator Barker!" She smiled up at him.

"Isn't that something?" Barker muttered as he headed for the door. His voice was a little hoarse.

# · 20 ·

The rest of Cynthia's day at OSHA was spent in a frenzy of activity. She met with the team of hygienists. She called Carlos and explained to him what Mrs. Furillo had said about not reporting the workers to Immigration, and urged him to report for work. The men might panic, she told him. It would be helpful to have someone they knew there to translate.

When she was not working on the details, she was trying to sell the story—slipping into phone booths to call editors who had bought her work in the past, and then calling back and calling back, since they were always away from their desks and she was not reachable by phone.

By nightfall, she had repeated the facts so many times she felt that if someone asked her her name, she would say, "A Baltimore manufacturer has been using illegal aliens from the District to—"

At eight o'clock, she got the answer she had been waiting for: the promise of a major spread in the Sunday paper for a long introspective piece, providing the finished product was as good as she promised and delivered to them by Friday noon.

Her glee rapidly turned into anxiety: Would it be as good as she promised?

At eleven o'clock that night, Cynthia drove to the barn; the OSHA team followed in another car. She parked on the street and, along with the others, stared up at what had to be a picture of serenity: white snowy hills topped off by a rustic barn with light flickering out the opened door.

As they made their way up the hill to the barn, Cynthia found herself lagging behind, shivering in the coldness, overwhelmed by a desire to be someplace else—anyplace else.

They got to the door and walked in. Just walked in. The light was almost blinding in contrast to the darkness outside. The barn's fluorescent ceiling lights cast a strange off-white glow that reverberated off the metallic paneling on the interior walls in a dizzying brightness, giving the room an iridescent grayness. The workers were scattered all over—small wiry men, dark ants barely discernible against the structure's vast brightness, lifting and lowering and pounding and carrying in total silence. No one spoke.

The sound of the machinery, however, was deafening. The assembly line rumbled. The parts clattered as the men shifted them. A loud, vibrating, stamping noise was coming from the other end of the barn.

The OSHA group stood unnoticed at the entrance, looking for someone to receive their official speech. Cynthia scanned the group nervously and finally spotted Carlos, just a few yards away. He did not see them. No one did.

Cynthia felt like laughing. Suppose OSHA launched a raid and no one noticed?

Finally the worker closest to the door looked up. A blank stare, bizarre in its total lack of reaction. The leader of the OSHA group approached him. "Hello, we are from—"

The worker's mouth opened, but his eyes seemed glazed over, his facial muscles fixed in a deathlike paralysis. He pointed to the other end of the barn. Gradually other workers looked up, including Carlos.

Carlos ran to the other end of the barn and returned with a large, paunchy, middle-aged man wearing a mask and white cover, like the other workers wore, but with a Baltimore Orioles baseball cap on his head.

The OSHA leader began to speak again. Halfway through the second sentence, the man in the baseball cap waved his hands and shook his head. "I dunno nothing. I just work here, work for the man who pays my salary. Do whatever you want. I dunno. I dunno."

The team of hygienists put on their protective gear and walked in.

By this time, all the workers had noticed the team, and all work had stopped, but no one moved. Each man stood at his station staring, just staring. Cynthia pointed out Carlos to the OSHA team leader, as she promised she would. The OSHA man walked over to Carlos, instructed him, and Carlos stood on a crate and yelled the words in Spanish to the group.

Cynthia waited at the door. That had been the agreement. She was not permitted inside. She watched as the hygienists set up their equipment, watched as they measured and sampled, watched as the men lined up in silence and passively submitted to the blood tests, watched as the American foreman paced back and forth nervously, until one of the OSHA team sat him down and began asking him questions and writing down his answers.

For more than an hour she watched, hypnotized by the scene, shocked by the total passivity of the Hispanic workers. Not once, during all the time she stared, did she see one of the workers interact with another or even so much as open his mouth to speak. She could not stop staring at their eyes—dark, haunting eyes, devoid of expression, devoid of emotion. Was it the effect of the chemical or the effect of years of nomadic living? Whatever, the look in their eyes gave the whole scene a nightmarish quality.

Finally, Carlos came to the door. "They said they don't need me anymore," he said. He was breathing heavily. "Can we go? Please can we go?"

They walked to her car. When they got in, Carlos put his head in his hands and sobbed. Just sobbed. Cynthia put her hand on his shoulder and patted him gently.

"I don't know why—" he cried. "I just—"

"Shh," Cynthia said softly. "I know why."

He sat up and wiped his face with his hands. His breaths were coming in hiccuping puffs, like a child trying to suppress tears. "Let's go," he said. "Please, let's go."

Cynthia pulled the car away from the curb.

After a while, Carlos began to breathe more regularly. "I

think the foreman told them everything," he said. "I heard him say 'Synco'. That's all I know. At least twice I heard him say 'Synco.'"

Cynthia took a deep breath and smiled as she exhaled.

"They thought it was bad—the people from the government? 'Despicable.' That's what the man at the chemical bath said to the lady working with him." Carlos was hugging himself, trembling a little. "Why do you think it freaked me out?" he asked Cynthia. "It wasn't a surprise or anything, the raid."

"Oh, probably just a mixture of a whole lot of emotions coming together," she said. "Francisco's death, the feelings you've developed for the workers, and the shock too. It's one thing to suspect. It's quite another to have your suspicions confirmed like that."

Carlos contemplated that, and gradually Cynthia noted a change in his demeanor. He sat up straighter, threw his shoulders back, and began nodding, slowly at first, but then faster, with conviction. "The American government really works!" he declared finally.

She stared at the road.

"You have to feel proud, being in a country like this," he went on. "A country that protects even illegal workers from dangers! Those OSHA people, I was really impressed with them. How about you?"

Cynthia thought of her morning begging the low-level OSHA bureaucrats to do something. But then she thought of Patricia Furillo. "You're right."

"It *was* kind of a nightmare tonight," Carlos summed up. "But then it was kind of good for me, I think. See, I've been real angry lately—about the green card and all. But, you know what? It's worth waiting for. I know that now."

Cynthia eyed him fondly. Carlos Ramirez had managed to come up with a new little philosophical pearl to assure sleep.

But then, she told herself, he was not alone. She had a pearl of her own. "The really remarkable thing," she began excitedly, "is that we caught them cold. They had no idea we were coming. No one had warned them!"

"Who could have warned them?" Carlos shrugged. "After all, no one knew we were on the trail but you, me, and Jed."

"Mmm." She gazed rapturously at the road ahead. "You, me, and Jed."

Cynthia stayed home from work Tuesday to begin writing her article. After spending three hours circling the story, she was feeling frustrated.

She went into the kitchen and poured herself another cup of coffee. She went into the bathroom and brushed her hair. She took her dirty jogging clothes off the floor and dropped them into the hamper. As she began to brush her teeth, she lectured the reflection in the mirror.

"This is Tuesday," she told herself. "You have exactly half a day and three nights to write this story, and you are getting nowhere. You have already practically blown today."

Well, if worse came to worse, she could always take another workday off and . . .

She glared at herself in the mirror. "Get on with it!"

Suffused with new energy, she went back to the living room, but she walked past the desk and the typewriter and kept going. In circles. The problem was, she had no answers yet. The chemical analysis on the workers had not been completed. Theodore Selebri had been officially cited by OSHA, but she had no idea what his penalty would be, what his lawyers would do. How could she write a story without an ending?

Without a theme, really. If Selebri were convicted, and his company fell into ruins, that would be a story. If Selebri got off scot-free, the stinker, that would be a different story, but still a story. What good could come of a story with neither verdict?

She walked around the coffee table and headed back to the kitchen, telling herself her coffee wasn't hot enough.

She saw the eyes again, those dark, expressionless eyes. She felt a chill creeping down her spine. Why hadn't she been able to get them out of her head?

Back to the facts. She was a reporter, not a photographer. The facts. But she did not have all the facts.

The eyes came back. This time, instead of trying to blot them out, she squinted, looking for a meaning behind them.

She thought of the millions of tourists from all over the world who flocked excitedly with cameras and children to the nation's capital—to the White House and the Congress and the memorials and the cherry blossoms—and then she thought of the motley, disheveled group of Washington's illegal guests, who lived on city streets and in flophouses oblivious to the tourist attractions just blocks away. Criminals, all, but whose only real crime was wanting to earn money to send home.

And then there was Carlos, the most pathetic irony of all. Carlos who so enthusiastically and ardently pledged allegiance to a country that would not give him a green card.

Ironies. All she had were ironies. She considered another irony: a reporter who had managed to wangle a well-placed spread for megabucks and who could now not find a story.

She leaned on the kitchen counter and swished the coffee around and around in her mug. And then her head cleared. Of course. There was her story. Right there, in the eyes and in the ironies. How could she have been so stupid?

She marched back to her desk and sat down, oblivious to the fact that she had left her coffee in the kitchen. She reached into her desk drawer, fumbled through the cassettes, and put the one marked "Francisco" into her tape recorder. She sat and listened to the whole interview, taking copious notes. When the tape finished, she pulled the piece of paper she had been writing on out of the typewriter, threw it in the wastebasket, and scrolled in a new one.


"To us!" Brittany Spinnet proclaimed ceremoniously as she raised her wine glass.

"To us!" Pamela Ricci and Cynthia chimed in.

The waitress came to take their orders, and Brittany and Pamela sat in shock as Cynthia ordered the club sandwich platter, plus an order of pasta, and then, as an afterthought, a bowl of gumbo as well. "I'm absolutely famished!" she gasped as she reached for a roll.

"Well," Pamela snickered to Brittany, "he's sure improved her appetite, hasn't he?"

Cynthia's eyes twinkled in feigned innocence. "Who?"

"Who?" Pamela shouted. "Who! The man who answers the telephone when I call! The man who's kept you so busy we never get to see you anymore!" She picked up a roll, broke it in half, and began buttering it. "So? When do we get a chance to meet this mysterious Jed Farber who is so witty on the phone?"

"Soon." Cynthia buttered her roll. "I promise. It's just—everything is so crazy right now. I'm working on a story with a Friday noon deadline, and—"

"Actually," Brittany said, "I've already met him."

Cynthia gave Brittany a suspicious look, and then turned to Pamela, her eyebrow raised. "Was it my imagination, or was that uttered with a note of disdain?"

"No," Pamela agreed, "not your imagination."

Cynthia looked at Brittany askance. "Is the wicked fairy about to rain on my parade?"

Pamela broke out laughing. Cynthia joined her, confident that all the rain in the world could not dampen *this* parade.

"Well," Brittany went on, her eyes swirling around with the wine in her glass, "not really 'met him.' I mean, not that he'd remember. I used to see him all the time at parties when he was working in the Senate. Very, very hairy chest, as I recall."

Cynthia whirled on her. "And how the hell did you get a close-up view of his hairy chest?"

"Relax," Brittany giggled. "Just from pool parties, is all. I remember seeing him at summer swimming parties, fundraisers, that type of thing." She continued gazing into her wine glass. "Big nose. If I remember correctly." Slowly, her eyes traveled up to Cynthia's. "Isn't he . . . uh . . . Jewish?"

"Yup. Is that a problem for you, Britt?" Her tone turned steely.

"No. No, uh, not at all. It's just, well, it's kind of a change of pace for you, isn't it?"

Cynthia smiled tightly. "If so, then I'm overripe for a change of pace."

"I also heard he had a real chip on his shoulder." Brittany focused again on her wine glass. "Dated a lot, but never for long. Dated 'em and dropped 'em. That kind of thing. I'll tell you, he really got around!" She turned to Cynthia. "He's divorced, right?"

"Right. His former wife lives in Maryland. She's an interior decorator or something like—"

"Anna Farber?" Pamela gasped. "Spelled 'A-n-n-a,' but pronounced 'honuh,' as in 'your honuh, the judge'?"

The color drained from Cynthia's face. "You know her?"

"Oh, do I ever. Do I ever! She stole a client from me, really *stole* him, and that's highly unusual in my business. You fight like crazy to win customers, but once you do and you've ordered their stuff, it is a no-no—pure sacrilege—for someone else to move in. But she did. I had this guy's place all planned and half done, and Anna Farber met him at a party, took one whiff of his bankroll, and began wondering out loud—tactfully, to be sure— if this and that was *really* his taste, suggesting improvements, playing to his ego."

Pamela pointed her roll at Cynthia. "Anna Farber is the kind of woman who, as a girl, played up to boys by saying things like 'Oooh, you're so big and strong!' and actually managed to pull it off. And, she's still doing it. 'Oooh, you have such an artistic flair!' she told my client. 'You need someone who can direct you, not dominate you'!"

Cynthia leaned forward with interest. "Is that really what she's like? A manipulator?"

Pamela leaned back in her chair. "Well, what does her former husband say?"

"That she's an immaculate, gorgeous, painted, petite iceberg."

Pamela chomped on her roll. "He's perceptive. I'll give him that. I'd add 'bitch,' bitch of the classic variety, and I'll tell you something else," she said very seriously, pointing her butter knife at Cynthia. "I'd watch out for psychiatric disorders in any man who spent a long period of time living with Anna Farber, especially a man who willingly chose to spend a long period of time with Anna Farber. I'd say you and she are as different as two people can get."

"Maybe he's ready for a change of pace too!"

"Is that what he says?"

"He doesn't talk about her much."

"Yeah? Concentration camp survivors don't like to talk much about their pasts either, but there are still plenty of scars."

"Well, they're not readily apparent with him, if there are."

"Scars often aren't readily apparent—especially the deep, emotional ones."

"My God, will you listen to the two of you!" Cynthia shouted. "I can't believe it! I haven't even gotten to tell you anything about the man, and you're already insisting he's funny-looking and emotionally scarred!"

"I'm sorry," Pamela apologized.

"Yeah, me too," Brittany said. "I certainly wasn't trying to make him less appealing for you."

"Don't worry," Cynthia said icily. "You couldn't, even if you wanted to."

"Well, I mean, I didn't want to influence you against him."

"And I meant it. You couldn't."

The two of them looked at Cynthia with shock. "You're really sold on this one, aren't you?" Pamela murmured.

Cynthia beamed. "Absolutely. One hundred percent."

Brittany reached over and put her hand on Cynthia's. "Now, Cyn . . . are you sure this isn't just a rebound thing? After Rob Diamond?"

"Leave her alone!" Pamela thundered. "She's right. We're being complete bitches." She turned to Cynthia. "Tell us about him. C'mon."

Cynthia shrugged and smiled. "He's wonderful," she said dreamily. "I think he's absolutely wonderful, and beautiful too—hairy chest, nose, and all—and he's very sexy. He's such fun. He has a fantastic sense of humor, and an exciting mind . . ." Her eyes rolled up to the ceiling. "Oh, hell, it all sounds so clichéd, but it's hard to generalize, especially when your two best friends have put you on the defensive! I'm just thoroughly, a thousand percent in love with him. That's all."

"But Cyn—"

"And you two know me well enough to know that I've never felt this way before. Not so completely."

"Are you in this to the limit?" Pamela asked intently. "Would you actually want to marry him?"

"Marry. Well, that's a bit farfetched," she sidestepped. "The subject hasn't really come up."

"There!" Brittany shouted, holding up a finger. "You *do* have doubts!"

Cynthia smiled. "Doubts about his asking me. That's all. It's a little early. I only met him about a month ago."

Pamela leaned forward. "But if he did?"

"In a minute. Yup. Oh, yes." She played with her napkin.

"All I know is he is someone I'm both excited by and completely comfortable with. I love living with him, being with him, all the time. I feel a little as though I've been role playing with men for years, trying to be whatever I think they want me to be. With Jed, I can just relax completely and be myself. He actually likes *me*! Myself!"

"I've never heard you come on like this," Brittany muttered, as though she were reproaching a child who was misbehaving.

Cynthia burst out laughing. "I've never felt like this before!"

"Will we like him?" Brittany asked, frowning.

"I hope so. I certainly hope so." Cynthia got a gleam in her eye. "Because I would hate to have to stop seeing my two oldest, dearest friends."

"You'd do that?" Brittany asked indignantly. "Him over us?"

"Oh, Britt, I'm just teasing."

"And threatening a little too." Pamela gave Cynthia a significant look.

Cynthia laughed. "That too."

"Okay, then. When do we get to meet him?" Pamela asked, sipping her wine. "How about this weekend? After you finish the story deadline?"

"This weekend's no good. We're going to West Virginia with his kids. Sylvia—you know, the woman in my office? She offered us her cabin for the weekend."

"That sounds wonderful." Pamela sighed. "Out in the country . . ."

Cynthia frowned. "I hope so. I'm a little nervous about it. Sunday is Jed's birthday, and, well, the kids say they've never celebrated his birthday, so I got all excited about having a big birthday party, and we've bought all these presents, and the kids are writing poems, and I was planning on cooking all sorts of special things . . ."

"Walt Disney!" Brittany burst out laughing. "Sounds like you've been writing for Walt Disney lately!"

Cynthia looked at her. For the first time she seemed uncomfortable. "You think it's corny?"

"A bit! Playing house and making a birthday party for Daddy?"

Cynthia's eyes clouded as she turned from Brittany to Pamela. "Too corny? Do you think it's too corny?"

"Well," Brittany said, "did it ever occur to you that maybe Jed Farber never celebrated his birthday before because he didn't *want* to celebrate it? Because he thought such celebrations were a little bit tacky? Kind of kitsch?"

Cynthia stared straight ahead, her eyes large and frightened. "Yes, as a matter of fact. It occurred to me last night, right after I chose a recipe for the birthday cake. I spent half the night wide-awake in bed worrying about it." She turned to Pamela, in search of support. "Part of me is worried he'll hate it, but the other part of me thinks that—well, he's a very family person, very sentimental. I guess what made me think of doing it in the first place was the feeling I had that he'd love something warm and familial like that. And that, with the divorce and everything, he'd been deprived of it." She shrugged. "I just thought it would make him happy. I really want to make him happy. He makes me so happy. So—"

Pamela raised an eyebrow. "All I know is I'd be a little leery about playing house with somebody else's children." She sighed. "Especially if they were Anna Farber's children."

Cynthia stared at Pamela in silence, hoping for a second thought, some encouragement, but Pamela just looked up at the waitress who had brought their orders. Cynthia stared down at hers wondering why she had ordered so much food. Suddenly she didn't feel the least bit hungry.

"Oh, I guess the American van driver saw a group, a bunch of Latinos," Carlos said slowly. "But the workers saw themselves as solitary islands—Chileans, Ecuadorans, Hondurans, Mexicans—separated from each other by national prejudices and the knowledge that, since this was a job for people with no papers, everyone was hiding something."

Cynthia turned off the tape recorder and went back to her typewriter. She had spent two nights now in the world of the men who worked in the chemical factory. Her guide was Carlos Ramirez. Over and over again, she had played the tape of her interview with Carlos.

To the delight of his schoolteacher parents, Carlos Ramirez

had learned to read at the age of four, and from that time on had never considered himself anything less than promising.

True, the promise became shakier with the destruction of his village in El Salvador, the death of his father, and the sudden migration to the United States. But the shakiness was temporary.

In Washington, D.C., Carlos had found firm ground once again, mastered English in a few months, and excelled academically. The promising one was now thriving in the land of unlimited promise. The problem of the green card, the daunted hopes for college, were just temporary setbacks, dim in comparison to the light of the promise, the brightness of the hope for the future.

And then, suddenly, Carlos Ramirez had found himself working with men without hope, sitting in a van every night and every morning with men who saw no future.

The more she wrote, the more Cynthia slipped back as the narrator, pushing Carlos to the front.

The men's lives became starker when seen through Carlos's eyes. The ironies were more powerful when left for the reader to grasp from Carlos's perspective.

The story Cynthia finished writing in the early hours of Friday morning was lovingly crafted, and, she had to admit, damn good. It was Carlos Ramirez's story.

Her confidence went up several notches when she delivered the manuscript at noon on Friday. The editors were ecstatic.

# · 21 ·

All the way to West Virginia, Lisa and Timmy scrambled around excitedly in the backseat of the car, asking questions, making plans. Would they be able to ice-skate? To go sledding? Could they toast marshmallows?

In the front seat, an undercurrent of adult electricity was being channeled into group discussion. But it was there—heightened by unanswered questions, the hunger of a week-long separation, and the knowledge that, in just a few more hours, they would be alone, together, at last.

The group excitement turned to delight when they got to Sylvia's mountain retreat and discovered a large, thoroughly frozen pond, deep snow, and a big, rustically beautiful house. Jed built a fire in the living-room fireplace, where they cooked hot dogs and toasted marshmallows and capped the evening off telling ghost stories.

When Jed finally emerged from the final round of "good-night kisses" in the children's bedrooms, he silently refilled their wine glasses and plopped down beside Cynthia in front of the fire. "Hello, stranger."

"Five whole days," she gasped.

"Worse," he commiserated. "Five *nights!*"

They sat very still, staring into each other's eyes, their lips just inches away and moving closer.

She backed off. "Words first," she announced, taking a sip of wine. "What the *hell* have you been doing all week?"

He stared into the fire. "Did you write a story?"

"Yup."

"Is it good? I mean, *really* good?"

"I brought you a copy." She shrugged. "The editors thought so."

"The editors?" He turned to her with interest. "You've sold it?"

"It'll be coming out in Sunday's *Herald*," she said smugly. "A really big spread."

"The Sunday paper!"

"Shh! You'll wake the kids!"

"The Sunday paper!" He whispered it this time, but his voice still squeaked a little. "I don't believe it! Damn, I'm proud of you!" He looked at her for a long time, as though he really was proud of her, proud and pleased.

"Will that be your client's reaction?" she asked, wide-eyed.

He turned back to the fire. "Theodore Selebri has decided to return to his former attorneys, Gadson and Abel, for representation on this one," he chuckled.

She was thoroughly confused. "How come?"

"A . . . uh . . . conflict of interest." Jed took a large gulp of wine and stared at the log crackling in the fireplace. "Selebri called and told me he needed help with some problems that had come up with OSHA about this factory outlet he'd constructed— an outlet he'd set up to cut costs."

Cynthia stared at him.

"I asked where the factory outlet was. He told me it was a renovated barn out near Frederick. 'A barn!' I pretended surprise. 'Near Frederick! Oh my God, Ted, I don't think you should tell me any more. I've got a funny feeling I'm dating the woman who's working on a story about that barn!'"

Jed turned to Cynthia beaming. "Silence on the other end. 'Carbon tetrachloride,' I said. 'Right, Ted?'

"'Duh, right,' says Selebri." Jed sighed wistfully. "It was then that I realized there'd be no more calimari at Mama Rosa's."

Cynthia frowned. "When exactly did this phone call occur?"

"Tuesday morning—at two A.M., right after the OSHA raid."

"He woke you up Tues—"

"Didn't wake me up," Jed corrected. "I'd been up all night,

frantically calling your number and getting no answer, fearing, as a matter of fact, that something terrible had happened to you." He grinned at her. "Actually, Selebri put me to sleep. His call assured me you were doing fine—doing just what you *should* be doing!"

Jed's eyes got serious. "I hate to tell you this, but I did some checking on my own, and the way the law is, I could have gotten Selebri off with nothing more than a little fine. Francisco's autopsy showed possibility only. Had it shown carbon tetrachloride as the definite cause of death, Selebri could have been prosecuted as a criminal and sent to jail. But even then, only if there was some highly motivated activist in the prosecutor's office. As it is, Selebri will probably get off without scars." He turned to Cynthia. "Does that mess up your story?"

"No," she sighed. "It fits right in." She turned to Jed. "But I don't understand. Why the silence all week? Why the forced separation?"

"Selebri's the only ball-bearing manufacturer in the region. As soon as Carlos mentioned ball bearings, in the car that night, I figured Selebri was the culprit. Besides"—he shook his head in disgust—"it fit right in with what I knew of the guy's modus operandi. However, since he had never confided in me about the plant, I was under no obligation to warn him. Still, I figured it was important to keep things clean. You were already on the trail. You didn't need my help. Quite the contrary, I decided, the best thing I could do was to remove myself completely and let you wrap things up on your own—which, it appears, you've done brilliantly!" He hugged her.

She put her head on his shoulder.

"I'm sorry about making the speedy getaway in your car in the snow that night," he said. "I knew you'd probably made the ball-bearing connection too, and I was certain it was just a matter of seconds before you started blaming me as an accessory to Selebri's sins."

Cynthia stared at the fire, wondering whether she'd appear less brilliant if she confessed that she had not made the connection then, that, in fact, she'd cried herself to sleep that night, certain Jed no longer loved her.

"But then I said to myself, 'Hey, Cynthia certainly knows

you well enough to know you would *never* willingly defend a shit like Selebri.'"

Another brilliant conclusion that had escaped her. Cynthia closed her eyes, overwhelmed with guilt for suspecting he would.

He kissed her hair and then her forehead and the guilt slowly melted away into gratitude, and then longing. Her eyes were moist when they stared up into his. "I love you, Jed."

He pulled her close. "What'll it be?" he whispered in her ear. "Your bedroom or mine?"

The entertainment highlight of Saturday morning was Jed on ice skates. The three of them all howled as, together, they lifted him back up off the ice, propped him up, and set him on his floundering way, again and again, while all the time Jed ranted nonstop about the "idiocy of a sport that goes out of its way to make walking difficult."

Late that afternoon, while the children were sledding and Jed was shut up in a bedroom reading Cynthia's article, Cynthia began cooking the birthday dinner. The more she cooked, the more anxious she got.

She envisioned Jed, who probably hated birthdays and had intentionally never celebrated his, shifting around uncomfortably during the festivities the children had planned, creating hurt feelings and then—a birthday dinner with Lisa's head turned irrevocably toward the wall.

She lifted the top of the large casserole dish and wrinkled her nose at the odor. The birthday dinner. Another of her terrific ideas.

She had a second casserole in the oven by the time Lisa and Timmy returned.

"Where's Daddy?" Timmy asked as the two charged into the kitchen.

"In the bedroom," Cynthia said, "reading the article I wrote." She jumped up. "It isn't all that long, my article. We'd better get ready. Timmy, you stand guard in the living room by the fireplace. Lisa and I will put candles on the cake. Now, when he comes out of the bedroom," Cynthia went on, "say something like 'Dad, we need another log on the fire,' but say it really loud, so we'll hear."

"Okay." Timmy jumped up and closed the kitchen door behind him.

"Now, when Timmy gives the signal, I'll go out first, and then you two follow with the cake." Cynthia's fingers were trembling as they stuck in the birthday candles.

They heard the bedroom door open. "Dad!" Timmy screamed. "We need another log on the fire."

"Okay, okay, don't get so excited." It was Jed's voice. "Where's Cynthia?"

"I'll get her!" Timmy yelped at the top of his lungs. He came bounding into the kitchen. "Quick!" he shouted at Cynthia. "He's lookin' for ya!"

Cynthia walked out and eyed Jed with trepidation. He smiled at her. Beamed was more like it. His eyes were so affectionate, so pleased. Warm blood began to replace the frozen liquid in her veins. He liked the article. He really liked it.

Jed walked over and put his arms on her shoulders and just stared at her, somewhat dreamily, for a while. "It's wonderful," he said slowly. "Absolutely wonderful. The drama, the way you manage to . . ."

Over Jed's shoulder, Cynthia saw the kitchen door open, and then close, and then open again. This time a cake topped by flickering lights emerged, with a frail but determined chorus:

"Happy birthday to you, happy birthday to you, happy birthday dear Daddy . . ."

Jed jumped and whirled around. He looked at Cynthia in a mixture of terror and confusion as she joined the chorus. "Happy birthday to you!"

Lisa and Timmy stopped in front of him, holding the cake. Jed turned to Cynthia. "Is it . . . uh . . . my . . . uh. . . ?"

The cake began slipping from Lisa's grasp. "I *told* you he wouldn't remember!" she shouted gleefully.

Cynthia grabbed the cake just in time. "Tomorrow," she hissed at Jed as she put the cake down on the table next to the fire. "February twenty-second. Tomorrow."

"Blow 'em out, Daddy!" Timmy was jumping up and down. "And make a wish. If you're smart, you'll wish for what I got you!"

Jed stood in a stupor, a man suddenly jolted out of his natural habitat and into an alien one. Cynthia's blood began running cold again.

Lisa took his hand and led him over to the table. "C'mon, Daddy, it's easy."

He followed her, his face expressionless. "I just didn't realize, I guess." He turned on Cynthia. "How did you know?"

"Blow, Dad, will ya!" shouted Timmy.

Jed looked at each of the three of them and smiled faintly. He took a deep breath and blew out all the candles.

"You can't eat it now," Timmy instructed. "We just wanted you to know what it was we were celebrating."

Cynthia and Lisa went to the kitchen and emerged with the presents and the champagne. Still stunned, Jed obediently opened the champagne bottle that was handed to him. Cynthia poured two glasses of champagne and two of ginger ale. She sat down on the floor by the fire next to Jed, handed him a glass, and raised hers: "Happy Birthday."

Lisa and Timmy followed in imitation. "Happy Birthday, Daddy!"

Jed lifted his glass and took a massive gulp.

"The poems!" Timmy shouted, scrambling out of his father's lap. "Before he opens the presents, we gotta read the poems!" He turned to Jed. "Lisa drew fancy pictures all over hers, but mine's better."

"Poems?" Jed turned to Cynthia in confusion.

Lisa jumped up. "Can I go first? Oh, please?"

"Go ahead," Timmy said smugly. "Save the best for last."

Lisa stood up, took a long breath, and exhaled slowly.

"C'mon!" yelled Timmy. "Hurry up!"

Lisa gave her brother a look of contempt and then began reading:

> *"There is a picture on my wall*
> *It's of a dark-haired man who's tall*
> *A man who's strong with lots of charms*
> *He holds a baby in his arms*
> *She's smiling."*

Lisa smiled at Jed.

He smiled back.

She went on . . . and on and on. It was a very long poem, so long that the final line of each stanza was punctuated by growls from her impatient brother.

As she shushed Timmy, Cynthia noted Lisa was playing to an audience of one. Her large, almost black eyes looked up at Jed expectantly at the end of each line, searching for approval, then radiating pleasure.

Daddy. The first love of every girl's life.

Cynthia became oblivious of Timmy's restlessness, entranced by the intensity between the poetess and the subject of her poem.

> *"She knows he yells and pulls his hair*
> *And gets upset because he cares.*
> *He knows that though she gets real mad*
> *Above all else, she loves her dad.*
> *That's why they're smiling."*

Lisa looked up at Jed and shrugged. "That's, um, the end."

Silently, he held out his arms. As Cynthia and Timmy applauded (Timmy begrudgingly), Lisa crawled into Jed's arms and Cynthia felt her eyes fill with tears.

"Okay, okay, guys, ready for the big show?" It was Timmy, poem in hand, pacing jocularly back and forth before the fire.

"Ready!" They shouted.

"Okay, here goes:

> *Some dads are crazy.*
> *Some dads are wreckers.*
> *I got a dad*
> *I can beat at checkers.*

Happy Birthday!"

They all broke into applause. Timmy's grin showcased his missing front tooth. With a flourish, he bowed majestically. "Thank you, thank you. I told you mine was best!"

After Jed opened his presents, Cynthia went back to finish dinner, and Jed helped the children set up a game of Monopoly.

Cynthia was slicing cucumbers into the salad bowl when Jed

came into the kitchen. He turned her away from the counter and put his hand under her chin, gently lifting her eyes up to meet his. "Thank you."

He bent down and kissed her. Then he watched his fingers as they played with a lock of hair on her forehead. It was a gesture he resorted to when he was uncomfortable with what he was about to say. "For so many years, I've lived this strange, fragmented life. I don't think I realized until tonight how fragmented it was. Somehow, you managed to bring me and my children together the way I think I've always wanted it to be." His hand roamed from her forehead down the side of her face as he looked at her.

She wiped a tear from her eye with the back of her hand.

"What's with this crying?" he said irritably. It was another gesture he used to undercut self-consciousness. "That's the second time tonight!"

She sniffed. "I'm just ridiculously sentimental. Family feelings always get to me." She looked at Jed. "Don't you ever cry?"

"Naw."

She shook her head and finished slicing the cucumbers. "But you're so sentimental. Gruff on the outside, but complete mush underneath." She put the cucumbers into the salad. "I definitely would have pegged you as a crier."

"I used to be."

"When?"

"Let's see—when Bambi's mother got shot, for starters. That's the first time I remember. And then, oh gee, I used to cry over sad books all the time." He picked up a carrot and began scraping. "Happy moments, too. I remember when Lisa was born. Anna cried all during labor, but as soon as the doctor said, 'You have a beautiful, healthy baby girl,' I fell apart. Tears all over the place. Same with Timmy."

Cynthia smiled. "Then, when did you stop crying?"

The misty expression in Jed's eyes evaporated. His face hardened, and he began clenching his teeth, causing his jaw to jut out in quickening beats. His casual carrot scraping suddenly became an act of vengeance. The strokes got deeper, longer, until Cynthia put her hands over his to stop the motion. "Jed?"

"June twenty-fourth, nineteen seventy-eight." He said the

words in monotone, but his face radiated anger—more than anger, Cynthia realized: hatred. It was a look totally alien to the man she knew. It lasted only for a second, but that second was enough to make Cynthia not want to ask any more questions.

She turned around quickly and began slicing an onion.

"Hey," he said, "that's the second time tonight you've done it!" The lighthearted tone was back in his voice.

"Done what?"

"Distracted me from what I wanted to tell you. That article is absolutely wonderful." He picked up a tomato and began cutting it. "There is drama in the story itself, but there's a lot more than that. You really get into the men, the life. Francisco is a short story unto himself, and *Carlos*—" He shook his head. "I've liked Carlos a lot in person, but I'm absolutely crazy about him in your article! Everyone will be." He pointed the paring knife at her. "Mark my words, Carlos will do well after this comes out.

"I read it through three times," he said slowly. "The writing is superb. Beautifully crafted."

Cynthia threw her arms around him. "You have made my night!"

He laughed and then pulled back and looked at her. "That article's very different from your others."

"You only read the lawyer exposé."

"Not true." He smiled shyly. "I read every single one you've written—the unabridged Cynthia Matthews—in the library last week. Hell, I had a lot of time on my hands!"

"You're kidding!"

"Nope. Good reading. Each one was a very sharp bit of reporting."

She beamed.

"But cold."

She stopped beaming.

"Shrewd, clever, exacting—but icy cold."

"And this one?"

"Warm. Loving, even, in a way. You carve each of these characters out with such care and sensitivity."

"It's a different story."

He shook his head. "Hell, you could have made it into an exposé on the wicked manufacturer! You chose, instead, to look into the men. It's only different because you chose to make it different."

"Then it's you."

"Me?"

"You've made me different. Or maybe you've made me back into what I used to be. I don't know." She walked back to the salad bowl.

"Which was?"

She smiled back at him. "A crier."

He played with the carrot scraper.

She turned to him. "Mark my words, Jed Farber, I'll turn you back into a crier too."

They stood looking at each other for a while in silence. Then he walked over to the oven, pulled out the big casserole dish, and set it on the burner. "What are we having?" he asked, picking up the lid.

She whirled around. "A surprise!" she screamed. It was too late. He was already staring down into the dish, a look of shock on his face.

He turned to her, pleading to be told he was wrong.

Her expression told him he wasn't.

The shock turned to horror. He bent down over the dish and sniffed.

Horror confirmed.

He looked at her as though ready to kill and then the Jed Farber laugh began—the slow, internal rumble, growing louder and louder. "You didn't!"

She giggled. "Well, I thought—"

"You bitch!" he howled. "You did! How the hell—" he said, approaching her with the carrot peeler.

"Shh! The kids are all excited."

"Oh, I'll bet they are," he said, holding the scraper up like a knife. "I'll bet they are, and you have your little joke, don't you? Your secret little joke."

He kissed her instead of stabbing her, but broke out laughing in the middle of the kiss. "You bitch!" he whispered, and kissed her again.

"Dinner's ready," she called out merrily as soon as his lips left hers. She grinned.

He scowled.

Lisa and Timmy burst into the kitchen, causing the door to open so quickly it slammed against the wall.

"Easy, easy!" Jed shouted.

"Daddy." Lisa sighed. "Go sit at the table and behave like the guest of honor."

Jed obeyed, but not before giving Cynthia a pointed look.

With a flourish, the children helped set the table in the living room, as Jed sat at the head, silently working out an appropriate reaction.

Lisa insisted on candlelight. She lit the candles and Cynthia brought out the salad, then a baking dish with something white in it, then the big casserole.

"What are we having?" Jed asked innocently.

Lisa and Timmy squirmed in their seats excitedly.

"It's a surprise, Dad," Timmy said. "Just wait until you see!"

Jed reached over and ceremoniously lifted the top off the casserole dish. His jaw dropped. "No, it can't be!"

"Yes!" Lisa screeched. "It is!"

"Pot roast," proclaimed Timmy. "Grandma's special recipe!"

"I—I don't believe it!" Jed shouted, thankful for the time he'd had to rehearse. "How did you ever get the recipe?"

"Cynthia had Lisa call Grandma for it," Timmy said.

"Grandma was so excited," Lisa gushed. "She gave me the recipe for her special noodle kugel too."

Jed eyed the nondescript white slop in the baking dish. "Yes, she did," he said slowly, the grin frozen on his face. "She certainly did."

"Are you surprised?" Timmy asked.

"Surprised!" Jed shouted, giving Cynthia the fakest smile he could come up with. "I'm . . . I'm more than surprised. I can't believe it. You know, Grandma's pot roast is a real birthday tradition."

"That's what she said," Lisa squealed happily.

Cynthia piled Jed's plate high with food and handed it to him. He picked up his knife, but then put it back down. If Cynthia had been true to his mother's recipe, the meat would just roll over and fall apart into little pieces once nudged gently with a fork.

\*   \*   \*

Late that night—very, very late, after Jed had crawled out of Cynthia's bed and made his way back to his own bedroom—Cynthia lay on her back, staring out the window next to her bed. There was a bright full moon in the stark wintry sky, and its brilliance mirrored her feelings. Happy. So very happy. She could not remember any time in her life when she had felt so thoroughly happy. She smiled at the moon and gradually drifted off to sleep.

Across the hall, Jed was enjoying the contented drowsiness he felt enveloping him, the darkness of the room, the memories of Cynthia, the heaviness of the blankets on top of him.

He wanted it to snow. He wanted the heavens to open up and deluge the whole area with so much snow, they would never be able to leave the cabin. If only they could be forced to spend the rest of their lives here, just the four of them, isolated, protected from the dangers, the temptations lurking in the rest of the world, bound together by nature's forces. Forever.

Enjoying both that dream, and the real memories of the evening, he rolled over and felt his body become slowly overwhelmed by the delicious sensation of oncoming slumber.

He woke up four hours later, saturated with sweat, restless in the heat of the heavy blankets on top of him. He kicked the blankets off, and twitched restlessly.

What was he doing? What had he done? He had never let go like this before, not since he had grown up and learned what "love" could do to you.

He had done something worse than just letting his guard down. He had let his children fall in love with her too. How was he to know she was going to launch this big public relations campaign, for God's sake? How was he to know she would attract them the way she attracted him, understand them the way she understood him? Oh, she was a shrewd one, moving right in on all of them, making herself indispensable, the glue that held them all together.

He pulled the blankets back up to stop his shivers, and he told himself this was middle-of-the-night angst. Silly emotionalism. But his body was pulsating and his mind was darting, into one dark corner, then into another.

All the wonderful things that had happened in the course of the day now repeated on him with negative force: What would he do when it ended? What would his children do? It would end. It always did. And the pain this time would be insurmountable.

# · 22 ·

Miranda opened Senator Barker's office door and stuck her head in. "Mr. Jackson is here for your four o'clock appointment," she whispered. "But Thad Rankerman is on line six from Des Moines. Thad says it's very important that he speak to you as soon as possible. He sounds kind of upset. Would you like to talk to him before I usher Mr. Jackson in?"

"Yes, Miranda. Thank you."

Senator Barker sat very still for a while, stroking his jaw pensively and staring at the blinking button on his telephone. He had been waiting for this call, ever since he had heard from Jimmy Farnsworth. Thad Rankerman's contact in the opposition camp had apparently come through.

He sighed, and when he finally picked up the telephone, he did so reluctantly. "Hello, Thad."

"Something's about to happen," Rankerman blurted out. "Something bad for us!"

Barker nodded slowly. "Now, just calm down, Thad." His voice was commanding, but soft. "Tell me what you know and how you know it."

"My contact? The one I told you about?"

"Mmm-hmm."

"All she'll tell me is that they're jubilant. They've found out something's about to break. A story, I think maybe a newspaper article."

"Mmm-hmm."

"From what I can get, they, uh, seem to feel this will mean the end of our whole campaign!"

"Well, perhaps they're just a mite overexcited, Thad."

"I don't think so. Really, I think this, whatever it is, could be devastating. Do you have any idea what it could be?"

"No, Thad." Barker swallowed, suddenly overwhelmed with sympathy and affection for this young man who had worked so hard—for all of them, who had worked so hard. "But we'll handle whatever it is. You just relax now, and keep me posted."

Barker hung up the telephone and sat in a stupor at his desk. He had done all he could. He had known—from the moment he'd opened up like that to Cynthia Matthews—that this could happen. Oh, he could try to put up all the impasses in the world, but if she had really been determined to get her story . . .

He stared at the picture of his wife and small children that sat on his desk. His eyes met those of Penny Barker, smiling out at him from the frame. With tears in his eyes, he forced a smile that duplicated hers, held his hands out, palms up, and shrugged.

"Damn!"

Jed hopped off the living-room sofa and rushed to the front door. Cynthia was grimacing in the entry, carrying a bouquet of half-dead flowers and two overloaded shopping bags, one of which had just ripped, spewing its contents onto the rug.

"I would have been happy to go shopping with you," Jed said, tossing a head of lettuce back in the bag. "Why didn't you call me?" He picked up the rest of the food and carried it into the kitchen.

"I did call," she said, following him. "The line has been busy. Do you know what it feels like to call and call your own phone number and have the line busy all the time?"

"I was fulfilling my role as your answering service. Brittany called and so did your sister, Georgine. Both wanted to know how the weekend went. I gave each a glowing report." He chuckled. "Brittany seemed surprised, Georgine delighted." He began unpacking the groceries. "I've decided there are two distinct advantages of my living here. One is I get to meet your friends and relatives."

"And the other?"

He chortled. "The other is my mother doesn't have the phone number!"

She pulled a cellophane package out of the bag. "How about chicken for dinner?"

"Chicken is fine." He looked up. She was trying to revive the flowers. "Okay, who is the son-of-a-bitch?"

"What?"

"The son-of-a-bitch who gave you flowers!"

She looked at him coyly. "Jealous?"

"Yeah!"

"Good."

"Who?" He halted the unpacking process, his hand on his hip.

She laughed at him. "My whole office. They were so great. They all came in early, and when I walked in, they had put up a big banner on the wall that said 'Great Story!' and were applauding and—they gave me these." She put the flowers in a vase. They drooped. She cut their stems and tried again. They continued to droop. "Well," she said, finally giving up, "it's the thought that counts. Personally, I prefer roses anyway."

"You've mentioned that several times. Are you by any chance hinting?"

"Me?"

"I have told you," he went on gruffly, "that I feel flowers are for funerals."

"You have told me, and that has dramatically altered my desire for flowers. What a price to pay!"

She watched as he put the vegetables in the refrigerator. "Oh, Jed, the best part is—you were right. The article has really turned out to be a boon for Carlos. The newspaper's been deluged with offers of help—everything from immigration lawyers volunteering their services, to colleges. A community college in Virginia says they're willing to go out on a limb and enroll him!" Her eyes lit up. "And they're right on the metro line, so he could just commute!"

Jed walked over, bent down, and kissed her. Snugly nestled in his arms, with Carlos en route to college and acclaim pouring in for her story, Cynthia decided that this had to be one of life's all-around high points. Besides, her sister Georgine had even got to meet Jed on the telephone!

"Well," she said, looking up at him, "what did you think of my sister?"

"I liked her. It felt very comfortable, like talking to you." He hesitated over whether or not to put the lettuce away in the refrigerator, and seemed to decide to keep it out for dinner. "We commiserated over what it was like to have prepubescent daughters, and we commiserated over the trials and tribulations of living with you."

They liked each other. She was certain of it, and delighted by it. "I'll bet you talked for hours," Cynthia groaned. "You two are the biggest talkers I know."

"Now there you go again, underestimating yourself!" His eyes twinkled. "Georgine sure knew a hell of a lot about me—down to the battery-powered socks my son gave me as a birthday present."

Cynthia blushed.

"The fact that Selebri was my client, the details of my mother's pot roast, the fact that I have a volatile temper—"

Cynthia was crimson.

"My sexual preferences in bed."

"No!"

Jed belly-laughed. "That was a test. Thank God you passed!"

She kissed him on the cheek and began putting together flour and spices to dredge the chicken. "How was your day?"

"Deadly dull," he said, rinsing the lettuce. "How was yours?"

"Worse. I got assigned to cover a filthy-rich shopping-center mogul who was touring the nation's capital."

"Now that's an unusual story, even for Capitol Radio!"

"Well, to be fair, the man has some newsworthiness. He's running for office. His sightseeing tour involved a stop at the Farm Credit Administration, where he lambasted the 'paper-pushing bureaucrats' who are driving 'our farmers off their land,' and a stop in Congress, where he launched a tirade against all those 'weak-kneed liberals' who are supporting the down-and-outers with welfare benefits, while the good, clean, hard-working folks are losing their jobs."

She began dredging the chicken in flour. "His oratory was quite dramatic. Unfortunately, Gardiner insisted that I do a one-on-one interview with him."

"Why did he want that?"

She shrugged and wiped a strand of hair from her eyes with the back of her hand. "Oh, probably just because the man's so wealthy. Gardiner is always trying to cuddle up to the moneyed set."

She put some oil in the frying pan. "He told me to make sure I told the man who I was and where I worked." She began cooking the chicken. "Poor Gardiner. If he wanted to flatter the man with a forceful radio spot, it backfired. The man is terrific at fire-and-brimstone put-down speeches, but he sure is lacking in the how-to-do-it-better department. He kept tripping over statistics and putting his foot in his mouth during the interview."

"And which did you report?"

"Both. But his presentation was greatly weakened by the latter." She grinned devilishly. "And by the sound bite I used of an official from the Farm Credit Administration, who succinctly and articulately underscored the holes in his rhetoric." She chortled as she turned the chicken pieces. "Gardiner will probably have a fit when he reads it. He hadn't returned from his lengthy lunch when I left."

"Who is the guy?"

"Hmm? Oh, his name is Heffer, Hal Heffer."

Jed's head darted up from the salad bowl. "Hal Heffer!"

"Yes. Do you know him?"

"*Know* him? Hell, he may not mean anything in Washington, but anyone who knows anything about Iowa politics knows him! The bastard plans on being the state's next Senator!"

"True, but that is a long way off. He hasn't even won the Republican nomination yet. And frankly, if today is any indication of his knowledge on the issues—"

"He doesn't *have* to know the issues. The guy could buy his own Farm Credit Administration! He owns shopping centers all over the Midwest. Oriole Shopping Centers—I'm sure you've heard of them."

"Oriole? You're kidding! They're all over Indiana. He must be loaded! But where exactly does he stand politically?"

Jed tossed the sliced onions into the salad. "Right wing—as in fascist!"

"No, seriously, what confused me today was his blasting the present administration. Isn't he a Republican too?"

"Oh, that's his strong suit, see? Heffer's neither Republican nor Democrat. The Republican he's running against in the primary is a normal Republican, so right now he's blaming the administration. Next, he'll zero in on the incumbent Senator, the Democrat, using the same jargon. 'A new idea.'"

"But don't the voters see that?"

"The voters see slick ads."

Suddenly everything clicked in Cynthia's head: *Heffer* was the one! *He* was Gardiner's benefactor, the source of his future job! Yes, that had to be it. It all added up: Chris Channing's talk about the rich Iowa backer, the right-wing slant of Capitol Radio assignments of late, Gardiner's move to keep the articulate sound bite of Senator Barker—Heffer's ultimate opponent—off the air. Gardiner's voice purring "Introduce yourself, Cynthia. Tell Mr. Heffer Capitol Radio is very much interested in his views."

She wiped her hands off with a dishtowel and ran toward the telephone.

"What are you doing?"

"Calling Chris Channing."

"Why call—"

"Damn." Cynthia slapped her hand on her hip. "They've got their answering machine on."

"But what—"

She held up her hand, waiting for the message tone. "Hello Chris," she said, grinning. "This is Cynthia and I just wanted to tell you that I've figured out your puzzle. The magic name is Hal Heffer!" Laughing, she put the receiver back in place. Jed looked at her as though she had gone out of her mind.

"Remember I told you that Chris has been working up this case against Gardiner? Well, he's convinced that some—"

The phone rang.

"That's probably Chris!" she chuckled, moving back to the phone. "He is really bonkers over this thing." She picked up the phone. "Hello? Oh, hello!" The tone of her voice changed completely. "I'm so glad you called." She pulled the extension chord and walked out of the kitchen into the hallway. "I was actually going to call you, to thank you. It was just marvelous. . . ."

Her voice faded and so did Jed's interest in the conversation. It wasn't Channing. He was sure of that. It was someone Cynthia did not seem to know very well. She sounded polite and a little formal.

He finished the salad, and made a dressing. He was turning the chicken when Cynthia walked back into the kitchen. She held the receiver out to him. "Jed," she called out gaily, "it's your mother!"

He froze.

Cynthia pressed the receiver into his limp hand. "Lisa gave her the number here," she cooed. "Apparently *you* forgot to."

"Hello. I was just getting ready to call you!" His face reddened as Cynthia coughed conspicuously. "Let me tell you, you were the hit of the weekend, even in absentia. Uh-huh . . . uh-huh . . . Yup, she sure did. Well, Cynthia's a great cook, and she adhered to your recipe rigidly. It was terrific. Not quite as good as yours"—he winked malevolently at Cynthia—"but, I mean, you know, it takes practice. This was her first time . . . Yeah, I got the card." Jed moved out into the hallway, and Cynthia went back to cooking dinner. A minute or two later, Jed reentered the kitchen and put the receiver back on the hook.

"That wasn't long."

"Well, she had already blown more than her usual three-minute allotment on you! I . . . we . . . don't usually talk that long."

"No kidding! Absolutely everything she knew about me she had heard from Lisa!" Cynthia looked at him accusingly. "Here I've been talking about you nonstop to Georgine, and you've hardly mentioned me."

"Hey, a mother is different from a sister. A man never tells his mother anything."

"Oh, well then, maybe I should try calling your sisters!"

"Set the table!" he ordered.

She began putting forks and knives on the kitchen table.

"Not in here. In the dining room!"

"The dining room? Since when do we—"

"Tonight!"

Obediently, she began carrying the utensils into the dining room. When she got there, she gasped. Two-dozen long-stemmed red roses stood in a vase at the center of the table.

She looked at him wide-eyed. "Does this mean I'm dying?"

"No." He wrapped his arms around her from behind as they both gazed upon the velvety bouquet. He kissed her on the neck. "It means you are the author of a terrific story, and the creator of a very special birthday party."

# · 23 ·

"It's Chris Channing for you on line two!"
Sylvia Berg shouted, waving the telephone receiver as Cynthia returned from lunch.

"Okay," Channing demanded as soon as Cynthia picked up the telephone at her desk in the workroom, "how did you figure out Gardiner's find was Hal Heffer?"

"Why, Christopher," Cynthia purred, "I thought for sure you were one step ahead of me on this! Didn't you know what my assignment was yesterday?"

"Just got back this morning. We took a long weekend at my folks' place," Chris explained. "Surely you must have known I was away when I didn't call to congratulate you on that fantastic article you wrote!"

They talked about the article, and Cynthia told him about her assignment to cover Hal Heffer the day before. "Gardiner's been out of the office all day today. I checked the log for yesterday, though, and there is no mention of the spot I wrote."

"What happened to it, then?"

"I don't know. And I won't until Gardiner comes in. He didn't issue it, that's for sure. I guess he didn't want me messing up his hopes for the future!"

"I don't think that's a possibility," Chris said grimly. "I hate to tell you this, but as far as I can tell, the deal with Heffer is firm. Gardiner probably wanted you to do the spot because he saw it as a friendly gesture, as icing on the cake.

"I know for a fact he and his wife have signed a contract for a house in Iowa. I gather it's just a matter of time before Gardiner'll be announcing that he's found a stimulating new job in the shopping-center business," Chris went on. "You should be job hunting! Cashing in on the very positive reaction to your Sunday story."

"I plan to. Started thinking about it over the weekend, as a matter of fact."

Chris sighed. "I still can't figure out what he's done to endear himself to Hal Heffer."

"Hey! A word of advice in return, Chris. Cash in on your research results and treat Gardiner as a thing of the past. Over. Stop diverting your energies into useless avenues."

"*He's* useless, that's for sure. A complete sleaze. It just kills me that he gets away with being one, that he—"

"What really kills you is the fact that he hasn't sold out Capitol Radio's journalistic integrity, thereby giving you an excuse to expose him."

"He tried to! He would have if he could have!"

"But the fact is, he hasn't," Cynthia said softly. "The fact is, he has probably managed to get himself a high-paying job on the up and up. *That's* what kills you. Take a piece of friendly advice—forget him."


As he returned from a late-afternoon meeting, Jed Farber stared down the corridor in disbelief. His usually fastidious, businesslike secretary, Yvonne Bailey, was sprawled leisurely in her desk chair, the telephone receiver pressed to her ear, giggling like a schoolgirl.

As Jed got closer, Yvonne Bailey saw him and stiffened visibly. "Oh, here he is now," she told the person on the other end of the telephone. "Just one moment."

Her eyes were still sparkling merrily as she pressed the hold button and looked up at Jed. "Senator Barker for you on line oh-five," she announced seriously. Then she shook her head from side to side and began laughing again. "He is one very funny man!"

Jed went into his office, hung up his coat, and picked up the telephone. "Well, Senator, I'm delighted you decided to take time out from your busy travel schedule to add some merriment to my secretary's life!"

"Poor girl needs a little mental activity!" Barker retorted. "Seems like her boss isn't putting in much time on the job these days!"

"And what is that supposed to mean?"

"That we've both been very busy men of late," Barker said. "I've been working, and you've been playing."

"Who have you been listening to?"

Barker's bear-laugh poured forth from the receiver. "I'll never tell! Listen," he said, abruptly changing his tone, "I've got to run because I'm late for a meeting, but I'd like to talk to you tonight."

"It has to be tonight?"

"Yup."

Jed blinked. Barker's requests for meetings were rarely so insistent. "Well, I have a Bar Association dinner, but I could back out if—"

"No. I don't want to interfere with your plans. I have a dinner too. How about afterward? Say around ten—at my house?"

"Sure, I could do that."

"I'll see you then."

Well, Jed thought wistfully as he hung up the telephone, so much for any "playing" tonight. Frederick Barker rarely slept, and was oblivious to the fact that other people did. A Barker session scheduled to begin at ten would be likely not to get underway before ten-thirty and could go on forever. Barker usually got a second wind around midnight.

Still, it had been a long time since Jed had got a call like this one—a call for a command appearance. He played with the pen on the desk in front of him, wondering what the subject was. He realized it could be just about anything. The two of them had been pretty out of touch recently. That made him sad.

He thought about the evening ahead, and felt another twinge of sadness, but for a totally different reason. He picked up the phone and dialed Capitol Radio.

Gardiner Weldy leaned back in his "executive" swivel chair. He waved his hands over the arms of the chair with a flourish, and then, with the grace and drama of a prima ballerina, he gently joined the fingertips of his right hand to the fingertips of his left.

He peered at Cynthia across the finger sculpture. "The story was unacceptable."

"On what grounds?" she asked.

"I did not want to say anything in front of the others," he sighed laconically, "but you were assigned to cover Hal Heffer. You were *not* assigned to do a hatchet job on the man."

"I covered Heffer. I reported what he said."

"You reported that he spoke inaccurately."

She leaned forward. "In fact, Gardiner, he *did* speak inaccurately. Surely you would not have condoned my reporting a statement as fact that was factually incorrect." She was enjoying this.

"Cynthia, Cynthia," Gardiner sighed, "why do a hatchet job on a man with a vision, a rising political star?"

"But isn't that our job? To point out the flaws to the public before it is too late? To inform them?"

"Oh, Madam News Business." Gardiner chuckled. "Our own Madam News Business!" Cynthia's pleasure diminished. Gardiner was enjoying this too. He leaned across his huge mahogany desk and cast upon her the affectionate look of a worldly savant indulging a sweet but naive young follower. "I didn't issue it, my dear, and you will be grateful to me some day. Hal Heffer is *not* someone you want as an enemy."

Cynthia was chilled by his certainty as well as by the implicit threat.

"I did it for you, my dear Cynthia. Out of affection."

She started to protest, but chose instead to set an example for the invisible Chris Channing: Forget it. Time to move on. She nodded curtly and walked out of Gardiner's office.

"Bad news!" Sylvia chirped, waving a pink message slip.

Cynthia laughed and looked back at Gardiner's closed door. "That seems to be the theme of the day." She glanced at the slip. It was several lines long in Sylvia's difficult-to-read handwriting. She handed it back. "Sylvia, you know it by heart, I'm sure. Translate."

"Jed says he won't be able to make it tonight. Senator Barker's asked him to come out to his house in Maryland after the

Bar Association dinner, and Jed says evenings with Senator Barker tend to go on forever. He'll call you tomorrow morning."

Senator Barker. Cynthia's face sobered.

"He sounded very apologetic," Sylvia offered in an aside.

Cynthia's eyes narrowed as she headed for the workroom. Why the meeting? To celebrate Jed's victory? The fact that he had brilliantly managed to channel Cynthia's interests into a *different* free-lance story?

She chastised herself for being unfairly suspicious, but, at the same time, the euphoria she had been feeling all day vanished.

At ten o'clock, Jed Farber pulled into the driveway of Barker's big, rambling Victorian house in Chevy Chase, and for a moment it felt like old times, as though he were arriving for a late-night work session on some legislative proposal. But only for a moment.

Suddenly, he was struck instead by how much his life had changed since those days, how old he felt. In the past, he would have arrived at ten with an open-ended evening ahead. Tonight arriving that late had wrecked his whole schedule.

The house seemed to have changed too. He saw only a few isolated lights in the cavernous structure. The rooms that had once been filled with people—Penny Barker and her charity groups, the teenage Barker children and their friends, eager legislative assistants—were now dark.

"Isn't this place a little big for you these days?" Jed asked as Barker opened the door and stepped back, still wearing a suit and overcoat. Jed realized his host had barely beaten him there.

"And good evening to you too!"

Jed laughed. "No, I was just thinking it must get pretty lonely in this huge house all by yourself."

"It would," Barker agreed, looking around, "but I'm never home."

"Then it must be really empty."

"Who cares, if there's no one around to know it?"

"You win," Jed chuckled, hanging up his coat. "Sorry I even brought it up. I should have remembered, you don't handle change well."

"An astute observation," Barker grumbled as he took off his own coat. "Less significant, however, coming from someone who's lived in the same damn apartment for seven years—one he described when he moved in as 'just a transitional step'!"

Jed looked at the filled backpack, hiking boots, and assorted outer gear resting against the wall in the entry. "Have you become an outdoorsman?"

"No." Barker grimaced. "That's Buzzy's. He arrived here last Thursday with a group of friends, and ambitious plans to hike along the Appalachian Trail. I left for Sioux City on Friday. When I got back yesterday, he was gone and the gear was here."

"That means he made it back alive, at least."

"It means the litter has grown," Barker said acerbically. "The family may have dispersed, but they keep leaving behind droppings every time they come. Sissy was here with her crew of babies a few weeks ago, and I'm still stumbling over broken toys and disposable diapers in odd corners."

Jed laughed as they walked into the living room. "You love it and you know it," he said affectionately. "It's nice having the grandchildren come by, the grown kids . . ."

Barker grinned in his own inimitable way: The lines of the face complied, but the eyes stubbornly refrained from lighting up. "If you say so. You always know best. Or at least you're always very convincing. For how many years have you been telling me I'm a good father, and telling them I'm a good father, and been such a slick orator you've just about convinced us all?" He patted Jed on the shoulder. "It's been very therapeutic. We all feel very fortunate, whether we deserve to or not!"

Jed wondered whether there were problems with the Barker offspring. Was that the reason for the meeting?

Barker turned on a light, revealing an absolutely immaculate living room.

Jed stared, shocked by the lifelessness on the one hand, the familiarity on the other. His former home-away-from-home had taken on a museumlike ambience.

"Lucille still comes regularly to clean," Barker said, reading Jed's thoughts.

"She sure does." Jed's eyes traveled around the room, stopping abruptly when they got to a large vase filled with fresh gladiolas on the side table. He smiled in recognition.

Barker's eyes followed Jed's. "Never understood why Penny liked them," the Senator grumbled. "To me, gladiolas look somewhat like multicolored pole lamps."

"A fact, as I recall, you brought up every time she filled that vase with gladiolas!" Jed laughed. "Just before you complained about the florist's bill."

"Well, I still complain about that," Barker stormed. "Every week when I pick up a new batch. Ridiculous, what florists charge these days just for a bunch of flowers!"

Jed turned to him, his eyes a little misty. "But you still buy them every week?"

Barker shifted around uncomfortably on his feet. "Figured she'd want me to," he said gruffly. "Gives things a kind of consistency."

Jed put his arm around the Senator's shoulders and gave a quick squeeze.

"I'll get you something to drink," Barker said, walking over to the bar. "Relax and dirty it all up a bit. It'll make me feel more comfortable after you go home and it'll give Lucille something to do tomorrow." He turned around. "Hey, do you know how to make a fire?"

"Yes."

"Make one—will you?" He beckoned to the fireplace. "I love fires and I don't know how to make 'em. Penny always made them. Penny or one of the kids."

"Want me to teach you how?" Jed asked, moving wood from the pile next to the fire place.

"Naaw." They both said it at the same time and with the same lazy inflection. They laughed—Jed in the living room, Barker from the kitchen.

"You might show Lucille, though," Barker chuckled. He returned from the kitchen with a filled ice bucket. He made two drinks as Jed lit the fire.

Jed sat down in his regular chair by the sofa. Barker handed him a glass of wine and sat down in his big armchair next to Jed. For a while they just sat, staring into the fire, totally comfortable with each other, the setting, the fire. Barker's eyes moved from the fire to Jed and he studied him for a while. "Your secretary's right," he said.

Jed looked up suspiciously. He remembered the vision of

Yvonne Bailey laughing that afternoon. Barker had a knack for getting close to secretaries through telephone relationships.

"She says you've been damn happy lately," Barker said gruffly in a mildly accusatory tone.

Jed smiled and looked back at the fire. "She didn't say 'damn.' The 'damn' is yours."

"Yeah, but the 'happy' is yours. Look at you, sitting there all relaxed—'laid out' as the young people say."

"It's laid back!" Jed laughed. "'Laid out' is what finally happens to old people. When have you had the time to get to know my secretary? She's relatively new at the firm."

"Hell, she's there all the time! You're not! She's the one I talk to after hours when I give you a call from Iowa! The choice is talking to your secretary or listening to the phone ring and ring and ring at your apartment. It's no wonder she and I have become friends. Yvonne, right?"

"Yvonne. Right." Jed frowned. "She's never told me you called."

"We agreed she wouldn't. Didn't want to cramp your style." Barker took a sip of his drink. "What's she like?"

"Yvonne?"

"No, dammit! *I'm* the expert on Yvonne, remember? I'm talking about the sweet young thing that is taking you away from your law practice and making it damn difficult to get hold of you. What is *she* like?"

Jed looked back into the fire. "Wonderful, actually," he said slowly. "I told you about her before. She's very beautiful and very smart—a reporter and a free-lance writer." He turned to Barker. "I remember when we were talking that night in your office about a month ago, you asked whether with all these professional women walking around, men and women got a chance to share dreams."

Barker looked at Jed intently and took a long pull on his drink.

"I think you meant sharing life, really, being interested in the same things, laughing at the same things, just thoroughly enjoying one another on many, many levels." He looked back at the fire. "Well, we do, she and I. It's very different from anything I've ever had before."

Barker leaned back in the armchair and rolled his eyes across the ceiling. "Well, boy, you had nowhere to go but up!"

Jed smiled, but he kept staring at the fire. "I'd like you to meet her."

"I'd like that too," Barker said gently. He watched Jed, and he frowned. "For the first time all night, now, all of a sudden, you're not relaxing. Look at you! Suddenly your muscles are all tensed up. Those eyes have that old darting look in them. Looks like you're about to jump right into the fire!"

"Don't be silly." Jed sounded testy.

"I'm not being silly, boy. You're being evasive. If she's so great, why are you getting all tense? Does she make you tense?"

"No!" Jed said loudly. "Not at all." His voice got softer. "Not when I'm with her. When I'm with her, I feel, if anything, calmer, and more relaxed than I ever have in my life."

Barker chuckled. "You've finally found a tonic, eh?"

Jed laughed, and then became serious again. "It's just . . . when I'm not with her, the whole thing is . . . too right. When I think, I get tense, anxious about it."

Barker groaned. "Jed, as I have told you at least three times a week for all the years I've known you—stop thinking! Lord, you're worse than Cassius!"

Jed laughed. He looked at Barker affectionately, and then his gaze turned to the clear-colored liquid and the slice of lime in the glass Barker was holding. "What the hell is that? Gin and tonic? On a cold wintry night by the fire?"

"It's almost March. That's nearly spring."

"Who drinks gin and tonics in February?"

Barker grinned smugly. "Not me." He handed the glass to Jed.

Jed took a sip and winced. "Club soda."

Barker nodded.

"Since when?"

"Since that night when I uttered that profound question about sharing dreams, a question, I hasten to add, that I have no recollection of whatsoever."

Jed beamed. "Good for you!"

"A good seven hours before, let the record show, seven

hours before you suggested diplomatically that I cut back on my drinking!"

"I was just worried—"

*"You think too much!"*

"Said the teetotaler."

"No, sir, not me. I'm not one of those born-again anti-alcohol types." He held up the glass. "This junk that helps you raise your bubble count but not your spirits. This is a temporary thing for me."

"Until when? Until the campaign's over?"

Barker looked at Jed uncomfortably and then turned back to the fire. "Those damn radio ads give me a pain in the ass—you heard them? 'I didn't realize I had a problem,'" Barker said in an un-Barker-like lilt, imitating the voice in the commercial. "'But now I do, and since I stopped drinking, I love my family and do well at my job and feel good all over, just because I've kicked the habit.' Hell, the anti-alcohol push bears a strong resemblance to the enticements that make people turn to alcohol and drugs in the first place—the feel-good-all-over promise!"

He got up and stoked the fire, which, Jed noted, did not need stoking. "Well, I've stopped, and the bad news is it isn't a panacea. I don't feel particularly wonderful. To tell the truth, I feel like I need a drink! And I plan to take one—"

"When?"

"When I don't feel I need one. When I know it will fulfill a pleasure, not a need."

Jed looked up at him, smiling.

"I don't like that look. It's the hero-worship look."

"How can you say that? No one knows better than I how infinitely flawed you are."

Barker continued stoking the fire. "How many more flaws you got room for?"

Jed laughed. "Want me to enumerate?"

Barker put the drink down on the table and went back to the fireplace, turning his back to Jed. "No, I want you to start thinking about adding a serious one to your list."

Jed's smile faded gradually. He looked at the silhouette at the fireplace, and felt a sudden outpouring of affection for the tall, gruff, somewhat paunchy man stoking a fire that didn't need stoking. This had to be the reason for the meeting. Whatever "this" was. "I think I can handle a couple more flaws," Jed said softly.

"Do you?" Barker whirled around. His tone was stern, almost angry. "I'm not so sure, Jed. It conflicts with your hero worship."

"Shit, the hero worship was your idea, not mine. Heroes are people you revere from a distance, usually in a cloud of naiveté. I know you too well, and I'm too old. You're not my hero. You're my friend, my father, maybe, my brother, my mentor."

"It's the mentor part that I'm talking about."

"Try me," Jed said, patting the cushion in Barker's armchair next to him. "Try me."

Barker sat back down in the chair and stared at the fire. "Tomorrow morning, I believe, the *Des Moines Press* is going to come out with a front-page story accusing me of soliciting PAC contributions in exchange for tax loopholes."

"Oh, hell, PAC contributions are limited to five thousand dollars a piece!" Jed shouted. "That would sure mean a hell of a lot of cheap loopholes!"

Barker closed his eyes and shook his head impatiently. "Not if you go after the whole industry. Not if you, say, approach the Washington lobbyist for the insurance industry, and say, 'Ralph, you get twenty or thirty or forty of your little member companies across this wondrous nation of ours to put up five thousand dollars each, and I'll take care of you.'"

Jed kept shaking his head. "I can't believe . . ."

"What can't you believe?"

"The *Des Moines Press* is a reputable newspaper. Why the hell would they print this kind of—"

Barker put his hand on Jed's arm and looked him in the eye. "Because it's true."

Jed just stared at him. He swallowed hard. He began shaking his head. "No!"

"Yes, Jed. Yes."

Jed got out of the chair and began slowly walking back and forth in front of the fire, staring at the floor. "You went to the insurance industry? You actively solicited their contributions?

311

You promised them outright you'd write them a tax break in return?"

"Yup," Barker said with a distant look in his eyes. "And not just the insurance industry."

Jed whirled around. "Why, for God's sake?"

"Good question. One I've been asking myself for a while now." Barker addressed his words to the fire. "I needed the money. That's the practical explanation. I suddenly found myself running against a man who grows dollar bills in shopping centers!"

"Running? He hasn't even gotten the nomination yet!"

"Yet." Barker scowled at Jed. "You haven't been *that* removed from politics. You know as well as I who's going to be running on the Republican ticket for the Senate in November—and who has spent his whole life running against me! And you know damn well that he's the most immoral, rotten, low-level—"

"So you decided to stoop to his level to keep the 'moral' man in the Senate?"

Barker slapped his knee and laughed. "Ain't it the truth!"

Jed paced.

Barker became serious. "Oh, to be fair to me, I was probably a little bit crazy at the time. Penny was dying. That seemed to make me even more determined to hold on to what I had left, to the one thing that has really mattered in my life. And I can say with all confidence"—his voice was getting louder—"that I am still, even with all this, the best candidate there is for the Senate from the state of Iowa." He ran his fingers up and down his glass. "That's a pretty sad commentary in and of itself."

"What proof do they have?"

Barker looked up at him, startled. He watched Jed pace. "My, you've learned to switch gears fast—right from idealist to defense attorney without missing a beat!"

Jed nervously ran his fingers through his hair. "What proof?" he repeated.

Barker sighed. "Plenty. More than enough. They have my voice on tape admitting it all."

"How the hell did they get that?"

"From an interview I did with a reporter, the reporter I talked to that night after you came to my office—the night, we both agreed in retrospect, I'd had too much to drink." Barker sighed. "Oh, I don't think it was just the booze that made me do it. The liquor loosened me, no doubt about it, but it was the burden of guilt as much as anything. It really bothered me. Made me downright crazy, to tell the truth."

"Damn!" Jed shouted, slamming his hand against his thigh. "I knew you were in no state that night for an—"

"Jed—it's over. I tried to minimize the damage. I took steps actively after the interview to hinder the reporter's information-gathering. But I knew all along my attempts would only work if the reporter willingly gave up the search." He grunted. "In the end, journalistic perseverance won out."

"That was a Des Moines reporter?" Jed asked in disbelief. "You were stupid enough to talk like that to a Des Moines reporter?"

"No," Barker said, taking a sip of his club soda. "It was a Washington reporter. I appear to be the beneficiary of one of those rare collaborations between the competing, usually fractious members of the Fourth Estate. A Washington reporter got the confession. A *Des Moines Press* reporter did all the legwork necessary to nail me."

"Why did they work together on it?"

"Damned if I know. I only got called by the Des Moines reporter, the guy who wrote the story."

"Then how do you know they worked together?"

"I know I made only one confession on tape, and I know the Des Moines reporter has it because he played part of it for me. The Washington reporter must have figured it would play bigger in Iowa. It will," he said grimly. "Front page."

"What did you say when Des Moines played the tape?"

"No comment." He smiled wryly.

Jed's pacing was getting faster. "Aren't you afraid of being prosecuted, for God's sake?"

"No," Barker sighed. "Not really. They were campaign contributions and campaign contributions don't benefit members of Congress personally. The bribery statute defines bribery rather specifically as taking 'a thing of value for himself.'" He looked up at Jed and smirked. "Surprised you don't know that, a smart young attorney like you!"

"I never had to deal with this issue before!" Jed practically choked on the words.

"Me neither," Barker said softly, shaking his head. "Me neither."

"How do they know for sure? Could they prove, with voice tests, that the voice on the tape is definitely yours?"

"They don't have to!" Barker roared. "It is!" He watched Jed pacing, his body pulsating, his mind ticking. "Jed—" Barker implored. Jed kept pacing. "Jed!"

Jed turned to him.

"Sit down," Barker ordered, rubbing his temples as though he had a colossal headache.

Jed sat down. He leaned forward with his elbows on his knees, staring at the floor.

Barker put his hand on Jed's arm. "Look at me."

Jed looked up.

"I told you, I tried to stop it, once I'd made the confession. Gave it a valiant try—but failed. Fighting it now would just make the whole thing louder and uglier. I don't *want* to fight it. Do you understand?"

Jed looked back at the floor.

"I've done a lot of thinking about this," Barker said, staring at his hand as it massaged the knob of the chair arm. "I want to admit it, and pull out. Sadly, reflectively, with as much grace as is left me, given the circumstances." Barker leaned back in the armchair. "I figure that's the best thing I can do—for me and for Iowa. I'd like to do a mea culpa, but point out the forces that drove me to it, the type of campaign Heffer is waging, in hopes, just maybe, of giving another Democrat a chance to beat the son-of-a-bitch in November."

"Like who?"

"Todd Greentree, I guess. He's the next in line. He's been—"

"He's a nothing, for God's sake! A bland nothing!"

"He's clean," Barker said. "He's honest. His instincts are in the right place. A nothing is infinitely better than a something, if Heffer is the something."

Jed just shook his head.

"I have a hunch something might backfire on Heffer. He's been waging a pretty ugly campaign. Once I'm removed from the race—bowing out majestically for the good of the state I have served so many years, throwing my support to a 'better man than I am' and underscoring the evil of our Republican opponent—Heffer's gonna lose his big target." Barker stroked his chin. "They're really good, solid people at heart, those Iowans. I think they'll do the right thing."

"If they're so goddamn good at heart, why won't they accept you, blemished record and all?"

Barker smiled. "Because they're that way. Hell," he chuckled, "if I were from Louisiana and did what I did, I'd probably pick up some extra votes." The smile turned dreamy. "But it won't play in Iowa. And that makes me kind of proud, the fact that it won't."

"And what the hell are you going to do? Open a candy store? Set up a little retirement law practice?"

Barker shrugged. "Maybe." He broke out laughing. "I could probably land myself a lucrative job with a Washington firm, just like all the somewhat tarnished lawmakers who've gone before me! This kind of thing plays pretty well in Washington!"

Jed was not laughing.

Barker stared at the fire. "I did something I have always considered reprehensible, and then went out of my way to expose myself." He shook his head slowly. "I was, needless to say, a very disturbed man at the time. But facing it these weeks, and dealing with it, has brought me back in a way. I may be on the verge of losing my career, but I think I've got my old self back." He turned to Jed, who seemed to be swallowing hard and shifting uncomfortably in the chair. "What I'm trying to tell you is—I can handle this, Jed. I guess I'm asking you to handle it too, to forgive me. You're the only one I've told. You're the only one I've been worried about."

Jed whirled around. "You've got to tell the kids before tomorrow morning! You can't let them find out in the news!"

Barker leaned his head back in the armchair and closed his eyes. "There you go again, making me into the perfect father and making them into caring offspring. Believe me, they won't—"

"I mean it. You have to call all three of them tonight."

Barker nodded, his eyes closed. "Okay, if it makes you

happy." He sat there for a while and then opened his eyes. "What about you?" he asked Jed.

Jed shrugged and looked away.

"I knew this would hit you hard. I just hoped—"

"It's the fact that you kept it from me as much as the act itself," Jed said, rising out of the chair again. He walked over and leaned on the fireplace mantel. "We've always talked. We've always opened up to each other."

"I didn't tell you before I did it, because I knew you would stop me and I didn't want to be stopped. I think I tried to tell you that night in my office," Barker said quietly, "but you didn't want to hear it."

"How can you say that? I had no idea—"

"You have an enormous capacity for love, Jed. You are devoted, passionate, giving. But over the years you have become arbitrary, brittle. Maybe I didn't tell you because I didn't want to lose you. Maybe you didn't want to hear because you didn't want to reject me."

"Where is all this pop psych coming from? This isn't you."

"What is me? A caring, deeply involved father? A pure and fastidiously honest lawmaker? If that's who you pledge your allegiance to, then I suggest you stop pledging!" He took a deep breath. "I never liked the pledging part anyhow."

"And what would you like me to do?"

"Accept me for what I am: a damn good Senator, albeit now somewhat flawed. An addicted politician who has quite selfishly put his work above everything and everyone else for most of his life. A man whose deepest parental involvement has *not* been bestowed upon his three offspring." Barker took a deep breath and looked up at Jed. "But rather, upon you."

Restlessly, Jed turned back to the fire. "If you'd even told me after the interview, together, maybe, we could have stopped the—"

"You're ignoring my request."

Jed turned to him. "Who was the reporter, anyway?"

Barker waved his hand irritably. "Oh, Jed."

"Who was it?"

Barker sighed. "A pretty young thing from that radio distribution service. What is it? Capitol Radio? Cynthia Matthews."

Barker shook his head. "A former farm girl," he said dryly. "Isn't that appropriate?"

Jed's entire body became rigid. Slowly, he turned back to the fire. "Cynthia Matthews?"

"Yeah. You've probably seen her around town. She's tall, blond, kind of leggy, you know? Sweet blue eyes." Barker grunted. "Deceptively sweet blue eyes, you might say."

Jed stood totally still facing the fire, his back to Barker.

"Do you know her?"

"No," Jed said.

"Jed?"

Jed whirled around and headed for the front closet.

"What are you doing?"

"Leaving," Jed said. "I need to think." He walked back into the living room, hurriedly putting on his coat, getting all entangled in it, actually. His face was ashen. "I can't . . . This is just . . ." He waved his hands in small, jerky motions and shook his head, at a complete loss for words. He spun around and walked out.

Barker heard the front door slam and then he heard a car motor. He sat very still in his armchair, staring into the fire as he heard the car pull out of the driveway.

Somewhere between Senator Barker's house and Bradley Boulevard Jed's mind snapped and Cynthia Matthews became Anna Farber.

If his innocent and adoring young wife who despised sex could have become an adulteress right under his eyes, then certainly the woman he had felt closer to than anyone else in the world could turn out to be a deceiver.

For a month he had lived out a fairy tale. It had given him highs like no highs he had ever experienced, but it had come replete with nagging suspicions and a growing sense of vulnerability.

The car that had peeled out of Senator Barker's driveway and sped down darkened streets, squealing its way around corners, now slowed to a controlled pace.

There was peace in having his worst fears confirmed—a perverse peace, granted, but a sense of peace nonetheless.

He threw the final plum into the pudding: He accepted the fact that his mentor—his father, his brother, his best friend— was not only a devious human being, but a corrupt politician.

The telephone was ringing when he walked into his apartment, but it took a while for the sound to register. When it did, it did not jar him. He simply turned off the phone bell in his bedroom and then in the kitchen.

His eyes were glazed as he walked into the bathroom and took out a few anatacid tablets and a few sleeping pills, and downed them all. He walked into the kitchen, and poured himself a stiff drink. Sitting down on the sofa in the living room, he sipped it as though it were medicine.

For more than seven years he had fought hatred, fought it although it was prevalent in the circle in which he traveled, fought it because it was contrary to his very being. He corrected that: contrary to the first twenty-nine years of his being. Tonight marked the beginning of a new acceptance of that emotion.

He felt his mind click, the adrenaline flow. It was very productive, this hatred—certainly more productive than his worrying about vulnerabilities.

He would nail her. He would nail her beyond belief. He would nail her the only way he knew how—as a lawyer, by building an airtight case against her.

# · 24 ·

When Chris Channing called the next morning, Cynthia was dressed for work and taking a last sip of her coffee.

"Have you turned on the news?" Chris asked.

"No. Why?"

"Is Jed there with you?"

"No. Chris? What's this all about?"

"You've been outscooped," Channing announced cheerfully. "The *Des Moines Press* has nailed Barker. The networks are reporting that the *Press* is running a big front-page story on how Barker exchanged tax loopholes for PAC contributions, detailing the industries. Barker's Senate office says he's going to have a press conference in Des Moines later today."

Cynthia plopped down in the nearest chair.

"Cyn? You there?"

"Yes." She gulped. "How did the *Des Moines Press* find out?"

"I don't know. Probably the same way *you* found out! Another drunken interview, maybe. I mean, a guy who goes around blurting out stuff like that to a reporter is a time bomb just waiting to go off, right?"

"I guess."

"Hell, I thought you'd be ecstatic! Someone took the story away from you! You can heave your little incriminating cassette now and relax. You're off the hook completely!"

"Yes. Thanks for calling, Chris." She hung up the phone and began pacing in circles around the kitchen. So *that* was what the late-night meeting had been about. The exclusive male fraternity of two mourning the loss of a Senate career! She saw Barker patting his accomplice on the back. "You did your best, Jed. After all, a man can only silence one reporter at a time. How many beds can you be expected to crawl into?"

Well, *she* might be off the hook, but Jed Farber was not.

She picked up the receiver and tapped out his number. She slammed the phone down when she got a busy signal.

Clean-shaven and attired in an immaculate three-piece suit, Jed Farber was standing at his kitchen counter, talking jocularly on the telephone.

"Yeah, I know calling you out of the blue like this at the crack of dawn is a little weird, old buddy, but I need to talk to you about something. No, it has to be in person. How about lunch at Benito's? We haven't had lunch there together in a hell of a long time. Great. See you then."

"Something's come up," Jed announced tersely when he called Cynthia at work later that day.

"I'll bet." She clamped her mouth shut.

"I won't be able to get to your place until late tonight."

"Whatever."

She spent the day standing over the wire machines in the office, watching the copy on Barker spew forth. She spent the evening pacing back and forth across her living-room floor, itemizing her case against Jed—all those remarkable "coincidences": One, he had picked her up at Lilah's party just hours after the Barker interview. Two, he had assiduously worked his way into her life. Hadn't he confessed himself that this was the first real involvement he'd had with a woman since his divorce seven years earlier? Three: He had diverted her attention by whetting her appetite for a totally different story—one on Carlos's chemical plant.

And what about the discrepancies that had been bothering her for weeks? How could two men who were so close talk to each other on the phone all the time without mentioning either Barker's transgressions or the name of Jed's romantic interest?

How indeed!

By ten o'clock that night, she had turned her big journalistic breakthrough on Synco into Jed Farber's carefully planted red herring, and she had transformed Jed Farber into Barker's accomplice, a culprit about to be backed into a corner and annihilated by her aggressive verbal assault.

It was only when he arrived at eleven and she faced him that she realized winning this argument would totally devastate her. She was also shocked by his demeanor. This was not an apologist bearing excuses. This was a man armed with his own list of accusations. It knocked the air out of her.

"Barker told me," he announced.

She blinked. Since when was his pal 'Rick' referred to as 'Barker'?

"He told me last night—about your interview."

"Oh, really?" she said sarcastically. "And you expect me to believe last night was the first time you'd heard about it?"

"Damn straight I do!" he roared. "Because that's the truth!"

"The truth!" she scoffed disparagingly. But when she looked into his eyes, she lost all her gusto. It was, she realized with shock, the truth.

"*You* never told me!" he accused.

"That's because I thought he should be the one to tell you what he'd done."

"Really?" The word was said loudly and was steeped in sarcasm, a tone designed to let the jury know the next question would be an important one. "So you made sure he would be forced to do so?"

She blinked to attention, along with the jury. "What?"

"Is that why you told the *Des Moines Press* about it? To force him to own up to me?"

"What are you talking about?" she gasped. "I had no contact with the *Des Moines Press*!"

"None whatsoever?" He turned his back to her, with his hands on his hips, his eyes staring up at the ceiling.

"None whatsoever!" It was true. Why did the words sound false? She had to elaborate. "They got that story completely on their own. Their story had nothing to do with the interview I did."

He whirled around and began walking toward her.

"There was no mention in their story about me, about my interview," she pointed out.

He smiled, but it wasn't a real smile. "Was that part of the agreement?"

"What are you talking about? What agreement?"

"Yours—with them. That they would not mention their source, the interview that triggered off their research?"

Her chest felt so tight she couldn't breathe. What was happening? Everything was confusing. "Jed, what are you talking about?" Somehow, saying his name, saying "Jed" made her feel better. "This is Jed," it told her. "You can relax. This is sensible, kind, fair Jed Farber."

"I know!" he shouted. "I know, so you don't have to continue this little game. Barker not only told me about the interview. He told me the guy at the *Des Moines Press* played the tape for him on the telephone."

"That's impossible," she said, getting up from her chair and running into her bedroom. She pulled the dresser drawer so hard it came out all the way, crashing to the floor. No matter. It was there, right where she had put it. She left everything else sprawled on her floor, grabbed the cassette, and ran back to the living room, holding out the cassette, victorious. "I have it still! Here it is! Right here! Look!"

"I may be naive," he said, scorning her tape, scorning her proof, "but I'm not stupid. Tapes can be copied."

She looked at him in shock, feeling strangely afraid. "You think I gave the *Des Moines Press* a copy?" Her words were barely audible.

He just stared.

She stared back. She could meet those eyes, even if they were a stranger's eyes. "I did not!" She said it with conviction. "How can you even *think* such a thing?"

"Barker said he only made one confession and that was to you." He walked toward her, backing her into a corner of her own living room. "He said they played *your* interview for him."

"That's impossible. I've never copied the tape, and it's never left this apartment."

He kept moving toward her. "Are you saying that Barker's lying?"

"Yes! If he said that, he's lying!" As soon as it came out, she knew that was the wrong thing to say. Senator Barker never lied—not Jed Farber's Senator Barker.

"He had no reason to lie. He doesn't even know I know you. He had no reason to bring up the tape if it weren't true."

"And I had no reason to give the tape to the *Des Moines Press*! If I'd wanted to do the story, I would have done it myself."

"The interview was done before we got together." He was looking away now, walking toward the jury. "Isn't it just possible you started to do the story, and then stopped because you knew I would be furious?"

"No!"

"And decided to cash in whatever chips you had by giving it to the *Des Moines Press*?"

"No!" She screamed it this time. She was right. She was telling the truth. She had to scream. "I did no such thing! I have never played or copied that tape for anyone!" She turned to him, waiting for him to see the truth in her eyes. But he didn't look.

He talked to the window instead. "Just as you never had an affair with Rob Diamond?"

Her jaw dropped. "What the hell has Rob Diamond got to do with this?"

"I had lunch with him today." He turned to face her. "You may have conveniently forgotten, but he seems to think he had an affair with you." He savored the words, relishing his ace. "Is he lying too?"

"You went to Rob Diamond to ask about me?" she gasped, both shocked and furious.

"Answer my question."

She couldn't, because the answer wasn't right. The truthful answer was not really the truth. "You went to Rob Diamond behind my back?" She felt violated.

"Answer my—"

"Yes, I had an affair with Rob Diamond!" She was on her feet again and screaming, heading toward him. "I never said I didn't have an affair with Rob. I just—"

"But you acted horrified when I—"

"Oh, it was his idea, not mine! He only did it because he

knew I was on a trail that would lead to him, and he was determined to stop me. So he decided to play to me, to flatter me, to make me—" She stopped, again finding herself backed into a verbal corner. Where were they all coming from, these corners? "It didn't work." She said it flatly.

"Were you in love with him?" The prosecutor was well prepared.

"No." Honesty in hindsight. She assured herself she could pass a lie-detector test on that response.

Jed raised an eyebrow. "That's not what Rob says."

"What I say doesn't count?" she asked in outrage. "What *he* says does?"

"Well, under the circumstances, you have to admit—"

"Under *what* circumstances, exactly? You're taking the words of a corrupt Senator and a proven felon over mine? Those are your circumstances? For God's sake, Jed, face it!"

"No!" A blood vessel was pulsating on the side of his head. "What we have here is an ambitious bitch ready, willing, and able to use anyone she can to further her professional career!"

"Oh, no we don't!" She paused to regain her composure. "What we have here is a totally innocent woman, guilty of only one thing, and that is being stupid enough to fall in love with a man who feeds on distrust."

"If that's love, I'd hate to see hate," he snickered, putting on his coat. "I'd hate to see even mild disinterest!"

"Says who?" she hissed at his back as he headed for the door. "Says Selebri's lawyer? Says Barker's disciple? Says Diamond's buddy? With credentials like that, where the hell do you get the balls to march in here and accuse—"

"Go to hell, goddammit!"

She continued the diatribe mentally when she heard the door slam shut behind him. Sleep with dogs and you get fleas! Associate with the scumbags of the world and you begin thinking like them, acting like them, seeing scheming, conniving people everywhere!

She paced back and forth, infuriated by his audacity, that pigheaded certainty that kept him from comprehending she was telling the truth.

It was more than that. It was his unwillingness. He really *wanted* to make her into the villain—actually enjoyed doing it!

Sick, that's what he was. Demented.

She pictured him, suddenly coming to his senses, rushing back, filled with remorse, apologizing, begging. . . .

She walked over and bolted the door.

Lucky, that's what she was—fortunate to discover Jed Farber's true colors before she got in any deeper.

She hoped his car crashed into a tree. She hoped he suffered, really suffered.

She walked in and out of rooms, slamming objects down on tables.

She never wanted to see him again. Out! Out of her life forever!

She marched angrily into the dining room, but then stopped dead when she saw the bouquet of roses at the center of the table. She reached out and gently stroked a delicate bud, suddenly desperate to scramble up, out of the nightmare and back to the past—yearning for the warm, comforting arms of the man who could be as gentle and caressing as the velvety petals before her.

Tears began streaming down her cheeks.

That man who had been in the living room, hurling accusations and hatred, that was an aberration. The real Jed Farber was right here, in the vase, and the truth was, her life was meaningless without *this* Jed Farber.

She sat down in a chair and, her face in her hands on top of the table, she cried—cried and sobbed and wailed—mourning the death of the only thing in the world that meant anything to her. She became more and more hysterical, intentionally self-starting the crying each time the sobs subsided by reminding herself of funny anecdotes, special moments.

Gone. No more.

She kept it up for a long time, until there were no tears left.

As she sat up, inborn practicality crowded in around her sniffles.

Wasn't she mourning a bit prematurely? Yes, she was innocent—condemned by a man refusing to see that innocence. But on the other hand, he was innocent too. He was *not* a Barker plant, of that she was certain. No one could fabricate that rage, that fury. It had to be spontaneous, the result of his shock at

Barker's confession and his belief that Barker was right—that she had given the story to the *Des Moines Press*.

So what was she left with? An honest man who did not trust her. She grimaced. Some gift, that. Some prize!

Oh, but he *was* a prize.

"Ambitious bitch, ready, willing, and able to use anyone she can to further her professional career!" She heard the words in her head, but worse still was the vision of his face when he had said those words. It was the same expression she had seen in the kitchen at Sylvia's cottage when she had asked him when he'd last cried.

Hatred. That's what it was. Her hands trembled. Hatred—this time directed solely at her.

She closed her eyes, hoping that would remove the vision. It did not work. So she opened her mind, instinctively searching for a way to change the look, a means of convincing him she was not a deserving target for that look.

She got up and began pacing around the living room. Obviously, Senator Barker had lied to Jed.

But why? It made no sense.

Still, there was no other plausible answer, no way the *Des Moines Press* could have possibly got her interview. She had retrieved that tape tonight from the very spot she had left it in the back of her dresser drawer. Untouched.

Untouched? She played with that a while. Had someone come into her apartment and taken the tape when she was not home? "Borrowed" it, and then put it back?

Oh, how, for God's sake? Who? This was no cloak-and-dagger mystery!

She continued pacing, pushing herself. There had to be a perfectly logical explanation. Find it.

Suddenly her body chilled and she put her hand over her mouth. She saw her emerald-green knit outfit—hanging in the closet at Capitol Radio.

Lathered up and shaving in front of his bathroom mirror, Jed complimented himself on the way he was handling this. The magical chemical concoction of pills and alcohol had worked for the second night in a row. He would now go to the office, hold all calls, and immerse himself in work.

Work was the panacea. Work blotted out everything. He would continue working and gradually the things he was blotting out would become less important, until finally they just faded away.

He washed the remaining lather off and dried his face with a towel. He viewed it in the mirror with satisfaction: unscarred, upbeat, definitely on top of things. He stared at the dimple in his chin that he had come to think of as *her* dimple. She made such a big fuss about it all the time. When he realized what he was doing, he looked away.

"Chris? It's Cynthia. Are you up?"

"Just barely," Channing grunted. "Hon, it's only six A.M.!"

She sat back in the kitchen chair. "Well, I have a present for you, something you've been looking for for a long time—a way to nab Gardiner Weldy."

"What the fuck are—"

"Are you awake enough to hear?"

"Uh, well, yeah, I guess so."

"The *Des Moines Press* story? That was based on the tape of my interview with Barker."

"Who says?"

"Barker. He told Jed the reporter played the interview for him—to pressure a confession, maybe."

"But, Cyn, don't you have the tape?"

"Yup. Right here, right now, in my hands. My guess is they got a copy."

"How? If you never—"

"There is only one time the tape was out of my sight." She closed her eyes, on automatic pilot now, reciting the statement she had spent the night crafting. "I went back to the office after the interview to change for a party I was going to that night. I left the tape at Capitol Radio overnight, at Gardiner's insistence. 'Consider this office your home, Cynthia dear.' That's what he told me. Gardiner knew I was going to interview Barker."

"But, Cyn, think: How could Gardiner have known ahead of time what Barker would say?"

"True, Gardiner couldn't have known the interview would be as incriminating as it turned out to be, but there might have been rumblings picked up by Heffer's people that Barker was vulnerable. His wife had just died, after all. The word might have gotten out that he was drinking a lot or something like that."

She played with the telephone chord. "My guess is Gardiner got a request to just go fishing. He might have even taken the initiative himself, decided to see if there was something I'd pick up that could be turned against Barker, maybe even turned around, twisted in a way that could be a problem for Barker. Gardiner was probably ready to splice the tape creatively, if it came to that. It all figures."

"So you're saying—"

"If my memory serves me right," she went on, "you told me the calls had been going from Gardiner to Heffer for a long time. Then you said the calls and mail started going in the other direction. I may be wrong, but I think you said the turning point—the time when the phone calls suddenly reversed themselves—was the week of January twenty-seventh."

"What phone calls?"

"The phone calls you told me you monitored through Sylvia and Capitol Radio's phone records!" she snapped. She rubbed her eyes and reminded herself that Chris Channing was at a disadvantage. He had not stayed up all night piecing this together.

"Don't you see, Chris? The interview with Barker was on January twenty-fourth. Gardiner came back to the office late that night—after suggesting I leave my interview gear there overnight—and made a duplicate. The duplicate of that highly incriminating interview with Heffer's key opponent is what endeared Gardiner to Heffer. What made Heffer suddenly show interest, call him repeatedly, probably offer him a job in the end, even!"

"Jesus. It all fits."

Cynthia took a deep breath. Relief. She could feel the wheels turning in Chris Channing's head, at last.

She found herself thinking along with him in silence, pacing herself, knowing where he was. How many times had they paced each other this way?

"There's just one problem," he said after a long silence.

"No problem," Cynthia said curtly. "There's Jimmy."

"Who's Jimmy?"

"I don't know his last name. To everyone he's just 'Jimmy.' He's the overnight guard at the building. Everybody who walks in after closing hours signs Jimmy's register. I remember he was getting ready to quit for the night when I came in Saturday morning to retrieve my equipment. If Gardiner came in late that night, he's got to be on Jimmy's register."

"I'll check." She knew he would. She felt like a sick person who'd gone to a very good doctor. If there was anything to find, Christopher Channing would find it.

"Chris." She closed her eyes and rubbed her temples. "That interview was done on my own time for a free-lance story paid for by *America Magazine*. It was done with my personal tape recorder, and it was recorded on a cassette I purchased myself. You know how careful I always am not to use any Capitol Radio materials for free-lancing."

"I know."

"What I'm saying is—"

"That the interview was your property, that by suggesting you leave the tape there, and then using it, Gardiner Weldy stole your private property."

His adrenaline was building. She could hear it in his voice. She felt very thankful.

"So you've finally come around," Chris said happily. "You want to nail Gardiner too!"

She opened her eyes. "I'm targeting an audience of one. Jed thinks I gave that tape to the *Des Moines Press*."

"You're kidding!"

"If nailing Gardiner can convince Jed, then by all means, crucify him."

Cynthia called the office and told Sylvia she had the flu and would be out the rest of the week. Her eyes lingered on the telephone after she hung up.

She told herself it was just a matter of time before Jed called to apologize. The hysteria of the moment would pass. Jed had been upset—devastated by what Barker had done. What *Barker* had done. He would realize soon enough that he had misplaced that rage by directing it at her. He was, after all, a rational, intelligent, compassionate human being.

What's more, he was in love with her! She started mentally tallying up the evidence amassed over the past weeks that proved he loved her, loved her as no one else ever had, but then she stopped herself.

Silly emotionalism.

He would call. In the meantime, she could use this extra time productively. She sat down at her desk and made a list. She would read all the newspapers, magazines, and books lying around the apartment she had not had time to read. She would cook. There were so many new recipes to try.

She spent the next two days in a frenzy of activity, moving from one project to another, disturbed by the shortness of her attention span, and the fact that it seemed to get shorter and shorter as the hours passed and Jed did not call.

When she looked around the apartment Friday night, Cynthia had the eerie feeling she had been sharing her quarters with an invisible roommate. Who had left all these books opened and lying around? Who had scattered red roses all over the place? Who had left all the uneaten food sitting on tabletops?

Chris Channing called repeatedly with news: The Capitol Radio phone records showed a call from Capitol Radio to Heffer's home at eleven-twenty P.M. on January twenty-fourth, the evening of Cynthia's interview with Barker.

He had been unsuccessful in reaching Jim O'Neil, the *Des Moines Press* reporter who had broken the story on Barker, but he would keep trying.

He had uncovered some remarkable things about Gardiner's past. Did she want to hear?

No, she told him. Just the tape. Just the Des Moines connection.

# · 25 ·

Jed Farber stared at the Bullets game on the television set in his living room, sipping his drink. Tonight he had reversed the order slightly, drinking ahead of the pills. He wanted to be knocked out, but not right away—not until he was sure the kids were asleep.

He did not feel well. Nothing he could put his finger on, really, he just didn't feel well. He had a headache, and although he had consumed more alcohol tonight than usual, it wasn't taking. It wasn't easing him the way it usually did.

What's more, he had no idea who was winning the game, although he had been giving the screen his undivided attention for half an hour.

It was understandable under the circumstances. He had put in one hell of a day. For a good twelve hours, he had kept the activities going nonstop, so neither of his children had time to pick up any stray vibes. Not that he was sending out any, but you could never tell with Lisa and Timmy. They seemed to sniff out everything.

He had begun by announcing, "Bad news. Cynthia has to work all weekend."

Then, by pretending to be every bit as depressed by the news as they, he had succeeded in nipping any suspicions in the bud. When they had asked about next weekend, what had he come up with? The brilliant morsel: "I sure hope she can make it!"

331

Sheer genius. The policy—string the children along and after a while they will hardly feel the loss—was off to a perfect start.

Jed took a long gulp of his drink. And after a while *we'll* never feel the loss.

Chris Channing called late Saturday night. He had made contact with Jim O'Neil, the Des Moines reporter.

At last. Cynthia collapsed into a chair in the kitchen. "When did he get the tape?"

"January twenty-eighth—the Tuesday after the interview."

"How did he get it?"

"In an envelope with one of those computer printout address labels on it," Chris explained. "He said it was the same kind of stick-on all his press mailings from the state legislature come in. In a big state legislature press operation, those things are accessible to a whole range of people."

"So, what do you think? Gardiner mailed the tape to Heffer, and one of Heffer's contacts got the label?"

"Better," Chris chuckled. "Gardiner flew out to Iowa on Sunday, January twenty-sixth. Sylvia's got receipts of the trip. It was on Capitol Radio's account."

"Fabulous!" For the first time in three days Cynthia felt elated. "Why didn't O'Neil use the tape?"

"He couldn't figure out where it came from, and who the mystery woman was. I gather, from what he said, that Gardiner must have spliced most of your voice out, leaving in only what was necessary for transition. O'Neil figured—intelligently—that writing a story about a tape that mysteriously came in the mail would deflate the facts, if anything make them suspicious from the beginning."

"So what did he do?"

"He began checking around on Barker the way you were going to, using the bare details of the tape and looking for facts to support them. He said he hit a few impasses and almost gave the whole thing up. He had no luck pinning down Barker's recent travel itineraries, for example. And that guy Barker mentioned on the tape—Ralph Buddington?—he was no help at all. As a matter of fact, Buddington was so tight-lipped, O'Neil said, it made him pretty sure the confession was true.

"When no one else broke the story, O'Neil decided the 'mystery woman' had handed him an exclusive. He said he knew it had to be a painstakingly precise case in order to work, and that took a hell of a lot of time and legwork—translating the tax bill, finding out what parts Barker had authored, checking out the interest groups Barker had alluded to on the tape. It wasn't until last Monday that the final piece of documentation he needed came through from a developer in Philadelphia. Tuesday morning, February twenty-fourth, he made the call to Barker."

"What was Barker's reaction?"

"O'Neil says the Senator denied it at first, but without enthusiasm. When O'Neil played him the tape, Barker shut up completely. Just said 'No comment.'"

"What's interesting is that the tape served two functions—it gave O'Neil a place to begin checking, and it gave him a weapon to hold over Barker's head so he couldn't deny the facts. But aside from that, it was never used. O'Neil never mentioned it in the story."

"So what?"

"Well, had it not been for your connection with Jed, and his with Barker, you would have never known anyone stole your tape. And since Gardiner did not know about those connections, he had every right to believe you would never find out." Chris Channing sighed. "I can't decide whether that's luck or genius on Gardiner's part."

"What if I had decided to break the story myself?"

"All the better! Two stories! They gave it to O'Neil for insurance. To make sure there'd be a big splash in Iowa's most prominent newspaper. Heffer's people are starting to open up, and, from what I've gleaned, Heffer's campaign people were hoping you'd write a story too."

"I see."

"Can I ask you one favor?"

"Sure."

"I can't prove Gardiner's role in all this, but I can suggest it heavily. You're the one who got the exclusive interview and only let the tape out of your sight that one night. Would you let me write that? Explain what happened, your decision not to do a story, and why."

"Anything you want." Her voice was a monotone. Cynthia

333

shut her eyes, satisfied now that Chris Channing was handling everything admirably, and desperate to turn off the sound. "Anything you want. I don't care." She opened her eyes. "Not Jed though! No mention of Jed!"

"No, no," Chris said quickly. "Jed Farber is completely irrelevant. Except, of course, to you."

Jed pulled off Sunday with less aplomb. By the time Daddy dropped Lisa and Timmy off at home Sunday afternoon, all three were grateful the time had come to part.

Back in his apartment, Jed upped the dosage of both sleeping pills and alcohol Sunday night, but he still had a lot of trouble falling asleep. When slumber finally came, it was short-lived. He found himself jolted awake by a nightmare in the middle of the night.

"A dream," he told himself, trying to ease his body back to sleep. "It was just a silly dream." But his head throbbed, and his stomach ached, and his body was dripping with sweat. He turned to the clock: two-seventeen.

Oh, great. He had managed to eke out one hour and forty-seven minutes of sleep. He pulled up the blanket. No good. His body was shaking all over. He reconsidered his chemical elixir: Tomorrow night he'd cut back on the sleeping pills.

He pulled the blanket up over his head and buried his face in the pillow. He wouldn't move. He would just stay this way, and sleep would come. He clutched his gut just below the top of the rib cage—that familiar place—and he wondered whether someone had actually cracked his skull with a blunt instrument in his sleep. Why else would his head be pounding so mercilessly?

Sleep would come, goddammit.

At five-oh-six, Jed declared the night over and got out of bed.

He took a shower. Just the thing for the chills, a hot shower.

He took a few aspirin. Just the thing for a headache, a few aspirin. Then he remembered his stomach and drank a glass of ginger ale. Aspirin was acidic. Just the thing for a headache but not for an ulcer.

At five-fifty-seven, he was pacing around his living room, allowing himself to think for the first time since he'd left Senator Barker's house almost one week before.

334

It didn't fit. It wasn't that his case against her lacked anything. It was airtight, for God's sake. That ridiculous tape she had shaken in his face—as though he were too stupid to know you could copy tape—that just convinced him he was right. After all, she had agreed, hadn't she? There was no other way the *Des Moines Press* could have got that tape.

Yes, the case was airtight, all right.

It was just the defendant that did not fit. Walking around in circles in his living room, he simply could not believe that the woman with whom he had spent most of the hours of the last few weeks would do such a thing.

Hell, she had just pulled the wool over his eyes, blinded him, that's all.

But be practical. What was the motive for her deception?

That was easy. Status. A professional connection. She was ambitious, that was for sure. She had wanted whatever credit she could get for her big exposé.

But couldn't she get a hell of a lot more credit for breaking the story herself? Why not just ditch him and go for broke?

His head throbbed.

He went into the kitchen and poured himself a drink, a drink to celebrate: his first Monday morning sunrise, about to happen.

Just a little drink. It would help his head. The aspirin wasn't doing shit, that was for sure.

He took a sip and felt better right away. Nothing like a nice hot cup of scotch at six o'clock in the morning.

He walked into the living room. Back to business. Back to motives. Why would she put together such an incredible package just for him? He was not rich or glamorous or something so terrific. "Farber" wasn't exactly a name that opened doors.

He laughed and drank some more. That was for sure. The name Farber was certainly no guarantee of a better life. Except, just maybe—if her idea of a better life was one she would share with him.

He stood still and stared at the carpet, granting himself what he knew was a special luxury: a moment of considering that possibility.

But, of course, it didn't figure. Jed Farber, ultimate catch?

He laughed at himself. Even Anna was smart enough to know that wasn't true.

He took another gulp, closed his eyes tight, and cringed at the deception. All those wonderful days and nights Cynthia had been keeping it all from him, listening to him go on and on about his buddy Rick Barker, while all the while plotting Barker's demise with a cohort at the *Des Moines Press*. What kind of a life could there be when the foundation was deception? He had had one marriage like that, thank you, and he had an ulcer to prove it, didn't he?

He walked to the window. An anemic little strain of orange-red was flailing its way out from behind the apartment house across the way. Sunrise in Bethesda.

He was in no shape for work.

Well, then, the hell with work. He drank to that. The hell with work.

He'd put in enough hours lately. He had nothing big scheduled for this week, no court appearances, no important meetings.

What was it Rob Diamond had said? "St. Thomas is nice this time of year."

He toasted Rob Diamond. He toasted Diamond's fortunate travel agent.

"St. Thomas is nice this time of year." Why not find out for himself?

Why not, indeed? He and Rob had shared something else, hadn't they? Those deceptive blue eyes. Why not share the blue skies of Diamond's St. Thomas too? All it took was one call to the office to tell them he would not be in this week, and another call to a travel agent.

He raised his glass. He made a toast: to St. Thomas, and a new life.

Then he he toasted the Bethesda sunrise.

Then he toasted his mother, who would pee in her pants if she knew her upstanding Jewish son was drinking scotch at six o'clock in the morning. He threw back his head and laughed. It sounded funny in the empty apartment.

# · 26 ·

Gardiner Weldy had called Sylvia from Iowa Saturday night and told her to assemble the entire Capitol Radio staff in the conference room Monday at three-thirty for an important announcement. So Cynthia went to work on Monday.

She had, in fact, spent all Sunday involved in productive activity: Her résumé was ready for Xeroxing. Her apartment gleamed. Her freshly washed hair sparkled. A Monday at work was a logical follow-up.

Sylvia was both silent and solicitous at the office, asking no questions, but looking at Cynthia with great concern, insisting, in fact, that Cynthia try a piece of homemade chocolate cake.

Jake Weinstein, the most thoroughly self-absorbed person in the world, was suddenly gazing at Cynthia as though he was worried about her, talking to her with gentle affection. He even went out and bought her a ham-and-cheese sandwich at lunchtime.

The combined odor of Sylvia's homemade layer cake and Jake's mustardy sandwich wafted up from Cynthia's desk to her nose, causing her to feel nauseated. During a brief interlude when no one was in the workroom, she tossed both offerings into the wastepaper basket next to her desk, and topped them off with some newspaper sections.

Why was it she was finding food so repulsive these days?

And why was everyone suddenly trying to feed her?

Was she that thin? She tried to remember how she had appeared the last time she looked in the mirror, but she couldn't remember when that was.

Well, however she seemed, she was really better. Much better. Ready to go forward and stop looking back. In control of herself again. She did not feel good. As a matter of fact, she was very shaky. But physically, not mentally. And physically shaky was much easier to bear.

At precisely three-thirty, the staff was assembled in the conference room, waiting restlessly for the man who had called the meeting in the first place.

Brian dragged on his cigarette. "No champagne, eh, Sylvia?"

Sylvia smiled and shrugged. "No champagne."

"Well, then, I'd hanker a guess this is no celebration." Brian leaned back, and put his feet on the conference table, an act Gardiner deplored.

"No celebration as far as Gardiner is concerned," Jake said brightly. "Maybe that means we're all getting raises!"

Suzie laughed.

"Maybe he fired himself!" Brian chortled.

Sinc squinted his eyes at the human barometer, Sylvia. He frowned. "I don't think it's good news," he said, still staring at Sylvia.

Sylvia looked up pointedly over her bifocals. "All he told me was 'Call a meeting.' No more."

The mood in the room changed from restless camaraderie to communal discomfort.

"Where is he coming from?" Brian asked.

Sylvia turned her hands palms up and shrugged. "Who knows with him? He called me from Iowa, Saturday night, and told me to set up a staff meeting."

"Did he say he was setting out on foot?" Jake asked.

"Shh," Suzie whispered as they started to laugh. "I just heard the front door."

"Hello, everybody," Gardiner said as he breezed into the conference room.

Not his "winning smile," Cynthia observed silently, rather a "sincere, we're-all-one family" smile. She wondered how Gardiner was going to pull this off and still leave the room in one piece.

Brian took his feet off the table.

Walking as though his body were on wheels, Gardiner glided to the armchair at the head of the table. They all stared in silence as he used his spotlight to do a lot of busywork, pulling down his shirt cuffs, checking his gold cufflinks, smoothing his trousers. Finally, he took a long, cleansing breath and stared solemnly at his hands, which were clasped before him.

He looked up and his eyes traveled slowly around the table, saluting each staff member individually, but with an unusual "death-in-the-family, we-must-be-brave" smile.

"Sad news," he said as he stared at his fingers, which were now spread out in front of him. "Very, very sad news."

Everyone else began staring at his hands too, looking for a clue.

Gardiner looked up suddenly, his eyes wide, his forehead furrowed. "I'll begin with the bottom line," he said quickly. "I have to. That's only fair. We are no more. Capitol Radio can not go on."

Suzie gasped. Sinc leaned forward in his chair. Jake stroked his beard feverishly. Brian lit a new cigarette.

Cynthia sat frozen like a statue.

"I've tried," Gardiner sighed. "I've tried for months now. For months, I have been cutting back on my salary, trying to make the books balance, trying to find investors, trying even to find buy-out potential, but," he sighed, shaking his head, "I have come to the realization that it is hopeless. And"—he looked up, around the table—"I can't keep going on in the red, with no hope in sight."

"You mean Capitol Radio is folding?" Brian asked in disbelief.

Gardiner reached out and put his hand over Brian's. "Yes, Brian," Gardiner intoned. "I'm afraid it is."

"When?" They were all asking now, more alert than they had ever been at a Gardiner meeting.

With a pained but sincere look, Gardiner gazed around the table. "As soon as you can each find other employment," he said sadly. "I won't leave any of you in the lurch." He thrust his body across the table. "I will write you all stellar recommendations—because you all deserve them—and we will see to it that you all find other jobs!"

"What if we took salary cuts or something?" It was Suzie's earnest soprano.

"Suzie," Gardiner said, at last finding a pair of eyes that would return his melancholy gaze, "you don't deserve a salary cut. I wouldn't ask that of you—of any of you. For one thing, that would not make enough of a difference. The debts are too high. And for another, this is a group that merits more, not less!" He pounded his fist on the table.

"Could we see the books?" Jake asked.

"Jake!" Suzie gasped.

"Well, I just thought . . ."

"Jake . . ." Gardiner sighed sadly. "Take my word for it. This is, after all, my livelihood too. I *am* Capitol Radio. It was my dream."

They all began asking practical questions: How long? What could they expect? Severance pay? Should they keep coming in?

Cynthia shifted uncomfortably in her chair, aware that there was one fact missing—a fact she knew was essential to Chris Channing's record. Her senses were dulled, however, her body lethargic and immobile. She told herself sternly to do something, but the command did not stimulate a response.

Sitting next to Gardiner at the table, Sylvia leaned over and gently put her hand on Gardiner's arm. He turned to her. She tilted her head and looked at him with warm, maternal concern.

"Gardiner," she murmured, "what will *you* do?"

His chest heaved. "I've been unwilling to tell you all, because I was afraid it would discourage you. I tried and failed to find anything in journalism." He stiff-upper-lipped his way around the table. "But I'm really not the journalist each of you is. Each of you! And I've dealt with that. It was painful, but I've dealt with it." His head began bobbing slowly again. "And so I've accepted a little job in business, not even in Washington . . . out in Iowa, of all places. I'm going to work for a company that builds shopping centers." He shrugged self-consciously.

The sighs around the table were sympathetic and embarrassed.

"Which company?" Sylvia pushed subtly.

"Oriole," Gardiner said. "It's name is Oriole."

Cynthia looked up to find Sylvia giving her a significant look over her bifocals. Sylvia had successfully solicited the missing fact for Chris's record. Cynthia acknowledged the accomplishment with a nod.

Gardiner left immediately after the meeting. Sylvia rushed to the telephone, Cynthia guessed to call Chris.

Sinc, Jake, Brian, and Suzie paced the floor in the work-room, voicing their fears for the future in loud, demonstrative outpourings. What would they do? How could he thrust this upon them so suddenly? Their reactions were predictable: Jake sneered at Gardiner's mismanagement. Sinc worried out loud about his house payments. Suzie collapsed in tears. Brian began chain-smoking his way through calls to contacts.

Cynthia watched it all passively from her desk chair. It was sad. So sad. But she couldn't feel it.

In a fog, she lifted the telephone receiver on her desk and dialed Jed's law firm.

"Yvonne? Hi, this is Cynthia again. Is Jed, by any chance, available?" She sounded gay. She told herself she was sounding gay and lighthearted.

"No, he's going to be out of the office all week, Cynthia."

"All week? How come?"

"Darned if I know." Yvonne laughed. "I assumed you would! All I know is he called in early this morning, sounding happy as a lamb and announced he was going on a vacation!"

Cynthia's eyes got larger. "A vacation?"

"To St. Thomas, he said. Can you imagine? Out of the clear blue like that? 'St. Thomas is nice this time of year.' That's what he said. Just that he was going to St. Thomas and he wouldn't be back in the office until next Monday! Can you believe—"

Cynthia hung up the phone.

When Cynthia left Capitol Radio Monday night, she knew she would never be returning. She did not mention that fact to any of her coworkers. Nor did she turn around and give the office a final look as she yelled "See you tomorrow!" over her shoulder and walked out the door.

In a daze, she followed her normal procedures—taking the metro to her regular stop, walking the three blocks to her apartment house, removing the letters from the mailbox in the lobby.

She was in her apartment, sorting the new bills that had arrived, when there was a knock at the door.

"Carlos!" The familiar sight of the boy grinning impishly before her jolted her system, bringing back all the happy memories. She felt her energy returning. "Well, look at *you*!" she gushed, taking in the pressed slacks, sports jacket, and crisp white shirt collar sticking out from the top of his navy-blue sweater.

"Busy?"

"Never too busy for you!" She stepped aside.

He strutted past her jauntily, and turned around. "The *new* me," he corrected, pulling back the sports jacket to reveal a "Pearson College" emblem in the upper-right-hand corner of the sweater.

"You've enrolled? Already?"

"Yup, took the metro out today. Oh, it's too late for the winter semester. I don't start until June. But I figured, while I was out there—I mean, no harm in getting outfitted now, right?"

"Damn straight!" She followed him into the living room.

"Man, I'm ready," he said, sitting down on the sofa. "Really psyched. Kind of like a jock who's spent hours priming himself for the big match. Know what I mean?"

She sat down, taking him in with pleasure. "I sure do."

He looked around. "Jed home yet?"

"No." She consciously maintained her smile. "He's out of town this week."

"Well, then, I'll just get all dolled up again next week, so I can come back and show him!"

"I'll make sure he doesn't concoct a batch of chili to celebrate," she giggled, playing out the fantasy, comforted by it. If the old Carlos was real, then certainly the old Jed must be too. "So, what does a college kid do when he has four months to wait for the semester to start?"

He shrugged. "Daydreams a whole lot—while he continues working as a busboy at Rico's Restaurant. Actually, I can't stay long," he said apologetically, looking at his watch. "I've got to leave time to change before I report for work. But first"—he looked at her expectantly—"how about some advice from the only real reporter I know?"

"Advice?"

"Well, uh . . ." He moved closer. "Let me just try something out on you."

"Shoot!"

"Every Saturday night at exactly ten, the same guy walks into the bar we have in the front room of Rico's. He's Hispanic, well-dressed—more than just well-dressed. The guy's flashy, know what I mean? And big, real big. Definitely thug material."

Cynthia nodded.

"The guy hangs his coat up on the coatrack, and sits down and orders a drink. 'Scotch on the rocks.' That's all he ever says. He gets his drink, and downs it in about ten minutes."

Cynthia shrugged. "So?"

"Wait. Let me finish." Carlos leaned closer. "Now, while he's drinking, Rico—the owner?—he sneaks over to the coatrack and stuffs a big envelope in the inside pocket of the guy's coat. At exactly ten minutes after ten, every single Saturday night. Then the guy slaps money down on the bar counter, gets up, puts on his coat, and walks out the door. About two minutes later, this guy sitting in the corner of the bar—another thug-looking type, this one with a big mustache—gets up and walks out the door after him." He sat back and folded his arms over his chest. "Well? What do you think?"

She cracked up. "I think it's amazing you get any busing done!"

"Hey, c'mon!" He tilted his head. "Hispanic mafia maybe? Rico making a payoff? The second toughie sitting there to let him know he either pays up or gets his balls busted?"

She leaned forward, suddenly interested. "Is there such a thing? A Hispanic mafia?"

Carlos's face turned red. "Well, uh, in *my* scenario, yes!"

Cynthia broke out laughing.

"Still," he persisted, "it could be something interesting. A possible story!"

"Could be," she admitted.

"So, then, your advice is what? To keep watching?"

"Definitely keep watching. If only for the distraction!"

"Hey, c'mon on. Seriously!"

She sighed. "You want my real advice?"

"Yes!"

"Look for a logical, boring explanation." She winced. "I hate to tell you this, Carlos, because I fear it may discourage your vocational pursuits, but, well, most times there's a logical, boring explanation."

"But just maybe—maybe not!"

She winked at him. "Maybe not."

He played with a button on his sports jacket. There was something else on his mind. "You're internationally famous, you know."

"I am?"

"Yup." He grinned at her. "As of this very moment, every single relative I have in El Salvador has received a copy of your article. My mother made sure of that."

She raised an eyebrow. "And how many of them understand English?"

"My mother enclosed a lengthy explanation." He looked a little bashful. "One that kind of boils down to—this is about Carlos. This says Carlos is terrific."

She beamed at him. "A rough translation, but apt."

He lifted his head up and really looked at her, his large brown eyes devoid of their earlier cockiness, filled now with gratitude. He swallowed. "Thank you."

"Now, Carlos—"

He held up his hands to silence her. "Come on, you've got to listen. It's only fair. I spent a long time on the preparation!"

"A speech?" she whined. "Don't tell me you've got a speech!"

"Two things gave me the courage to come over here and deliver it. One was that, well, there were things I wanted to tell you."

"And the other reason?"

He grinned at her. "I figured you'd be even more uncomfortable listening to it than I'd be saying it!"

"Get on with it, then," she groaned, burying her face in her hands.

"Okay. First of all, I don't need to tell you the article

changed my life, right? I mean, hey, just feast your eyes on Mr. College here!"

She laughed, shaking her head.

"I just wanted you to know about the personal stuff—how much you and Jed—how much the two of you've changed my outlook."

She watched as he stood up and began walking around the living room.

"See, I've always known that this was the best country in the world—politically and economically—but I've always felt Americans were real cold. 'Not like us.' That's what my mother always says about the people she works for. 'They're not *family* people like us.'"

He began nodding affirmatively at a distant wall. "Well, you and Jed, you're 'family people.' You really *care*." He laughed a little. "Man, I'll never forget the sight of you—facedown in that snowdrift at the factory at six o'clock in the morning? You were funny-looking, really—but absolutely determined to take that damn picture!"

He turned to her. "And I'll never forget your tears for Francisco," he went on softly. "Geez, I swear, I keep seeing them all the time—tears for this illegal Guatemalan laborer falling down what has to be just about the most American face in existence."

She looked away.

"And the way Jed yelled at me that night for wanting to take chances with my life by continuing to work? This big-shot lawyer actually worried about my safety, like he was my father or something."

He chortled. "Remember how dumb he looked the night we rushed Francisco to the hospital? Wearing that expensive suit, but all rumpled and covered with snow?"

She nodded, chuckling.

He gulped and stared soberly into space. "And the way he kept insisting, all the time, that what the two of you were doing—getting up in the middle of the night to rush someone you didn't even know to the hospital—that it was perfectly normal, the only thing to do."

He sat down on the stool at the foot of her chair. "I guess all I'm saying is you two are really special—'family people.' I mean, even my mother would say so! You're like us. No—" He shook his head, thinking. "You're better than that." He looked up at her. "You're what I hope to become."

Cynthia's eyes were huge and moist, her lips tugged into a smile. "Thank you," she whispered. She leaned forward and kissed Carlos on the cheek. "Maybe you should give up ideas of journalism, Carlos, and go into politics. You're quite a convincing speaker."

A dark cloud seemed to pass over his eyes. "It wasn't just a speech. I really meant it."

"I know you did." She squeezed his hand. "And, in case you can't guess by all my sniffles, it meant an awful lot to me to hear it."

He stood up, and she followed him to the door. "Family people—" she mumbled, thinking. "You know, in a way, more than most other American cities, Washington is a town of immigrants."

"No kidding!" Carlos grunted sarcastically.

"No, I'm not just talking about immigrants from other countries. Washington's filled with *American* immigrants—like me and Jed. Immigrants from places like Ballard, Indiana, and Brooklyn, New York. Places where you grow up surrounded by family values."

"So you're saying they bring those values to this city?"

She thought about Jed in St. Thomas, taking the Rob Diamond sun cure, dropping her as though what they had never existed. "They bring them, and then they lose them." Her visage hardened. Now it was all coming back—the coldness, the hurt. "Some immigrants master the art of assimilation," she snapped. "In a short period of time, they adopt the hardened cultural attitudes of their new environment."

She seethed. Jed had certainly made a speedy transition, hadn't he?

"You okay?" Carlos was standing in the hall, giving her a funny look.

"I'm fine, Carlos," she said, shooting him a steely smile as she closed the door. "Just fine."

"I'm fine," she instructed herself, leaning back against the door.

It was time to start really feeling "fine" again, time to follow Jed's lead and declare the past over.

She faced the facts: She was, obviously, replaceable. When would she realize she she was just one in a million and stop entertaining these romantic dreams of being a one-and-only?

Right now.

She was just as much a veteran of Washington social customs as Jed Farber. She, too, knew how to switch gears the well-practiced way, by blotting out the hurt and rising above it.

Her jaw stiffened. Get on with it, then!

Cynthia awoke Tuesday embued with raw energy and determination. She spent the day writing individual letters to accompany her résumés, gathering packages of her writing samples, having them professionally duplicated, and then tracking down the addresses of potential employers.

The phone kept ringing when she was home, interfering. She reassured her sister, Georgine, that she was fine—over it. She reassured Brittany and Pamela. She told Sylvia she was just busy job-hunting, and ignored the pregnant pauses.

Late Tuesday night, Chris Channing called. "Cyn, this thing is getting bigger and bigger. You wouldn't believe what I'm—"

"What would you like me to do?"

"Well, um, would you object to my contacting Senator Barker?"

"No, not at all. Whatever you want."

"It's just that I keep uncovering stuff on the dirty campaign Heffer is waging. I think this might turn out to be a much bigger story than I thought."

It tired her. Christopher Channing and his insatiable thirst for stories. It tired her. "Whatever, Chris."

"By the way . . . Cyn?"

"What?"

"I tried calling Jed Farber a couple of times."

"You *what*?"

"Well, it was Sylvia's idea. You know, to try to set the record straight—"

She felt the blood rush to her face. "*This is none of her business!* Why *ever* would you—"

"Hey, calm down, will you? Look, I never got through. I just thought I'd tell you. And they say he's out of town in—"

"St. Thomas. Don't try again. Do you hear me, Chris? It's over. I'm perfectly comfortable having it over. And if I am, Sylvia can damn well be too."

She hung up the phone and stared at it, the purveyor of interruptions. She reached under the box, and turned it off. She walked into the kitchen and turned that telephone off too. She sighed with relief. No more noise from the outside world.

Cynthia sat down at her desk and counted the envelopes she had filled with résumé packages. Ten thus far—and all with out-of-town addresses.

An opened suitcase with one bathing suit tossed in lay on the chair in the living room of Jed Farber's apartment. It had been sitting there that way for two days, ever since Jed had taken it out of his closet Monday morning.

The suitcase was surrounded by litter—strewn newspaper sections, books lying open and facedown on tables and chairs, plates caked with uneaten food, partially filled glasses, pill containers, liquor bottles, and an empty vat of Pepto Bismol.

Oblivious to it all, Jed sat back on the sofa in sweat pants and an undershirt, stroking the three-day stubble that had accumulated on his chin, thinking.

Why had she looked so comical?

Well, for starters, her face was white and her nose was bright red—right at the tip. One of her problems, she had said plaintively, was that whereas other people got rosy cheeks when they were out in the cold, for some reason she got only a rosy nose.

He had suggested she try breathing through her cheeks. She'd thought that was funny.

Jed pulled himself up from the reclining position on the sofa and put his elbows on his knees, propelling his weight forward. The position usually eased his ulcer pains somewhat.

The red nose. That was part of it. And the hat. That big, ugly gray knit hat she had found in one of the closets in Sylvia's cabin. She pulled it way down, over her eyes, practically, so you just saw a big gray head and her red nose.

The baggy jacket and the old pants intensified her clownlike appearance. So did the tattered, old ice skates.

She said she wore them for reasons of vanity: They proved her feet were still as small as they had been when she'd got the skates, at the age of fifteen.

But the effect was not the stuff of which vanity is made. The effect was so clumsy, and kind of adorable too. Certainly a striking contrast to glamorous little Lisa, who was wearing her sleek ice-skating satins and performing her classy figure eights.

Cynthia was so comfortable out there on the pond, comfortable enough not to give a damn about how she looked. She was in her milieu. That whole weekend at Sylvia's she was in her milieu. He liked her milieu.

Except for the ice skating. Well, at first, that is. He had almost killed her for insisting he try to skate, pulling him out on the ice, where he proceeded to fall on his ass, causing Lisa and Timmy to collapse with laughter.

Very funny.

"You know how and I don't," he had protested. "There are skaters and there are nonskaters."

"Really?" she'd asked, continuing to hold his arm, continuing to show him how. "Just as there are Jews and non-Jews?"

What exactly had she meant by that?

He hadn't thought about it then. He'd been too busy trying to stay up. And he had forgotten about it later, when he actually started getting a kick out of skating. It wasn't all that difficult, after the first couple of times around the pond.

What had she meant?

Part of her rejection theme, maybe. A prophesy? She knew what was coming, after all.

It was getting harder and harder to ignore the facts. His stomach was on fire and the flames were flaring out in all directions, shooting cramps up and down his body.

He gritted his teeth and leaned farther forward. He put his hands on the coffee table and pushed most of his weight forward onto his hands. A little better. A slight easing. He closed his eyes and tried to see her in the silly gray knit hat again. He liked the look, found it comforting.

But it didn't work this time. He opened his eyes and stared at the hands before him on the coffee table.

He saw white knuckles.

He got up quickly. Too quickly. He felt as though he had left half his head behind on the sofa. Where were these headaches coming from?

The stomach first. One thing at a time. He walked directly to the medicine cabinet in the bathroom, where he opened a new jar of ulcer tablets. He took two. No, three. He walked back into the living room. Then into the bedroom. Back to the living room.

He tried to daydream. That had been working lately, the daydreams. But he was keenly aware of the fact that this whole thing was escalating out of control. He had started with pills and booze, working himself up to greater and greater levels with less and less relief. He'd found solace occasionally over the last few days when he'd let himself think about the good times . . . often getting so caught up in how good they were that he'd temporarily forgotten reality.

And now that wasn't working so well either. Now he was popping pills and anxiously orchestrating fantasies in search of a feeling of relief that was becoming more and more elusive.

He decided to call a doctor. He went to the phone, but when his fingertips touched out a number, it was not the doctor's. It was Cynthia's.

He looked out the window. Dark. It was night. Tuesday night. No. Wednesday night. Whatever. It was night. She'd be home.

What would he say? He had no idea. "Help" maybe. "Please help."

He paced, bent over slightly, as it rang. After a while, he realized it was ringing too much. There was no answer. He hung up and went into the kitchen.

There was no more scotch. No more bourbon. No more gin. He pulled out an old, somewhat sticky bottle of some kind of liqueur. He didn't look at the label. He just poured a healthy amount of it into a glass.

Warm. Warm going down, helping his head. Thank God for that. He'd pay for this later—he knew that—but at least he'd get a little relief now.

He hoped the ulcer pills had got there first—wherever "there" was.

He walked into the bedroom and lay down on the bed. He put his hands over his eyes. It helped at first. But he couldn't stop his hands from shaking, and the jerky tremors made his head go crazy with pounding.

Finally, he drifted off to sleep.

When he woke up, he heard groans, moaning groans, getting louder and louder. He realized they were coming from him. He was doubled up on the bed, clutching his stomach, paralyzed by a pain unlike any he had ever felt before.

Oh, it hurt. Oh, God, how it hurt. He wanted to die. Anything, just to stop the pain. Please, oh, please God stop the pain.

His whole body was soaking wet, and he was squeezing his stomach and the squeezing seemed to be causing terrible sounds to come out of his mouth, gasps and moans.

He was going to explode. He felt as though his whole body were going to explode. Nausea. Such terrible nausea. Nausea and pain. Sick. He was going to be sick.

He pulled himself off the bed, and, doubled over and still making frantic sounds, he ran into the bathroom. He leaned over the toilet and felt his whole body heave violently.

Wretched-tasting stuff poured out of his mouth. He opened his eyes. It was red. Bright red. He gasped and swayed, off balance because he was still clutching his stomach, still engulfed in burning cramps, barely able to breathe.

His body heaved again. This time he kept his eyes open. He gagged in horror at the blood-red vomit spewing out of his mouth and into the toilet.

His legs gave way. His head smashed against the corner of the sink as he passed out on the floor.

When he came to, lying flat on his back, staring at his bathroom ceiling, he knew two things: His ulcer was hemorrhaging. And he wanted to live.

## · 27 ·

Most reporters began in the hinterlands in hopes of gaining enough experience to qualify them for a future job in a major media market. Cynthia was bucking the trend, an experienced journalist seeking work in the smaller markets, and she was finding many receptive editors. By Friday, fully twenty résumé packages had been mailed out, seven of them preceded by telephone calls, five of which elicited very interested responses. There were two almost-firm offers from Indianapolis—one from a television station, the other from the city's major newspaper.

Satisfied that there were jobs out there, she decided to wait for written responses to her mailings before making a decision. A budget analysis convinced her her savings and severance pay from Capitol Radio was ample enough to carry her through a couple of months of unemployment.

She purchased and mailed a birthday present for her mother, although it was three weeks early, and complimented herself for being ahead of time for once.

Continuing her policy of escape through accomplishment, she kept her telephone turned off. She cleaned out the closets and cabinets in the apartment that had needed a thorough overhaul for months, relining the shelves in her kitchen in the process, and hauling a load of old clothes off to Goodwill.

On Friday night, the apartment was spotless, its owner taut

as a violin string and looking for a new challenge. The only thing left was the kitchen floor. She approached the task with gusto.

By noon, Saturday, the kitchen table and chairs were stacked in a heap in the living room, and Cynthia, in jeans and a sweatshirt, was on her hands and knees in the far corner of the kitchen surrounded by utensils: a pail, a sponge, a scouring pad, and a scrub brush.

Saturday's the day we wash the floor, wash the floor, wash the floor.

Well, one Saturday every ten years, perhaps. She decided the need to scrub one's kitchen floor by hand came twice in the life of an apartment: after you moved in and before you moved out.

The scouring pad was leaving pink suds all over the square, but she could see the gray turning to off-white underneath as she rubbed and rubbed, and it felt very satisfying, peeling off years of scum, cleaning up. Cleaning up her life. Her hand ached a little, but it was worth it.

It felt good, releasing the physical energy, accomplishing something specific, and keeping the world at bay with her telephone turned off. That was something she had learned this week—the pleasure of keeping the world at bay. She winced at all those soppy songs about people needing people. It was being able to get along fine without anyone else that was the ultimate accomplishment. It had taken her a long time to realize that, but she did now, and the realization would change her life for the better. She was certain of that.

Around and around some more.

The fact was, there was absolutely no one she wanted to talk to. That made her feel good—invulnerable, really.

She sat back on her haunches, wiped the hair out of her eyes with the back of her hand, and evaluated: not clean enough. She leaned forward again. Around and around.

She thought about the job offers from Indianapolis. She had not mentioned them to her sister because Georgine would have got all excited, prematurely excited. Cynthia could not make up her mind about them.

Why not? Why not head back to the home state after almost fifteen years of pioneering in the other world? Wasn't it time to go back? Time to give up? Fifteen years of trying to make it in the big world had yielded the distinct sense that she was simply not that eager to make it, hadn't it?

She pressed harder on the scrub brush.

Around and around.

Indiana.

She took the sponge and wiped the square. Perfect. Her mother would be proud. She laughed a little. It was the truth: This was definitely something her mother had hoped she'd grow up to do well some day.

Well, she'd fulfilled one person's goals for her at least.

There was a knock at the door. She shuddered, discomforted by the thought of an intrusion from the outside world.

Another knock, louder this time. The noise upset her.

She dried her hands on the dirty towel still hanging over her shoulder and went to the door. A door-to-door solicitor, probably. Better to get rid of him quickly than to have him keep knocking.

"Senator Barker!" Her body chilled as she said the name. She was furious at herself for heeding the knock, furious and frightened. The nightmare was coming back.

"Hello." He was holding his hat in his hands, attired in an expensive-looking suit, tie, and formal overcoat. Still, he looked every bit as tired as he had that night in his office. The sense of déjà vu made her stomach queasy.

"May I come in?" he asked, standing very still out in the hallway as she gaped.

No. She wanted to say "no."

"Yes, of course," she said, stepping aside, feeling her safe, private world crumbling as he walked by her.

"May I take your coat?" she asked as she shut the door. She prayed he would say he wasn't going to be that long.

"Yes. Thank you." He took it off, and she put his hat and coat in the hall closet. Her hands trembled as she wrapped the coat around a hangar.

Senator Barker was standing at the entrance to the living room, staring at the kitchen table and chairs.

"Excuse the mess," she mumbled. "I was just washing the kitchen floor."

He smiled and nodded.

She walked into the living room, wondering if this was really happening. He followed her in, and they both sat down, she on the sofa, he on her delicate blue velvet Victorian chair. She realized instantly it was a mismatch: Senator Barker's bulk and the chair's miniature lines.

"I came by to say thank you," he said, leaning back in the chair, and then, realizing he could not really lean back, shifting around awkwardly in an attempt to find a comfortable position. He ended up leaning forward stiffly. "I've been talking to your friend quite a bit—Chris Channing—and he explained to me the circumstances surrounding the tape."

She hated him, just as she hated the "circumstances surrounding the tape." Old history. Leave it buried. Please leave it buried. Leave my home.

"Chris said he was going to contact you." She stared at her fingers in her lap as she said it, hoping she was making Senator Barker as uncomfortable as his presence was making her. She had a feeling she was.

"Well, yes. For his story. I've been helping out a little with the Iowa connection. Our interests kind of coincide on this one," Barker grunted. "Might be able to get Weldy and Heffer in one blow."

Cynthia intentionally showed no reaction.

"The story's going to be a big one. Not only in Washington. There's a lot of interest, he says, in syndicating it out in the Midwest, certainly in Iowa."

"I didn't know that."

"I know you didn't. Channing says he's been trying to call you, but can't get an answer." Barker looked up at her. "A lot of people can't get an answer here."

She heard the words and felt her entire equilibrium suddenly threatened by their innuendo. She looked down at her knee and played with the seam of her blue jeans.

"Anyway, I came for something else. I wanted to thank you. I think it was a damn decent thing you did, deciding not to—"

"Rotten journalism," Cynthia snapped, her eyes flaming. "It's not going to win me any respect in newspaper circles, let me tell you, backing off a top story like that."

Barker looked at her. His eyes seemed surprised at first. Then they squinted. "Well," the voice said slowly as the eyes scrutinized, "in human circles, it merits a lot of respect."

"I wouldn't do it again," Cynthia said, determined to provoke an explosion. "If I had it all to do over again, I'd go for the story."

Barker ran his fingers slowly along the rim of the table next to his chair. "Well, then," he said in his lethargic drawl, "I guess I should thank my lucky stars the timing was on my side." He smiled.

Her jaw clenched in frustration. What was it with this man?

"I think you'll feel better when you see Chris Channing's story," Barker plodded on. "From what I can tell, you come off as a heroine of sorts, and Channing certainly travels in journalistic circles."

Cynthia sat very still, monitoring her breathing, trying to make it even, calm.

"I've been hearing a lot of good things about you lately," Senator Barker said slowly, stroking the table.

He had an agenda. The man had an agenda and he was going to press on with it no matter what she did. She wanted to shout "Get to the point!" but at the same time, she had a feeling she did not want to hear the point.

"Can I get you a cup of coffee?" she asked, jumping up. "I was just going to pour myself a cup when you came."

"Well, fine," he said, smiling. "I could use a cup of coffee. Black, if you please."

"Black it is." She walked into the kitchen.

When she came back, he had switched to the sofa.

"As I said, I've been hearing a lot of good things about you lately," he began again.

She handed him the coffee, but walked with her cup over to the corner living-room window. It was as far away from the sofa as she could get.

"Here I thought you were such a quick reporter," he said lazily, watching her.

Her eyes darted frantically at the cars and tree branches and people walking by outside the window, seeking a focus.

"I throw out a line like that," he went on, "and you don't even pick up."

Mild words camouflaging a threat to her armor. She turned her back to him, as though shielding herself from the meaning. She shook her head. "No—"

"You don't even want to know who said it and under what conditions?"

She shook her head. "No. Please. No." She whirled around to face him. "I can't hear that. Not and maintain my sanity."

"Your san—"

"I'm very shaky just now. But I'm dealing with this pretty well. I—"

"'Dealing with this,'" Barker grumbled in disgust. "Where do you people pick up all these peculiar expressions?"

"Please!"

"All I know is you look a good ten pounds lighter than you did the last time I saw you," he snarled. "Your eyes look like they haven't been blessed with a good night's sleep in a mighty long spell."

"I don't need to hear this."

"You look like a wreck to me," he went on, "and I just spent an entire night with someone who's an even worse wreck." Barker took a sip from his coffee cup. "*Was* a worse wreck," he grumbled. "I think he's a little better now." He put the cup on the table and rubbed his eyes. "But it was one hell of a night."

"I don't want to know, can't you see that?"

Barker nodded slowly, taking his hands from his eyes. "I can see that."

"It's over!"

Barker shook his head and winced. "I can't see that."

"Would you be willing to let yourself care about someone you knew would never trust you?" Cynthia asked. "Someone looking— breaking his neck to find reasons to hate you? Someone who could drop you like that and never think about it again?"

"No," Senator Barker said emphatically. "Definitely not."

"All right, then." She went back to the window.

"But that's not the issue here. This is a case of misunderstanding brought about by very irregular circumstances."

"Distrust. This is an open-and-shut case of distrust."

"More like overreaction, I'd say. Overreaction on both sides."

She shook her head obstinately from side to side, her back to him.

Barker shifted restlessly on the sofa and stared at the ceiling, an uncomfortable matchmaker. "Now, I put in a lot of hours listening to him explore the reasons for his overreaction—" he said.

"You won't have to listen to any from me," she snapped.

"Good!" Senator Barker shouted. "Very good! That is welcome news indeed! This is not a role I'm particularly comfortable in."

"Then why are you here?"

He laughed a little. "Almost didn't make it. I've seen more of your neighborhood this morning than most residents. Enlightening place, this, uh, what is it called, this area?"

"Why are you here?" She yelled it this time.

"Jed seems to think he can't live without you," Barker said, staring into space.

"Bullshit."

Barker nodded, still staring. "That's what I told him. Exactly what I told him!" He picked up the coffee cup and took another sip. "Oh, it's part of the age. You know, the older you get, the more you realize that much of what you are is due to age. In your twenties and thirties, you think you *must* have this or you'll die." He laughed. "At sixty, I've learned I can go without just about everything and do just fine!"

"Well, gifted with that brilliant insight, what are you doing here?"

Barker lifted up his arm from the back of the sofa and dropped it back down in defeat. "I couldn't convince him of that fact. You people apparently aren't mature enough yet for brilliant insights." He grinned at her. "Can't 'deal with them,' as you would say."

"So you've come to save my life?"

"Hell no!" he roared. "Not *your* life! I don't know you from Adam." He watched her mischievously out of the corner of his eye. "Except, as I said, I have heard a lot of nice things about you. Oh, all overdone, I'd venture, shrouded in the melancholy melodrama of the moment." He played with the coffee cup. "No, this is for him."

"Jed sent you here?"

"Hell no! He would probably be very angry if he knew. I just got tired of watching him dial the phone and get no answer."

"Then why are you here?"

"Because, inadvertently, I believe I'm somewhat responsible for the, uh, misunderstanding in the first place." Barker got serious. "Because Jed is just about the best thing I've encountered in these sixty long, tedious, experience-enhancing years I've put in. I love him like a son. More, even. I'd go the limit for him. And this," he said with irritation, turning around to her, "this, as far as I'm concerned, is above and beyond the limit."

"Did it ever occur to you I might not be interested in him?"

"Yes," Barker said very slowly, suddenly losing his expansiveness. "Yes, it certainly did. That's why I decided to come. I figured a rejection from you wouldn't hurt me as much as it would hurt him. I don't think he could take that right now."

Couldn't take it, she scoffed to herself. Had the Caribbean sunshine made Jed Farber suddenly weaker? He had been perfectly able to take anything the last time she saw him—to take it and to dish it out. She stared at the top of the window, seeking escape. Her hands were shaking so much that the coffee in her cup was practically spilling over the top.

"And this, this sudden turnaround," she said, her voice quivering, "this feeling that he couldn't live without me, did this occur before or after you told him the truth about the tape?"

"Before," he said, staring at the assemblage of kitchen chairs in the distance. "Long before. He just learned the true story about the tape from me last night. He has been trying to contact you for a while now—from, er, a variety of places."

Cynthia snarled, picturing long-distance attempts from St. Thomas.

Senator Barker turned completely around on the sofa and spoke to her back. "See, I'd been trying to get hold of him ever since he stormed out of my house that night after I told him about the *Des Moines Press* story. But he wouldn't speak to me, wouldn't answer any of my calls."

"Really?" Cynthia asked sarcastically. "How surprising! How unlike perfect Jed!"

"I kept trying, until his secretary, Yvonne, told me he'd gone to St. Thomas. But it wasn't until your friend, Chris Channing, called me Thursday that I had any idea about the connection between you and Jed. I'd never realized *you* were the woman he'd been telling me about."

Barker played with the empty ashtray on the coffee table. "That made me realize how devastating the information I had given him must have been, and that worried me. Hell, Jed's not the type to decide to take off and forget it all on sunny beaches downing piña coladas!"

Cynthia turned and looked at him, suddenly alert.

"By Friday morning, I was a little frantic. I got the resident manager to let me in his apartment. It—" Barker waved away the memory with his hand. "It didn't look good," he sighed, running his fingers around the ceramic ashtray.

Cynthia walked away from the window, toward the sofa.

"So I started calling hospitals."

She gasped and put her hand over her mouth. "Hospitals?"

Senator Barker looked up at her. "I found him last night."

The blue eyes were enormous. She dropped down onto the sofa. "You found him in a hospital? Jed's in a hospital?"

He nodded.

"He's sick?" Her voice squeaked. She moved closer to Barker on the sofa. "How sick?"

"He's going to be all right."

"How sick?" she shouted angrily. "Tell me! What happened to him?"

"His ulcer hemorrhaged."

She put her hands to her head. "When? How?"

"Wednesday night. He apparently passed out, but came to and was able to dial nine-one-one. They called an ambulance."

"Oh," she murmured in a very little voice. She tilted her head, tears filled her eyes. "He was all by himself? All alone? He must have been—" She turned to Barker. "Is he really all right?" she demanded. Her face was ashen. Her whole body was shaking. "Is he in pain? Is he—"

"He feels pretty terrible at the moment, but the doctors say he'll be just fine."

"Why didn't you say all this right out?" Cynthia screamed,

standing up and flailing her arms. "How could you let him lie there while you went through this whole charade? Why didn't you get to the point?"

Barker took hold of her arm and met her eyes. "If I had," he said slowly, "what would you have done?" His eyes looked intently into hers. "Think now, what would you have done if I'd knocked on your door—which I only did because you've refused to answer your phone all week—if I'd knocked on your door and said, 'Jed is very sick in the hospital. Come'?"

She plopped back down on the sofa. "Slammed the door in your face," she murmured, appalled by the truth. She looked at him, shaking her head, crying. "What's the matter with me? Why am I so crazy?"

Senator Barker put his arm around her and patted her gently. "Damned if I know," he muttered. "But you're not alone, that's for sure. He's plenty crazy too." Barker shook his head slowly, lost in his own thoughts. "You look at these two smart, good-looking, promising young people, everything going for them on the outside, and you realize with shock that their interiors are filled with such strange wounds and insecurities."

He stared into space. "I spent all last night wondering why the brightest, freest, most liberated generation ever would go to such lengths to self-torment." He shrugged. "Maybe no society was ever meant to be so free. Maybe that's why those who are, develop these strange, crippling vulnerabilities." He grunted. "I'll tell you, honey, your swinging-single, double-income, high-living generation has created a whole host of unnecessary psychological handicaps for itself. Personally, I'd take going through the Depression and World War Two any day!" He looked at the young woman lost in tears beside him and realized he had been talking to himself.

He nudged her. She wiped her face with the back of her hand. "I—I was so terrible to you. I'm sorry. I—" She started crying again.

"Naw. No problem. You get to the point in life where it all rolls off your back." He nudged her playfully this time. "Another of the advantages of aging. You got a whole lot to look forward to."

"You loved him much better than I did," she mumbled, staring off into the distance. "You tried to find him. You didn't—"

"Hey," he interrupted, anxious to get the show on the road. "How about you go get your coat, and I drive you to a place where two crazy people can perhaps figure it all out together, while the older generation goes home and gets some sleep?"

She smiled up at him through her tears, and they both headed for her closet.

# · 28 ·

There was a splotch of brown on the off-white ceiling just above the bed in Jed's hospital room. It was the size of a hand, and the shape of a spill, with little trickling lines radiating out from its solid brown center. Jed had been staring at it for three days now.

Lying flat on his back, hooked up by intravenous tubes to bottles on either side of the bed and a catheter at the bottom, his views had been limited: the splotch or the vast expanse of off-white ceiling.

Had he lifted his head slightly or turned it to one side, he could have stared at the windowsill, but such movement hurt.

"Severe migraine." That was the medical diagnosis for his heavy head, "hemorrhaging ulcer" the learned assessment of his stomach ills, "stress" the official cause of both.

He accepted total blame for the cause, and was, as a result, terribly grateful to modern medicine for making such a valiant attempt at relieving his symptoms.

The liquid trickling through the tubes and into the veins in his arms managed to stop the pain entirely that first night, although, in the process, it had seemed to stop just about everything else as well, leaving Jed conscious but feeling comatose, wondering whether, by mistake, they had given him a frontal lobotomy.

Each time the dosage of the liquid stuff was reduced ("A

sign you're making progress!" the little nurse with the zesty smile kept telling him), he experienced an increase in both discomfort and alertness. He stared at the splotch on the ceiling yearning to return to comatose. Then he began yearning for something else. Since his speech was garbled by the tube they had heaved down his throat, he gave the zesty nurse Cynthia's phone number and asked her to call.

What was the message?

"Please come" was the message.

Please come. He was beyond pride. He was in need. He even hoped, he confided to the brown splotch on the ceiling, that the zesty nurse would dramatize the seriousness of his condition a little, if only to guarantee a visit. He was not only beyond pride, he was beyond standards. He did not care, quite frankly, if Cynthia Matthews were the Boston Strangler in disguise. He just wanted her there.

But there was no answer. That's what the zesty nurse reported back time and again.

"Still no answer!" she chirped as she brought in a new bottle to attach to his intravenous tube.

"Still no answer!" she whispered when she found him dozing.

"Still no answer!"

Coinciding with the "still no answers" were more happy proclamations of his progress—proclamations that were accompanied by further lessenings of the dosage of the wonder drug, the blessed comatose-inducer, and greater discomfort all around.

By Friday afternoon, he was telling the brown splotch on the ceiling that he had a terrible feeling he was "progressing" right back to the starting point: He was beginning to feel as bad as he had before entering the hospital.

"What the *hell* have you gone and done to yourself!" The roar of the voice did not match the deeply concerned visage of the bearlike presence bending down over him, gripping his hand.

Relief. Rick Barker. The Senator assuming command, talking to the doctors and nurses, insisting the painkillers be increased to a level that provided greater comfort. Rick calling Anna and telling her Jed would not be taking the children on the weekend; Rick calling Jed's mother and explaining all, but somehow managing to convince her there was nothing to worry about, her son was on his way to recovery; Rick helping him dial Cynthia's number again and again.

Still no answer.

Rick, all night in the darkness of the room, explaining to Jed about the tape, and then calming him. Listening and listening and listening as the words struggled out of Jed's mouth, helping him look for answers. Finally, Rick's deep, strong voice, showing him how to put the pieces back together, assuring him he could be put back together.

At three o'clock in the morning, Jed stopped staring at the brown splotch and turned gratefully to the large shadow hovering over him at the side of his bed. "It's so much more comforting to have a parent than to be a parent," Jed mumbled hoarsely. Barker broke out laughing. Jed drifted off to sleep with the sound of that wonderful belly laugh rolling through his head.

He awoke to find Barker nodding off in a chair next to his bed. He sent him home to get some sleep.

And then it was back to the telephone. Still no answer.

Georgine. Her sister, Georgine. He called Indianapolis information, but there were three office listings for attorneys named Philip Miller, and he had no idea what suburb Georgine and her husband, Phil, lived in.

His head was getting heavier.

He had never loved anyone as much as he had loved Cynthia, and he had never treated anyone so cruelly.

His head throbbed. He put his right arm over his eyes, taking care not to twist the tubes in the process. For a while it helped. It blotted everything out.

He heard something at the end of the bed: a sound, by the door. A nurse, maybe. He took his arm off his eyes and looked up. Someone was standing at the foot of his bed. The room was a little dark. Rick had made them turn off the lights because they bothered Jed's head, and the pressure of his arm over his eyes had temporarily blurred his vision. He blinked, trying to get his eyes to focus.

He saw a figure. A person standing very tentatively, sort of supporting himself by holding onto the bed's foot board. A woman. A woman's hair. Blond hair. A blue down coat.

Cynthia?

"Cynthia?" The name came out in a raspy tone he couldn't believe belonged to him.

She didn't deny it. She mumbled something he couldn't make out.

He cleared his throat. "Cynthia?"

"Yes."

She was walking toward him now, and even in the gray daylight with blurred eyes, he could tell. Oh, God. It *was* Cynthia. He couldn't see her face clearly, but it was Cynthia, and she was nervous. Very nervous. Trembling a little.

But she was moving so slowly. He pulled himself up, impatient, wanting to get to her instead of having to wait until she got to him. But his elbow gave way and the sheer weight of his head made him fall back against the pillow.

She moved faster. She sat down on the side of the bed. She leaned forward, over him. He felt her put her hand gently on the side of his face.

So much to say. So many carefully planned things to tell her, all outlined clearly in his head, all laid out logically, systematically, in order of importance. But all he could do was bury his face in that hand. Such a wonderful feeling, that hand, so cool on his hot face. That hand, oh, that hand.

"I'm so sorry," he said. Again, the sound was scratchy.

"I know," she whispered, kissing him now. Lightly. So lightly. He felt he was floating away with the touch. "I'm sorry too." He felt her hands slip under his shoulders, until her arms were underneath him, holding him, hugging him.

Oh.

His head was swirling. He closed his eyes and put his arms around her, tightly around her, squeezing the prize at last, squeezing so hard.

Then his whole body was swirling along with his head, building up into some kind of crazy tidal wave. He felt everything building up inside him, building up until it exploded into funny muffled sounds on her shoulder, and then into louder sounds.

He realized he was crying, and he couldn't stop. It kept getting louder and louder, exploding all over the place. Soon he was sobbing and forgetting completely who he was and where he was. He was twisting and crying out isolated words. "Cynthia" ... "hurt" ... "crazy" ... "sorry" ... "hold me, hold me."

The words were coming out of his mouth in gusts, just as the tears spurted from his eyes, and just as involuntarily. Words without sentences, nothing to explain what they meant, nothing to hold them together, just words, plaintive words, words he couldn't stop.

All he knew was that she was there, right there holding him in her arms, riding his screams and his heaves, never letting go.

# · 29 ·

Cynthia got out of the elevator but then stopped. She saw a shadowy male figure in the distance, backing out of her apartment, closing the door, rattling the knob a little to make sure it was locked, and then heading down the corridor toward her.

The frown on her face melted into a smile of recognition as he got closer. "Carlos!"

He jumped. "Oh . . . hi!" He seemed surprised to see her. "I was just, uh, keeping Jed company while you were on your job interview. Back a little early, aren't you?"

"Yeah." She made a face. "It wasn't worth the time. Not as interesting as some of the other possibilities." She nodded toward her apartment. "Want to come in for a while? Extend the visit? We haven't—"

"Naw." He shifted from foot to foot. "I've got to report for work."

She nodded in reflex, but then thought for moment. "On Monday?" she asked, squinting at him. "Isn't Rico's closed Monday nights?"

"Yeah, uh, well, yes—for customers, that is. But see, he likes the employees to show up anyway to—you know, clean up and all."

"Mmm." Carlos was certainly anxious to exit.

"Another time!" She watched for a second as he headed for the elevator, and then proceeded on her way.

"Oh, uh—Cynthia?"

She stopped and turned around.

"Rico takes in a lot of cash on Saturday nights," he yelled to her. He was grinning, but he had a sheepish expression on his face.

"Huh?"

"And he gets nervous having all that cash around late at night, when the customers get drunk and a lot of unsavory types come in." He pressed the elevator button.

If there was a point, she was missing it. "Carlos?"

"So he has his brother-in-law, Alfredo, come by, and pick up the extra cash and drop it in the night deposit box at the bank."

Had the boy gone batty? She shook her head. "But what—"

"And, just to be sure Alfredo makes it safely to the bank, Alfredo's friend Pedro follows him there." The elevator door opened and Carlos walked in. "At ten past ten, every single Saturday night."

"Oh!" Cynthia's eyes lit up. "No Hispanic mafia!"

The door closed, but she heard Carlos's voice groaning loudly as the car descended. "A logical, *boring* explanation!"

She was still giggling when she walked into her apartment. "Hi there!" she called out. "How's my patient?"

"Mending rapidly. You're back early."

"Yeah," she laughed. "What a dull job! Ten minutes into the interview, I decided to accept the other offer." She hung her coat up in the closet. "I just bumped into Car—" She heard an explosive pop come from the bedroom. *"Jed!"* she gasped, running in. "Jed?"

She stopped at the entrance.

Vases filled with spring flowers lined the dressers, windowsill, and tables around the bedroom. In a sweater and jeans, Jed Farber lay on top of the bed, propped up by a pile of pillows, an opened champagne bottle oozing vapor in his hands, a grin on his face, and a tulip nestled behind his right ear. Two empty champagne glasses stood on the night table next to his side of the bed.

"Have you gone—"

"Happy spring!" He toasted her with an empty glass.

Her eyes roamed around the room in shock. "Where on earth did you—"

"Carlos Ramirez, my man in the neighborhood. Carlos did the shopping for me."

Well, that explained the guilty look and speedy getaway in the hall. But why?

"It's going to be spring in just a week or two. I thought we should celebrate."

She frowned suspiciously, tilting her head to one side. "Jed?"

He fluffed up the pillows next to him on the bed and winked, beckoning her. "C'mon. You've been so busy taking care of me. You need a celebration."

Shaking her head slowly, but laughing a little as she did, she kicked off her heels and crawled on her hands and knees across the bed to him.

He poured champagne into one of the glasses, put the bottle back in the ice bucket on the night table next to his side of the bed, and handed her the glass.

"I'm supposed to drink alone?"

"Nope. Got some doctor-prescribed bubbly here for myself too." He lifted a bottle of ginger ale off the floor, filled his glass, and clicked it against hers. "To spring!"

He put his arm around her. She snuggled closer to him, sipping the champagne and looking around the room. "The flowers are beautiful. It does look awfully dreamy." Her eyes traveled from the vases to the smoothed-down bedspread and the comforter folded neatly at the foot of the bed. She looked at him in shock. "My God, Jed, you even made the bed!"

"Don't misunderstand, now." He pointed a finger at her sternly. "This is not a policy change. This is a once-in-a-lifetime gesture. You know—for ambience."

"Ambience?"

"Actually, I contemplated returning to the scene of my last romantic outburst," he chortled. "But I figured it was too long a drive from here to the emergency room at D.C. General Hospital."

"Jed?"

"I would have preferred that little French restaurant we went to on our first date," he went on expansively, "but I didn't want to wait for the doctors' okay. This was the best I could come up with under the circumstances."

"Jed, what on earth is this about?"

His face suddenly sobered. He swallowed and turned to her. "Will you marry me?"

She choked on her champagne. "A formal proposal?" she cried, coughing and sitting up abruptly.

"You expected some other kind?"

"No . . . I mean . . . it's just, well, so old-fashioned!"

"Don't you see," he said softly, playing with her hair. "We are two old-fashioned people who have been thoroughly messed up, over the years, by trying to move in sync with a fast-track, swinging, new-fashioned existence." He took a swig of ginger ale. "I say from here on out we go with old-fashioned."

She smiled at him affectionately. "I guess I just thought we'd—well, that it was sort of understood, without saying anything specific."

"How the *hell* do you get married without saying anything specific?" he roared. "You don't just wake up some morning and realize that you've miraculously been wed, you know! It takes blood tests, for Christ's sake! You gotta get a license, among other things. It takes a specific moment in time when you absolutely—out loud—make the commitment."

"I agree." She leaned back against the pillows and looked up at him, her eyes suddenly radiant. "Yes, Jed, I will marry you." She took a deep breath and let it out, smiling. "With the greatest pleasure."

He let his head fall back against the pillows and closed his eyes. The deep, internal Jed Farber laugh began rumbling. He sat up abruptly as it exploded. "You will? Really!"

"Surely you can't be surprised."

"No. Yes. Well, happy. That's all. Damn happy!" He leaned back against the pillows and grinned at her.

She looked at him intently. "Now, this is an old-fashioned commitment, not a new-fashioned one."

"What does that mean?"

"You're stuck for life," she deadpanned. "I don't *do* divorces."

"Oh, really?" he laughed. "Up to now, as I recall, you haven't done marriages either!"

She stared him down.

"'Til death do us part," he whispered.

She smiled and rolled over on her stomach. "I can't think of a more wonderful commitment," she said, running her fingers down his face. "There is nothing in the world that would make me happier than spending the rest of my life with you." She kissed his cheek and then nestled her head between his chin and his collarbone, standing her champagne glass on his chest.

"I love you, Cynthia." His voice was choked.

She closed her eyes and moved her head around under his chin. "I love you too."

He cleared his throat. "I promise, I'll make you very happy."

She looked at him askance. "I should hope so. That was a quid for my accepting your formal proposal."

"You'll be relieved to know that I have thought about it a great deal lately, and I've decided I get much more pleasure out of making you happy than I do out of making you miserable."

"Now, *that's* reassuring!"

They both broke into giggles, but gradually, as they gazed into each other's eyes, their amusement faded away.

He reached out, pulled her close, and then kissed her—very seriously.